Praise for Mary Kubica:

'Brilliant, intense, and utterly addictive. Be prepared to run
a gauntlet of emotions!'
B A Paris, author of *Behind Closed Doors*

'With *Every Last Lie*, Mary Kubica spins an utterly
mesmerizing tale of marriage and secrets.'
Megan Abbott, author of *You Will Know Me*

'Perfect suspense.'
Buzzfeed

'Grabs you from the moment it starts.'
Daily Mail

'Gets right under your skin and leaves its mark.
A tremendous read.'
The Sun

WITHDRAWN

'Sensational.'
Metro

'Fans of *Gone Girl* will embrace this.'
Lisa Gardner

'Memorable and riveting.'
Lovereading.co.uk

'Stunning – Kubica is an author to watch.'
We Love This Book

'*Single White Female* on steroids.'
Lisa Scottoline

EVERY LAST LIE

MARY KUBICA

ONE PLACE. MANY STORIES

This novel is entirely a work of fiction. The names, characters and
incidents portrayed in it are the work of the author's imagination.
Any resemblance to actual persons, living or dead, events or localities
is entirely coincidental.

HQ
An imprint of HarperCollins*Publishers* Ltd.
1 London Bridge Street
London SE1 9GF

This paperback edition 2017

1
First published in Great Britain by
HQ, an imprint of HarperCollins*Publishers* Ltd. 2017

Copyright © Mary Kyrychenko 2017

Mary Kubica asserts the moral right to be identified
as the authors of this work. A catalogue record for this
book is available from the British Library

ISBN: 9781848456600

Printed and bound by
CPI Group (UK) Ltd, Croydon, CR0 4YY

Our policy is to use papers that are natural, renewable and recyclable
products and made from wood grown in sustainable forests. The
logging and manufacturing processes conform to the legal
environmental regulations of the country of origin.

EVERY LAST LIE

To Mom & Dad
My biggest fans

CLARA

They say that death comes in threes. First it was the man who lives across the street from my father and mother. Mr. Baumgartner, dead from prostate cancer at the age of seventy-four. And then it was a former high school classmate of mine, only twenty-eight years old, a wife and mother, dead from a pulmonary embolism—a blood clot that shot straight to her lungs.

And then it was Nick.

I'm sitting on the sofa as the phone beside me starts to ring. Nick's name appears on the display screen, his familiar voice on the other end of the line like any of the other thousands of times he's called. But this time it's different because this is the last time he will ever call.

'Hey,' says Nick.

'Hey yourself.'

'How's everything going?' he asks.

'Just fine,' I tell him.

'Is Felix asleep?'

'Yup,' I say. The way new babies have a tendency to do, up all night, sleep all day. He lies in my arms, rendering me immobile. I can't do a single thing but watch him sleep. Felix is four days and three hours old. In seventeen more minutes he will be four days and four hours old. The labor was long and intense, as they nearly all are. There was pain despite the epidural, three hours of pushing despite the fact that delivery was supposed to get easier with each subsequent birth. With Maisie it was quick and easy by comparison; with Felix it was hard.

'Maybe you should wake him,' Nick suggests.

'And how should I do that?'

My words aren't cross. They're tired. Nick knows this. He knows that I am tired.

'I don't know,' he says, and I all but hear the shrug through the telephone, see Nick's own tired but boyish smile on the other end of the line, the usually clean-shaven face that begins to accrue with traces of brown bristle at this time of day, along the mustache line and chin. His words are muffled. The phone has slipped from his mouth, as I hear him whisper to Maisie in an aside, *Let's go potty before we leave*, and I imagine his capable hands swapping a pair of pale pink ballet slippers with the hot-pink Crocs. I see Maisie's feet squirm in his hands, drawing away. Maisie wants to join the troop of other four-year-olds practicing their clumsy leg extensions and toe touches.

But, Daddy, her tiny voice whines. *I don't have to go potty.*

And Nick's firm but gentle command: *You need to try.*

Nick is the better parent. I tend to give in, to say *okay*, only to regret it when, three miles into our commute home, Maisie suddenly gropes for her lap and screams that she has to go with a shame in her eyes that tells me she's already gone.

Maisie's voice disappears into the little girls' room, and Nick returns to the phone. 'Should I pick something up for dinner?' he asks, and I stare down at Felix, sound asleep on my still-distended stomach. My chest leaks through a white cotton blouse. I sit on an ice pack to soothe the pain of childbirth. An episiotomy was needed, and so there are stitches; there is blood. I haven't bathed today and the amount of sleep I've reaped in the last four days can be counted on a single hand. My eyelids grow heavy, threatening to close.

Nick's voice comes at me again through the phone. 'Clara,' he says, this time deciding for me, 'I'll pick up something for dinner. Maisie and I will be home soon. And then you can rest,' he says, and our evening routine will go a little something like this: I will sleep, and Nick will wake me when it's time for Felix to eat. And then come midnight, Nick will sleep and I will spend the rest of the night awake with a roused Felix again in my arms.

'Chinese or Mexican?' he asks, and I say Chinese.

These are the last words I ever exchange with my husband.

* * *

I wait with Felix for what feels like forever, staring at the filmy black of the lifeless TV, the remote on the other side of the room hiding beneath a paisley pillow on the leather settee. I can't risk waking Felix to retrieve it. I don't want to wake Felix. My eyes veer from TV to remote and back again, as if able to turn the TV on through mental telepathy, to eschew that all-consuming boredom and repetition that accompanies infant care—eat, sleep, poop, repeat—with a few minutes of *Wheel of Fortune* or the evening news.

When will Nick be home?

Harriet, our red merle Border collie, lies curled into a ball at my feet, blending well into the jute rug—part of the furnishings, and also our guard. She hears the car before I do. One of her ticked ears stands on end, and she rises to her feet. I wait in vain for the sound of the garage door opening, for Maisie to come stampeding in through the steel door, pivoting like a little ballerina across the wooden floors of our home. My stomach growls at Nick's arrival and the promise of food. I'm hungry.

But instead the noise comes from the front door, a businesslike rapping against the wood, and Harriet knows before me that it's not Nick.

I rise from the sofa and open the door.

A man stands before me, his words evasive and out of reach. They float in the space between us like lightning bugs, flying swiftly away as I try to gather them in my hands. 'Are you Mrs. Solberg?' he asks, and when I say that I am, he says, 'There's been an accident, ma'am.'

He wears a black woven shirt, a pair of black woven pants. On his shirt there are patches, a badge. The car parked in my drive reads *Serve & Protect*.

'Ma'am?' asks the man when I don't reply. Felix lies in my arms like a sack of potatoes. His body slumps, inert, still sleeping and growing heavier with time. Harriet sits at my feet, glaring at this strange man.

Though my ears hear the words, my brain can't process them. Sleep deprivation I blame, or maybe it's denial. I stare at the man before me and wonder: What does he want with me? What is he trying to sell?

'Can it wait?' I ask, pressing Felix to my chest so he can't see the moist patches of milk that stain my shirt. My insides feel heavy; the lining of my legs burns. I limp, an effect of giving birth. 'My husband will be home soon,' I say, promising, 'any second now,' and I see the fabricated pity that settles upon the man's desensitized face. He's done this before, many times. I tell him about Maisie's ballet class, how Nick is driving home as we speak, how he will be here any minute. I tell him how he was stopping only to pick up dinner, and then he will be home. I don't know why I say so much. I open the door wider. I invite him inside.

'Would you like to wait inside?' I say, and I tell him again how Nick will be home soon.

Outside it is nearly eighty-five degrees. It's the twenty-third of June.

There's a hand on my elbow; his hat is in his hands. He steps inside my home, sure to cling to me so that he can brace Felix's soft spot should I fall.

'There's been an accident, ma'am,' he says again.

* * *

The Chinese food we usually eat comes from a small take-out restaurant in the town next to ours. Nick has a thing for their pot stickers, me for the egg drop soup. The restaurant isn't more than five miles away, but between here and there lies a rural road that Nick likes to take because he prefers to avoid the heavy traffic of the highway, especially during rush hour. Harvey Road is a flat, level plane; there are no hills. It's narrow, two lanes that hardly seem suitable for two cars, especially along the bend, a sharp ninety-degree angle that resembles an L, the double yellow line that dissects it met with disregard as cars drift blindly across it to make the hairpin turn. A chain of horse properties run the length of Harvey Road: large, modern houses surrounded by picket fences, harboring Thoroughbreds and American quarter horses. It's the high-end version of rural, tucked in a nook between two thriving suburbs that snowball with droves of department stores, convenience stores, gas stations and dentists.

The day is sunny, the kind of glorious day that gives way to a magnificent sunset, turning the world to gold at the hands of King Midas. The sun hovers in the belly of the sky like a Chinese lantern, golden and bright, glaring into the eyes of commuters. It sidles its way into cars' rearview mirrors, reminding us of its dominion in this world as it blinds drivers moving into and away from its glare. But the sun is only one cause of the accident. There's also the sharp turn and Nick's rapid speed, I'm soon to learn, three things that don't mix well, like bleach and vinegar.

That's what he tells me, the man in the woven shirt and pants, who stands before me, bracing me by the elbow, waiting for me to fall. I see the sunlight slope through the open front door and gain entry into my home, airbrushing the staircase, the distressed hickory floors, the hairs on Felix's vulnerable head in a golden hue.

There are words and phrases equally as elusive as *accident* had been: *too fast* and *collide* and *tree*. 'Was anyone hurt?' I ask, knowing Nick has a tendency of driving too fast, and I see him in my mind's eye force some other car off the road and headlong into a tree.

There's the hand again at my elbow, a sturdy hand that

keeps me upright. 'Ma'am,' he says again. 'Mrs. Solberg.' He tells me that there was no one there. No witnesses to the scene, Nick taking that turn at over fifty miles per hour, the car being propelled into the air by the sheer physics of it, speed and velocity and Newton's first law of motion that an object in motion stays in motion until it collides with a white oak tree.

I tell myself this: if I had asked for Mexican for dinner, Nick would be home by now.

* * *

The fluorescent lights line the ceiling like a row of stalled cars at a stoplight, one in front of the other in front of the other. The light reflects off the corridor's linoleum floors, coming at me from both directions as everything in that one, single moment comes at me from both directions: Felix with a sudden, single-minded need to eat; men and women in hospital scrubs; gurneys ferrying by; a hand on my arm; a solicitous smile; a glass of ice water set in my shaking hand; a cold, hard chair; *Maisie*.

Felix disappears from my arms, and for one split second I feel lost. Now my father is there, standing before me, and in his arms sits Felix as I fold myself into him, and my father holds me, too. He is thin but sturdy, my father. His hair is nothing more than a few faint traces of gray on an otherwise smooth scalp, the skin darkened with age spots. 'Oh, Daddy,' I say, and it's only there, in my father's arms, that I let the truth settle in, the fact that my husband, Nick, lies lifeless on an operating table, brain dead but being kept alive on life support while a list of organ recipients is procured: Who will take my husband's eyes, his kidneys, his skin? A ventilator now breathes for him because Nick's brain no longer has the ability to tell his lungs to breathe. There is no activity in the brain, and there is an absence of blood flow. This is what the doctor tells me as he stands before me, my father behind me, like a pair of bookends holding me upright.

'I don't understand,' I tell the physician, more because I refuse to believe it than I don't understand, and he leads me to a chair and suggests that I sit. It's there, as I stare into his brown, disciplined eyes, that he explains again.

'Your husband has suffered from a traumatic brain injury. This caused swelling and bleeding in the brain,' he says, knotting his arms before his thin frame. 'A brain hemorrhage. The blood has spread over the surface of the brain,' and it's sometime there that he loses me, for all I can picture is an ocean of red blood spilling onto a sandy beach, staining the sand a fuchsia pink. I can no longer follow his words, though he tries hard to explain it to me, to choose smaller and more rudimentary words as the expression on my face becomes muddled and confused. A woman stops by, asking me to sign a donor authorization form, explaining to me what it is that I'm signing as I scrawl my name sloppily on a line.

I'm allowed into the trauma center to watch as a second physician, a woman this time, performs the very same tests the male doctor has just done, examining Nick's pupils for dilation, checking his reflexes. Nick's head is shifted to the left and the right, while the physician watches the movement of his steel-blue eyes. The doctor's eyes are stern, her expression growing grim. The CT scan is reviewed again and again, and I hear these words slip into the room: *brain shift* and *intracranial hemorrhaging*, and I wish that they would put a Band-Aid on it so that we could all go home. I will Nick's eyes, his throat, to do whatever it is they need for them to do. I beg for Nick to cough, for his eyes to dilate, for him to sit up on the gurney and speak. *Chinese or Mexican?* he'd say, and this time I would say Mexican.

I will never eat Chinese food again.

* * *

I say my goodbyes. I stand before Nick's still-alive but already-dead body and say goodbye. But I don't say anything else. I lay my hand on a hand that once held mine, that only days ago stroked my damp hair as I pushed an infant from my body. A hand that only hours ago cradled Maisie's tiny one as they skipped through the door—she in a pale pink leotard and tutu, he in the very same clothing that is now sprinkled with blood, clipped from his body like store coupons by some nurse's hurried hand—to ballet class, while I stayed behind with Felix in my arms. I run a convulsing hand along his hair. I touch the bristle of his face. I lick my thumb and wipe at a swatch of fluid above his eye. I press my lips to his forehead and cry.

This is not the way I want to remember him, here on this aseptic bed with tubing stuck into his arms and throat and nose; pieces of tape plastered to his face; the machines' grating beeps and bleeps, reminding me that if it weren't for them, Nick would already be dead. The appearance of his face has changed, and suddenly I realize that this is not my Nick. A terrible mistake has been made. My heart leaps. This man's face is covered with contusions and is swollen so that it's no longer recognizable, not to me, not to his hapless wife, another woman who will soon be informed her husband is dead. They've brought some other man into this room—mistaking him for Nick—and his wife, this poor man's wife, is now wandering the monochrome hospital halls wondering where he is. Perhaps he, too, is a Nick, but *my* Nick is somewhere else with Maisie. I stare at this torpid body before me, at the bloodstained hair, the pale, ductile skin, at the clothing—Nick's clothing, I thought only moments ago, but now I see it's an insipid blue polo shirt that any man could wear—that's been pruned from his body. This is not my Nick; I know this now. I swivel quickly and scurry through the curtain partition to find someone, *anyone*, so I can proclaim my discovery: the dying man on that hospital bed is not my husband. I stare a completely bemused nurse right in the eye and demand to know what they've done with my husband.

'Where is he? Where is he?' I beg, latching on to her arm and joggling it up and down.

But of course it is Nick. Nick is the man on that hospital bed. My Nick, and now everyone in the whole entire hospital is looking at me with pity, feeling thankful that they're not me.

When I'm done they lead me to another room, where Maisie sits on a hospital table beside my father, fervently filling him in on the fundamentals of her ballet teacher, Miss Becca: she's pretty, she's nice. The hospital staff has told me Maisie is fine, and yet there's a great wave of relief that washes over me at seeing her with my own eyes. My legs buckle at the knees, and I latch on to the door frame, telling myself it's true. She really is fine. I'm feeling dizzy, the room orbiting around me as if I am the sun and it is the earth. Felix is there in my father's grip, and in Maisie's hand is a lollipop, cherry red, her favorite, which dyes her tongue and lips bright red. There is a bandage on her hand—*just a small laceration*, I'm assured—and on her face is a smile. Big. Bright. Naive. She does not know that her father is dead. That he is dying as we speak.

Maisie turns to me, still bubbly from an afternoon at ballet. 'Look, Mommy,' she says, 'Boppy's here,' which is her nickname for my dad, and has been since she was two years old and couldn't enunciate her *r*'s or her *g*'s. She sets a sticky, lollipop-coated hand on his, one that is three times the size of hers. She's completely indifferent to the tears that plummet from my eyes. Her thin legs dangle from the edge of the examining table, one of her shoes lost in the maelstrom of the crash. The knee of her tights is torn. But Maisie doesn't mind. One of her pigtails has come loose, too, half of her corkscrew curls trailing her shoulders and back while the rest is held secure.

'Where's Daddy?' she says, squinting her eyes past me to see if Nick is there. I don't have it in me to tell her what's happened to Nick. I envision her sweet, innocent childhood thwarted with three words: *Daddy is dead*. She stares out the door frame, waiting for Nick to appear, and I see her pat her tiny stomach and tell me she's hungry. So hungry she could eat a pig, she says. *A horse*, I nearly correct her for the erroneous cliché, but then realize it doesn't matter. Nothing matters anymore now that Nick is dead. Maisie's eyes are hopeful, her smile wide.

Until they aren't.

A Code Blue is announced over the loudspeaker system, and at once the hallway is a flurry of activity. Doctors and nurses go running by, a crash cart getting shuttled down the linoleum floors. It's loud, the wheels thunderous against the floor, the items in the cart rattling in their metal drawers. At once, Maisie cries out in fright, bounding from the table and dropping to her knees, gathering herself into a ball on the floor. 'He's here,' she whines, and as I, too, fall to my knees and gather her into my arms, I find her shaking. My father's and my eyes meet.

'He followed us here,' Maisie cries, but I tell her no, that Daddy isn't here, and as I fold Maisie into my arms and stroke her bedraggled hair, I can't help but wonder what Maisie means, *He followed us*, and why, in a matter of seconds, she's gone from being hopeful of seeing Nick to scared.

'What is it, Maisie?' I ask. 'What's wrong?'

But she only shakes her head and closes her eyes tight. She won't tell me.

NICK

BEFORE

Clara stands before the kitchen sink in a striped crewneck T-shirt that surges at the center. Our baby. The shirt has a stretchy look to it, like spandex, so that it lies smoothly over the bump. From the back, you wouldn't know she was pregnant. Her dark denim jeans hug tightly to her curves, that stretchy elastic panel that holds our baby in place hidden beneath the extended length of the T-shirt. But from the side is a different story. From Clara's side, where I stand watching, completely hypnotized as she scrubs a Brillo pad along the surface of a frying pan, wiping away bits of cooked-on egg, her midsection swells to an unreasonable expanse, bumping into the sink. Red Tabasco sauce trails along the banded stripes of the T-shirt, over the hump that is always in the way.

Soon her maternity shirts will no longer fit.

We've begun to guess that she's got a linebacker tucked away inside her womb, a pro boxer, a budding defenseman for the Blackhawks hockey team. Something along those lines.

Clara sets down the Brillo pad and rubs at the small of her back, arching from the weight of our baby. Then she picks up the pad and gets back to work on the frying pan. A haze of hot air rises from the waterspout and into the air, making Clara sweat. These days, she is always hot. Her legs and feet swell like a middle-aged woman fighting the ugly effects of gravity, ripe with edema, so that she can no longer stuff her feet into her shoes. Along the armpits of the striped T-shirt, the blue begins to yellow with sweat.

But still, I stare. My Clara is exquisite.

'Jackson,' I say as I force my eyes away from my wife and gather the breakfast dishes from the table: Maisie's unfinished cereal bowl, my clean plate. I dump the crumbs into the trash can and load the dishwasher with the bowl and plate, a spoon.

'Too trendy,' Clara replies, eyes never swaying from the frying pan or the hot water that falls into the stainless-steel sink from a faucet I've recently replaced. Our home, a turn-of-the-century Craftsman, is incessantly a work in progress. Clara wanted a newer home; I wanted one with character, personality. A soul. I won, though oftentimes—my evenings and weekends consumed with fixing things—I wish I hadn't. 'He'll forever be one of three Jacksons everywhere he goes,' she says, and I relent to this, knowing it's true.

I try again. 'Brian,' I say this time, knowing I haven't met a Brian in recent years who was younger than twenty-five. My Brian will be the only Brian who's still a kid, while the rest are thirtysomething, balding businessmen.

She shakes her head. 'Too conventional,' she says. 'Might as well call him William or Richard or Charles.'

'What's wrong with Charles?' I ask, and peeking at me with her grassy green eyes, Clara smiles. Charles is my middle name, given to me by my father, also a Charles. But for Clara this won't do.

'Too conventional,' she says again, shaking her head so that ribbons of hair sway on the surface of the striped shirt, all the way down her back.

'How about Birch?' Clara suggests, and I laugh out loud, knowing this is the root of dispute: names like Birch. Or Finbar. Or Sadler, names she proposed yesterday and the day before.

'Hell, no,' I say, going to her and embracing her from behind, setting my chin upon her spindly shoulder, wrapping my hands around her bulging midriff. 'My son will not be a Birch,' I assert as through the T-shirt the baby kicks at me: an in utero high five. He agrees. 'You'll thank me later,' I say, knowing how sixth-grade boys have a predisposition for picking on boys named Birch and Finbar and Sadler.

'Rafferty?' she asks, and again I groan, my fingertips finding their way down to the small of Clara's back, where they press on those aching joints and nerves. Sciatica, her obstetrician told her, describing the softened ligaments that were causing pain, the shift in her center of gravity, the added weight. There was no doubt that Baby Brian was going to be a big boy, much bigger than Maisie—clocking in at seven pounds, eight ounces—had been.

Clara soughs at the pressure of my touch. It feels good, and yet it doesn't all at the same time. 'Isn't that some kind of ribbon?' I ask, pressing gently on her back, seeing Clara's meticulously wrapped holiday gifts all trimmed with red and green rafferty.

'That's raffia,' she says, and I laugh into her ear.

'Need I say more?' I ask. 'Raffia, *Rafferty*. What's the difference?'

'There's a difference,' she tells me knowingly, shooing away my hands from her back. She's had enough of my massage, for now, but she'll be back for more tonight, after Maisie is tucked in bed and Clara spreads drowsily across our mattress and begs for me to rub, directing my fingertips to the spots it most hurts. *Lower*, she'll say, and *To the left*, sighing when together we've found the spot where little Rafferty's head has lodged itself into her pelvis. She can no longer lie on her back, though the only thing in the world she wants to do is lie on her back. But the OB said no, that it isn't good for the baby. Now we sleep with a body pillow pressed between us, one that takes up more space than me, and I know it's only a matter of time before I find myself sleeping on the floor. Maisie has been wandering in, too, of late, concerned about her mother's swelling belly, knowing that soon she'll have to share her home, her toys, her parents, with a baby boy.

'Why don't you sit down?' I say to Clara, seeing that she is tired and hot. 'I'll finish the dishes,' I say, but Clara won't sit down. She's stubborn. It's one of the many things I love about her.

'I'm almost done,' she tells me as she continues to scour that frying pan.

And so instead, I collect the shreds of Sunday newspaper from the breakfast nook where Maisie sits quietly, staring at the comics, the *funnies* as she likes to call them because that's what Clara says. At the table, she giggles, and I ask, 'What's so funny?' plucking a piece of leftover Lucky Charms from her chin. Maisie doesn't say, but she points a gooey little finger at the paper, an image of a gargantuan elephant squishing some sort of prairie animal flat. I don't get it, but still I laugh, ruffling her hair with my hand. 'That's funny,' I say, as an image of the latest terrorist attack floats before Maisie's eyes while I pile up the paper for the recycle bin. I see her eyes jump at the image, leaping from comics to the front-page news: an inferno of fire; a building collapse; bits of rubble obstructing what was once a street; people with heads in their hands, crying; law enforcement agents walking around, toting M16s.

'What's that?' asks Maisie as that gooey finger finds its way this time to an image of a man with a gun on a street in Syria, red blood reduced to a dusty brown so it isn't evident that it's blood. And then, without waiting for a reply, Maisie's finger travels to a woman standing behind the man, caked in tears. 'She's sad,' she tells me, an interested expression on her pale face, one that proudly asserts an aggregate of freckles now that the heat of summer draws near. She's not concerned. She's too young to be concerned about the woman in the newspaper, crying. But still she takes notice, and I see the question there in her confused expression: *grown-ups don't cry.* So why is this woman crying?

And then Maisie asks the question out loud, 'Why?' as her eyes and Clara's eyes land on mine at the very same time, Maisie's curious, Clara's stymieing. *Why is the woman sad?* Maisie wants to know, but Clara wants this conversation through.

For Clara, when it comes to Maisie, ignorance is bliss.

'Time for you to get dressed, Maisie,' Clara says as she finishes rinsing the frying pan and sets it in the drying rack. She takes a series of short, quick strides across the room to gather the rest of the newspaper in her wet hands, struggling to bend to the floor to recoup the pieces I've dropped. My Sunday morning routine and also Clara's pet peeve: my dropping the newspaper to the ground. As she bends, her hands clutch her midsection, as if worried if she bends too far down, our baby will fall out.

'I'll get it,' I tell Clara as she drops what she's collected on the image of the buckled building, the crying woman, the humongous guns, hoping to erase the photograph from Maisie's mind. But I see Maisie's curious eyes and know she's still waiting for my reply. *She's sad*, those eyes remind me, begging, *Why?*

I set a hand on Maisie's, one that all but disappears in mine. On the kitchen chair, she squirms. Holding still for a four-year-old is near impossible. Her rangy legs kick willy-nilly beneath the table; she shifts erratically in her chair. Her hair is a mess and her pajamas are clotted with spilled milk, which will start to smell rancid the longer it sits, that *spilled milk* smell that often clings to kids. 'There are lots of people in this world,' I tell Maisie, 'some bad, some good. And some bad person hurt this woman's feelings and made her sad. But you don't have to worry about that happening to you,' I say quickly, before Maisie's mind has a chance to go there, to envision the collapsed buildings and the M16s here in our safe, suburban neighborhood. 'As long as Mommy and Daddy are here, we won't let anything like that happen to you,' and Maisie beams and asks if we can go to the park. The sad woman is forgotten. The guns are forgotten.

The only things on her mind now are seesaws and monkey bars, and I nod my head and say okay. I'll take her to the park, leaving Clara at home to rest.

I turn to Clara, and she gives me a wink; I did good. Of my little spiel, she approves.

I help Maisie from the table, and together we find her shoes. I remind her to go potty before we leave. 'But, Daddy,' she whines, 'I don't have to go potty,' though, of course she does. Like every other four-year-old in the world, she resists potty breaks and naps and anything green.

'You need to try,' I say and watch as she scampers off for the bathroom, where she'll leave the door open wide while she uses the step stool to climb up on the toilet and pee.

It's when she's gone for a whole thirty-eight seconds and no more that Clara comes to me, pressing that baby bump into my body, and tells me that she'll miss me, her words like some sort of voodoo or black magic, making me melt. She has a power over me; I'm under her spell. For the next forty-five minutes, while I'm romping around the playground with Maisie, my pregnant wife will be at home missing me. I smile, filled with warmth. I don't know what I ever did to deserve this.

Clara stands tall, just inches shy of my own six feet, un-showered, smelling of sweat and eggs, but beautiful beyond compare. In my whole life, I've never loved anyone as much as I love Clara. She kisses me in this way that only Clara could kiss, gauzy, diaphanous lips that brush the surface of mine, leaving me completely satisfied and yet greedy and wanting for more. I set my hands on the disappearing curves of her waistline; she slips hers under the cotton of my shirt. They're damp. She leans into me over the bulge of our baby, and again we kiss.

But as always, the moment passes too soon. Before we know it, Maisie comes skipping down the hall from the bathroom, calling out for me loudly, 'Daddy!' and Clara draws slowly away in search of bug spray and sunscreen.

Maisie and I pedal off down the sidewalk while Clara stands on the front porch, watching us go. We haven't gone more than a house or two when I hear a voice, grouchy and rude. Maisie hears it, too. She also sees her friend Teddy sitting on his own front lawn, picking at the grass, trying to tune out the sound of his dad screaming at his mom. They stand in an open garage, our neighbors Theo and Emily Hart, and it's pretty damn quick when Theo thrusts her against the garage wall. I slam on the bike brakes, but tell Maisie to pedal on ahead. 'Stop when you get to the red house,' I say, a redbrick home just about half a block away.

'Everything okay over there?' I call across the street, stepping off my bike, ready to make a run for it if he attempts a second assault. I'm expecting a response from Theo—something curt and rude, probably even threatening—but instead it comes from Emily as she wipes her hands on the thighs of her jeans and pats down her hair, stepping away from the garage wall as Theo hovers behind her, watching like a hawk.

'Doing great,' she says, with a smile as phony as spam email. 'Beautiful day,' she adds, then calls to Teddy, telling him to come inside for a bath. Teddy rises at once, not all gun-shy and reluctant as Maisie is when we suggest a bath. He does as he's told, and I wonder if it's simple compliance or something more. Something more like fear. Emily doesn't strike me as weak—she's a tall woman, a fit woman—and yet that's exactly what she is. This isn't the first time I've seen him buttonhole her with my own two eyes, his hands on her in a way that verges on abuse. If he does this out in the open, what does he do behind closed doors?

Clara and I have had this conversation more times than I can count.

You can't help someone who doesn't want to be helped.

I watch Emily and Teddy disappear inside, hand in hand. As I continue off down the street, hurrying to catch up with Maisie, who hovers at the end of a driveway waiting for me, I catch sight of Theo and his death glare.

CLARA

The grief comes at me in many ways.

I spend my mornings with sadness, my evenings in melancholy. In private, I cry. I can't bring myself to confess to Maisie why Nick is not here, and so I've taken to lying, to telling the girl who stands before me with pining eyes that her father has run out, that he's on an errand, that he's at work. I rely on tired responses—he'll be home *soon*; he'll be home *later*—thankful when Maisie smiles and prances gleefully away, telling me okay. Granting me amnesty, a reprieve. Later I will tell her. Soon. My father comes and my father goes. He brings dinner and sits beside me at the table and tells me to eat. He sets the food on the fork tines, the fork in my hand. He offers to take Maisie to the playground, but I say no, too afraid that if Maisie leaves without me, she also won't come home. And so we stay and get soused in sadness. We get marinated in it and submerged. We let the sadness steep into every inlet of our beings, making us tender and weak. Even Harriet the dog is sad, curled into a ball mopishly at my feet, while I hold Felix all day long, staring blankly at Maisie's cartoons on the TV screen. *Max and Ruby*, *Curious George*. Harriet's ears perk up at the sound of passing cars; a pizza deliveryman at the home next door sends her flying to her feet, mistaking the noise of an idling car for Nick. *It's not Nick*, I want to tell her. *Harriet, Nick is dead.*

Maisie points at something on the TV screen, laughing, tendrils of copper hair canopying her eyes. She's completely content to watch talking bunnies on the television set for eight hours a day, eating bags full of microwave popcorn for breakfast, lunch and dinner—asking of me, *Did you see that?* and I nod my head lifelessly, but I didn't see. I don't see anything. Nick is dead. What's there left to see?

But when I am not sad, I'm angry. Angry at Nick for leaving me. For being careless. For driving too fast with Maisie in the car. For driving too fast, period. For losing control and launching headfirst through the air and squarely into that tree, his body continuing to hurtle forward while the car suddenly stopped. I'm also mad at the tree. I hate the tree. The force of the impact wrapped the car around the old oak tree on Harvey Road, while Maisie sat in the back seat, on the opposite side, miraculously unharmed. She sat there as around her the duralumin of the car caved in like a mine collapse, trapping her inside, while in the front seat, Nick breathed his last self-sufficient breaths. The cause: Nick's warp speed, the sun, the turn. This is what I'm told, a fact that is repeated ad nauseam in the papers and on the news. *Crash on Harvey Road leaves one dead. Reckless driving to blame.* There is no investigation. Were Nick still alive, he would be given multiple citations for excessive speeding and reckless driving, to name a few. In no uncertain terms, I'm told that this is Nick's fault. Nick is to blame for his own death. He is the reason why I've been left alone with two young kids, a fragmented car and hospital bills. As it turns out, it's quite expensive to die.

If only Nick had slowed down, he wouldn't be dead.

But there are other things I'm mad about, too, besides Nick's lead foot and recklessness. His supply of running shoes strewn behind the front door, for example. They enrage me. They're still there, and in the mornings, tired and hazy from another sleepless night, I trip over them and feel livid that Nick didn't have the courtesy to put his shoes away before he died. *Damn it, Nick.*

The same can be said of his coffee mug abandoned on the kitchen sink and the newspaper spread sloppily across the breakfast nook so that sections of newsprint cascade to the ground, piece by piece. I pick them up and slap them back on the wooden table, angry with Nick for this whole blasted mess.

This is Nick's fault; it's his fault he's dead. The next morning Nick's alarm clock screams at him at six o'clock, as it always does—a force of habit, as is Harriet who rises to her feet in the hopes of being walked. Today Harriet will not be walked; tomorrow Harriet will not be walked. *Your husband, ma'am*, that police officer had said, before he welcomed Felix and me into his patrol car and drove us to the hospital where I signed an authorization form, renouncing my husband's eyes, his heart, his life, *was driving too fast*. Of course he was, I tell myself. Nick always drives too fast. *The sun*, he blamed, and again, *He was driving too fast*.

Was anyone hurt? I asked obtusely, expecting the officer to say no. No one. Oh, how stupid I've been. They don't send officers to collect the next of kin when no one's been hurt. And then I feel angry with myself for my own stupidity. Angry and embarrassed.

I let Maisie take to sleeping in my bedroom. My father warns me that this isn't a good idea. And yet, I do. I let her sleep in my room because the bed is suddenly too big, and in it, I feel small and lost and alone. Maisie is a restive sleeper. She talks in her sleep, mumbling quietly for Daddy, and I stroke her hair, hoping she will mistake my touch for his. She kicks in her sleep. When she wakes in the morning, her head is where her feet should go and vice versa.

As we settle into bed at seven thirty in the evening, Felix cocooned in his bassinet by my side, Maisie asks me for the umpteenth time, 'Where's Daddy?' and I reply with the same vacuous response, 'He'll be home soon,' and I know that Nick wouldn't do it this way. This isn't how Nick would handle things, were I the one who was dead. Oh, how I wish I were the one who was dead. Nick is the better parent. He would use words, gentle words, euphemisms and colloquialisms, to explain. He would set her down on his lap, and swathe her in his benevolent arms. *Resting in peace*, he would say, or *In a better place*, so that Maisie would imagine me in Disney World, napping on a bed in the highest tower of King Stefan's castle with the exquisite Sleeping Beauty, and there would be no sadness or incertitude over the fact that I was dead. Instead she would forever envision me lying on a luxurious bed in a beautiful evening gown, my hair framing my face, a crown set on my head. I would be elevated to status of princess. Princess Clara.

But not Nick.

'When will Daddy be home?' she asks me, and I run my hands through her hair, force a smile and issue my boiler-plate response: 'Soon,' turning quickly away, attending to a disgruntled Felix so she will not see me cry.

* * *

The day of Nick's funeral, it rains, as if the sky itself is commiserating with me, crying along while I cry. The sun refuses to show its culpable face, hiding behind the safe-guard of blubbery, gray rain clouds that fill the sky. In the distance, the clouds reach formidably into the sky, a Mount Saint Helens of clouds. Connor, Nick's best friend, stands beside me, on the left, while my father is on the right, Maisie snuggled in between my father and me. As the priest com-mits Nick's body to the ground, we scatter handfuls of earth on top of the casket.

Maisie holds my hand as our feet sink into mud. There are rain boots on her feet, teal rain boots with puppies on their shaft, to pair with the black A-line dress. She's tired of asking where Nick is, and so she stands unsuspectingly as her father is lowered into the ground.

'What are we doing, Mommy?' she asks instead, won-dering why all these mournful people have gathered under a canopy of black umbrellas, watching as a crate is buried in the ground, much in the same way that Harriet buries her bones in the backyard.

'This is unacceptable,' Nick's mother says to me later as we drift away from the cemetery to our parked cars.

My father says, 'You should tell her, Clarabelle,' which is his nickname for me, one I've grown to love, but once de-spised. In the distance, Maisie skips along with a younger cousin, only three years old, both oblivious to the obvious sadness that imbues the air along with the laden humidity. Outside it is hot and muggy, gnats and mosquitoes proliferating before our eyes. I push Felix in the baby carriage, plodding over the pitted lawn and around the granite headstones. Dead people. I wonder how they died.

'I'll tell her when I'm ready,' I snap at the both of them, my father and Nick's mother. When I am not sad, I'm mad. My father means well; Nick's mother does not. She's never liked me one speck, though these feelings weren't meant to be mutual. And yet they are.

Only my father comes to my home after the funeral. The rest drift in their own direction, hugging me in these awkward, strung-out ways before saying goodbye. They don't stay long for fear that death and bad luck are contagious. That if they stick around me too long, they might just catch the bug. Even Connor makes a quick departure, though before he goes he asks if there's anything he can do for me, anything I need. I say no.

Emily is the only one who lingers for more than two and a half seconds. 'Call if you need anything,' she says to me, and I nod my head, knowing I won't call. Her husband, Theo, stands behind her by three paces or more, checking his watch twice during the twenty-second exchange, and at seeing him Maisie bounds to my side, clutching me tightly by the hand, her body half hidden behind mine. She lets out a feeble cry, and Emily pities the child, saying, 'Poor thing,' as if Maisie's fear has something to do with Nick's death rather than Theo. Emily is a neighbor, the kind I spend lazy afternoons with on the front porch, killing time while our kids play, my Maisie and her Teddy, who is also four. Teddy, short for Theodore, named after his dad who goes by Theo. Theo and Emily and Teddy. Except we don't let Maisie play with Teddy when Theo is there. Theo is a gruff man, prone to violence when he's angry and sometimes when he's not. Emily has told me as much, and we've all heard his voice— Nick, Maisie and me—resounding through open windows and across the still summer night, screaming at Emily and Teddy for reasons unknown.

Theo terrifies Maisie as much as he does me.

'Promise me you'll call,' she says before Theo lays an autocratic hand on her arm and she turns, walking away with the rest of the drifters who flee the cemetery, one step behind him all the way through the lawn. I promise nothing. It isn't until they're out of view that Maisie finally lets go of my hand and steps from the safety of my shadow.

'Are you okay?' I ask her, peering into her eyes, and when she can no longer see Theo or Emily, Maisie nods her head and says that she is. 'He's gone now,' I promise her, and she smiles cautiously.

In my home, my father doesn't stay long, either. He can't. There is my mother, of course, sitting at home with a paid babysitter while my father attends to me. He is pulled in two directions. He can't care for both her and me.

'She's been seeing things,' he tells me reluctantly. 'Hallucinations, like the doctor told us might happen. A black crow sitting on the curtain rod,' he says, 'and bugs.'

I grimace. 'What kind of bugs?' I ask.

'Ants,' he tells me, 'climbing the walls.'

'Go to her,' I say, disheartened to hear my mother's dementia has taken a turn for the worse. 'I'm fine,' I assure him, as I set a hand on his thin, liver-spotted arm, and grant him permission to leave. Felix is asleep; Maisie is twirling around the living room, obliviously dancing.

As my father's car pulls out of the driveway, I see the resignation. He isn't sure he should leave. I give him a thumbs-up to be sure. *I'm okay, Daddy.*

But am I?

* * *

That night Maisie sleeps with me again. She toddles into my bedroom with her scruffy teddy bear in her arms, the one that used to be mine. She's all but eaten an ear off, a nervous habit that's picking up speed. She stands at the foot of the bed in a nightgown of spring bouquets, dahlias in every shade of pink—fuchsia, salmon, cerise—her feet covered in white ankle socks. Her copper hair hangs long down her back, gnarled and bumpy, the tail end clinging to a rubber band.

'I can't sleep, Mommy,' she says, gnawing on the ear of that poor bear, though we both know it was only three and a half minutes ago that I kissed her good-night in her own bed. That I pulled the sheets up clear to her neck. That I kissed the bear's downy forehead and tucked him in, too. That I told Maisie, when she asked for Daddy to tuck her in and give her a kiss good-night, 'He'll be up just as soon as he gets home,' hoping that she didn't see or hear the blatant lie.

Felix is in my arms, and with a *pat, pat, pat* to the back, I slowly ease him to sleep. He wears his yellow sleep sack, likely hot in the torrid room. The air conditioner, it seems, has stopped working. What does one do about a broken air conditioner? Only Nick would know, and again I find myself mad that Nick would leave me with a broken air conditioner and no clue what to do. Nick should have made a list of such contingencies, were he to suddenly die. Who should repair the air conditioner, mow the lawn, pay the newspaper boy?

The windows are open. The ceiling fan whirls above us, as in one queen-size bed, Maisie and I sleep. Harriet the dog lies at the foot of it, Felix just three feet away in his bassinet. I don't sleep because I have stopped sleeping. Sleep, like most things these days, evades me. The room is dark, save for the night-light Maisie insists upon because she is afraid of the dark. But the night-light casts shadows on the darkened walls, and it's these shadows that I stare at as Felix sleeps and Harriet snores, and Maisie orbits the bed in her sleep, like space junk orbiting the earth, pulling the thin cotton sheet from my sweating body.

And then, come 1:37 a.m., Maisie sits upright in bed.

She talks in her sleep as much as she talks when awake, and so the grumbles that issue from her mouth are of little concern. They're incomprehensible, mostly. Drivel. Until she begins speaking of Nick, that is. Until her eyes dart open, and she goggles me, her green eyes wide and scared. Her clammy little hand gropes for mine, and she calls out, she cries desperately, pleadingly, 'It's the bad man, Daddy. The bad man is after us!'

'Who, Maisie?' I ask, shaking her gently awake. But Maisie is already awake. At the foot of the bed, Harriet stirs, and beside us, Felix begins to cry. A small cry, merely fussing. He stretches his arms above his head, and I know in the moments to come his small cry will escalate into a full-out squall. Felix is ready to eat, and, as if in preparation, my chest leaks through my gown.

'Him!' she says insufficiently as she sinks low under the bedcovers and tosses them above her head. Maisie is hiding.

Hiding from some man. A bad man that is coming after her and Nick. But Maisie knows nothing about bad men, or so I believe, and so I try to convince myself that it's only make-believe, the hunters who killed Bambi's mother or maybe Captain Hook coming after her and Nick in a dream. But as she says it again, wide-awake and far more terrified this time for it to be make-believe—*the bad man is after us!*—my mind makes up for Maisie's lack of details, imagining a bad man trailing Nick and her down Harvey Road, and at this my heart begins to pound, my hands to sweat more than they are already sweating.

'Maisie,' I plead, as mollifying as I can, though inside I'm anything but relaxed. But Maisie is under the bedcovers now, and she is not speaking. When I try to touch her, she screams out, 'Stop!' and then she goes silent, like some sort of toy whose batteries have just died. She'll say nothing, though I ask and then I beg. And when the begging is ineffective, I find myself becoming angry. It's out of desperation, only. The reason I become angry. There's a desperate need to know what it is that Maisie's prating about. What bad man? What does Maisie mean?

'If you tell me, Maisie, we can get donuts in the morning,' I say, with the promise of a Long John slathered in strawberry icing.

I promise other material things, as well—a new teddy bear, a hamster—hoping to lure her out of the pitch-black, suffocating world beneath those sheets. But that world beneath the sheets is also safe for Maisie, and so she won't come.

By now, Felix has begun to scream. 'Maisie,' I say again over the sound of Felix, trying to pry the covers from her hands. 'What bad man?' I ask desperately, and it's speculation only when I probe, 'Was the bad man in a car?' and from under the covers I sense the nod of Maisie's head and hear her tiny voice whisper, 'Yes,' and at this I gasp.

A bad man. In a car. Following Maisie and Nick.

I stroke Maisie's hair and force myself to take measured breaths, trying hard to remain calm as the world crumbles around me, and I find it harder and harder to breathe.

'The bad man,' Maisie blubbers again as I slip her teddy bear beneath the sheets and into her clammy hands, asking sedately, 'Who, Maisie, who? What bad man?' though inside I feel anything but sedate. Who is the bad man that was following Nick and her? Who is the bad man that took my husband's life?

And without sitting up in bed or sliding the covers from her face, she thrums, her voice masked by the density of the sheets, 'The bad man is after us. He's going to get us,' and with that she flies out from under the sheets like a rocket and into the master bath, where she makes haste of slamming closed and locking the door with so much zeal that a frame falls from the wall and smashes onto the floor, shattering into dozens of pieces.

NICK

BEFORE

There was no way I could have known that morning as I stood at the foot of our bed, watching Clara sleep, the way our lives would change. I stood there for longer than I planned to, staring at her as she lay on the bed sound asleep, completely transfixed by the movement of her eyes beneath their lids, the curve of her nose, the delicacy of her lips and hair. I listened to the sound of her breathing, flat, even breaths interrupted by the occasional gulp of air, the thin blue sheet pulled clear up to her neck, hiding our baby, so that it swelled with each breath.

I stood at the foot of the bed watching Clara sleep, wanting nothing more than to climb back into bed and spend the day wrapped up in each other as we used to do, to run my hands over the ballooning belly and spend hours trying to come up with a name for our baby boy.

There was no way I could have known, as I leaned over to plant a kiss on Clara's forehead, that outside a storm was brewing, a supercell storm that would soon tear through our lives, and that all that unstable air moving around the atmosphere was waiting for us just outside the front door.

There was no way I could have known that I was running out of time.

* * *

Outside the bedroom door, Maisie stands, arms crossed across herself, her hair standing on end. She's still half asleep, her eyes trying to adjust to the traces of light that come in through a hallway window. She rubs at her eyes. 'Morning, Maisie,' I say in a whisper as I drop down to my knees and take her into my arms, this tiny little thing that collapses against me, tired and tuckered out. 'How about we get you some breakfast and let Mommy sleep for a while?' I suggest, hoisting her into my arms and carrying her down the stairs, knowing how Clara's nighttime sleep has been interrupted of late, always trammeled by her inability to find a comfortable position to sleep. For the last few weeks, the leg cramps have woken her in the middle of the night, either that or the baby kicking in earnest to get out. *He's got his days and his nights all mixed up*, Clara said, though I find it hard to believe there's some sort of timetable in utero, that the baby has any notion of when is night and when is day. But maybe.

I can't do anything about the cramps or the kicking, but I can occupy Maisie for a while so that Clara can sleep.

I warm frozen waffles in the toaster oven and serve them to Maisie at the coffee table with a side of syrup. I brew my coffee—decaf, as if I am pregnant, too; my vow to Clara that she doesn't have to suffer through this pregnancy alone—and pour Maisie juice. I turn on the TV for Maisie and set the kitchen timer for an hour. 'Please, don't wake Mommy until after two episodes of *Max & Ruby* or when the timer rings,' I say to her, adding, 'Whichever comes first,' before planting a kiss on her forehead, too, one which is still waxy from sleep. 'Did you hear me, Maisie?' I ask, and, 'When can you wake Mommy?' just to be sure Maisie was listening and that she heard. Maisie is a smart girl—sometimes too smart for her own good—but she's also four, eyes and ears lost to the cartoon bunnies that now fill our TV screen.

'When the timer rings,' she says, eyes not meeting mine. Harriet sits at the floor beside her feet, ever hopeful that Maisie will drop her waffles to the floor.

'Good girl.' I stuff my feet into a pair of shoes and find my car keys. 'See you later, alligator,' I say, opening the garage door to leave.

'In a while, crocodile,' says Maisie, mouth stuffed full with food.

I make my way to the garage. I'm not halfway there when a text comes through on my phone, and I stop midstride to see who it is, groaning already because of course it's bad news. Good news never arrives at 7:00 a.m. in the form of a text message.

Take your time, it says. Another cancellation. Wilsons flew the coop. —N

CLARA

Morning. A stay of execution for those who are grieving. The first few marks of sunlight appear in the darkened sky, bringing oxygen back to the stifled world and making it easier to breathe.

I wake on the floor beside the bathroom door, Felix spread lengthwise on my extended legs. The door to the bathroom, as I jiggle the glass knob for the eighteenth time, is locked. It's an antique, a 1920s fluted crystal glass knob; we no longer have the key. Perhaps we never had the key, but this didn't matter, not until Maisie took to locking herself on the wrong side of the door as she did last night when she cried out, *The bad man is after us. He's going to get us*, before scurrying from bed.

She won't come out.

There is glass everywhere, lying unprotected on the floor.

For four hours now, she's been on the other side of the bathroom door and I've listened as her frenzied cry died down to a quiet drone, her requests for *Daddy* lessening as she sobbed herself to sleep. And now the sunlight appears, chasing the shadows away from the walls.

For hours I've replayed Maisie's words over and over and over again in my mind: *The bad man is after us. He's going to get us.* 'Please, Maisie,' I beg for the forty-seventh time. 'Please, come out.'

But Maisie won't come out.

* * *

Maisie sits at the breakfast nook staring vacantly at three microwave pancakes set before her on a plate. There was only one squirt of syrup remaining in the bottle, and so her pancakes are mostly dry. But that's not the reason she won't eat. On the table before me, there is nothing, no food. I, too, won't eat. Not until someone makes me, which will be soon. My father fills a mug of coffee for me and brings it to the nook, setting it on the wooden slab before me.

He pats my head. He tells me to drink. He tells Maisie to eat her pancakes.

In my bedroom upstairs, the bathroom door lies flat, the hinge pins tapped out of place with a nail and a hammer. My father talked me through it on the phone. He didn't need to come, I told him. We were fine. Maisie was fine, Felix was fine, I was fine. But my father didn't believe for one split second that any of us were fine. Maybe it was the panic in my voice, or the fact that Maisie had locked herself in the bathroom overnight and, on the mosaic tile floor, cried herself to sleep. I don't know. Or maybe it was Felix, thrown into a state of hysteria once again, his tummy empty, and me too busy removing hinge pins from a raised panel door to feed him, after sixty-seven unsuccessful attempts to lure Maisie out on her own devices.

I can't be in two places at one time.

'It's okay to ask for help,' my father tells me now as Maisie stabs at those pancakes with a kid fork, some sort of adorable cow printed on its grippy, teal shank. But she doesn't eat the pancakes. She mangles and dismembers them. She mutilates the pancakes. 'You don't have to do this alone, you know.'

But I am already alone, aren't I? No matter how many people are here in this house with me, I am still alone.

My father has yet to go upstairs, to see the bathroom door lying listlessly on its back, the picture frame's shards of glass sloshed across the floor, the stash of rumpled tissues into which I cried a small lake, my eyes now so red and puffy they're practically swollen shut.

'I did ask for help,' I tell my father as he hands me my own plate of microwave pancakes sans syrup, with instructions to eat. 'That's why you're here.' He fills his coffee mug with soapy water at the kitchen sink and swirls it around before plunging a dishrag into the ceramic. He won't leave that mug for me to clean. He is a lean man, too lean, the hair on his own head reminiscent of that on Felix's head. He dresses like an older man with the waistlines too high and the patterns of his collared shirts no longer in style but now considered vintage. On his wiry frame, his clothes droop and sag, his body getting swallowed by the fabric. He's aging far too quickly for me.

'Did you find the check?' I ask him, remembering only then the missing check from my father's tenants, a two thousand dollar rent payment that he endorsed but never deposited into the account. My mother is to thank for this, to be sure, my mother who is ever wandering about, misplacing things. The missing check was an exigent matter in the days before Felix's birth and Nick's death, somehow forgotten in the upheaval of the last few days, though it was less than a week ago that Izzy and I sat together, combing through my parents' belongings for it, and coming up with nothing. Izzy, the paid babysitter, who watches over my mother when my father and I aren't there. Izzy's own parents died when she was eighteen and then nineteen—heart failure for one, followed by stage-four leukemia for the other—leaving her to care for an eight-year-old sister. Now, ten years later, she's working hard to earn money to put the sister through college.

Izzy has been with my mother since the dementia began, or rather since we knew she had dementia and was not simply distracted and absentminded. She works for one of those home health agencies and, as my father says, is a godsend. Her hair is a short cropped cut—somehow decidedly masculine and feminine all at the same time—bleached white, and often adorned with flowers, her body decked out in an odd bricolage of things: skirts and tights, gimmicky jewelry, ornate socks pulled clear up to the knees. She has a silver pendant on a rolo chain, one that bears her name on a charm in an easy-to-read typeface, large enough for the elderly and disabled to see. Large enough for my mother to see, and when she gazes at her disoriented as she often does, Izzy plucks that trinket from around her neck and holds it out for my mother to see. *Izzy*, it reads.

Izzy cooks, she cleans, she micromanages my mother in the bathtub with reminders to wash this and to scrub that. She's a babysitter to a degree, there whenever my father can't be and sometimes when he is, to assure that my mother doesn't hop in the car and decide to take it for a spin, or serve herself a bowl of cat litter and eat it with milk and a spoon, both of which she's done before. More than once. *Why do you even have cat litter when there is no cat?* I'd asked my father at the time, and he shrugged his shoulders and said my mother insisted on it. Of course she did. Because to her there is still a cat, poor Oliver who was run over by a truck years ago.

She still sees him sometimes, hiding behind the curtain panels.

But the incident that takes the cake is the time she decided to give Maisie's hair a trim, disappearing stealth-like into the kitchen and coming back moments later with a pair of scissors in hand. When we asked her why she did it, she said, *Clara's hair smells pungent*, as Izzy drew her from the room that day while Maisie plummeted to the floor, crying. *Like a dirty old sponge. That's why. I can't even get a comb through it anymore. It needed to be trimmed. It's disgusting.*

Clara's hair.

My hair.

My mother has needed more and more assistance of late, no longer sleeping through the night, becoming nocturnal and spending her nights pacing the home, oftentimes crying for no apparent reason at all. Her brain no longer receives messages from the bladder that she needs to pee, and as a result she wets herself almost every day. She fought the illness tooth and nail once, using memory games, crossword puzzles, reams of sudoku. She memorized nursery rhymes to prove to herself that she could do it, and then waltzed around reciting the words to *Simple Simon* without a clue as to why. She read the newspaper; she exercised more and as often as she could, remembered to take her vitamins. She discovered that eating salmon helps with memory retention and took to eating it day in and day out, and she signed up for clinical trials to test the efficacy of experimental drugs. She pulled my old Simon memory game from storage and played it at great length.

Nothing worked; her mind continued to fade.

Izzy hadn't wanted me to help look for the missing rent check that day for obvious reasons: I was nine months pregnant and could hardly walk. *Why don't you take a load off*, she said to me as we drifted into my father's office together, and I tried logging in to his bank account online, to be sure my father hadn't deposited the check and somehow or other forgotten. My mother rarely left the house; it seemed the check had to be here somewhere, and yet it wasn't. But as I sat down at the computer and found the slip of paper where my father kept a listing of his accounts and passwords, I felt the first contraction. Izzy gently withdrew the computer mouse from my hand and told me in no uncertain terms to leave, to go lie down, staring at me with a look of genuine fear at the prospect of childbirth. She took care of all kinds—women with dementia, aging men suffering from incontinence—but she didn't deliver babies.

It's nothing, I'm sure, I told her, trying hard to catch my breath from the shock of it, from the sudden pain. *Just Braxton Hicks*, I said. But still, I left to go home and lie down while Izzy continued the search. I assured her I'd check the account later, from home, but by the end of the night, Felix

was born, and I, of course, had forgotten the password anyway, forgotten all about the missing check.

Now, standing in my kitchen, my father shakes his head.
The check has not been found.

'Don't worry about me,' he says. 'You have a lot on your
mind, and there's plenty more money where that came from.'
He pats my head in the way he did when I was just a girl,
a statement, which is really neither here nor there, but altogether true. I have many things on my mind, though one
thing eclipses all other thoughts this morning as I stare
blankly out the double-hung windows and into the backyard,
neglecting my pancakes as they drift from hot to warm to
cool. Outside it is hot, as hot as it is inside our now un-air-
conditioned home. Rain plays a game of hide-and-seek with
us, here one day before disappearing again for another six.
The lawn yellows with thirst, turning brittle in the sweltering summer heat. It is just after 9:00 a.m., and already the
mercury on the thermometer reaches eighty degrees. Birds
wait in vain on the perch of a backyard birdbath that has
long since gone dry. That is something Nick is in charge
of: feeding the birds, filling the birdbath. Even the birds
miss Nick, the American goldfinch sitting on the edge of
the resin birdbath, a female cardinal perched in the boughs
of an evergreen tree.

The bad man is after us. He's going to get us.

That's the one thought on my mind. In no uncertain
terms, Maisie has made it clear that Nick's car accident
was no accident at all. Maisie's words return to me again
and again, so many questions running through my mind.
Does Maisie know this bad man? This bad man in a car that
pushed Nick and her from the road? Did she get a glimpse

of him before the car went airborne, flying into the tree? I want to ask Maisie, but I don't want to upset her any more than she is already upset. And yet when my father steps from the room to gather laundry to wash for me, I lean across the breakfast nook and guardedly ask, 'Did Daddy see the man in the car, Maisie? Did he see the bad man in the car?' Her eyes turn sad, and she nods her head a negligible yes. Nick saw the man. Before he died, Nick saw the man who was about to take his life.

But before I can ask more, my father returns.

Like Maisie, I stab at my pancakes. I mutilate them, too. My father tells me to eat.

* * *

It just so happens that Felix has a well-baby check this morning with the pediatrician. 'You and Felix go alone and I'll stay with Maisie,' my father says as he removes the breakfast dishes from the nook. 'Take your time,' he adds. 'Izzy is with your mom.'

Normally I would object but today I agree. Today there are other things on my mind, and I know that if Maisie were there, standing beside me on the minced gravel that flanks Harvey Road, there would be questions.

And so I leave the breakfast nook and slip away to my bedroom alone, stuffing myself into maternity clothes because that's all I have that will fit. It doesn't matter that there is no baby in my womb; my body has yet to collapse back into its original shape. I'm still fat. My uterus cramps and clenches, trying hard to shrink down to size. Involution, it's called, the shrinkage of my uterus from a watermelon back to a pear, as lochia dribbles from my insides and every single atrium and artery and ventricle in my heart aches. My heart is broken, as is my womb.

It comes to me again in that moment, as I step into a pair of stretchy gray leggings and a sleeveless tunic top: Nick is dead. I reach into his dresser drawer, plucking undershirts out at random, pressing them to my face in an attempt to breathe in his scent, an intoxicating combination of deodorant, cologne and aftershave, finding that Nick's scent has been washed clean and replaced with lavender detergent, a realization that again makes me cry. I dig deeper into the drawer, smelling them all, hoping to find one on which his scent remains. But I find none. No undershirts that smell of Nick, but what I do find, tucked there beneath a dozen white undershirts, is a scrap of paper that for whatever reason piques my interest, paper where no paper should be. I set the shirts aside and grope for the scrap, finding a receipt to the local jewelry store in excess of four hundred dollars. The receipt is dated months ago, and under the line item it reads *pendant necklace*. Unconsciously my hands go to my neck, knowing there's no necklace there. Nick never gave me a necklace, nor is my birthday or our anniversary coming anytime soon. My stomach clenches. This necklace isn't for me.

Nick spent four hundred dollars on a necklace that wasn't meant for me? How could that be?

It's a mistake only, I assure myself, rummaging for excuses and coming up near empty. I decide that the receipt must belong to another man, to some other man who bought his lovely wife a four-hundred-dollar pendant necklace. A mix-up at the dry cleaner's, I also decide. Somehow or other, this receipt found its way from another man's shirt pocket into Nick's dresser drawer.

It makes no logical sense, and yet it's far better than considering the alternative.

There's no way in the world Nick was having an affair.

In the bedroom, I refuse to make eye contact with the shards of broken picture frame glass, or the bathroom door lying prostrate on the wooden floorboards—memories of Maisie's and my night. I don't look in the mirror to see the redness of my eyes.

I find the spare car keys and, with a kiss to Maisie's head and a pat on my father's arm, Felix and I leave.

NICK

BEFOЯE

Stacy is waiting for me in the parking lot when I pull into work. In her hands rest two Starbucks cups, one for her and one for Dr. C, both containing an overdose of caffeine. She holds them out to torment me and says the exact same thing that's on my mind, 'Two more months,' because we both know I'll be celebrating my baby's arrival with a venti coffee, fully loaded, to make up for nine months of caffeine withdrawal.

The headaches were stymieing at first, enough that I almost caved after the first two days. Like some sort of alcoholic on a drinking binge, I sneaked into the closest chain coffee shop twice a day and stood in line, standing there with no intent to buy, inhaling the aroma of freshly brewed coffee to see if it was enough to jump-start my day. One time I even ordered a double espresso, but before the barista could hand it to me, I changed my mind. Trust is one of the pillars of a good marriage, the foundation a marriage is built upon. I had made a promise to Clara, and I intended to keep it.

Now, as I hold open the door for Stacy and she and her two cups of coffee pass through, I tell myself only two more months to go. Two more months until I can drink caffeine, too. 'Your perseverance is quite impressive, my friend,' says Stacy as I follow her into the dental practice that bears my name on the front door, Solberg & Associates Family Dental. It's a space that's entirely chic—and not at all my style—Clara's design because it was the only way she'd say yes to my idea of starting my own practice. To me, it just made sense. There were more start-up costs initially, but in the long run we, Clara and me, would see the financial benefits of owning our own practice, as well as being blessed with financial independence that working for another practice would curtail. That's the way I explained it to Clara anyway, a few years ago as we sat at the breakfast nook of the fixer-upper we'd just bought for a steal, well below asking price because my negotiation skills weren't half bad, Clara's disinterested eyes glazing over as I went on and on about the costs of a tenant upfit to an existing commercial structure, dental lenders, malpractice insurance and operating fees—employee salaries, office equipment, the pricey drip coffee maker I'd go nine months without being able to use.

As it was, I had an undergrad in business administration plus a DMD. It seemed the logical next step for me. I was in the know, a businessman with a doctor of dental medicine degree. And Clara, with full decorating authority and a liberal budget, agreed. In time. My credit was good enough, and so even though we had a house and cars to pay for, my hefty student loans, securing a loan wasn't a big deal, even one in excess of four hundred grand, though I had to get life and disability insurance to go with it, money set aside to cover my debt should I die. It was a formidable proposition, and yet, at twenty-six, death wasn't likely to happen anytime soon. I also put our house on the line as collateral. Though the medical and dental industries weren't hit by the same recession that hampered other businesses at the time, I had to prove to the lender I wasn't going to default on the loan.

The space Clara and I picked out for the practice was close to home, less than nine miles, so that my commute was a mere thirteen minutes each way. We paid more to find space on a four-lane highway, on one of the main arteries in town, so that the thousands of cars that drove past each day would see us, Solberg & Associates Family Dental, and that we weren't tucked off on some country road that no one ever used. Clara agreed. Not right away, no, but in time she agreed, and eventually set to work ordering furniture to fill the waiting room, a wide-screen TV and expensive diversions for the kids: a sand maze and a play cube and a top-of-the-line roller-coaster table, because at the time she was newly pregnant with Maisie and could think of nothing but catering to kids. She subscribed to magazines and got a wire wall rack to hold them all. She insisted we line the floor with hardwood or tile, and I readily agreed, knowing that winter in Chicagoland is replete with slush and snow, and hardwood would be easier to keep clean. Of course it cost more than carpeting, but at a time when we were putting so much into the practice, it seemed so easy just to throw a little more in. And a little more, and a little more. Clara and I were both consumed with this false sense of free money, forgetting somehow that sooner or later we'd need to pay it all back, convincing ourselves that defrayment would come in the form of small payments, and by then business would be booming anyway and money wouldn't be a concern at all.

Clearly we were wrong.

And now, as I walk into the office and watch Nancy at the front desk, Nancy the receptionist, reprinting a receipt because she's managed to drip her cocoa on it so that blotches of brown sully the words on the receipt, I wonder how much the additional sheet of paper is costing me, how much for the toner and the electricity that keeps the printer functional, how much I pay Nancy, kind, affable Nancy whom every patient likes, to sip her cocoa and answer the phones and spill her drink on the receipts.

There was a time when I didn't think about any of it, but now I can't help but think of it all, every last penny I no longer have to my name. The truth of the matter is, I'm in dire straits and I don't want Clara to know. I've tried to think of ways to turn a quick and easy profit before having to admit to her that the practice is crumbling, our life savings nearly gone. I've looked into everything I can think of to make extra cash: dog walking on my lunch break, taking a second job in the evenings and telling Clara that I've expanded my hours again, selling my own plasma, selling my sperm. Selling drugs. I could get my hands on all sorts of pharmaceuticals—the perks of being a dentist—and then sell them on the street to middle-class moms. Heck, I have even considered heading to Vegas and betting everything I have on roulette, but the cost of a hotel and an airplane ticket quickly sapped that idea, as well as the need to explain to Clara where I'd been.

And then, in these moments of total desperation, when

my self-pity gets the best of me and I can barely see beyond the *past due* notices to think logically, my mind drifts to the notion of *Russian* roulette—one round in the chamber of a revolver—wondering if Clara might be better off without me around. It is morbid, which really isn't me. I like to think of myself as a glass-half-full kind of guy. And yet it is natural, human nature, when the stress gets the best of me, to think to myself, *I wish I was dead.*

CLAЯA

'He's losing weight,' the pediatrician says to me. Her name is Dr. Paul, and I can't help but wonder if some male ancestor ever had the misfortune of being named Paul. Paul Paul. The room is happy, and there is a panorama of farm life painted on the otherwise white walls: a horse, a pig, a spotted cow.

'Mrs. Solberg,' she says to me, and I force my thoughts to the baby on the baby scale, Felix, who cries from the sudden coldness of the hard plastic tray on which he lies.

'He's losing weight.'

Dr. Paul asks how the nursing has been going, and I lie and say fine. Just fine. I've nursed a baby before. I'm an old pro. And yet I've never been a widow before. This is wherein the fault lies, the reason why Felix is not eating well, why he is losing weight. Widowhood is all new to me, and it's here that I struggle, though I don't tell the doctor this, but I don't need to because everyone in the whole entire world now knows that I am a widow, that my husband is the one who took the turn out on Harvey Road too fast, that he crashed the car into a tree, that he did it with our four-year-old daughter in the back seat, that he's dead.

'Some weight loss after birth is normal,' she tells me, 'but Felix has continued to lose weight since we visited him in the hospital. He's lost over fourteen ounces since he was born. This is of concern,' she says, though her eyes lack judgment. I'm not being criticized. Dr. Paul is simply concerned. She lays a hand on my arm and asks again, 'How has the nursing been going?' and this time I tell her.

* * *

I'm decidedly opposed to roadside memorials. It seems a silly way to honor a beloved family member who's now dead. And yet I find myself purchasing a white wooden cross at the local craft store, and a spray of flowers, burgundy and pink, because it's premade and on display at the florist shop. I don't have time to special order; I want it now. The cross itself seems glib. It's not as if we go to church, not often, though we had Maisie baptized because Nick's mother said Maisie was bound for perdition if we didn't. The only times we've been to church since are when Mrs. Solberg is in town, when we dress up in our Sunday best and slide into the spartan pew, pretending this is something we do.

But still, I buy the cross to go along with the floral bouquet. It seems the thing to do.

I drive to the scene of the accident, where a red-winged blackbird sits on a thin telephone wire watching me, like a tightrope walker, its gnarled black claws clinging tightly to the cord. Its black feathers shimmer in the late-morning sun, a single patch of red and yellow blazoned upon its side. It sings a brassy, emphatic song, and from somewhere in the distance, perched in the cattails of a roadside ditch, a female returns its call, quieter and less emphatic than the male. They parley back and forth, back and forth again, making plans to meet, and as I stand there on the side of the road, the sun bearing down on me and making me sweat, the car parked less than ten feet away, Felix inside with the window rolled down, the male red-winged blackbird leaves his perch and swoops down into the cattails to find his mate.

The houses in the area reside in one of those green housing developments with their energy-efficient designs, a neighborhood composting program, a community garden. The homes are all faux farmhouses, too clean and modern to be real farmhouses. There are horses in their enormous backyards, beautiful light bay and dapple gray horses enclosed in pointed picket fences, their snouts rising from the grass to see what it is that I'm doing as I return to the car and retrieve a small treasure from the trunk: the spray of funeral flowers, the white wooden cross.

I'm opposed to roadside memorials, but without it, I'd have no reason to be here, to see if what Maisie says is true, that there was another car on the road with her and Nick, one that made them crash.

I lay the flowers on the roadside; I dig away at the earth to make room for the cross. Cars pass by and wonder what it is that I'm doing, but then they see the cross, the flowers, and they know. They drive slower, more thoughtfully. They take the turn with deliberation. They stay in their lane, never allowing their cars' tires to crisscross the double yellow line and into mine. This roadside memorial serves as a reminder and also a warning: this is what happens if you don't slow down. You die like Nick has died, losing control of the car along that hairpin curve and slamming into the tree at breakneck speed.

But what if this is not the way it happened? What if what Maisie says is true, that there was another car on the road that fateful afternoon? Everyone loved Nick. He had no enemies, none at all. Whatever transpired on this street had to be the worst kind of luck, a simple act of being at the wrong place at the wrong time. A case of road rage, a drunken driver.

There's no way that someone set out to intentionally harm Nick.

The tree itself shows signs of abuse. I kneel before the tree, pressing the pointed edge of the white wooden cross into the ground. This isn't an easy thing to do. The earth is arid and shows no signs of giving in. It's stubborn like me, as I step on the crossbar with the sole of a shoe and force it into the ground. Another car comes soaring down the road too quickly, sees me, and steps on the brakes so that tiny pebbles come skittering across the street toward my feet.

It's a tall tree, a firm tree, one with much girth. But still, there is a wound. Bits of bark hang loosely from the tree trunk, the innards of the tree exposed. I run my hands along the rugged bark, feeling suddenly sorry for the tree. Will the tree die?

Behind the tree there is nothing, only cattails and open fields and grass. Wildflowers line the gravel of the street. There is only one tree and the absence of a guardrail where a guardrail should be. The only thing around for Nick to hit was the tree. What are the odds of this?

The homes with their horses stand over a hundred feet

away or more, their inhabitants likely not seeing a thing until the ambulance arrived, and then the fire trucks and police cruisers to lug Nick and Maisie from the shattered car. It was only then that the noise and the chaos lured them from their homes to see what the fuss was about. The police didn't bother speaking to the residents because there were no open-ended questions that needed clarification. Nick was speeding; he took the turn too quickly and died.

But what if that's not the way it happened? What if Nick was killed?

It's deserted around here, and though there are homes nearby, I feel strangely alone. Or not alone, but rather like I'm being watched. I turn quickly, but there is no one there. Not that I can see. My eyes rove the surroundings on the other side of Harvey Road, the haggard trees, the mounds of grass. But I see nothing. And yet I can't shake the feeling, as if I'm the target on the other end of a sniper scope.

Is somebody here?

Was someone here, watching Nick as he crashed?

A slow trepidation creeps under my skin, and suddenly I'm scared. I move quicker now through my tasks. Like an archaeologist searching for artifacts in sand, I examine the concrete of Harvey Road for signs: tire prints in the dirt; black skid marks along the surface of the road; remnants of broken car parts. Something to tell me that what Maisie says is true, that there was another car on this road with her and Nick that made them crash. But there are none. The evidence has been washed away by the daily flow of traffic up and down Harvey Road.

But this I know for sure: the mangled car that was re-moved from the tree only showed damage at the site it impacted the tree, on the driver's side. If the car had collided with another car, there would have been evidence of this on the car and on Maisie. Maisie would have sustained much more than a small laceration that has already healed. But Maisie was fine, as was the passenger's side of the car.

I decide: Maisie must be wrong. I push aside those thoughts of being watched. I'm being silly; I'm not thinking clearly. I've let my imagination get the best of me.

Nick was driving too fast. He took the turn too quickly. It's Nick's fault that he's dead.

* * *

On the way home, my cell phone rings. 'Hello?' I ask, pressing the device to my ear as I drive down the highway in an older, run-down part of town, past the cheap motels and adult stores, where I know that one day soon ever-inquisitive Maisie will point to them and ask what they are and what they sell.

'Is this Clara Solberg?' asks the silvery voice on the other end of the line, and I say that it is. 'Mrs. Solberg, I'm calling from Dr. Barros's office, your mother's internist. You're listed as an emergency contact,' she says, and at once my breath leaves me, and I ask, 'Is everything all right?' envisioning my mother and father with Maisie at the office of Dr. Barros. My mother has fallen again and hurt herself, maybe, or she's mixed up her pills and has taken too many of the wrong ones.

'Everything's fine,' the woman assures me. 'I'm calling from billing. Just a question on an unpaid bill,' she says, going on to tell me how my father's check for their last visit with Dr. Barros bounced. 'We've been trying to contact him before sending the bill to collections. That can be such a headache,' she says. 'We left messages at home, but he hasn't returned our calls.'

It's so unlike my father, and yet I'm struck with an instant pang of guilt, knowing my father has brushed aside his own obligations to care for mine, keeping me company, making my meals, doing my laundry, watching my children, when he should be caring for my mother and himself.

Money has never been a problem for my father. Between my father's pension, the rental property and more, he should be making a sufficient income. It will be a few years still until he can dip into social security, but he has been planning for retirement since he was twenty-five. He's prepared for this.

'It must be a mix-up with the bank,' I tell this woman. 'How much was the bill for?' I ask, and she tells me, confirming an address for payment, which I scribble onto a sheet of scratch paper while parked at a stoplight, waiting for the light to turn green.

'I'll take care of it,' I assure her, begging, 'Please, don't send the bill to collections. I'll speak to my father,' though I won't. What I'll do instead is send a check to the office of Dr. Barros because, after everything my father has done for me, this is the least that I can do. The last thing I want is to make him feel stupid for the oversight, or to make him embarrassed.

Dementia isn't contagious, I remind myself as I have so many times before, though the first indicators of my mother's dementia were slight. Could these be the warning signs? Bounced checks. Not returning phone calls.

No, I tell myself. My father is simply preoccupied with my life.

I end the call and instantly the phone rings again. 'Yes?' I say this time, fully expecting to hear the same voice on the other end of the line. The receptionist from Dr. Barros's office calling already to tell me that the check has been found. But it's not the receptionist this time.

'Did I catch you at a bad time?' The voice is apologetic, and at once I say, 'No,' feeling myself soften and relax at the sound of Nick's best friend, Connor, on the other end of the line, the anguish in his voice as palpable as that in mine. Connor is the only one in the world who loved Nick as much as I did, though in a different way, of course.

'There aren't any good times anymore,' I confess, and we sit in silence on the phone until Connor breaks the stillness by saying to me, 'We don't have to do this alone, you know?' and I remember then what they say about misery loving company.

* * *

When I get home that afternoon, Maisie is crying. My father has his feeble hands on her shoulders trying to console her, but Maisie won't be consoled. She turns her back to him, taking two tiny steps away from where he sits. The tears roll unfettered from her eyes and down her freckled skin as she and my father linger in her bedroom, an odd-shaped room with sloped ceilings, a bedroom that is all pink. Hot pink, carnation pink, pink pink. On her bed lies that poor, pathetic bear with its ear all but chewed off. The bed is as Maisie left it last night before she plodded into my room, blaming insomnia for the reason she couldn't stay in her own bed. Her walls flaunt pricey, custom-made art: a princess in a pink tutu, a giraffe with a rose tucked behind its ear. Her bed is thin and narrow, a spindly Jenny Lind bed, which sags under even the meager weight of my father; it's draped by a pretty pink tulle canopy, which hides the guilt of his earnest eyes.

He has told her about Nick. At this I fill with anger. He never liked Nick; Nick was never good enough for his little girl, and then years later when she finally arrived, for Maisie. Nick was unemployed when we met, a student hard at work on a dental degree. He was eager and goal-oriented and a hard worker to boot; that's the way I saw it. But my father only envisioned the ever-growing debt of a doctoral degree, and the complete lack of income while I supported Nick as he achieved his dreams. When Nick decided to go into private practice, and we dipped into money I'd earned doing event and portraiture work—spending my weekends with a camera at the weddings of people I didn't like or know—to rent a space and purchase dental equipment, my father could hardly contain his disappointment and dismay. *That man*, he told me of Nick, over four years ago as we cut the ribbon of Nick's new space, one that would flourish over the next few years, expanding to include a partner and more clients than I could count, *will only bring you down*, he'd said. And now, standing before him, feeling like the rug has been pulled out from under my feet, I wonder if he was right.

'Daddy,' I say, stepping quickly into the room, towing Felix by the handle of his infant seat, a contraption that must weigh thirty pounds. 'What's going on in here?' I ask, setting the weight of Felix and the baby seat gently to the floor.

But before my father can reply, Maisie cries out with doleful eyes, staring at me in despair, 'He's dead. He's dead.' And I feel my heart begin to ache, the tears spring to my eyes. My father, too, has eyes that are red-rimmed, though I want to point an accusatory finger at him and say that this is his fault; he is to blame. He had no business telling Maisie about Nick.

Maisie scurries to my side and wraps her arms around my lower limbs quickly and without warning, so that I lose my balance and nearly fall. 'It's okay,' I say mechanically as I stroke her hair while glaring at my father inches above her head. 'Everything will be okay.' My words, my motions, are robotic, perfunctory, lifeless.

This isn't the way Nick would do it. He would drop down to Maisie's level and gather her in his tender arms; he would say something, anything, other than these mendacities. It is not okay. Everything will not be okay. I'm lying to Maisie; I'm a liar.

'Clara,' my father bleats, an attempt at an apology, but I hold my hand up to him—I don't want to hear it. This news, this information wasn't his to share. It was mine.

It's my father's fault that Maisie is clinging to my legs and crying.

'Look, Mommy,' Maisie says then, drawing slowly away from my legs. She slips a sticky little hand inside my shaking one and draws me to her dresser, a long white bureau with a mirror. There are things on top of the dresser, many things that Maisie points to at random: a pair of princess underpants, a doll, the stethoscope from a toy doctor kit, a used tissue. There are photographs slipped into the frame of the mirror: Maisie and Nick; Maisie and me; Maisie forced to stand beside my mother, two and a half feet out of reach because she is scared of my mother, as I would be, too, if I were four; Maisie and her boppy, my father, who watches on now not saying a thing.

I step forward and follow the route of Maisie's finger with my eyes. She points to a jar, one of my old mason jars with holes punctured in the top of the metal lid. I move closer, not knowing why the jar is here or how it's come to be here.

Inside the jar is a twig, shorn from a tree. It's a thin twig, a copper brown. There are leaves inside the jar— green leaves, a scrunched-up handful of leaves as if Maisie grabbed on to a tree and tugged—and sheaths of grass covering the bottom of the jar, a deathbed upon which lies a lightning bug spread out on its back, all six inert legs up in the air, its tail no longer sparkling. It doesn't move.

'We forgot,' Maisie voices to me pathetically, the tears streaming down her eyes. 'He's dead.'

My eyes move to my father's in silent apology. How this lightning bug has come to live and die in a mason jar inside Maisie's bedroom, I don't know, but this is what I know: my father has done nothing wrong.

'How did a lightning bug get inside your room?' I ask, but Maisie's eyes become shrouded with guilt; her face flames red, and she shakes her head. She doesn't say and I don't pry. It seems trivial now, how this bug has come to be here. She still doesn't know a thing about Nick. For all intents and purposes, Nick is fine. That's all that matters.

'These things happen,' I say mechanically. 'Everything will be okay.'

'When will Daddy be home?' Maisie pleads, wanting someone who can console her better than I can, and I turn away from Maisie's beseeching eyes and say, 'Soon.'

* * *

We bury the lightning bug. We dig a hole two inches by two inches in the ground with the end of a stick and lay the insect inside. Harriet stands in the yard behind us, keeping watch. My father has gone for the day with the promise that he'll be back tomorrow. 'Why, Mommy, why?' Maisie asks over and over again as I dig the hole and lay the bug inside. The bug has a name, or so it seems: Otis. I don't ask how it's come to have a name; truth be told, I don't care. I sprinkle a handful of dirt over the lightning bug's corpse, grateful that Maisie doesn't make the easy connection between this grave and Nick's. 'Why are you doing that, Mommy?' Maisie asks as I drizzle the dirt and pat it gently back into the earth with my fingertips. I suggest she find a rock to serve as a marker for Otis's grave, and again Maisie asks, 'Why?' but she scampers off in search of a rock without waiting for my reply, Harriet following closely behind.

* * *

In the evening a knock comes at the door. It's dark outside, far too late for Maisie to still be awake. And yet she is, sprawled on the couch in front of the TV, watching preschool cartoons because I haven't the energy to put her to bed. I'm on my laptop in the kitchen, trying to pull up the Chase website in an attempt to access my father's accounts. I'm thinking of the unpaid bill to the office of Dr. Barros, and wondering if my parents are in some sort of financial distress about which I should know. I try hard to call to mind my father's password, an odd mix of letters and numbers that's near impossible to memorize. I try only twice and then give up, worried that after too many unsuccessful attempts, the account will be locked and my father notified. I don't want to ask him about it for fear of making him feel bad, and yet I have my concerns. What if my father has less money than I think? What if my father has less money than me?

At hearing the knock, I go to the door and unfasten the lock. I pull the door open a crack, peering outside, and there find Connor standing on my front stoop in a black T and vintage wash jeans. In his hands are a helmet and gloves; a motorcycle is parked in the drive. Connor isn't a tall man, standing just a couple inches above my own five-eight height, with brown hair and eyes, the kind that make women swoon. His smile is sympathetic, a contorted smile that's meant to be both a smile and a frown. His heart is heavy, as is mine, but the half smile proves that he's trying.

'Connor,' I say, and he steps inside, wrapping his arms around me and pulling me into a warm embrace, and it's there, in his arms, that I close my eyes and press into him, allowing myself to believe for just one split second that I'm in Nick's embrace, that it's Nick's arms that hold me tight.

'Clara,' he says.

I've known Connor for half a dozen years, Nick's dental school friend turned employee. But Connor was never quite an employee to Nick but rather a partner, one he collaborated with about patient care as well as business expenditures and what to get the office ladies for the holidays. Before we had kids, Nick and I shared many double dates with Connor and whatever girl he was dating at the time, but after Maisie was born, that type of lifestyle—basement dance clubs and parties in rooftop bars—no longer fit the bill and Connor was left going stag. Connor doesn't have children of his own; he doesn't have a wife. He's the perpetual bachelor, abounding with good looks and charm, but lacking in commitment. He was engaged to a college sweetheart once, a woman for whom he would have gone to the moon and back, as Nick has told me by way of Connor's drunken admission. They planned the wedding, church, hall and all, and then she changed her mind, having met some other man the night of her bachelorette party, breaking Connor's heart. Nick and I often reasoned that never again would he pop the question to anyone, no matter how in love he was. As the saying goes, once bitten, twice shy.

I draw away from him and watch as a handful of bugs let themselves in through the open front door, making a beeline for the chandelier that hangs above us, a Medusa type contraption with chrome light bulbs twisting out like the snakes of her hair. I close the door, and Connor follows me to the kitchen, ruffling the hair on Maisie's head as we pass through the living room; she is so intent on her cartoons that she hardly notices, though from the corners of her sleepy mouth I detect a smile.

The lighting in the kitchen is dimmed. Dinner dishes remain in the kitchen sink, our uneaten meals evident as the food hardens and grows cold in the red glazed bowls, chicken soup warmed in the microwave from a can. It's the best that I can do. Neither Maisie nor I could eat it.

'I should have come sooner,' Connor says, eyeing the leftover food, the guilt in his voice tangible as he leans against the kitchen sink, pressing his hands into the pockets of his jeans. But I shake my head and tell him no. The last thing I want is for Connor to feel any sort of guilt for not coming to see me sooner. He, too, has been grieving.

'It doesn't matter,' I say, reaching into the refrigerator to snatch one of Nick's old beers from the door, handing it to Connor though he never asks. I crave a glass of wine, just a few ounces of Chardonnay to help blur my sensibilities and make me indifferent and numb, but knowing the effects of alcohol on a breastfeeding infant, I make the decision to abstain.

'None for you?' Connor asks, but I shake my head and tell him no. He runs his hand through his hair, making the strands stand on end. He snaps open the beer with a bottle opener and drinks in a mouthful. 'How have you been holding up?' he asks, though I don't need to tell him. The bags beneath my eyes say enough, that and the swelling and redness, the fact that I haven't slept for more than two hours at a time since before Felix was born, something that was only exacerbated by Nick's death. I can no longer blame Felix for the lack of sleep. Now I blame Nick.

'I've been having trouble sleeping,' I confess, and Connor says, 'Me, too,' and it's only then that I see the dark circles beneath his eyes like mine. His skin looks sallow, jaundiced; he's anxious and strung out. His eyes drift throughout the room from the stove top to the travertine tile, as if searching for Nick, finally settling on the beer in hand. He avoids my gaze.

'I remember the day I met Nick,' he says while picking at the wrapper on his beer, pulling it off in tatters, a pile of them gathering in his hand. His voice is quiet, subdued.

He goes on to tell me about the first time he and Nick met, crossing the campus to a shared class. It's a story I've heard before, though only ever from Nick. They were in dental school, slowly chipping away on the many hours of labs, lectures and clinical practice before they'd be given a degree. They'd never spoken before, but the class was small, twenty students at best, and Connor had his eye on some girl, a brunette who also happened to be Nick's lab partner. It was the reason for his introduction, the reason they became friends. Over some girl.

After graduation, Connor got a job working under an experienced dentist in town while Nick went into private practice. For a couple years it went on this way, until Connor's ever-increasing dissatisfaction with his job got the best of him, and he quit to come work for Nick.

'I haven't even begun to think how I'm going to support myself,' I admit to Connor. Since Nick's death, I haven't yet sorted through the mail, too terrified to see what awaits me there. The envelopes I pull every few days from the mailbox get tossed to a pile on the floor just inside the front door. Bereavement cards, mostly, those bearing their *With heartfelt sympathy* and *May you find peace and solace* sentiments, but also bills. Estimates of Benefits from the insurance company already telling me which of Nick's hospital expenses they will and will not pay. A notice from the library of fourteen picture books that are a week overdue, each costing me five cents a day so that every day I tally up another seventy cents for the library, and still I can't get myself to return the books. I haven't the energy for it. Bills, bills and more bills. Catalogs for items I can no longer buy.

I had a savings account once, nothing extravagant, but an adequate savings account, money set aside for a rainy day, but we ended up putting each and every penny into Nick's practice. We'd see the money back, he said, and promised me it was worth it. Had I told my father this he would have said no, but I took Nick's word and invested every cent. The practice was Nick's dream. Who could refuse a man his dream? Not I, said the fly. And so I said okay, and handed over all my money so that Nick could fulfill his dream while I set mine aside. My own photography studio. That was my dream.

Even our home is a money pit, constantly in need of repairs or renovation. The only thing left I have of value is the dental practice.

'I don't know what I'm going to do,' I confess to Connor, 'about the bills. The mortgage. The hospital payments. Car payments. Saving for college, Maisie's wedding. How will I afford health insurance?' I ask, thinking of Felix and his well-baby checks every two months, all running over with pricey vaccines. Without waiting for an answer, I say to him, 'I can look for a job, but if I work, who will watch Maisie and Felix? How will I ever afford child care?' knowing my father is out of the question. He's too busy caring for my mom, and an in-home nanny or a day care would cost me nearly five hundred dollars a week. 'The dental practice,' I say to Connor, 'it's the only thing I have left.' But a dental practice is nothing without a dentist. Without Nick here, the practice is meaningless.

A look of confusion crosses Connor's face. 'You don't know?' he asks, and I implore, 'Know what?'

But he doesn't answer right away. He drinks his beer, three long, slow swigs while I wait for him to reply. 'Know what?' I ask again as he sets his finished beer on the countertop, and I reach into the refrigerator for another one.

'There have been some layoffs,' he says in a tight-lipped way, as if he doesn't want to say the words aloud, as if he wants to sugarcoat them like he's speaking to a child. 'Nick had to let some people go.'

But I shake my head and tell him that I didn't know. 'Who?' I ask and, 'When? Why?'

'A month ago, maybe more,' he says and my heart sinks. It slides from my chest and plummets somewhere down to my stomach, where for a single moment I think that I will be sick. I grip the countertop, my knuckles turning white. Why didn't Nick tell me about the layoffs? I imagine the ladies who work at the front desk, Nancy, with her predilection for hot cocoa with mini marshmallows, and Stacy, a math wiz, matter-of-fact and thorough; she's a crackerjack with the bills. Are they gone? Have they been fired? And what about the hygienist, Jan?

'Financial trouble,' he tells me, and I sharply inhale, my fears overwhelming me as I wonder desperately about all the things I don't know. Nick paid the bills; he handled the finances. I handed them over willingly and without question when we were married and turned a blind eye to all fiscal matters. I could barely compute simple math; I wasn't good with numbers. The last thing we needed was me paying the bills.

'Why wouldn't Nick tell me?' I wonder aloud, and Connor shrugs his shoulders and says that he doesn't know. He thought for sure Nick would have told me. And now, standing in the weak glow of the kitchen's dimmed recessed lighting, I wonder: If Nick could keep this secret from me—if he could go weeks without alluding to financial trouble, if he could lay off employees and not mention it to me—then what else wasn't he telling me?

What else don't I know?

* * *

That night Maisie asks to sleep with me. She treads lightly into my bedroom as I tuck Felix into the bassinet, seven and a half minutes after tucking Maisie into her own chambray sheets and pulling the quilt up clear to her neck that way that Daddy does it. *Snug as a bug in a rug.*

'I can't sleep,' she tells me, crossing the room where I've recently swept the broken picture frame glass, and I ask, 'Did you try?' to which she nods her little head so vigorously that hair falls in her eyes. She clutches the teddy bear by a single leg, the deplorable thing hanging upside down. He's nearly gone blind thanks to Maisie's unending chewing, the plastic brown eyes about to fall from their place, hanging on now by a single brown thread. I pull back the sheets and welcome her in, grateful that someone is here and I don't have to spend the night alone. Maisie happily obliges, rushing to the bed and hopping inside, right where Nick should be. She sets her head on his pillow, her body failing to fill the space where his body once lay, his warm arms wrapping me in a cocoon while I slept, a leg tossed across mine, growing heavier in time. The air is imbued with the fresh scent of Johnson & Johnson Baby Wash and the sweltering summer air that eases itself uninvited into the open window and again makes us sweat.

It's the middle of the night when Maisie wakes up screaming.

'The bad man!' she yowls in a piercing voice, and then, straight on the heels of the first desperate declaration, 'The bad man is after us!' she shrieks as my heart begins to dash. She's crying beside me, sitting upright in bed, clutching the bed pillow as if she believes it is Nick. The tears fall from her eyes like the rushing water of Niagara Falls, urgent, the kind that can't be slowed down.

I lay a shaking hand upon Maisie's clammy one, and say to her, 'Shhh,' but she pushes me away with so much might that I all but tumble from my side, latching on to Felix's bassinet for support as it lurches precariously on its stand. Felix, rattled from sleep by the sudden shove, begins to cry, a cry that easily trumps Maisie's and my own cries. Felix's cry quickly escalates into a caterwaul as Maisie hides her head under the pillow to try to smother the noise or to hide from the bad man who trails her. I don't know why it is that she hides, though I can imagine because I, too, want to climb under a pillow and hide.

'What bad man?' I ask loudly, over the sound of Felix, as I slip from bed and slide my hands under the weight of him, lifting him from the bassinet. 'Shhh. Shhh,' I croon to Felix now, standing beside his bassinet and trying to sway him back to sleep. 'What bad man, Maisie?'

'The bad man,' screams Maisie redundantly, her voice muffled by the pillow. As my eyes adjust to the darkness of night, I begin to see Maisie's legs kicking persistently at the bed before she pulls them into herself and throws the sheets up over her tiny body. I scrabble around inside Felix's bassinet for his abandoned pacifier, for something, anything, to silence the insistent sound. He's upset, scared, maybe even a bit pissed off that Maisie and I woke him from sleep.

'What bad man, Maisie? What man? Tell me about the man,' I beg frenetically as I slide my arm from the spaghetti strap of a tank top and place Felix against my chest. It is not quite time for him to eat. By my count, Felix shouldn't eat for another hour, and yet the pacifier is nowhere; there's no other way to stop his screaming than to let him suck on me. As his gums latch down, my breasts begin to protest. The nipples are cracked, the skin dry, riddled with a bloody discharge; my breasts are hard and sore and unimaginably clogged. Like water held back by a beaver dam, the milk refuses to flow at the same pace Felix would like—a trickle rather than a surge, and so he slurps and slurps to little avail, making my chest crack and bleed. *How has the nursing been going?* Dr. Paul had asked in the exam room, and I'd lied, *Just fine*, before telling her the truth: the pain, the broken skin, the low milk supply. What I expected was a haranguing on breastfeeding, but what I was given instead was a way out. *There are other ways*, she told me before listing them for me: infant formula, a breast pump, donor milk.

Maisie won't tell me about the man, and I want to tell her that she's wrong, because I've spoken to the police and I've read the newspaper articles. I've been at the scene. They all seem to corroborate the same truth, that Nick's speeding was the cause of the crash.

'Tell me about the man,' I say again, and when she won't, I ask Maisie to tell me about the car. She's told me already that the man was in a car, and I picture him racing after Nick on Harvey Road. 'Was it a red car?' I suggest when Maisie says nothing. She shakes her head negligibly; it was not a red car. 'Was it blue?' I ask, to which she replies with another shake of the head. 'Was it a black car, Maisie?' I ask this time. 'Was the car black?'

This time she doesn't shake her head. Her response instead is a long drawn-out cry, a wolf howling at the moon, as she runs from the bed and from the room, calling over and over again for Daddy. She flees the bedroom in search of some other room where she can hide, the bathroom door still removed from its place and lying on the wooden floorboards, which I trip over in an attempt to catch my four-year-old daughter before the click of a lock bisects Maisie and me. In my arms Felix is no longer pressed to my chest, but now trying to imbibe anything he can find: my nightshirt, his hand, my hair. With a handful of my hair in his mouth, he no longer has the ability to scream.

It was a black car. A man in a black car. If what Maisie says is true.

I drop to the floor before Nick's office door and ask three times for Maisie to come out. 'Please, come out.' On the other side of the wooden pane I hear her cry, and imagine Maisie's tiny body splayed across Nick's ikat rug, her tears getting absorbed by the weft threads, the frosty grays with the citron stripes. Or maybe she's hurled herself over the arm of Nick's club chair, hugging the tufted back, pretending that it's Nick.

When she doesn't come, I make my way out to the garage in search of a nail and a hammer.

I'm becoming an old pro at this.

NICK

BEFOᴙE

Her name was Melinda Grey, and I should have known right away, when she walked into my office some six months ago, that she was a problem patient. We'd talked about them in dental school somewhere in between local anesthesia and oral pathology. Problem patients. You wouldn't have known it to look at her, for her small size seemed to contradict the barracuda she was. She was a pleasant-looking woman, approaching middle age, with soft brown hair and benign eyes, the kind that made great contact when she talked.

Ms. Grey presented as a phobic patient. She blamed it on an extensive dental history complete with emergency everything—root canals, abscesses, a fractured tooth—and a habit of choosing dentists with a lousy bedside manner because they tended to be cheaper, their appointment openings more readily available than someone like me, who had a calendar full of patients, until I met Ms. Grey, at least, and then suddenly I had time in my day to spare.

Her dental insurance was lousy, which she admitted to me, another red flag. I should have ended our appointment there and had Stacy look into coverage before I did any work, but Ms. Grey was the last appointment of the day, an emergency walk-in, and she was in a great deal of pain. The tooth was decayed; that I could clearly see. It would most likely need to come out. I offered a root canal as an alternative to extraction—a root canal, which would cost her three grand or more with the crown—but she shook her head and said that was more than she could afford. The tooth was a molar anyway, and she didn't care to save it. By comparison, an extraction wouldn't surpass a couple hundred dollars at best, and, seeing as Ms. Grey had no plans for an implant and intended to leave a hole in the back of her mouth that no one would see, the procedure would be relatively cheap.

It was a simple extraction. The tooth was completely above the gum line and required only a local anesthetic. I used nitrous oxide to help calm Ms. Grey's rattled nerves. I lifted and pulled the tooth with my elevator and forceps; I packed the wound. I sent her home with pain relievers, though I made the decision not to prescribe antibiotics because, in my professional opinion, they were overprescribed, a problem that led to antibiotic resistance and a whole host of other bad things. I was strictly opposed to the use of blanket antibiotics. Ms. Grey was forty years old and completely healthy. She didn't need antibiotics. Still, as always, I told her to keep an eye out for signs of infection: puss or other discharge, the formation of an abscess, fever or excessive pain. I said it out loud, maintaining eye contact so I was sure she heard. 'There's always some degree of pain following a tooth extraction,' I remember saying, perched there beside Melinda Grey on my burgundy stool, unpinning the bib clip from around her neck, wiping the last of the bloody saliva from her lip with a napkin. 'What you want to keep an eye out for is excessive pain. Severe pain or swelling in two or three days from now. If you feel like something's not quite right or if you have any questions— any at all—please, don't hesitate to call.' And she nodded her head as if she heard.

I told the hygienist to make sure Ms. Grey had my business card before she left, one that listed the office number as well as my cell phone, which I always gave out so that I could be available to my patients twenty-four hours a day. It seemed like the ethical thing to do. I never wanted my patients to feel they were lacking for care. I also told my hygienist to schedule a follow-up appointment for Ms. Grey in one week, so I could be sure the wound was healing as it should be.

Ms. Grey never called. She never returned for her follow-up appointment.

What I failed to realize was that one of my hygienists was out for the day, home sick with a strep throat infection that had already blitzed half our staff, and the other was up to her neck in patients, taking on the workload of two. In the middle of all that chaos she had apparently forgotten to have Ms. Grey give informed consent, signing a simple form that indicated she knew the risks associated with the procedure.

I also didn't realize it was the beginning of the end for me.

CLARA

A new air-conditioning unit costs upward of five thousand dollars, installed. To have the existing unit repaired—assuming repair is even possible—would cost in the vicinity of one hundred to nine hundred dollars, depending on what needs to be fixed.

'How old's the unit?' asks the HVAC guy on the other end of my phone line, and I say that I don't know. He walks me through a number of estimates before I thank him for his time and set the phone down, tallying up the prices in my mind, though not those for the air conditioner. Nick's wooden casket cost two thousand dollars; embalming, which oddly enough wasn't required by law, was an additional eight hundred. These are the figures I add up in my mind. The funeral home charged us for near everything, from the preparations of the body—combing through Nick's blood-tinged hair, dressing him in his Sunday best, a refrigeration fee of fifty dollars a day and more—to a service fee for the funeral director, who was quickly making a killing off my loss. I sprang for the prayer cards, forty bucks for a hundred, with Nick's handsome face printed on the front in black and white. I thought it looked classy, stately, but Nick's mother said I should have used color; the black and white made them dated, she said; they made Nick look old, though Nick would never grow old.

The cemetery, too, charged an arm and a leg for the cost of the plot, the cost to dig the plot, the cost of a headstone and the graveside service, for all of us to stand around the uncovered hole and cry. But that wasn't all. There was still the cost of a hearse to carry Nick's body from the morgue to the funeral home to the cemetery, the cost of flowers that I didn't want or need, but were tradition, as the funeral director told me, and so I ordered those, too, sprays of white that filled the church.

The credit card has been maxed out.

I can't afford to fix the air conditioner or have it replaced. For now we will have to sweat. My father wants to help, he's told me, with the funeral fees. 'Please, no,' I said, laying a hand on his arm. My parents aren't lacking for money, and yet retirement put them on a fixed income, which my mother's never-ending medical expenses chip quickly away at. It will be years still until social security and Medicare kick in. *But there is money*, my father has said, though I've told him no. 'Please, no,' I said, wanting him to save that money for his and my mother's needs, remembering the bounced check from my mother's internist and trying to decide if it was for lack of money, or a simple mix-up with the bank.

Nick's mother and father have money, but never once have they offered to help.

* * *

In the afternoon Maisie, Felix and I drive to the store. It took great cajoling for Maisie to climb in the car. There were many things she wanted to do apart from grocery shop. A new episode of *Max & Ruby* was about to begin, she was thirsty, Maisie—who never likes to pee—needed to pee. Three times. And then once inside the car, coaxing her into the car seat and beneath the smothering straps of a five-point harness was another matter, a feat only accomplished after handing over my smartphone with its Candy Crush app. Oh, how Maisie loves her Candy Crush, matching her pieces of candy and swiping them from the screen. With the phone in hand, she almost forgot she was confined to a chair, in the type of contraption that only days ago collapsed under the burliness of a white oak tree.

But for me, the fear was still there.

Maisie's hand goes to the harness, and I snap at her, 'Don't touch it. Leave it be,' hoping she won't see the swelling or redness of my eyes. Undoing her own harness has become Maisie's latest pursuit. She's discovered that pressing the buttons will undo the whole darn thing and set her free, though her fingers are too small, her fine motor skills too gauche to do it herself. And yet she tries, quite an undertaking for a four-year-old, but something she'll figure out soon enough. 'Play your game, Maisie,' I say so that her mind will go elsewhere and forget about the car seat straps. And it does.

We drive. As we make our way down our street of older historic houses, past the park and the small shops of an upscale suburban downtown and through newer, cookie-cutter homes, the momentum of the car lulls Felix to sleep.

Known as one of Chicago's five collar counties, ours flanks the city to the south and west, one of the fastest-growing counties, an area that added almost two hundred thousand people over the course of just ten years. A Cooper's hawk sits perched at the top of a utility pole, eyes appraising the fields for its next meal. Maisie sees this and points a finger out the window. 'Birdie, Mommy,' she tells me, and then to Felix, who's sound asleep. 'See the birdie, Felix?' I tell her that I see. Felix says nothing.

Suburban sprawl they call this, when the expanding population spills into rural America, making Chicagoland home to over ten million people. Our suburb is often outclassed by some of the more sought-after towns around, and yet the new construction in our area is second to none; for half the money you get twice the house, a promise that lures people in droves. The schools are top-notch, the demographics just what Nick and I were looking for when we purchased our home: a white-collar community with a median age of thirty-two. There would be plenty of kids for ours to play with. Good kids. Good kids whose college-educated parents made over a hundred thousand a year. Crime in the community was limited to theft mainly; violent crimes almost didn't exist.

As we drive through the cornfields, past newer subdivisions that flaunt their energy-efficient and custom-made homes, Maisie idly kicks the back of the passenger's seat and chants, 'Faster, Mommy, faster.' Maisie likes to do things quickly. But I will not speed despite Maisie's request; I know better than to speed.

We work our way to the main hub of town. I park in the grocery store lot, sliding in between a minivan and a pickup truck, and heft Felix and his baby carrier from the car, urging Maisie to follow suit. But Maisie doesn't follow suit.

'Come on, Maisie,' I beckon. 'The sooner we finish, the sooner we can go home.'

But Maisie just kicks her feet against the back of the passenger's seat, refusing to come. She grips my phone in her hands, the annoying Candy Crush theme music making my head ache. 'Come on, Maisie,' I try again, changing tack. I say this time, 'You can play the game inside.'

But Maisie doesn't come.

I gather a shopping cart from the rack outside and set Felix and his carrier inside, moving to Maisie's side of the car. Snatching the phone from her hands, I listen to Maisie squeal. She fights me as I unfasten the harness and try to force her arms and legs to the other side of the woven strap. 'No!' she says as she kicks her hot-pink Crocs at me.

'Get out of the car right now,' I insist, and it takes every ounce of patience I have not to snap. Fatigue and grief are a lethal combination, though I can't give in to despair. I might have lost my husband, but Maisie has lost her father. Though she doesn't quite know it yet, she, too, has been hurt. I stroke her hair and ask nicely for her to come.

'No, no, no, no, no,' she bleats as I wrench her small body now—all thirty-seven pounds of her—out of the car and onto the concrete, holding her hand too tightly so that Maisie cries out in pain. By now Felix, too, has begun to cry, awoken by the glaring afternoon sun, which blares in his half-open eyes. The car has stopped moving, the undulating motion that lulled him to sleep gone. He whimpers first, and then he screams, and I grope at my pockets for something to plug the leak. I find his pacifier and stuff it into his mouth, less gently than I would have liked to, and begin to push the cart with one hand while dragging Maisie with the other across the lot.

All that I want is infant formula. Infant formula and baby bottles.

'We'll be in and out in three minutes,' I promise Maisie, but three minutes is a lifetime to a child. The warmth of the day engulfs us the second we step from the air-conditioned car, heat rising up from the blackened asphalt beneath our feet. The store seems suddenly so far away as Maisie schleps along with tiny, baby-sized steps, her hand trying to wiggle free of mine. I make promises; I offer rewards. 'We'll get popcorn when we're through,' I say, telling her how we can swing by the food court on the way out. 'A Slurpee, too,' I say, hoping that the promise of a frosty soda drink will make Maisie pick up the pace. But Maisie doesn't pick up the pace. If anything, her feet slow, her hand pulling back on my hand so that there's the sensation of swimming upstream. The single word—*no*—continues on repeat as I push Felix and tow Maisie through the parking lot while passing mothers turn with steely eyes to stare, and I see in their eyes the judgment, the condemnation, the disapprobation. Oh, how easy it is to judge when we don't know. Maisie's feet drag along the concrete, her objections becoming more and more shrill as she quietly—and then forcefully—screams, 'No!'

It's then that Felix's pacifier manages to fall from his mouth and onto the blistering tar; in one fell swoop, I pick it up and stuff it back into his mouth before he has a chance to notice its absence, not caring what dirt or germs now live on the end of that plastic device but needing him quiet. His idle sucking resumes, though Maisie is now completely inert, standing in the middle of the parking lot, pointing. Pointing and crying. Pointing at a car, a black car, though from the distance I can't see its make or model. All I know is that it is black and dusty, the cause of Maisie's sudden and inexplicable tantrum.

Her body has begun to shake uncontrollably; urine creeps from below the hem of a knitted dress and down the inside of her wobbly leg, collecting in the sole of her hot-pink Crocs. Maisie, who has already peed three times before we could leave. One wouldn't think there was any more urine left to pee. But there it is, the amber liquid trickling to the asphalt as Maisie manages to wrench her hand free of mine and makes an attempt to run. I blame the sweat for this, the slippery moisture slathered between our hands, as she sprints across the parking lot without looking for cars, so that another driver must slam on the brakes to keep from hitting Maisie, issuing me a dirty look as she does.

I'm so sorry, I'm so sorry, I mouth as I steer the cart across the lot to try to reclaim the little girl who now darts pell-mell through the rows of parked cars. I am faster than Maisie, this much I know, and yet with Felix and the shopping cart in tow, I'm not as sprightly as she. I can't squeeze through the rows of cars like Maisie can, going this way and that like the steel ball of a pinball machine. My heart races, waiting for the blare of a car horn, the squeal of brakes, a little girl's agonizing cry.

'Maisie!' I call to her over the still summer air. 'Maisie!' I scream, so that half the town's population, it seems, turns to see what the fracas is all about, pointing in lukewarm concern at the little girl running recklessly through the parking lot, two matted pigtails streaming down her back. Felix again loses his hold on his pacifier, but I can't be slowed down. Over the sound of my own screaming, Felix, too, begins to scream. I grab Felix from the shopping cart and begin to run, though the weight of his infant carrier slows me down, my legs like lead.

Others in the parking lot turn to look at Maisie, but none do a single thing to stop her. Instead their eyes travel to me, wondering what kind of mother I am that I let my daughter run like this through a crowded parking lot. Don't I know how dangerous this is?

'Clara?' I hear a voice then, kind, concerned. I turn. Emily, my neighbor and friend. She stands too closely and places a hand on my arm, and I see her little four-year-old, Teddy, obediently standing by her feet, without the need to hold hands. 'What's happened, Clara?' she asks, her desperate voice mimicking my own. 'What's wrong?'

'Maisie,' I say, and before I can tell her or even point to Maisie off in the distance, streaming through the rows of cars that gleam in the afternoon sun, Emily tells Teddy to stay with me and then takes off in a sprint. Emily is a fast runner, much faster than Maisie is, without the baggage that slows me down. I watch as Emily's own long black hair billows behind her, her legs sailing through the parking lot with ease, closing the gap on Maisie, and collecting my little girl into her arms just like a good mother would do.

But not me. No, not me.

Rather, I stand idly by while some other woman saves my child.

'No, no, no, no, no,' says Maisie as she is returned to me, tears streaming from her eyes. She's sweaty, her hair glued to the hairline. She kicks in Emily's arms, wanting to be free. But Maisie doesn't look at either of us, not Emily nor me, but rather at that black car, now parked two and a half rows behind us so that it's near impossible to see. But I follow the route of Maisie's terrified eyes to where the car should be and am absolutely certain that's where she looks because she's told me already, or rather implied it, that it was a black car that took Nick's life, puzzle pieces I've gathered from Maisie's cagey innuendos and placed together with care.

'Stop this, Maisie,' I say about her outburst, though I cling to her, my heart still pounding, knowing I was one distracted driver away from losing a child. How easy it would have been for a car to hit her, just one driver checking an incoming text message in the parking lot or peering over a shoulder to reprimand a child. That's all it would have taken, one split second of distraction as Maisie tore across the parking lot and into their path. 'Do you know what could have happened to you? You have to be more careful, Maisie. You have to hold an adult's hand in the parking lot. Always,' I say, and then again, more forcefully, 'always.'

'Thank you, Emily,' I say to the woman who stands before me, watching but not judging. 'Thank you, thank you. I don't know what would have happened if...' But I don't finish the sentence; I can't bear to say the words out loud. My hair, too, clings to my sweaty face; the sweat pools beneath my arms and in the crooks of my knees. Everywhere there is sweat.

'It's all right,' she says, and, 'No bother,' though her eyes inquire about Maisie's outburst, and I palliate the truth by saying, 'She doesn't want to go grocery shopping. She'd rather stay home and play,' though I make no mention of the black car, which has her instantly terrorized, or the fact that my four-year-old has some latent belief that my husband was killed.

'Grocery shopping is so hard with the children,' Emily bemoans with a dramatic eye roll, though her little Teddy stands obediently beside her, carrying the plastic shopping bag. 'Would you like to come home with Teddy and me?' asks Emily then, as she squats at the knees and leans in close to Maisie, her voice subdued in a way meant for kids' ears. 'Give Mommy a break for a while?' And as Maisie nods her slow approval, Emily rises up and says to me, 'If it's okay with you, Clara. Maisie can play with Teddy for a while. Let Felix and you shop. It would give me a break, too—they can entertain each other,' she says, assuaging my immediate concern with, 'Theo is gone this week. An auto show in Massachusetts. He won't be home for a few days,' and at this I nod my head numbly. I say okay, though still I have reservations about sending Maisie off with someone else, and yet there are other things on my mind, which trump these reservations.

'She's had an accident,' I say apologetically, and Emily tells me it's no bother. She can borrow something of Teddy's while the clothes dry. 'If you're sure,' I say, and Emily says she's sure. 'Just let me move her car seat,' I say, but Emily says not to bother. She has an extra booster seat Maisie can use, and so instead I press my lips to Maisie's forehead in a simple adieu.

I have only two things on my mind.

Infant formula.

Black car.

NICK

BEFORE

Connor is laid out in the dental chair when I come into the exam room. He's flat on his back, staring up at *The View* on the ceiling-mounted TV, feet crossed at the ankles, hands folded across his abdomen. It isn't just his predilection for being lazy that's lured him to the TV, or the fact that some supermodel is the featured guest. Not today anyway. We both had patients scheduled for 11:00 a.m., both of whom failed to show. *Two more flew the coop*, is the way Nancy told us about it, while sipping from her mug. They were siblings, which made it better somehow, just one mother or father deciding to take their children's dental work elsewhere, rather than two separate individuals beating a hasty retreat. There were any number of things working against us, but two in particular stood out: a surfeit of bad online reviews of late, which I was certain were all one Melinda Grey with countless aliases, and a new dentist in town, Dr. Jeremy Shepherd.

Dr. Shepherd was the kind of practitioner with top-of-the-line everything, lavish prizes for referrals, direct mail flyers that promised free new-client exams complete with X-rays, forcing my clients to jump ship. I couldn't blame them. Word on the street is that he's an upstanding guy, handsome, a philanthropist—he's apparently done charity work in Africa with the Global Dental Relief, providing free dental work for hundreds of impoverished people, which is something I've always wanted to do, but never found the time. He has an orthodontist and an oral surgeon on staff so that they can serve everyone's individual needs. There is no need to see a specialist elsewhere. And if a patient refers a friend, they're entered into a raffle to win a Weber grill, black porcelain, sixty inches tall by sixty inches wide, with three stainless-steel burners and cast-iron cooking grates, along with all the fancy cooking utensils and an apron that reads *BBQ Master* to boot. I've been on their website, staring covetously at the grill. It was almost enough to make me jump ship, too.

Clara caught me one night staring at the grill online, coming up from behind, warm hands reclining on my shoulder blades as I quickly minimized the screen. It was months ago, when Clara was still comfortable and trim, and the baby inside her belly was only as big as a brussels sprout and not yet a honeydew.

'What's that?' she asked, but I said nothing because by then it was gone.

'No, really,' she spurred, reaching over my shoulder for the wireless mouse, so that she could maximize the screen. Clara is many things—warm, kind, breathtaking—but she's not dumb.

And so there it was again, staring me in the eye. That grill.

'You're looking for a new grill?' Clara asked, sitting beside me at the table, hand now resting on my knee. 'What's wrong with the grill we have?' she asked, and I claimed that one of the burners didn't work, and the flame took forever to ignite. It wasn't true, of course—our run-of-the-mill grill worked just fine—but Clara bought it for the time being. And so there that night, with Clara by my side, I checked the price of a similar grill online, wondering if I could host a grill giveaway, too, and try to reclaim the patients I'd lost to other dentists around town. Maybe if I had my own grill giveaway for patient referrals, they'd return, like migrating birds returning to a nest year after year. But that was only a pipe dream, of course.

'Maisie in bed already?' I asked, hoping to derail or at least defer this conversation for the time being. I didn't like lying to Clara.

'Yes,' she said, because I hadn't yet raised my eyes from the computer screen to see that she wasn't being trailed by a tired child. 'She's out cold,' said Clara, and then she returned her attention to the grill, hand on my knee, spinning tiny circles on the fabric, moving higher up my thigh. 'Do we have the money for a new grill?' Clara asked, seeing the way my eyes scoured the website for a grill—those exorbitant price ranges filling me with inexplicable hatred toward Dr. Shepherd, who, like me, was only a man with a dream, and a better business sense it seemed. My body didn't pay attention to the pursuits of Clara's puttering hand, didn't even notice. Any other day I would have noticed. But in that moment I was intent on only one thing: getting that grill.

What Clara didn't understand was that this grill meant everything to me. That my practice, our family, our sustenance and livelihood all hinged on a Weber grill. It was hyperbole, and yet it wasn't. My business was going to hell in a handbasket, and I had to figure out a way to make it stop. But I didn't tell this to Clara, who had a brussels sprout in her womb and didn't need to worry about anything more. It wouldn't do any good for both of us to worry, and anyway, somewhere deep inside my mind I stupidly believed a grill could save me, could save us, could change the expected course of our lives.

'What about something a little less fancy?' Clara asked, as I drooled over the stainless-steel burners and the cast-iron cooking grates. *But I don't want another grill*, I nearly whined. *I want this one.*

It struck a nerve in me, that for as hard as I worked and as much as I sacrificed for my job and my patients, I couldn't afford a grill, any grill, whatever grill I pleased. But it didn't make me angry. Instead it left a void, and I found myself feeling desperate to fill it.

I gazed at Clara then, about to explain with logic and reason why this was the grill I needed to have, seeing for the first time what I'd been blind to see, as she nuzzled into my ear and whispered this time, lips pressed to cartilage so I could feel her words all the way down to my toes, 'I said that Maisie is out cold.' Clara sat there beside me, hair falling shamelessly into her eyes, lips painted a bloodred, which for Clara only ever meant one thing, and as she breathed into my ear this time, 'She's out like a light,' I felt my hands rise to her, holding on tightly to what was already mine, terrified for the first time in my life that if I let go I might just lose her, too.

Clara meant everything to me, I reminded myself. Not the grill. Not the money.

Only Clara.

I grabbed ahold of her hands and drew her to me as Clara's fingers worked their way down the buttons of my shirt with only one thing in mind, not caring for one millisecond that the blinds throughout the home were open wide, inviting neighbors to view the scene: the way I raised Clara onto the tabletop, leaning into her, relieved that Maisie still slept in a toddler bed then, with knob covers on her bedroom door handle. There was no way for her to come toddling into the kitchen to find Daddy trying hard to wriggle out of his pants as Mommy wrenched the shirt from her arms, dropping it like hot lava to the tile floors.

'Trust me,' I said, sliding my hands under the hem of a flouncy skirt, the one that vaunted Clara's spun-out legs, which happened to be the first thing I fell in love with about her: those legs. Those persuasive legs, which she wrapped around me then as if she knew all along this hang-up I had with her legs. She did it on purpose: the skirt, the legs, Maisie in bed earlier than was the norm so she could catch me before my evening torpor set in, the three beers I'd already consumed starting to slow my movements, to have their way with my mind. She pressed her lips to mine, kissing me deeply and completely, as I buried myself into her, trying to think about Clara and only Clara. Clara wanted me in a way that only she had ever wanted me. She gave my life purpose and meaning.

I drew back and stared at her then with ambitious eyes,

eyes that would convince her we had money to spare, my intransigent movements trying hard to elicit a sense of power and greed rather than what it really was: burgeoning despair. 'We have money,' I whispered into her ear, and in reply she let out a long, euphoric sigh that had nothing at all to do with money. Nothing at all. I was the only one still thinking about the grill and money. 'Plenty of money. Money to spare,' and for a bat of an eye I imagined Clara and me as Demi Moore and Woody Harrelson, making love on straps of hundred dollar bills.

But of course we don't. We have no money. Not then and not now. Not enough, at least.

And it's not just thanks to Dr. Shepherd, either.

In the last six months, four new dentists have moved into the area, and competition is fierce. Add to it the impact of social media, all these *Moms of such-and-such* groups on Facebook recommending doctors and dentists to their thousands of online pseudo-friends. Just one person has a bad experience at my office, and within minutes, three thousand people know about it. Clara follows these groups online, so it isn't a groundless fear; it's genuine. She showed me a post months ago, a mother complaining that my hygienist Jan was snarky with her child. The truth of the matter: she was, but she needed to be, as the little boy had a series of cavities lined up between his teeth and refused to sit still as I injected him with shots of Novocain. Jan wasn't out of line, but she was firm. There were seventy-some comments on the woman's Facebook harangue, all recommending new dentists around town, words like *caring* and *compassionate* peppering their replies, none of which pertained to me.

Clara and I dismissed it at the time, until the coming weeks when patients started dropping like flies.

Though I didn't tell Clara about this. I didn't want her to worry.

I also didn't tell Clara that I sneaked into her Facebook account when she was fast asleep, and pulled up the same group account. There was a poll running, about which doctors and dentists the ladies of town most preferred. Of the twenty-plus dentists listed, I was ranked number eleven. This didn't bode well for a successful business.

The top-ranking position went, of course, to Dr. Shepherd.

In the middle of the night while she was sleeping, I managed to figure out how to hide these group posts from Clara's newsfeed.

And now, standing there in an empty exam room, Connor asks, 'What are you going to do about this, Boss?' as *The View* breaks for commercial and the TV screen fills with an ad for some revolutionary cleaning product, which promises to get through even the most uncompromising mildew and mold. Daytime TV. He sits upright in the chair, idle, waiting for me to reply. *What are you going to do about this, Boss?*

Boss. The very word galls me. When business is going well, Connor and I are partners, but when it's not, I'm the boss and it's my problem to solve. That's why my name is on the front door. I cut the checks, I pay the bills. I'm the one who put my entire life on the line for this, the one who stands to lose it all.

I sit down on the hygienist stool and sigh. 'I don't know,' I admit, rubbing my forehead and asking, 'What do you think we should do?'

He admires himself in the mirror. 'That's what I asked you.'

The problem with Connor is that he hasn't changed a bit since he was twenty-three; he's still the same guy I met in dental school, often moseying through the office doors ten minutes late, bleating about the enormity of his hangover and how much he had to drink the night before. He's a loose cannon, which, at twenty-three, made for a good time, but at this point in my life makes him a liability. Our friendship has been petering out lately, many heated conversations ruining what was once a strong bond—another thing Clara doesn't know about, because I don't want her to worry, and also because Clara loves Connor almost as much as she loves me. Almost.

The days have begun stretching longer, whole chunks of time where Connor—Dr. C, as he's favorably known by the clients and staff—and I sit twiddling our thumbs, watching daytime TV. I've dropped an innuendo here and there about how stupid it is having two dentists around with nothing to do. I've made comments about how these days, there's really only enough work for one dentist, not two. I hoped that Connor would catch my drift and start looking for a new job, but so far he hasn't taken the bait. Instead he's said something useless like, 'You'll figure it out,' or, 'I'm sure the answer will come to you,' and even though it frustrates me to no end, I'm not sure I have it in me to lay him off, if that's what I need to do.

Clara adores him. Maisie, too. He's on his best behavior any time he sees them, fawning over Clara's latest hairstyle or Maisie's new dress, presenting them with gifts. But Connor also has a temper and a habit of drinking too much. I could easily fire him for a whole host of things, but there's a part of me that's worried it might throw him off the deep end if I do. I've watched Connor give a crippling uppercut to some guy, all because he'd taken his stool at a bar when Connor was gone three minutes to piss. It had nothing to do with the stool itself, but the girl on the other side of it, five foot nine with long brunette hair, eyes like chocolate and a skirt so short she might as well have left it at home. Connor's date who some other guy dared to flirt with while he was gone. At twenty-three, I might have watched on, applauding, but, now, instead I heaved Connor out of the bar before they could call the police.

He's a loose cannon.

And I never want to be on the receiving end of that uppercut.

I brought Connor on board when business was booming and I had a ton of new clients, who I barely had time to see. I did it as a favor to him, and also to me. I'd tried expanding my hours to accommodate patients with long workdays like mine, but it took its toll. I was tired, grouchy and only saw Clara for about an hour a day when one or the other of us wasn't asleep. I wanted better for our marriage. Her father had been a workaholic when she was a girl. Mine had, too. They were the kind of men who were home for dinner—sometimes—and around on the weekends on occasion. Clara and I hardly ate dinners together, and conversations were limited to the essentials: *Can you pick up milk on your way home? Did you mail the mortgage payment?* I didn't want my children growing up wondering all the time when I'd be home, whether or not I'd be at their soccer games or school plays. I wanted them to know I'd be there.

And so I hired Connor, and we divvied up the work. Connor took half of the patients, and the practice continued to expand. Now, I could be home more for Clara and Maisie, and be the husband and father I always wanted to be.

Until Melinda Grey and Dr. Jeremy Shepherd walked into my life, whether purposefully or inadvertently. Then everything changed.

I knew there was a problem when some medical malpractice attorney inquired about records for Melinda Grey shortly after we'd submitted her unpaid bills to claims. Months had gone by since that emergency tooth extraction. She never returned to me for follow-up care, nor did she pay the bills that Stacy sent her, not the first, the second or the final notices. And so Stacy sent it along to a claims agent to collect the couple hundred dollars we were due. This was protocol; it's what we did when a bill wasn't paid on time. But when a lawyer started fishing around for medical records, I wasn't surprised. Sooner or later a complaint would arrive, asserting negligence.

I did my due diligence and discovered that Ms. Grey incurred a severe infection after that tooth extraction, one which sent her to the hospital with a face so swollen she could hardly breathe. Thousands of people are hospitalized for dental infections each year and, of these, a few dozen die. Thankfully Melinda Grey didn't die, though her problem was exacerbated by the fact that she didn't come in for her follow-up appointment or call me when symptoms began to appear: the discharge, the swelling, the pain. I would have put her on an antibiotic and cleared it up right away, but that wasn't in Ms. Grey's plan. She claimed that she didn't know the risks involved with the procedure—proved by the fact that there was no informed consent on file—and that I was negligent by not prescribing antibiotics on the day the surgery was performed.

Other doctors might have prescribed antibiotics not because she needed them but as a precaution. But it wasn't an egregious mistake; it wasn't even a mistake. In my professional opinion, I did the right thing.

There was a part of me that knew what was coming all along, a malpractice suit, though I couldn't bring myself to admit it to Clara, who, at six and then seven months into a grueling pregnancy, didn't need to be bothered with bad news. There was also the fact that in some ways I was ashamed by the imminent suit, this assertion of negligence that marred everything I've tried to do, to provide the best possible care for my patients. I'd always tried to be a decent human being, but this suit made me less than that, turning me into one who was inattentive and sloppy. It made me look bad.

In the days and weeks that followed, I began prescribing blanket antibiotics to my patients anytime I so much as made them bleed. Evidence of my own guilt. When the time came, the offense would eat this up, I knew, but I couldn't resist. The last thing I wanted was another one of my patients to end up in the ER with an infection headed to the brain, swelling that cuts off the airway.

Sooner or later I knew that Ms. Grey would sue me and that we'd settle, though the question of wherein the settlement demand would lie was something that started keeping me awake at night, little dollar signs floating before my eyes.

I lay in bed, estimating the cost of Melinda's hospital stay, IV antibiotics, pain management, emergency room fees, not even taking into account pain and suffering. I wondered what her monetary demand would be, twenty-five thousand, fifty thousand. I don't know. I have malpractice insurance, but wondered still what a malpractice suit would do to my reputation and practice. I saw Melinda's face when I closed my eyes, her sweet, genuine eyes, and sometimes I wanted to strike her with a fierce uppercut. I've spent my nights thinking of that, me beating the life out of Melinda Grey, so that when I woke up in the morning I was exhausted from not sleeping and from all of the exertion, from pummeling the woman who's trying to ruin my happy life.

I started Googling things. Strange things. I'm not sure why. Like how to get myself out of this mess. I came across some message boards, practitioners in similar positions that I now found myself in. Apologizing to the victim, some said, was paramount. Vital. I came across all sorts of statistics online that said malpractice suits were often dropped when a practitioner apologized for his or her error. But the fact of the matter was that I hadn't made an error. And admitting that I had would make me look bad.

And so I started looking at other options, wondering what would happen if I'd have done away with Melinda Grey's records when her lawyer first asked for them, if I'd have taken a match to the practice and watched the whole thing burn, records and all.

But it was too late for that now.

Other avenues of escape crossed my mind as well, like running away or faking my own death. It seemed extreme, and yet as I lay there in bed at night—Clara spread out beside me, me wishing the gentle purr of her breath would be enough to lull me to dreamland, as well—I pictured myself living in Dubai, on the coast of the Persian Gulf where, as far as I knew, they couldn't extradite me to the United States. When the time came I'd send word to Clara, Maisie and the baby, and they'd join me in Dubai. How to do it, I didn't know. It was all just a fantasy, one that grew more elaborate in time so that on those strung-out nights that I couldn't sleep, I started thinking about just how I'd do it, how I'd disappear, and I came up with this: leaving my car abandoned somewhere, with blood at the scene. My blood. Not too much to bleed out, but enough to cause concern—and then catching a red-eye to Dubai.

CLAƧA

I sit in the back seat with Felix pressed to my chest, the both of us draped in a black-and-white houndstooth blanket so that passersby can't see as he tries in vain to siphon milk from my breast. I do it as a force of habit, though I couldn't care less what bystanders see. My eyes are focused on the black car, which has sat inactively in the parking lot now for eighteen minutes since I watched Emily, Teddy and Maisie climb into Emily's own sedan and drive away.

Aluminum wheels, black with chrome accents, a three bar grille. Illinois license plates, though not the standard Illinois plates but rather specialty plates, the H and the I embossed on the aluminum plate for the hearing impaired. The hubcap is missing on one of the wheels, the left rear tire, which I convince myself over the next ten minutes—as Felix and I begin to bake in the unventilated car—is from where that car sideswiped Nick, elbowing the car from the road and into a tree. I reach for my phone from the diaper bag and start snapping photos of the vehicle from where I roost: the color of the car, a close-up of the license plate, the missing hubcap.

There's something about this car that frightened Maisie, and I have to know what it is. Does this car belong to the *bad man*? I'd ruled the idea out already—Maisie's suggestion that someone intentionally killed Nick—but now I wasn't so sure.

My smartphone can't zoom in closely enough to capture the license plate number, and so I draw Felix from me and burp him briefly before replacing him in the infant seat. He protests quietly, but soon he will be asleep. I have the wherewithal to grab an extra burp rag from the bag before springing from the car with Felix by my side, plonking his carrier back into a shopping cart and taking off across the parking lot for that black vehicle.

I try to be discreet about it but also wary, for whoever owns the car could be anywhere, watching me. Perhaps the owner was sitting at his own perch, watching as I fed Felix, as I snapped a photo of the car to give to the police. Watching as Maisie tore through the parking lot, zigzagging between cars. Watching as I hollered for her; watching as Maisie cried. Perhaps there was some sort of ecstasy in it, some sort of rapture or bliss. Perhaps he got off on our palpable fear, made apparent to everyone who viewed the scene, my screaming to accompany Maisie's tireless *no, no, no, no, no.*

I edge across the parking lot, with my phone in hand. I warble quietly to Felix to make believe I'm just a mother with a child, off on a shopping expedition. That there is no ulterior motive here.

I silence my cell phone and move insidiously across the asphalt, snapping photos of the car on burst mode, capturing twenty pictures with a single click, in an effort to increase the odds that one will display the license plate number, proof for the police that this is the car that took my husband's life.

I don't look at the car but keep my eyes on Felix the entire time.

And that's when I see a man making his way toward me.

He's a middle-aged man, late forties or early fifties with hair everywhere—a mustache and beard, tufted eyebrows, unshorn sideburns, messy hair. Black curls slink through the neckline of a black T-shirt that sports a Harley-Davidson and a single word: *Shovelhead*. I have no idea what it means. His arms are thick, lined with muscle. There are sweat marks on the pits of the shirt. His eyes are a fierce blue.

The man carries a shopping bag in one hand, and in the other a case of beer. Budweiser. I have never been a beer drinker, but Nick always was. His Labatt Blues still line the refrigerator door. I haven't had the strength to part with them; I wonder if I ever will.

The man looks at me and says, 'Afternoon, ma'am,' and my legs turn to paste, hardly able to sustain my own weight.

Is this the man who's taken my husband's life?

The external portion of his hearing aid rests behind an ear as verification that this car, with its hearing impaired designation, is his car. On his arm is a tribal tattoo that runs the entire length of the skin, from his wrist to the sleeve of the black T-shirt, a tattoo with sinuous lines and intricate patterns, which I try to burn into memory so later I can discover what it means. I nod my head, but I don't reply, as Felix and I pick up the pace, scurrying across the parking lot more quickly now, quite certain that as I run, the bad man's penetrating eyes follow me.

* * *

I buy infant formula and baby bottles. I dart through the self-checkout line and pay cash. I don't pay any attention to the kind of formula that I buy, nor the bottles.

Back inside the car I call Emily, letting her know that our one stop has now transformed into two. 'The bananas,' I tell her, 'were unripe. Too green. Maisie won't eat the ones that are green,' and so we need to go to another store to find ripe bananas for Maisie to eat. 'Do you mind?' I ask, but Emily says no, of course not, that I should take my time.

'Get some coffee, too,' she says, telling me how the kids are playing so well. She tells me about a new coffee shop that has just opened up in town. 'You should try it,' she says. I thank her for the tip and assure her I'll go.

Of course it's not true. None of it is true. Maisie won't eat bananas whether they're yellow or green or something in between. Apples are the only fruit she'll eat, diced up bits of Gala apples with the peel completely removed, though right now it doesn't matter a thing about apples or bananas. I'm not going to another grocery store or the coffee shop. I'm going to the police.

* * *

The police station in town is new. Constructed just in the last few years, it's a large redbrick building with an American flag that hangs outside at half-staff, tucked away on an industrial road beside an indoor sports facility and a bottling manufacturer that employs hundreds of people in town. There is also a fire station and the railroad track, one whose trains are constantly stopping on the tracks and interrupting the flow of traffic. It's more than a headache for commuters but also a safety concern, those frequent times the locomotive splits the town in two, separating diabetics from the local hospital, the police from foul play.

I park in the lot and walk inside.

I stand before a large counter as if I'm at a doctor's office or a bank, and when a quasi-receptionist in uniform asks how she can help me, I tell her I need to speak with a detective. She says that someone will be with me shortly. There are chairs to wait in, black padded chairs with a heavy-duty steel frame. They aren't in the least bit comfortable.

I wait for nearly fifteen minutes for a Detective Kaufman to arrive, hearing the sound of his footsteps before he appears. By comparison, he's a short man, five foot nine or five foot ten, enough that as I stand from the chair, I meet him eye to eye. His hair is raven, mottled with flecks of gray. Though the hair on his head is sheared quite short, there is a curl to it, an obdurate wave combed backward, away from the tan eyes. His mustache and beard are well groomed, trimmed and brushed, also flecked with gray. There is a swarthiness to his complexion and on his face, a sad, somber expression.

I've never seen this man before. There was no detective at the hospital when the officers in uniform informed me that my husband was dead, or dying, because there was nothing to investigate then. It was an open-and-shut case. Man drove too fast, flew off the road and into a tree. Case closed.

But now it might be something more.

Detective Kaufman leads me to a small room and invites me to sit down on a hard plastic chair. I follow behind as he leads the way, trailing the single squeak of a pair of leather shoes. The room reminds me of a workplace lunchroom, with a round table that seats four, and four hard plastic chairs. Blue. The walls, too, are painted blue, cinder block walls painted blue like lapis lazuli. Metal grids and drop tiles line the ceiling, interspersed every now and again with plastic light panels, which make the room artificially bright. There is no window. There is a counter lined with an unwashed Keurig machine, a microwave, a forgotten paper plate and, on the floor, a watercooler sans water. The bottle is bone-dry.

'I'm Clara Solberg,' I say, and he says to me, 'I know who you are,' as I slide sideways into the blue plastic chair.

This could make me blush, and yet it doesn't. I'm beyond that point in my life when being embarrassed comes with ease. My husband is dead. I feel nothing anymore but grief.

'My husband,' I go on, as if I didn't hear him at all, 'is the one who was killed out on Harvey Road. Seven days ago.'

'I know.'

We're a town of nearly forty thousand people, not the kind of town where everyone knows everyone. But in the age of social media, news spreads quickly. The newspaper had asked for a photo of Nick to include with their report: *Crash on Harvey Road leaves one dead.* I tried unavailingly to find a photo of Nick alone, but all I could dig up was Nick and me. Nick and me standing on the limestone bluffs of Peninsula State Park, overlooking a frigid Green Bay; at the top of Eagle Tower, enjoying the view; kayaking. The newspaper had asked for family photographs, the kind of image that would trigger sympathy and boost ratings and sales, but I wasn't too keen on having Maisie's face splayed across the black-and-white newsprint to make someone else feel sad. I wasn't too keen on having Maisie's image made public for any reason, but especially not to trumpet the fact that her father was dead.

I chose a photo of Nick and me. The next day it appeared in the local paper and online. By afternoon, it had been spread around the internet a bazillion times. It appeared at random on friends' Facebook feeds—my tragedy quickly becoming theirs, people I didn't know leaving commentary on friends of friends' status updates about how they were so sorry for so-and-so's loss, as if my high school pal Amanda and Jill, the woman I spoke to at the gym on occasion, had lost a spouse and not me. *So very sorry for your loss, Jill*, said one Facebook friend to Jill. *What a horrible tragedy*, followed by the obnoxious inclusion of a cyber hug. Jill had never once met Nick. She didn't need a hug, and I found I was appalled by this cyber hug, truly and utterly aghast by the left and right curly keyboard brackets coming together in a warm embrace on my laptop screen, an anger that spiraled into the decision never again to speak to Jill.

And then that evening Nick's and my blithe faces aired on the news, and I watched in awe and disgust as Nick's story spread far and wide.

It doesn't surprise me that Detective Kaufman knows who I am.

'I wanted to talk to you about my husband's case,' I say, and at this his mouth parts in questioning. There is no case.

'You mean his accident?' he asks, and I shrug my shoulders, but I don't say yes or no. Accident implies that something has happened unintentionally and without deliberate cause. I'm no longer sure that's the case.

'I have reason to believe that foul play was to blame.'

I watch the expression on his face. A single eyebrow elevates, the other droops. He doesn't smile. For a long time, he doesn't say a thing.

And then, after a while he asks, 'And why is that, Mrs. Solberg?' His eyes never once wander from mine, as he sips lingeringly from a mug of coffee, taking his time. The room is cold, the air conditioner working overtime to counter the temperature outside. I feel suddenly awkward in the detective's eyes, repulsive and fat, the extra baby weight stuffed into the elastic panel of a pair of maternity pants. The dried sweat clings to my skin; my underarms begin to reek.

'My daughter has been having nightmares,' I say, trying to return his sustained stare. It's not so hard to do. 'She's been having nightmares about the accident. Flashbacks. Except that in these flashbacks there's a *bad man* following her and Nick. A bad man in a black car,' I say, taking the liberty of consolidating the stories and filling in the missing details. 'Perhaps there was another car out on Harvey Road that day, one that pushed Nick and Maisie off the road. Perhaps this car,' I say as I set my smartphone on the table between us and find the image of the car and a close-up of its license plate. Detective Kaufman narrows his eyes at the images on the screen, but they don't look for long.

'Your daughter told you there was a car following her and Mr. Solberg on Harvey Road?' he asks, and I nod my head and easily commit perjury.

'Yes,' I say, believing in her own way that Maisie did say these words to me. I asked point-blank if the man was in a car, and she said yes. When I asked if the car was black, Maisie let out a howl and ran, unlike when I asked if it was red or blue, to which she shook her head and said no.

'Why do you think this is the car?' he asks, and so I tell him about the scene in the grocery store parking lot this afternoon, my Maisie running helter-skelter through the cars in fright. I tell him how she wet her pants, how she screamed over and over again *no, no, no, no, no*. The detective seems disinterested in this. He doesn't write any of it down, nor does the expression of his face change.

Only when I stop talking does he speak.

I'm informed of things I never knew. How when Nick died, a crash reconstructionist was called to the scene. A crash reconstructionist, Detective Kaufman explains—as he brings me my own Styrofoam cup of coffee and a box of tissues—provides an in-depth analysis of a crash site, particularly those involving fatalities such as Nick's. This analysis includes how fast a driver was going at the time of impact, the road and weather conditions, whether or not homicide is to blame for the death, or manslaughter, or just bad luck. At the scene, measurements and photographs are taken, and the vehicle and roadway are analyzed. 'These days,' he tells me, 'most vehicles even come with their own black box, which may soon eliminate the need for crash reconstructionists. Event data recorders, they're called. They tell us things the deceased cannot, like how long it took for the air bags to deploy, whether or not the driver was wearing a seat belt, or if he stepped on the accelerator in the moments before impact, or the brake.'

My eyes move to him in question, wondering just exactly which Nick stepped on: the accelerator or the brake. I envision Maisie and Nick in the car together, riding down Harvey Road. In my vision, the windows are closed, the air conditioner is on. It was hot that day, and though Maisie likes to ride with the windows all the way down, the sun in her eyes, the wind in her hair, Nick would have objected. Nick has patience for many things but never humidity or heat. I see him with his sunglasses on, though my mind knows better than this; Nick's sunglasses now lie on top of his bedroom dresser, forgotten that day at home. He was in a hurry. Nick didn't have his sunglasses, but in my visions there they are, perched on the bridge of his nose, and he turns to Maisie and chants a few lyrics of a song he doesn't know. On the radio is the soundtrack to *Frozen*, while Maisie kicks her feet against the leather back of the passenger's seat, keeping rhythm with the music. In her hands, a book. A board book she chose from the basket of them that sat in the center of the back seat, *Goodnight Moon*, because this is how the paramedics found her, with a book in hand.

Detective Kaufman excuses himself from the room, and returns seconds later with a folder in hand. He pulls photographs from the folder and slides them toward me. 'I'm not sure if this is something you want to see,' he says, and I survey them indecisively. I, too, am not sure this is something I want to see. The rich red car folded around the oak tree. The side of the car crinkled into a ball like an old sheet of notebook paper, flattened and creased. Car parts scattered at random across the concrete: a side mirror, a headlight, a wedge of bumper, a hubcap. A hubcap, like the missing hubcap on the black car from the grocery store lot.

I've been told time and again what happened, how it was that Nick actually died. I've been told because I asked repeatedly, wearing on those around me. I needed someone to explain it to me, how a family car with five-star safety ratings could take my husband's life. The air bags did deploy, I've been told, but it somehow failed to protect Nick's head from the blow. It happened quickly, they said. In an instant. Nick and the air bag, they missed each other somehow.

In the image the detective shows me, black lines mark the road, skid marks, evidence of a car's tires braking quickly and leaving rubber along the surface of the road. As a girl, I used to have races with neighborhood friends—who could create the longest skid mark. We'd line our bikes up in the cul-de-sac and rev our imaginary engines. We'd bike as fast as we could for twenty feet or more, and then squeeze tightly on the hand brake, seeing who could create the longest and darkest skid mark, just like a pink eraser leaving gummy residue along a sheet of paper.

I run my fingers across the blackened lines and say to the detective, 'Skid marks. Nick slammed on the brakes. He tried to slow down.'

But Detective Kaufman responds, 'Funny how these little black lines can tell us so much about what happened at the site of an accident, leaving trace evidence behind on the concrete. We call these lines here yaw marks. They're a bit different than skid marks, which start light and get darker. Acceleration marks are just the opposite. They start dark and get lighter as the vehicle picks up speed. But yaw marks are different still. They're curved, for one, which tells us that the car was sliding sideways at the time of impact, that the driver took a turn too quickly and slid laterally. There are striations,' he says, running a single finger along the linear lines of what the detective has termed yaw marks. 'These tell us which direction the car was sliding,' he adds as he reaches out for another image where he can make clear the direction the car was sliding: right toward the burly white oak tree.

The other thing the detective elucidates with the point of his finger and a patronizing stare: the yaw marks present on the photograph are not in Nick's lane. They're to the left of center, on the wrong side of the solid yellow line in a no-passing zone.

'There were no skid marks at the scene,' he says quite plainly. 'Your husband never stepped foot on the brake, which we were able to authenticate when we pulled the vehicle's event data recorder. He hit that turn at the same speed as the half mile of linear road before it, which, suffice to say, was too fast. He wasn't paying attention; he didn't have time to anticipate the turn and slow down. The yaw marks reveal the way the car slid across the solid yellow line and into the base of the tree. The evidence puts Nick's speed around fifty miles per hour. Harvey Road is forty-five, but drops to twenty at the bend. We surveyed the surrounding street, well before and after the crash. Acceleration marks but no skid marks. Your husband sped up before the turn. But after, there was nothing.

'You know what happens when a car flees the scene of a crime quickly?' he asks, and I shake my head and say no. And he says it then like I'm dumb, dense, empty-headed. 'Acceleration marks,' he says, as if this is something I should know. He starts collecting the photographs before him, an indication that our conversation will soon be through.

'If someone ran your husband off the side of the road, they weren't going to stick around waiting for the police to arrive. They would have picked up speed and gotten the hell out of Dodge. You know what I think happened?' Detective Kaufman asks then, staring me straight in the eye. I return the stare, though baby Felix beside me has begun to grumble. 'I think your husband was driving too fast and took the turn too quickly. Maybe the sun was in his eyes and he didn't see the turn in time. Maybe he was distracted.'

It's then that I hear little Maisie's sweet voice in the back seat of the car, her hot-pink Crocs kicking the back of the passenger's seat inattentively, as if she doesn't even know she's doing it.

Faster, Mommy, faster, she says.

I force this notion from my mind. Nick knows better than to give in to the capricious whim of a four-year-old.

I remember the hubcap. The one missing from the black car, and also the one at the scene of the crash. I pull up the image on my phone, the black car with its missing hubcap. I set it beside the detective's own glossy eight-by-ten. I make it clear that this could be more than a coincidence, and he exhales heavily. His patience with me is wearing thin.

'How do you know that isn't your own hubcap?' he asks, but without waiting for my reply, 'Would it lessen your concern if I spoke to the owner of the vehicle?' he asks, and I say it would. It would help immensely. Detective Kaufman finds the close-up of the license plate number on my phone's photo album, and jots it down on a sheet of scrap paper. He tells me he'll contact the owner and let me know what he finds.

'One more thing,' he tells me before I can rise from my chair and leave. 'It came to my attention that Mr. Solberg had an Order of Protection filed against him,' he says, words that I find utterly farcical and so I laugh. It isn't a lighthearted laugh, but an unsettled laugh, one that gets the detective's attention.

'A restraining order?' I gasp, knowing how impossible this is. There's no way in the world that someone would file a restraining order against Nick. Nick is gentle, kind, a pacifist. He can't even raise his voice to me when he's mad. The detective is wrong. This can't be.

'Yes, ma'am,' he says, staring at me in a way that suggests he isn't wrong. 'A restraining order. You didn't know?' he asks, and it's mockery the way he says it. He's mocking me. I shake my head; I didn't know. 'An Emergency Order of Protection was filed against Mr. Solberg. He and the accuser were awaiting a date for the hearing for a plenary order, which would decide whether or not the Order of Protection was going to stick.'

'The accuser,' I say, more to myself than to the detective, a loaded word in and of itself, *accuser*, which would make Nick the *accused*. This can't be. 'This has to be a mistake,' I tell the detective. 'This is simply ludicrous. Nick couldn't hurt a fly,' I say.

'Maybe he would, maybe he wouldn't,' says the detective, 'but that was up to a judge to decide,' explaining to me that in three days' time Nick and this accuser were to attend a hearing to decide whether or not the emergency order had any merit or if it was a frivolous claim.

'I suppose we'll never know now,' he says, though in my mind I've already decided.

Nick would never hurt a fly.

'Who did this to Nick?' I ask, needing to know. When I think of restraining orders, I imagine maniac men with violent tendencies threatening their wives and children. I envision battered women in shelters, and scared kids who cling to their mother's gaunt legs, crying. I don't see Nick. My mind is reeling as I ask again, more preemptory this time, less polite, 'Who did this to Nick?'

It isn't a question this time. I demand to know.

The order is public record. I could go to the courthouse and request a copy of the filing if I wanted to, which is maybe the only reason why Detective Kaufman gives me the name. It's one I've never heard before, a woman who I soon plan to know anything and everything about. At the mention of her name, I feel a stabbing sensation in my chest because it is a woman. My mind recalls the receipt for the pendant necklace. Was the necklace for this woman?

Was Nick having an affair?

All the air suddenly leaves the room, and I find it hard to breathe.

I gather Felix and begin to leave, but not before the detective stops me one last time. 'There's something else,' he says, and I pause with my hand on the doorknob and turn. 'It's standard protocol to check the cell phone records in the case of a vehicle collision. See if the driver was on the phone at the time of a crash. Browsing the internet. Texting. Illinois is now a hands-free state, which I'm sure you know,' he says, and I know what he's getting at well before he says it.

'Your husband was on the phone at the time of the crash,' and though I want to quibble with him and claim that it's not possible, I see the expression on the detective's face and know that he's telling the truth. Nick, who never speaks on the phone while driving, was on the phone. And he wasn't speaking to me because before he left the ballet studio, we'd already spoken.

I'll pick up something for dinner. Chinese or Mexican? Chinese.

Who was Nick speaking to at the time of the crash? I wonder. I ask the detective about this. 'He was on the phone,' I say, 'with who?'

The detective stares at me for an extended minute or two before shrugging his shoulders and saying, 'I believe you were given Mr. Solberg's personal effects already. The items we were able to gather from the car. His phone should be there,' though already I'm telling myself that whoever it is, was simply a wrong number. It was a wrong number, and Nick, ever obliging and gracious, took the time to answer the call, to tell the caller politely that he or she had misdialed. And for this he died.

'I'm so sorry for your loss,' Detective Kaufman says prosaically, rising from the table and collecting my abandoned Styrofoam cup in his hand as I leave, bound and determined to figure this paradox out. Who was Nick speaking to at the time of the crash? Who filed an Order of Protection against him and, perhaps more important, why?

What secrets has Nick been keeping from me for all this time?

NICK

BEFO**Я**E

Most nights I go home with the best intentions of telling Clara exactly what's going on. It isn't that I'm purposefully trying to keep it from her. There aren't secrets in our marriage; that's a promise we made when we said *I do*, and one I plan to stick to.

It's more of an omission.

I think to myself as I drive home, *Tonight's the night I'm going to tell her*, but then I come in through the door to find Clara with a belly swollen three times its size and feet so inflated she can barely walk, setting the table for dinner. Maisie is sitting before the TV, surrounded by glue sticks and crayons, evidence that she didn't watch TV all day, but rather spent the day creating, and when I come in she runs to me, and I hoist her into my arms and tickle her as she laughs. She wears her leotard still, this pastel-pink thing with fluttery sleeves. Wrapped around her waist is a dainty pink skirt, with flouncy edges that remind me of lettuce leaves. Today is Tuesday, the day Maisie takes ballet. 'Where were you?' Maisie asks as I bring her back down to earth, the same question she asks every day though she knows good and well where I was.

'At work, silly,' I say, and she asks why.

'Taking care of my patients,' I tell her, and again she asks why. This is what kids do when they're four. But I'm smarter than a four-year-old, or so I like to think that I am, and so I ask Maisie where she was all day, and she says, 'Here, silly,' and she tells me about the spider she found in her bedroom, a big, black and hairy spider—'Maybe even a tarantula!' she exclaims—as big as a truck. She holds her hands out so that I can see the size of the spider, two kid hands spread a good eight inches apart so that it might have been a bunny or a squirrel or a hedgehog that she saw there in her bedroom, or it might have been nothing. 'This big, Daddy,' she tells me. 'The spider was this big.'

'There was no spider,' says Clara, coming into the living room in a pair of leggings and a stretchy white T-shirt that is stretched as far as it can go, so that I can see her belly button pressing through. Her hands are laced together, on the small of the back where it constantly hurts, and her eyes are full of fatigue. She's tired, physically and mentally, but still, she looks at me and smiles, and as she does, I liquefy completely and dissolve. Her hair is flat, and eye makeup is smeared beneath a single eye; evidence of a nap, of Clara sleeping while Maisie also slept. There is something yellowish smeared across the front of her white shirt and bread crumbs on her forehead, and still, there's no woman in the world as beautiful to me as Clara. 'It was lint,' she adds with a tired but amused smile. 'Not a spider,' she says, meeting Maisie in the eye this time, 'but lint.'

'It was a spider,' replies Maisie, also with a smile, and whether she's mistaken or lying, I don't know.

I squat down to Maisie's height and stare her in the eye. It's strange seeing the world from three and a half feet high. Maisie's eyes are green, like Clara's, a mossy green that stands out on the fair skin. In fact, she's all Clara, from her hair to her eyes, to her strong-willed demeanor. Pigheaded and stubborn in a way I adore. Neither Clara nor Maisie is ever wrong, or so they believe.

'Sometimes we see something that scares us a little,' I explain, 'and we make believe it's something that it's really not. Once, when I was a little boy,' I tell her, making this up as I go, 'I thought I saw a coyote in the backyard. I was playing all alone outside, and I was sure I saw a coyote pass through the yard. I screamed for my mom, and she came running to see why I was upset. I told her about the coyote. She looked all around, but sure enough, there wasn't a coyote there. There wasn't a coyote anywhere. It was only the neighbor's cat.'

'What did Grandma do?' she asks, her eyes wide with curiosity as her tiny little hands disappear in mine. 'Did she get mad?' she asks, but I tell her no, of course not, 'Grandma didn't get mad, but she did remind me of the story of *The Boy Who Cried Wolf*.'

'What's that?' asks Maisie. She's never heard the fable before, and as I hover there, squatting to kid height, she climbs on my bent knee.

'It's a fable,' I say. 'A story that's supposed to teach us something,' and with that I relay the story to my girl as

Clara watches on, clearly pleased. The story of the little boy who lied so many times that when he finally told the truth, nobody believed him. I don't lecture or scold, and I make sure to leave out the part where the boy gets eaten by the wolf. But Maisie listens and commits the story to memory, so that maybe, when the opportunity arises again, she'll think twice before telling a lie.

The contour of a passing car catches Clara's attention, the window's beveled edges tainting the view. With bare feet, she glides to the glass and peers outside, hands cupped around her eyes like a pair of binoculars. Across the street, beside a silver sports car that sparkles like diamonds in the sun, is Theo Hart, stepping out from the car. 'What's it this time?' Clara asks, as I lean into her from behind, chin resting on her shoulder, hands cupped beneath our baby boy.

I let out a long, low whistle. 'A Maserati,' I say, trying hard to contain my jealousy. 'Those go for over a hundred grand a pop. You don't see that around here every day.'

'It's not like it's his,' Clara spits, and then we stand and stare as behind us Maisie spins like a whirlybird around the room, arms extended in the air. A helicopter's rotor blade. *Look at me, Daddy. I can fly, I can fly.* Theo circles the car three times, a pair of Ray-Bans in his hand, eyeing his latest prize. 'He's such a scumbag,' she grumbles, and though he is, that's about the least offensive label I can think up. There are far worse names I can think up for Theo Hart.

'I wish she would leave him,' Clara says as I tell Maisie to be careful so she doesn't fall.

'Emily?' I ask.

'Yes,' Clara says. 'I saw them again,' she remarks, words muzzled so that Maisie can't hear. 'The bruises. His handprints. On her neck. She wore a turtleneck this time so that I wouldn't see. But I saw his hands, there on her neck. I wish that she would leave him.' She turns and presses herself into me, so that now Maisie begins to chant something she must have picked up at the playground where the big kids play, kids too old for the playground. *Mommy and Daddy*, she begins, forgetting altogether the line about the tree, and leaping straight to *K-I-S-S-I-N-G*. Clara grins now, pushing Theo and Emily out of her mind as, to Maisie's delight, she presses her soft lips to mine, whispering into my ear, 'I'm so lucky I have you.'

We sit down to dinner, though by now I've forgotten everything I planned to tell Clara when I got home, about the potential of a malpractice suit, the loss of clients. The lease payment I'm going to have trouble paying when the first of the month comes. It isn't a lie; it's an oversight. A memory lapse.

Instead we discuss baby names. We make no progress, but instead force eliminations. Enoch and Finch are out; so, too, are Edward and Tom. Clara is losing patience and starting to worry. 'What if we never find a name for the baby?' she asks, and I see the stress settle upon her in fine lines around the mouth and eyes. 'I don't want to be one of those couples that go a week or two weeks without naming their child, as if they didn't already have nine months to decide.' She lays her hand on her stomach, and looks to me pleadingly, her eyes so sad I almost give in to Finch. Finch Solberg. Almost. 'I want to be able to call him something,' she entreats, 'something other than *him*,' and I try to talk myself into that name, Finch Solberg, just to indulge Clara, to make her happy, but I can't do it. A finch is a bird, and I won't name my child after a bird.

'We'll think of something,' I promise her, 'we will. We'll think of something soon,' and my eyes travel to Maisie's, which are also staring at me, listening to the entire conversation. 'Put your thinking cap on, ladies,' I say. 'It's Operation Baby Name,' and at this Maisie giggles, but Clara doesn't seem so sure. Having a name for the baby would make the experience more real, would bring the unborn child to life.

That night as I tuck Maisie into bed, going through my standard *snug as a bug in a rug* routine, slipping the edges of the sheet beneath her torso and legs, she sits upright at once, undoing what I've just done. 'Maisie,' I groan as the sheet gets pulled from under her limbs and kicked to the end of the bed, not realizing yet that her eyes are locked out the bedroom window where the sun is in the slow, painful process of setting. This time of year it's harder and harder to get Maisie to go to bed because, as she likes to point out, *it's not dark outside*, even if the digital clock beside her head reads 7:53 p.m. Lights-out is 7:30. She's already spent twenty-three minutes procrastinating, and it seems she's not yet through.

'Daddy!' Maisie yelps, but before I can scold her I see that she looks scared. I rise from the edge of the bed and follow her gaze out the open window, eyes scanning up and down the street, seeing nothing. Nothing important at least. A boy playing basketball two doors down. The Thompsons walking their dog. A squirrel on the bird feeder.

'What is it, Maisie?' I ask as I turn the handle on the blinds and draw the curtains closed. 'What did you see?'

'The scumbag, Daddy,' she grumbles. 'The scumbag's

outside,' and though there's a part of me that wants to laugh, there's a part of me that fills with shame. *The scumbag.* Theo Hart. Maisie heard Clara and me when we were talking about Theo after work. We have to be far more careful about what we say in front of Maisie. She's listening. All the time, she's listening even when spinning dizzy circles around the room, pretending she can't hear.

I draw the blinds open one more time and look outside. Theo isn't there. The blinds are closed throughout the Hart home; the house is dark. I turn back to Maisie. First I tell her that she shouldn't use words like *scumbag*, and neither should Mommy or me. They're not nice.

But then I look her in the eye and say sternly, 'Secondly, Maisie, you know better than to lie. We just talked about this tonight. Remember the story of the boy who cried wolf?' I ask, and she nods her head, mouth open, ready to argue. I see the words forming in her mind: *But he was there*, she thinks, though I press a finger to her lips and whisper, 'Shhh,' before she can say them aloud. He's not there now. He wasn't there before.

And even if he was, he lives there. Theo Hart outside is nothing out of the ordinary, unfortunately. Maisie just wanted to try the word *scumbag* on for size. She wanted to delay bedtime, to get a reaction.

And so I put my poker face on and say that it's time for bed.

Knowing she has a tendency for dramatics when she's four, Clara and I better be at the top of our game by the time she turns sixteen, or we're going to be in trouble.

CLAЯA

In the parking lot of the police department, I pull up a search engine on my smartphone and type in the woman's name that the detective has given me, the accuser who filed an Emergency Order of Protection against Nick. The need to know is eating away at me; I can't wait until I get home. In the back seat Felix fusses, but this time my own urgency and desperation prevail. I search the name the detective has given me. Melinda Grey.

All the usual social media sites load, Facebook and Twitter, the woman's Pinterest boards. Her profile photo is hardly of herself, but rather a crystal-blue coastline with a palm tree set to the side, Hawaii or Puerto Rico maybe, the Virgin Islands. A woman stands at the center in a bikini top and a sarong, though she's at such a distance she's near impossible to see, an afterthought to the palm tree and the sea. Her Tweets are protected; her Facebook page is set to private. Only her Pinterest boards are public, but all I find there is an obsession with chocolate and handmade crafts. The White Pages online list an address on Parkshore, which I scribble quickly onto the back of my hand, but before I can investigate further, my phone rings.

'Hello?' I ask, agitated by the untimely phone call that pulled me away from Melinda Grey, from zooming in on her profile photo to see if I could catch a smidgen of eye color, a snippet of hair. Melinda Grey filed a restraining order against Nick. This woman, with her white bikini top and her splashy sarong, filed a restraining order against my husband. I couldn't even begin to estimate an age, and I can't say whether or not she's pretty, but my mind wonders why. Why did she file a restraining order against Nick? Was he sleeping with her? Were they having an affair?

I think of Nick's late nights, when he came home from work after Maisie and I were both in bed. Was he not at work at all, but rather with Melinda Grey? Maisie's words come to me, *The bad man is after us*, and I have to wonder if Maisie was certain it was a bad man, or if by chance it could have been a bad *woman* who was after her and Nick. The sunlight was so bright the day of the crash. How likely is it that in the heat of the moment, with the sunlight glaring into her eyes, Maisie saw the driver of the car that pushed her and Nick from the road—*if* some driver pushed her and Nick from the road?

'Clara,' says a kind voice, pulling me away from my thoughts of Melinda Grey. 'It's Connor,' he says, and I feel a great relief wash over me that for the moment I am not alone. That these questions, these uncertainties, are not all mine to manage. Connor is here.

And so I can't help myself. I just come out and say it.

'Was Nick having an affair?' I ask, tears already piercing my eyes, and the lack of a response is more than enough to say for certain that he was. Nick was having an affair. Silence lingers in the space between Connor and me for a full thirty seconds or more, and even then all he can muster is an unassertive *I don't know*, and I find myself apologizing. 'I shouldn't have asked you that. I shouldn't have put you in that position,' I say, reminding myself that Connor was Nick's best friend, not mine. Of course Connor would never betray Nick's trust.

'Clara,' he says regretfully, but I dismiss him.

'No,' I say. 'Please. Forget about it,' as I watch a train of mallard ducks waddle across the police station parking lot and toward a pond on the other side of the road. 'Forget I said anything. Forget I asked. What did you call for?' I ask then, remembering it was Connor who called me and not the other way around.

'I wanted to see if you were okay,' he says, and I curtly answer, 'I'm fine,' while wiping the tears from my eyes.

* * *

Twenty minutes later, I arrive in the doorway to Emily's home with an iced latte in hand, one from the new coffee shop in town. In the plastic cup the ice cubes melt, turning the cup sweaty.

'For you,' I say, as I call for Maisie to come, and thank Emily for taking her off my hands for a bit. 'You're such a good friend,' I say, though no words are mentioned about Maisie's tantrum in the grocery store parking lot, my pitiable parenting skills or the fact that Emily may have saved Maisie's life. My mind is reeling from the information I've been delivered in the last few hours: the fact that a woman named Melinda Grey filed an Order of Protection against Nick, the fact that they were having an affair, the belief that she—a jilted lover seeking revenge—pushed him from the side of Harvey Road. I wish more than anything that I could talk to Emily about this, and yet there's something so disgraceful about a cheating spouse that I can't bring myself to say the words aloud, not to Emily at least, of whom I've been so judgmental of her marriage.

'It was no bother,' she says to me as she invites me inside. I step into the foyer. Her home is meticulous, an art deco–style with bold colors and geometric designs. There isn't an item out of place, and at this I feel chagrined, knowing how my own home is a mess, in shambles, poor Harriet the dog left alone all day without a walk. She'll have found a corner to pee in by now, no doubt, and I'll scold her as if she should have opened the door herself and let herself out to pee. 'Really. Teddy just adores her,' she says to me. 'We should get them together more often to play.' And Emily asks whether or not I was able to get my shopping done, and I say yes, that I never would have were it not for her, and at this she smiles and says kindly, 'Anytime.'

Emily is the type of woman that—until you get to know her—women easily despise. She's lovely, with her hair the color of obsidian and flawless olive skin. Like other women, I despised her, too, the first time I laid eyes on her as she and Theo moved into the vacant property on our block, a grand Victorian-style home. It wasn't until later that I discovered that her warmth and compassion belied her beauty as if one couldn't be both, pretty and nice.

We went years without speaking, though by all accounts we should have been friends. We had so much in common, from concurrent pregnancies to children born just weeks apart, to husbands with hectic work schedules who left us to our own devices for ten hours or more each day.

But it wasn't until Maisie and Teddy discovered one another at the age of two and a half that Emily and I became friends. It was then that I realized she was sweet and kind, not at all the haughty woman I'd assumed her to be.

'Stay for dinner?' Emily asks of me, reminding me that Theo is out of town. She's a tall woman, as am I, but taller still, so that her eyes look down to mine.

'Of course,' I say, remembering, and, 'Massachusetts. An auto show,' but I shake my head and tell her no. 'I can't stay,' I say, and for a fraction of a second these words nearly follow: *Nick will be home soon.* It's habit, a force of nature. Nick should be coming home soon. But tonight Nick will not be home. Tomorrow Nick will not be home, and I'm afflicted by the sudden and painful reminder: Nick is dead. My hand goes to my mouth, but I refuse to cry. I will not cry, there in the foyer to Emily's home with Teddy and Maisie just upstairs. I feel the warm tears spring to my eyes, but I force them aside.

Emily's hand comes to rest on my arm. 'I'm so sorry, Clara,' she whispers, swallowing her own tears. 'I'm so sorry this is happening to you.' But I shake my head quickly and hold up a hand. I can't have this conversation, not here, not now. Because then I will cry, and I don't want the children to see me crying. I call for Maisie again, my voice louder now, unbridled and less repressed.

'I've left Felix in the car,' I tell Emily, imagining the

heat and humidity of the day enveloping his tiny little body, making him sweat. 'I need to go,' I say, my voice wavering, losing restraint, and then, nearly a scream for Maisie as the little girl appears at the top of the steps in Teddy's magician costume—the poplin jacket with its satin lapels, the red cape, the black hat—and asks if we're ready for the show. She and Teddy have a show for Emily and me to see, a magic act whereby they plan to turn a dollar bill into ten and make a sock randomly appear. I wonder if they can make Nick appear, too.

'We can't leave now,' says Maisie, with a frown upon her face, her ungovernable hair hanging in her eyes. She stomps her foot and demands of me, 'We can't leave before the show.'

And then I cry.

* * *

'Where are we going?' Maisie asks as I drive past our house and continue down the street. It isn't a question so much as a complaint. If she can't play with Teddy, then Maisie wants to go home. I stare down at the address I've scrawled on a hand, the same one that's now programmed into my GPS. Maisie begins to groan, 'Home, Mommy, home,' as our front porch fades from view.

I think fast.

'I could have sworn, Maisie,' I say as I inch the car through our neighborhood and toward the highway, 'that I saw a lost dog walking down the street. Can you help me look for the dog, Maisie, so we can get her home?' I ask as a means of distraction only, for there was no dog, though I go on to describe it for her, a big yellow dog with a purple collar around its neck, as Maisie presses her face to the windowpane, quietly searching for the lost pup, forgetting that she's tired and hungry, that she wants to go home. I turn on the radio to counteract the silence, watching as, in the rearview mirror, Maisie's toes begin to tap, her eyes glued out the window, and I pray that between the music and the dog, she'll be temporarily content.

Parkshore Drive is nearly nine miles south of our own home. At the onset of rush hour, it takes over fifteen minutes to get there, out of our neighborhood and onto the highway, bypassing gas stations and restaurants until the landscape becomes residential again and the houses return. The homes on Parkshore are retro and dated, circa 1950- or 1960-something, when sprawling ranch homes dominated suburban American life. The trees are tall and wide, the houses shrouded by leaves. As I pull onto Parkshore, there are half a dozen boys playing a game of baseball in the middle of the street. They part like the Red Sea before me, so that I can pass through.

'Do you see her, Mommy?' Maisie asks about the dog, and, 'Where did she go?'

'I don't know, Maisie,' I claim, peering over my shoulder to offer a placatory smile, reaching a hand back to pat her knee. I don't want to lie to her, but how could I possibly explain? 'Maybe somewhere up here?' I suggest as I roll along the road and toward the home that, according to the White Pages, is registered to Melinda Grey. I pull to the side of the street and stare at the low-slung home with its evergreen bushes and trees. It's not much to look at. It's small and plain, and now that I'm here, I haven't the first clue what to do. Do I park the car and walk to the door and knock? What would I say to her? Would I ask her outright if she and Nick were having an affair? Or would I make up some excuse as to why I'm here: a door-to-door sales rep maybe, or a missionary from the Church of the Latter-day Saints, here to evangelize and proclaim my faith, so that I can catch a glimpse of the woman who's taken my husband from me? I wonder what she looks like, as my imagination enlarges the wee figure in the profile photo, the white bikini top and the sarong, until she takes on supermodel stature, a bathing beauty with long, lean legs and enormous breasts.

But I also wonder about the restraining order. Do I call her out on it? Do I point my finger at her and demand to know why she sought an Order of Protection against Nick? There's no way in the world Nick did something to harm her.

But instead I stay in the car.

I don't go anywhere. I sit and wait for her to come to me, certain that if I wait long enough, I'll see her black car pull into the narrow drive, or that she'll step out from behind the front door to walk a dog or gather the mail or sit on the front stoop with a glass of wine and read.

But waiting with a four-year-old and an infant in the back seat is near impossible. A reconnaissance mission with children tagging along. It isn't easy to do. It's not long before Maisie begins to whine that she can't find the dog, that she can't find the dog *anywhere*, and I tell her how we must be quiet so we don't scare the dog away. 'If we stay here, Maisie, then maybe the dog will come to us,' I suggest, 'but we have to be quiet.' I press a finger to my lips, and ever-intelligent Maisie suggests that maybe food would help, that maybe if we left some treats outside the car the dog would come to us. Except of course that we don't have dog treats, no food other than some Goldfish crackers I keep stuffed in a plastic bag at the bottom of my purse, and so I open the car window and toss a handful of crackers outside and watch as Maisie waits optimistically for the dog to come.

The dog doesn't come.

Nor does Melinda Grey appear, though as six o'clock comes, a light clicks on inside her home, illuminating a living room.

'Stay here, Maisie,' I say, which is a completely needless thing to say, seeing as Maisie is strapped beneath her seat belt and can't go anywhere.

'Why, Mommy?' she asks, and it's an impulse when I lie to Maisie and tell her I thought I saw a flash of fur around the corner of the house and hightail it into the backyard of the home.

'I'm going to go see,' I say as I set my hand on the door handle and pull, and Maisie squirms in her seat, saying she wants to go, too. I look to the skies, grateful for rain clouds, and say, 'Rain is coming, Maisie. It'll be here any second. I don't want you to get wet.' Then I slip quickly from the car and close the door before she can object. I leave the car running, the keys in the ignition so that the air conditioner cools Maisie and Felix in the back seat, and like the flash of fur I supposedly spied, I dart across the street and high-tail it toward the backyard, too.

There's a window on the side of the house, one that joins to the same room where the light turned on. She's there, I tell myself. Melinda Grey is there. The bad woman is there.

I press myself in between the laurel hedging and toward the double-hung window on the west side of the home. The evergreen clings to my clothing, scratches my skin. A cobweb binds to my hair, and I try hard not to imagine its owner spinning webs in my hair or on my back. My feet sink into dirt. My shoes get dirty.

At the window, I rise up on tiptoes to see inside, careful not to be seen. I rise only so far that my eyes can see, the rest of me hidden beneath the window ledge. It's a living room, complete with a TV and sofa, a piano and a reclining chair. Like the house itself, it's a dated room. The carpeting is thick and plush, streaked with stains. A tile entryway buttresses the front door. Framed photographs line a taupe wall, but they're far away, the images impossible to see from this distance. I can barely make out colors or shapes, though I try. Oh, how I try. I squint my eyes and press closely to the window and try to make out Melinda Grey in the photographs. I rise up higher on my toes so that now my entire face is at window height, but the closer I press, the more the aluminum screen distorts my view so that everything is marred by silver lines.

I rise higher. I press closer so that the screen abrades my face, likely leaving dust on my nose and cheeks. I cling to the outer edges of the window and pull myself in. I forget altogether to breathe.

And that's when I see the eyes.

Blue eyes that are ever-so-slightly cross-eyed, an aqua blue that press against the screen from the other side, staring at me so that I clutch at my chest and nearly scream, falling quickly to the earth like a soldier at war, diving for the trenches. My heart beats fast, the blood circling my body so quickly that I feel woozy and sick.

And then I hear a name, my name, 'Mommy,' hissed at

me through the hedges, and as I part the bushes and peer to the other side, I see her, Maisie, standing before me.

'Is the doggy there, Mommy? Did you find the doggy?' she asks, her ginger hair falling into her sleepy eyes. I'm so taken aback at seeing Maisie here, out of her seat and on the other side of the street, that I forget the pair of aqua-blue eyes watching the two of us from the living room window, reaching for a phone to call the police, or a weapon, maybe, to prevent us from telling the truth about Melinda Grey and her black car chasing Nick down Harvey Road.

'How did you—' I begin to ask—*How did you get out of your car seat?*—but I see her in my mind's eye, her nimble fingers toiling away at the chest clip, a small thumb pressing hard on the release button as I stared through the window and into the home of Ms. Grey. An escape artist. My very own Houdini. I reach for her instinctively and tug her inside the bushes with me, and as she asks again for the dog, I whisper that the dog found its owner, that the dog lives here, that we don't have to look for the dog anymore, and Maisie, ever-resourceful and quick, asks, 'Then why are we hiding?'

It's then that my indiscretions slap me in the face, the fact that I am hiding in the bushes, lying to my child, stalking a woman I don't even know. The fact that even my four-year-old can see the stupidity in this is disgracing. What am I doing? I ask myself, staring at the dirt that clings to the soles of my shoes, the laurel leaves attaching themselves to my clothes.

What am I doing?

I force a smile. I try to think fast, to mollify Maisie, knowing we need to make a break for it and run away before we find ourselves in a world of trouble. 'I don't want the dog to follow us,' I say. 'If the dog sees us, she might want to come live with us. And I don't think Harriet would like that,' I claim.

'Another dog?' I ask, and Maisie shakes her head and agrees. Harriet would not like another dog in our home, she says, as I grab her by the hand and we duck and run, certain the aqua eyes track us through the lawn and to the car. I open the back seat and all but push her inside, quickly strapping the harness across her chest. I don't bother taking the time to reprimand her for undoing her straps, for getting out of the seat. For leaving Felix alone. For crossing the street without holding an adult's hand.

I'm far more guilty than she.

As I put the car in Drive, I peer cautiously one more time back at the home, certain to see Melinda Grey there on the concrete stoop, phone in hand, eyes glaring at me. My hands are sweaty and shaking, my head spins. Soon sirens will arrive, a whole police squadron to figure out why I've been trespassing on the Grey property, stalking Melinda. The blood rushes through my veins at an alarming rate, and as I turn skeptically, I'm half certain I'll see a block full of neighbors on the Grey lawn with Melinda as the ringleader of the mob, pointing an angry finger at me. I put the car in Drive and my foot on the gas, ready to escape quickly if need be.

But instead this is all I see. A small shape in the window, illuminated by the living room light. A slender body standing upright on the windowsill, a single paw raised to the screen. Other than that, there is nothing. No angry mob, no police. No Melinda Grey. The house is quiet and still.

It isn't until later when my heart has slowed and my head has stopped overthinking that I realize the aqua eyes I saw were that of a cat.

NICK

BEFORE

Sunday afternoon we get in the car and make the trip to Clara's parents' home, just a short drive from ours. She brings the same cinnamon crumb cake as always, one she buys from Costco because she knows it's something her mother will eat. We're still a good ten minutes from the house—a blah ranch in a retirement community just a few miles from our own home—but already Clara's hands are shaking, her knees jiggling on the passenger's seat beside me. On her lap, the cinnamon crumb cake rattles in her agitation, and I ask if she wants to set it down before she drops it. She says no.

In the car, on the drive to her parents' house, Clara says to me, 'We should have Connor over sometime. For dinner. It's been a long time since I've seen him,' and at the mention of his name I feel my arms and legs tense up and my face turn red. It's a completely innocuous comment; it means nothing, but still, I have this sense that Clara can see right through me. I look to her and say *sure*, and *okay*, hoping she doesn't see the obvious omission, how awkward and uncomfortable it would be to have Connor at my dining room table when, in the back of my mind, I'm wondering how and when to lay him off. I hear his arrogant voice in the back of my mind, egging me on. *What are you going to do about this, Boss?*

'When?' she asks, and I shrug my shoulders and say, 'Maybe next week?'

'I'll make tacos,' she says, and I say okay, though of course I have no plans to invite Connor to dinner.

Clara turns to Maisie and tells her how she wants her to say hi to her grandmother when we arrive. To make an effort to be friendly. 'Give her a hug, or at the very least, say hello,' she says, but immediately Maisie begins to protest vehemently, screaming that she doesn't want to.

'No, Mommy, no!' she demands, kicking hard at the back of the passenger's seat where Clara sits. Louisa scares the daylights out of Maisie. I know this, and Clara knows this. I don't blame Maisie for her fears. They're with good reason, and yet I hate seeing Maisie so scared.

'It's okay, Maisie,' I coax, reaching a hand into the back seat to pat her knee. 'Grandma's not trying to scare you,' I tell her. 'Pinkie promise, she's not. Grandma's just a little bit sick,' I say. This isn't the first time we've had this conversation.

At Tom and Louisa's home, we park the car and form a procession to the front door, me in the front, Clara in the rear, Maisie in between. Clara walks slowly, clutching that crumb cake, telling Maisie to be careful of her step and not to trip.

Tom yanks a baseball cap from his head as we step into the living room, eyes gaping wide at Louisa as she sits in her chair. Tom greets us all, and then bends down to Maisie's level to whisper into her ear. We watch on as Maisie creeps to her grandmother's side and waves flittingly, though her grandmother only stares. There is no whining, no crying, no begging and pleading, *Nooo!* Maisie simply does as she's told, though Louisa says nothing. That doesn't surprise me in the least bit, but what does surprise me, what has always surprised me, is this leverage Tom has on Maisie, not so much power but a pact. She'll do whatever he asks because she worships him just that much. If Tom leaned down and whispered into her ear to jump off a cliff, she might just do that, too.

Louisa is dressed up nicely when we come, her hair well groomed. We all know Izzy—the in-home caregiver who works untiringly to care for Tom and Louisa—is to thank for this. She keeps Tom's and Louisa's lives on track in a way that Clara and I can't; she tolerates Louisa's dementia, the confusion and the memory loss, the anxiety and mood swings, the tremors, the bathroom accidents, the aimless wandering. What I know about Izzy is relatively small, but I know there's a kid sister in college, and nearly every last cent Izzy makes goes to pay for tuition and housing at the U of I, while Izzy lives in a squalid apartment in one of the more crappy neighborhoods around town. Their parents died within a year of each other nearly a decade ago—the kind of tragedy that makes you stop for a minute to appreciate your own lot in life—and Izzy has since supported the sister, whose name I don't know. Izzy is a nice girl, dependable, maybe even a little too selfless for her own good.

Clara places a tender kiss on her mother's cheek and says, 'Hi there, Mom.' Maisie, scared as always, now clings to my leg, though Tom makes silly faces to conciliate her, and she giggles. How she loves Tom.

Visits as always start with a nonchalant medical report, such as, 'Louisa's having a great day today,' or, 'Louisa didn't sleep very well last night,' so we have an idea of how the day will go.

Today Tom says, 'Louisa's lost her glasses. We can't find them anywhere,' and we all spin in half circles to see if we can spot them, the clear plastic frames loafing on top of the TV set or on an end table. We don't. 'She keeps misplacing her things,' says Tom. 'Today her glasses, yesterday her mother's wedding ring,' at which Clara's eyes fall to Louisa's right hand, where she always keeps her mother's wedding ring, a silver antique with a wide band and intricate flowers that should one day be Clara's. It's not there; it's gone.

Clara puts her hand on Tom's arm in a comforting way, and says, 'Don't worry, Daddy. We'll find them. They have to be around here somewhere.' This, too—losing things—is a side effect of the dementia.

We sit around the living room and force conversation. It's awkward, all stilted and contrived. 'How about those Cubs?' I ask of Tom, and someone mentions the weather. And then again there's silence. Awkward and uncomfortable silence. I turn to Izzy for no other reason than to obliterate the silence, and ask how her sister is surviving college.

She smiles warmly and says, 'She's doing well. Thanks for asking.'

Izzy sits closely to Louisa's side, her hand on the armrest of Louisa's chair, ready and waiting to meet the woman's every need. Louisa is in a daze, staring at some spot just beneath the curtain hem, her eyes bounding back and forth as if she's got her eye on something, which she probably has. Something pretend.

'What's she studying?' I ask, because the awkwardness of Tom and Louisa's home is suffocating, and without some conversation to get us through the day, I might just choke and die. Also, it's not that often that anyone talks to Izzy when we're here. We tend to treat her as a home accessory or an appliance, maybe. It's not intentional, and yet so many of our visits are gorged with updates on Louisa's medical prognosis or whatever weird habit she's recently picked up, that Izzy gets overlooked. She's a pretty girl, a bit avant-garde, and if Connor were here, I'm guessing he'd have something offensive to say about the size of her hips. But I like her. Around her neck she wears a charm that bears her name, *Izzy*, which is genius if you ask me. Every time Louisa doesn't know who she is, she just shows her the necklace.

Izzy smiles, clearly pleased that someone is talking to her. Her face softens, her eyes perk up. The silence must be painful for her as well, and while Clara, Maisie and I get to make a break for it soon, Izzy is stuck here all day, earning money to pay for someone else's keep. 'She just changed her major,' she says to me, 'from chemistry to food science and nutrition. She wants to be a dietitian.'

'What does a dietitian do?' I ask, more for conversation's sake than because I really care. She tells me how they work with people who want to lose weight, or those with food allergies, teenage girls with eating disorders, among other things. 'Sounds like a worthwhile career. Helping people,' I tell her, 'must run in the family,' and Izzy smiles sadly this time and says that they learned it from their mother, who was an active volunteer at a crisis hotline before she died, taking calls and talking people off the literal and proverbial edge. A suicide hotline, which is one of those things I'm only beginning to grasp—suicide—realizing how desperate a person would have to be to take their own life. There were recent times, as the dental practice drifted closer and closer to complete bankruptcy, that I paused to consider how better off Clara would be without me in her world. I'm not one of those grisly types consumed with death, but more of a realist. Without me weighing her down, Clara could find another husband in an instant, one who wouldn't test her on the whole richer-or-poorer part of the wedding vows.

'She had a way with people,' Izzy confides, and the room turns quiet as a moment of silence passes for Izzy's mother. 'One conversation with her could change a person's whole outlook on life,' she says, and I wonder what her mother looked like. I have half a mind to ask more—about her mother, her mother's death, how difficult it would have been to have custody of a child when she was still a teenager herself—but Clara flashes me a dirty look, and I quickly change my mind.

Clara, nearly the entire time we're here, doesn't say a word. She's silent, eyes moving back and forth between Tom and me or Izzy and me, landing occasionally on her mom, who also sits unspeaking. Not until later does Clara finally speak, when her father calls the two of us aside for a private conversation. I follow Clara to the kitchen, my hand on the small of her back.

'What is it, Daddy?' asks Clara, finally coming to life. She touches her father's thin arm and asks if everything's all right. Being an only child has its downsides. The fact that all issues concerning her parents—financial, medical and otherwise—fall in Clara's lap is a heavy burden to bear.

'It's your mother,' he says, which doesn't surprise me in the least bit because it seems nearly every conversation with Tom involves some detail of what Louisa's done since we've last seen her. There are the odd facets, the calling for a cat that no longer exists, the screaming in public, the purpose-less walking around the house. Sometimes they have to do with Louisa's medications or the details of an appointment with the neurologist or GP.

'What about her?' she asks Tom.

'She's done something,' he says, and I can see the tension in his eyes, the shame. 'A couple nights ago. Tuesday,' he explains. 'Somehow or other she got ahold of the car keys,' he says, and already I know where this is going. He goes on to tell Clara and me how Izzy wasn't home at the time—it was nearly bedtime, and so Tom had sent her home for the night—and he'd fallen asleep on the sofa. Late afternoons and evenings are always hardest on Louisa, when the con-fusion seems worst. It was nearing eight o'clock that night, and, thanks to Louisa's intermittent sleep schedule, Tom was tired. She was restless all night, every night, stricken with insomnia, which meant that Tom also didn't sleep. I could see it in his eyes. He was exhausted. 'She thought she needed to make dinner,' he says, 'but there was no milk. I don't know what I was thinking leaving the car keys in my coat pocket, within reach,' he goes on, his words running over with shame and guilt, and Clara croons, 'It's okay, Daddy. It's not your fault. It's no one's fault.'

As it turned out, Louisa managed to take the keys and

walk right past Tom and outside. She managed to find her old car in the garage, one she hadn't driven in years, get the keys in the ignition and put the car in Reverse. She managed to drive a block or two until she swerved, crashing into Ed Ramsey's garbage bins that were lined up in preparation of garbage day. 'Thank God no one was hurt,' he says. 'Ed found her sitting there in the car, completely out of her mind. All she kept saying was that she needed milk, and so Ed thought for sure she was thirsty and brought her a glass of milk from inside while he waited for me to arrive. I should be mad at her—I could be mad at her. And yet she just can't help herself,' he says.

'Oh, Daddy,' says Clara. It's all she can say.

'Thank God no one was hurt,' he says again, and we all agree.

We're standing two feet into the kitchen so that Louisa can't hear. And yet we won't leave Louisa and Maisie together unattended, not after what happened last time. I still can't get the image out of my mind, Louisa coming after Maisie with a pair of scissors. It happened so fast.

It's about that time that Maisie loses the ability to sit still and rises up from the sofa to do a series of poorly executed ballet leaps across the room. Tom, Clara and I step back into the living room to watch the performance, and Clara, clapping her hands at Maisie's moves, says that Maisie has begun taking dance classes at one of the nearby studios on Tuesday afternoons. She goes on to tell them about the studio on the lower floor of an old refurbished furniture factory; about Maisie's teacher, Miss Becca; about the fact that in Maisie's class there are ten girls and one boy, a detail that Maisie repeats every time she comes home from

class. She's taken with his footless black tights and his white
T-shirts, and the fact that he is a *boy*. Maisie has never seen
a boy ballerina before. A danseur, it's called, not a ballerina,
which we only know because Clara searched the word on
the internet. We're sure Maisie has her first crush.

'Pretty soon,' says Tom, eyes focused on me, 'you'll have
to step up and help out with these tasks, son.' Tom has called
me *son* approximately four times in our marriage, and each
came with a scolding, often directed at the amount of money
we've invested in my practice. But this time, it's my parenting of which he speaks, my perceived disinterest in taking
Maisie to ballet. 'With a new baby, everything will change.
It won't only be Clara and Maisie anymore. Clarabelle will
have her hands full,' he says, and at this he winks in Clara's
direction, as if this conversation was preordained.

But Clara leaps to my defense. 'Nick is so busy,' she tells
him, 'supporting our family,' and I die a little bit inside,
wondering what Clara and her father would think if they
knew the truth about my crumbling practice. 'And besides,'
she says, 'he helps. He helps whenever he can.'

'You ever take Maisie to ballet?' he asks as Izzy hovers
in the background, wishing like me that she could become
one with the wallpaper and disappear. 'Go with Clara to all
those prenatal appointments?' and his insinuation that I'm
an absentee father strikes a nerve with me because that's the
one thing in the world I never wanted to be: my own father,
who always put his career before our family.

'I would like to,' I assert, but it's a pathetic excuse. Clara
comes to my aid again. 'I love taking Maisie to ballet,
Daddy,' she says. 'Watching her with her friends. Dancing.
Talking to the other mothers. It's therapeutic,' she claims,

'having other mothers to talk to. Parenthood can be lonely,' she says, and this is the first time she's mentioned it before, the suggestion that at home alone with Maisie, she feels lonely. Alone. I reach out my hand to touch hers in a silent acknowledgment. I heard her; I will do better. I will make every attempt to be around more.

It's the first time Louisa opens her mouth to speak.

'My Clara never could dance,' she says, her tone bitter and vitriolic. Except her eyes aren't watching Clara, but rather Maisie as she leaps gracelessly around the room. 'The poor thing,' she says. 'So ungainly. She was born with two left feet. Clara,' she snaps then at Maisie as she leapfrogs across the room, more of a toad than a graceful ballerina, landing on the flats of her feet and losing balance, tumbling to the ground in a stop, drop and roll fashion. 'Clara! Stop doing that, why don't you. You look like a fool. Like a goddamn fool. Don't you know you can't dance worth a damn,' she growls, humiliating both Clara and Maisie at the same time.

Only one of them cries.

Before we leave, Tom calls Maisie to his side, and again leans down to her height, pressing his lips to her ear. More secrets. She giggles merrily, as he wipes a tear from her cheek, forgetting already about her sadness of only two moments ago. As he speaks, her eyes stray to mine, and she smiles. What's this got to do with me? I wonder. What in the world is he saying to her about me?

In the car on the way home I try to talk to Clara about it. Maisie is in the back seat, reading a book, and the baby in my wife's womb is punting her insides. Clara has her hands folded around her midsection and from time to time flinches in pain. I reach with a single hand to lay it on top of her own and ask, 'Do you want to talk about it?' meaning her mother's dance commentary, her father's car keys, the neighbor's upended garbage cans, the fact that no one ever ate the cinnamon crumb cake and that at home, being a stay-at-home mother, she's lonely.

'I don't want to talk about it,' she says, though her hand binds to mine.

I try Maisie instead. 'What did your grandfather say to you inside?' I ask.

Her leafy-green eyes peer up to mine. 'When?' she asks— either naively or defiantly, I don't know.

'When he leaned down and whispered in your ear. Just thirty seconds ago,' I tell her, and she's quiet for a minute, but then she smiles and says, 'Boppy said that secrets aren't for sharing,' and focuses her attention out the window, already at the age of four, learning to tune out the sound of my voice.

'Look there,' she says. 'An airplane's in the sky.'

Both Clara and I look, but we see nothing.

CLARA

I set the dinner table for three.

Maisie comes bounding to the table, declaring jubilantly, 'Daddy's home! Daddy's home!' and it's only then that I realize my mistake.

There are too many plates and forks and spoons for Maisie and me.

'Oh, no, honey,' I say, 'Daddy won't be home tonight,' as I grievously remove Nick's plate from the head of the dining room table with shaking hands. With just Maisie's and my plates set it looks sad, and so I lift those, too, and bring them to the breakfast nook, which is narrow and more compact, the vacant space not so obvious without the extra room. I make baked macaroni and cheese for dinner. Maisie's favorite. I haven't made dinner since Nick has been gone, but tonight I'm trying as a way to offset my stunt at Melinda Grey's this afternoon. I pluck a treat for Harriet from the kitchen cabinet, an apology for scolding her as I scrubbed dry urine from the living room floor.

'Daddy won't be home for dinner tonight,' I say, followed by, 'He has to work,' as always feeling thankful when Maisie doesn't press me, wondering when Daddy will be done with work.

'Daddy always works,' she says, and I sense an ire settling in, an annoyance with Daddy's relentless work schedule. But Maisie doesn't ask more of me, demanding to know just when exactly Daddy will be home.

While dinner cooks, I pull up the Chase website one more time, deciding to have another go at accessing my father's account. If he's in financial distress, I need to know. The first password I attempt is denied. The password guidelines are bewildering, requiring numbers and letters, special characters, no consecutive or repetitive digits. It's not a simple birth date or name. When my second attempt is rejected, I give up, again not wanting my father to be notified that three unsuccessful attempts have been made to gain access to the system. He'd be insulted if he knew I was checking up on him, doubting his mental capacity and financial standing. My father has done so much for me. He's nearly all I have left. I can't lose him now.

Neither Maisie nor I eat much, and Harriet is entrusted with the leftovers, too. I send Maisie to the next room to turn on the TV, feeling somehow more at ease with the daffy voice of SpongeBob and his friend Patrick joining us in the room. It's not often that I let Maisie watch *SpongeBob*, but tonight she deserves this special treat. I let Harriet outside, allowing her to roam within the pickets of a red cedar fence before the wind ushers in a summer storm, and then return inside to move the dishes from the table and set them in the sink. All day long, the weathermen have been telling us about this imminent storm to come. The day itself has been bipolar, sun and then clouds, sun and then clouds, as if it couldn't quite make up its mind. An electrical storm has been forewarned, with a bounty of thunder and lightning, the possibility of flash floods and hail. It isn't here quite yet, but it's on its way.

I find my phone and my laptop again and get down to work.

The first phone call I make is to the life insurance company. I don't know how it works. Do I call them or do they call me in the case of a policyholder's death? Does a claim need to be filed, or do they simply *know* that Nick is dead? Do they read the obituaries? I wonder, knowing how daft that sounds, and yet I wonder it nonetheless. When Maisie was born, Nick took out a whole-life policy for himself, leaving me as the primary beneficiary and my father as the secondary one. My father was also to be given our children should Nick and I both die. Nick took out the life insurance because he wanted to be sure I was okay if something ever happened to him, a policy that was secondary to the one the dental lender required of him. They were two different policies, so that there would be no red tape should I ever need to access the funds.

And so I find the paperwork, and the toll-free number embedded on the documents—desperately in need of that life insurance money to cover the accruing bills, replace the inoperable air conditioner and more—and place a call to the insurance company. A woman answers, and I tell her how my husband has died, and I need access to his life insurance funds. It sounds so cold as I say it, and I immediately know why spouses are the first to be questioned for murder when life insurance is involved. How easy it would be to kill one's other half and then cash in for the rewards. I'm sure I sound like a money-grubber to this woman on the phone. I wish to tell her about the air conditioner and how it's not working, the interest that's quickly accruing on my credit card for Nick's funeral expenses. I want to tell her about my family, my children, four-year-old Maisie and Felix, the newborn, so that she'll see I'm not as avaricious as I sound over the phone. I have children, I want to tell her, a family to support.

But I'm guessing she doesn't care.

'You need to file a death claim and submit a certified copy of the death certificate,' she tells me, her words mechanical and unemotional. She doesn't say she's sorry for my loss; she doesn't offer an ounce of sympathy, and so I ask, 'How long until I get the money?' and she tells me the insurance company has thirty days to review the claim, and then, if all checks out, they'll issue a check.

'What do you mean *if all checks out*?' I ask. Do individuals submit paperwork of someone who isn't dead in the hopes of a great cash reward?

'Assuming there isn't any reason to deny the claim,' she says to me.

'Such as?' I ask. Why in the world would they ever deny a beneficiary their due funds? Seems a ruthless and cruel thing to do to someone who's just lost a loved one.

'Suicide, for example,' she explains. 'Our policies have a suicide clause where we'll deny payment if the policy-holder commits suicide in the first two years of coverage,' she says, but I tell her Nick has had the policy for more than two years, which is neither here nor there because there's no way in the world Nick intentionally drove the car into a tree with our child strapped in the back seat.

Or did he? Is it possible? I pause to wonder, latching on to the wooden table for support. Nick had been off in those days before his death, jittery and jumpy and on edge. I asked him about it; I noticed. He blamed fatigue, as did I. As my belly swelled in those final weeks of my pregnancy with Felix, it became near impossible for either of us to sleep. The charley horses were relentless, waking us in the middle of the night, those stabbing leg pains that forced Nick to massage my calves at 1:00 and 2:00 and 3:00 a.m. Maisie, anxious of the new arrival we assumed, stopped sleeping well, too, consciously or unconsciously worried that the baby would soon steal the show, and our love for her would be divided in two. The fatigue was wearing heavily on us all, and with Felix's arrival we were grateful for the pregnancy to be through.

In those days leading up to Felix's birth, Nick was a bundle of nerves. Two times he snapped at me, which was unusual for Nick. He raised his voice, he yelled, and I yelled back, calling him a name that now I wish I could take back. *Stop being an asshole, Nick*, was what I said. *You're being an asshole.* I wish more than anything that Nick was here, standing before me, and I could take it back. I want to reach out to him instead of the way I'd petulantly pulled away, wrenching my arms from his as he tried to hold me in vain. I could hold a grudge like no other.

And now I wonder: Was it me? Was it my fault? Did I send him into the arms of Melinda Grey?

It was so unlike Nick to lose his temper, but again, I blamed the exhaustion, the pressure of caring for two children instead of one. But what if it was more? There were mental health issues in his family, depression and schizophrenia; we'd discussed these when the decision to start a family was made.

But suicide? I think. No. Not Nick. Never. He had so much to live for, his practice, our family. He never would have taken his own life, not that way anyway, with Maisie in the car. But those with suicidal tendencies don't always think straight, and they're gripped with an overwhelming sense of desperation and despair, a frenzied need to make it all go away, to make it stop. I have this sudden vision of Nick, his foot pressing hard on the accelerator with that tree in sight, taking aim on it as he tore down Harvey Road with only one thing in mind: ending his own life. Tears spring to my eyes as I start to cry. Not Nick, I beg. Not Nick. But maybe he was plagued by guilt. Maybe he'd ended his affair with Melinda Grey and she threatened to tell me, and he could see no other way to remedy the situation other than by taking his life.

And then, the woman on the phone says, interrupting my thoughts, 'Or homicide,' explaining, 'sometimes in the case of homicide there's a delay as the claims representative works with the police department to ensure the beneficiary isn't suspected of the policyholder's death.'

The tears stop, and I become immediately defensive. 'I didn't kill my husband,' I say.

'I didn't say you did,' she says. She asks me for the policy number and I tell her. She'll need to send me a claims package, which will detail everything they need from me to complete the request. And then, from the other end of the line comes silence, as this woman no doubt types the policy number in and waits for the computer to think. But it goes on for far too long—that dreaded spinning pinwheel on the computer screen—and then the woman asks for me to repeat the policy number again. She's typed it in wrong, and the computer has doubtlessly told her as much. And so I repeat the policy number again, slower this time so she will type it in correctly, but again my words are followed with silence.

Far too much silence that I find myself growing quickly concerned.

'Is something wrong?' I ask.

'That policy has been canceled, ma'am,' she tells me, and I'm overcome with sudden and overwhelming dolor that makes it hard to breathe.

'What do you mean?' I ask. 'That's impossible,' I say, but I think that it's not impossible, that the dental lender has beaten me to the punch and that they have taken everything, my share and theirs. They've repossessed their loan from the life insurance meant for me. How can that be? I'm ready to fight for what is mine, to hire a lawyer and sue, but then, from the other end of the telephone line, the woman explains to me that four weeks ago—at which she rattles off some random date back in May—Nick canceled the life insurance policy. Nick did this; not the dental lender. The funds have already been paid out.

'That can't be,' I stammer, as I imagine Nick filching all that money he'd been squirreling away to protect the children and me should he die. 'There must be some mistake,' I say, my heart beating quickly, realizing that now, just like that, Nick was dead, and Felix and Maisie and I had nothing. Absolutely nothing. A house—unpaid for and still owned by a bank that Nick sent checks to each month—a mediocre college savings fund and debt. More debt than I could ever imagine, and growing daily at a substantial rate.

I tell the poor woman on the other end of the line that she must be wrong, my voice shaking and quickly losing control. I say that certainly she's made a truly asinine mistake. I say it three times, my voice getting angrier and more demanding each time. I ask to speak to someone else, to anyone else, to someone who's in charge. And when that someone comes on the line, I tell them how stupid that first woman was, and how they need to help me find my husband's life insurance funds now.

Now, I say it again just in case he misheard the first time. *Now*.

'The policy, ma'am,' this man states point-blank, his voice annoyingly composed and not bothering to apologize for the first woman's incompetence, 'has been canceled.'

'You're wrong,' I say, but he assures me I'm not. 'I'll prove it,' I say to him self-righteously, as I pull up the account online to see for myself, so that I can snap a screenshot and send it to him somehow, an image that shows the available funds in Nick's life insurance policy.

But instead I discover that the policy has indeed been canceled and the funds surrendered to Nick. My heart stops beating; my head spins. My hands become sweaty and clammy on the keyboard. I try hard, but I cannot breathe. *Breathe, Clara*, I tell myself. *Breathe*.

What did Nick do with the money, and why?

Nick has left me, and he has left me with nothing.

I hang up on the life insurance man.

I can't focus on this now. There are questions, more questions. So many questions. I will find a job, I will ask my father for help, I will beg Nick's parents for a loan. But why did he cancel the policy and squander the money away for himself? I have to know. Did it have something to do with Melinda Grey? I pull up a search engine and type her name in one more time, but this time, in addition to the social media sites I found earlier today while sitting in the front seat of my car, I scroll further down the hits and discover something I failed to see this afternoon. It's Melinda Grey's name there on the local police blotter, an entry dated many months ago. *Melinda Grey*, it reads, *of the three hundred block of Parkshore Drive, was taken into custody by the Joliet Police Department on charges of possession of a controlled substance.* And there is a mug shot, one quite unlike the imagined profile photo of the woman in the bikini and sarong, but rather one with thinning hair and blemished skin and depressed eyes, a woman older than Nick by a decade or two, with whom I couldn't possibly imagine he'd be having an affair. She isn't attractive in the least bit, and yet Connor told me as much. He told me Nick was having an affair.

But if Nick wasn't having an affair with Ms. Grey, then who?

And if they weren't having an affair, then why was he mixed up with this woman? Did it have something to do with drugs? Was Nick using?

In an instant it makes sense. Nick being out of sorts in the weeks leading up to Felix's birth. His moodiness and despondency. The fact that he cashed in his life insurance funds for quick and easy money with which to purchase drugs.

Melinda Grey isn't Nick's lover, I decide. She's his dealer.

Nick has been using drugs. Was he using drugs at the time of the crash? Was he *high*? Certainly the police would have tested for drugs or alcohol at the hospital after the crash, but maybe not. I have half a mind to ask Detective Kaufman about this, but then again, I don't want to put any suspicion into his mind. He's already convinced Nick is to blame.

I take a moment to gather myself and then scurry off to find the collection of personal effects that came to me from the morgue days ago—the car keys and his wallet, and Nick's cell phone.

But there are other things mixed up with Nick's personal effects, other things I didn't notice at the time but now I do. There in the bottom of the plastic sack I find a lime-green cap from a bottle of soda and a molded green army man, no more than two inches tall. It isn't the bottle cap but rather the army man that catches my eye, the kind of toy that is sold by the bucketful, each container filled with a hundred army men or more. I pluck the army man between my fingers and look the soldier in the eye. 'Where'd you come from?' I ask, but the army man doesn't reply.

I call to Maisie and, holding the figure out for her to see, ask if it's hers. She crinkles her nose in disgust, and shakes her head an obdurate no, pulling away from the toy. 'That's for boys,' she says as if the toy might be tainted with cooties or worse. She goes back to watching TV.

Why would Nick have a toy army guy? Maybe it's a mistake, I reason. Maybe some other body at the morgue came equipped with a molded green army man in the pocket of his or her jeans, and an inept mortician only thought that it belonged to Nick.

Maybe somewhere out there, a little boy is missing both his father and his toy.

I put the toy back in the bag. But there's more. Two blue oval pills in a pill package, each one less than a centimeter long. Not your typical ibuprofen or allergy medication, but something different. Nick didn't take any prescription medication, none of which I was aware. But maybe he did. Maybe he did and he just didn't tell me. Or maybe these are the drugs he was getting from Melinda Grey, prescription medication not meant for Nick to consume. I hold the pills to my eye and read the wording inscribed on each tablet, *Halcion*, and a dosage. A quick Google search informs me that Halcion is generally used to treat insomnia—which makes sense, we'd all stopped sleeping in those weeks before Felix was born—and yet the side effects are immense: aggressive behavior, depression, thoughts of suicide. My eyes linger on those words on the computer screen. *Thoughts of suicide.* Are these pills to blame for my husband's death? I access Nick's MyChart account, an online database where physicians keep medical records for patient use. The log-in is Nick's email address, and when I click the button for a forgotten password, it emails it to Nick, which I access easily, knowing the password to Nick's email account. I search his medical records and the listing of prescription medication. The last thing his doctor prescribed was amoxicillin to treat a sinus infection the previous winter. There's no listing for Halcion anywhere.

The pills didn't come from Nick's doctor. They came from somewhere else.

I set the medication aside for the time being.

The battery to the cell phone is dead and the screen fractured beyond repair. I dig a charger out of the junk drawer. It takes time to charge the phone well enough to power back on, though from the sad state of the screen, I'm surprised it turns on at all. The lock screen appears, a photo of Nick and me together, the shattered lines of the LCD screen splintering our faces. But still, Nick is handsome as ever, a youthful face immune to age. In the photograph, his smile is sublime, and I remind myself that Nick would never hurt a fly. Never. Memories of the restraining order flood me then, as I stare into Nick's kind, gentle eyes, knowing his hands never touched me in a way that wasn't compassionate or warm, that his words were never cruel or mean.

It must be a mistake; it has to be a mistake.

Drugs, restraining orders, affairs. This is not Nick.

I type in Nick's password—proof, I tell myself as I do, that there were no secrets in our marriage, though my mind is starting to doubt this—and click on the call log to see who he was speaking to at the time of the crash. It's a 206 area code, one that doesn't strike a chord with me, and so I open a search engine and type in the number. I picture Nick on the phone, his large, capable hands pressing it to his ear, whispering to Maisie in the back seat reading her book to *be quiet, Daddy is on the phone. Hello?* I see him ask, and then a moment of confusion passes across his handsome face as the caller on the other end asks for Amy or Natalie or Renata. *You have the wrong number*, he says, as suddenly that brewing bend in the road is before him and he doesn't have time to react, but rather takes the turn at a whirlwind fifty miles per hour, spiraling off the side of the road. This person on the phone must have heard him, I think; he or she must have heard the very last words my husband ever said, something irreverent, I'm sure, something profane, though Nick wasn't one to be profane. But I'm thinking that's exactly what he would have done as he lost control of the car and went soaring off the side of the road, said something like *Jesus Christ* or *holy shit* because that's exactly what I would have done. That's what I have to find out; that's what suddenly I have to know. What are the last words Nick ever said, and did he or she—this person with the 206 phone number—hear over the phone the sound of the car striking the tree; Nick's head impacting the tempered glass, making it smash; the metal of the car collapsing; Maisie calling out to her father, her desperate falsetto voice begging him to make the bad man go away?

Seattle, I discover, is home to area code 206. So, too, is Bainbridge Island, the city where Nick was born and raised. I've heard the stories about the humble little home not far from Puget Sound, less than a block from the harbor, so if he angled his head just right, he'd catch a glimpse of sailboat masts floating above sea. Until they retired, Nick's mother served as a docent at one of the museums, and his father was an anesthesiologist who took the ferry over to Seattle nearly every day, spending his entire life on call. That's what Nick has told me. But Nick left Seattle for college when he was eighteen and never returned. It wasn't that he didn't like it, but rather that by the time he'd received his dental degree and made the decision to launch his own practice, his parents were gone, retired to a humble little home in Cape Coral, not so unlike the one they left behind save for, of course, the winters and the rain. Their visits with us are limited and always brief, and now, with Nick gone, I'd dare say that the time between visits will continue to expand until they one day dwindle to nothing. Not that I mind. His mother always had someone else in mind for Nick's wife; no one in particular, just someone other than me. She's made that much clear.

I have two theories, then, two hypotheses: either the caller was a telemarketer, or someone who misdialed the phone. Nick doesn't have family in Seattle anymore. Just a coincidence, I tell myself, thinking how Nick hasn't uttered a word about Seattle in half a dozen years or more. I know nothing about Seattle, other than some tired fact about how it rains nine months out of the year. I fetch the phone and dial the number, waiting warily for someone to answer the call.

'Hello?' a woman says, and for whatever reason I'm discomfited by this, not quite sure what to say. Her voice is soft, delicate, ladylike. I should have prepared something ahead of time. I should have jotted down an idea on a scrap of paper so that I'd know what to say, if nothing other than my opening line. But as it is I can't speak, so that the woman on the other end of the line must say it again, louder this time in case I'm hard of hearing or downright deaf. 'Hello there?'

I clear my voice and try again, and this time words do emerge, but they are halting and inarticulate. 'Hello. You don't know me,' I say too quickly, so it all comes out as one concurrent thought. 'I was given your phone number. By the police,' but the words are too quiet, too tremulous, so that she asks me to repeat what I've already said. I say it again, louder this time, trying hard to flatten my words and pronounce each syllable at a time. I hear the voice of Sponge-Bob penetrating the walls of our home, the remote likely in Maisie's hand and Maisie pushing buttons at random so that SpongeBob and his pals now scream. I hear her giggle, nearly muted by the sound of the TV. It's been a while since I've heard Maisie laugh. 'I was given your phone number by the police,' I say again.

'By the police?' she asks abruptly, her voice riddled with confusion. And I say, 'Yes,' though it isn't exactly true.

'Do I know you?' the woman asks, and I can hear her voice transmitted through radio frequencies to me, where I sit at the breakfast nook, a single leg thrumming against the kitchen floor. There's a sudden reservation to her tone, an immediate doubt. Why would the police possibly have given me her phone number? Who am I and why have I called? She's nervous and filled with dread. Her mind scans through the people in her life, wondering whether or not everyone is okay. Have I called bearing bad news? Am I the personification of death, the Grim Reaper, coming to steal loved ones from her life?

'No,' I say. 'You don't know me. My husband, you see,' I tell her, my words emerging briskly, 'he was in a car crash. An accident, they say. A car accident. But I don't think it was. A crash, yes, but not an accident.' And then I find that I simply can't stop myself, and that I'm muttering quickly, telling some woman on the other end of the phone about Nick and Maisie and Detective Kaufman and some black car trailing them down the bendy road, a bad man, or quite possibly a bad woman. I tell her about the horse properties and the white oak tree, somehow or other winding my words back to Detective Kaufman and how the detective told me Nick was on the phone at the time of the accident, at which I shake my head and say it again, less sure this time whether or not it was a crash or an accident.

And at this, she breathes in sharply and lets out a long,

slow exhale before saying to me, 'Clara,' and I feel the Earth's axis shift as I lose balance, clinging to the edges of the breakfast nook so that I don't fall.

She knows me.

Outside, thunder grumbles through the sky, the day's dank air rising upward to collide with colder temperatures that hover in the atmosphere above. As expected, the rain starts coming down in sheets. The grass needs it, as do the trees, but for a little girl already traumatized by something, of which even she doesn't know, it's the last thing in the world she needs. Maisie, from the next room, cries out at the sound of thunder, abandoning *SpongeBob* to run to me, her hands pressed to her ears to muffle the harsh noise. A dog barks, and it takes some time for me to realize that it is poor Harriet, who I've sent outside, now getting pelted by hail and rain.

'I'm sorry,' I say into the phone as Maisie cries, putting my arms around Maisie and holding her tight. 'There's thunder. She's scared.'

'They say it's going to be quite a storm,' this woman says into the phone, and as she remarks on the muggy weather and the lack of rainfall, I come to realize that this woman isn't in Seattle as I'd imagined her to be, watching the orcas swim out on the briny waters of Puget Sound, but rather somewhere close, watching the sun pass from sight as the rain comes down in sheets. Like me.

Again Harriet barks, and this time I rise from the nook as Maisie clings to my hand, begging, 'Please, Mommy. Don't go,' and together Maisie and I step toward the back door, letting a sopping wet Harriet inside. The wind shoves the door into me, and I nearly fall, pressing hard against the weight of it to get the door to close. I turn the dead bolt and follow the dog's wet footprints inside where she stands before us, shaking her body dry, drenching Maisie and me at the same time.

'Who are you?' I beg breathlessly into the phone, and Maisie imitates me saying, 'Who, Mommy, who?' so that I must press a finger to my lips and whisper a silent, *Shhh*. I move to the kitchen window and lower the blinds, consumed again with that sense of being watched, the same sensation that preoccupied me out on Harvey Road. Is someone out there on my back lawn, standing in the rain, staring through the window at me?

The lights of the kitchen burn ablaze, a contrast to the darkness that is quickly falling outside. A stranger could see right in. They could see everything about this moment: me on the phone, Maisie clinging to my leg. Is this what they want, for us to be sad, confused, afraid? Is someone there, lurking in the backyard? I hesitate with the blinds only partly closed and scan the backyard quickly, fearing the trees. A dozen of them or more, big, tall oak and maple trees with much breadth, enough that a man or a woman could stand behind them and not be seen. The perfect hiding place.

I'm about to send Maisie to other rooms of the house to help lower the blinds, but then the thunder comes again, immediate and out of the blue, and like pent-up steam about to escape from a hot teakettle, Maisie screams. I press a hand to Maisie's mouth, asking again, beside myself now with a need to know who this woman is on the other end of the phone. 'Who are you?'

My heart is beating quickly; like Maisie, I feel like I

could scream. I whisper to Maisie, *shhh*, and to *be quiet*, and slowly remove my hand. But before the woman on the other end of the phone can reply, an abrading sound like nails comes from the door, and I feel my blood run cold, my legs stiffen, as Maisie says softly, delicately, her little arms clenched tightly around my leg so that I can hardly walk, 'There's a man at the door, Mommy. A man.'

'A man?' I beg, knowing that from this distance Maisie could not see whether there was a man at the door. In the kitchen we're out of sight, impossible to see from the beveled glass that lines the front door, but still, Maisie assures me with an inappreciable nod that there is a man at the front door, a man with a hat on his head and gloves on his hands. 'A hat and gloves,' I implore, 'in summer?' knowing it can't possibly be true. Despite the storm, it's much too hot outside, much too humid for a hat and gloves.

'Stay here,' I say to Maisie as I pry her fingers from my leg and move toward the front door, though what I want to do is climb under the breakfast nook and hide. But I can't let Maisie see that I'm scared. I ask the woman on the phone to hold on. I move away from the kitchen, telling Maisie again to stay, slipping past a disabled home security system that has been unarmed now for three years, since Nick and I agreed it was silly to pay the rates to keep it activated for nothing, and stare through the glass at the world outside. I peer into the yard, trying to see whether or not someone is there, a man in a hat and gloves, as Maisie has said, one who pressed his face to the window while I was in the kitchen and peered in, making eyes at Maisie.

But so far as I can see, no one is there.

But then the noise comes again, a scraping noise right

there at the door's wooden panel, and I jump, crying out. From the kitchen, comes a whimper. I breathe in deeply and gather the courage to open the front door just a bit, my body weight behind the door so I can slam it closed if needed.

But I don't need to.

I breathe a sigh of relief, grateful to discover that the noise is only the wind rattling a grapevine wreath so that it thumps again and again on the front door pane. No one is here, but then I think again of the wide-open expanse of our backyard, a man in a hat and gloves, and wonder if that's true. Did Maisie see a man, or no? Was it a man on the TV, like Curious George's dear friend, the Man with the Yellow Hat? Is that what Maisie means? I don't know. Is someone here, skulking behind those trees, peering through binoculars at Maisie, Felix, Harriet and me? I find myself wishing and hoping that I could arm the home security system right now, feigning a false sense of security knowing our home is being monitored from someone afar.

'Who are you?' I beg again of the woman on the phone as a burst of thunder cracks. On the other end of the line is the distinct sound of something dropping and shattering glass. A gruff male voice interjects, startling me even from the distance. 'Shit,' he says.

'Let me call you back,' the woman begs, but I say no. I say it more uproariously than I'd meant to, barking out the word so that even Harriet's eyes rise up to mine, her tail getting lost somewhere in the confines of her rear legs in fear. 'No!' Harriet's ears tumble; she looks sad. She thinks that I'm yelling at her. Harriet is a rescue dog, the kind with a sketchy past, an easy startle reflex and a habit of always being underfoot lest we decide to ditch her. She was Nick's dog before she was mine. Nick was the one who found her, suckered in by some sad ad on the TV for homeless and abandoned pets. He said he was running errands, and when he came home, at his feet was a dog, a sorry creature with patchy fur still healing from a mite infection and a ridge of bones that should have been hidden beneath fat and muscle but wasn't. It appeared to me that this animal had been starved. I didn't want to keep her. I said no. Chances were good that she wasn't going to make it anyway. But it was winter and outside the weather was deplorable; snow had begun to fall fiercely from the sky. *Tomorrow she goes back*, I said, but by morning I'd changed my mind.

'Please,' I beg. 'Please tell me who you are.'

'Tomorrow,' the woman replies, whispering quickly into the phone. The line crackles and I fear I'll lose her, thanks to the storm. 'Meet me,' she says. 'There's a park on 248th Street. Near 111th. Commissioners Park. I'll be there.'

'I know the place,' I force out. I know it well. I've been there with Maisie many times before. To Maisie it is the hippo park. They're all just nicknames to her, the hippo park, the whale park, depending on which structures catch her fancy. This one has a giant blue hippopotamus that children can climb through, in his backside and out the mouth. 'What time?' I ask, saying it twice for good measure, 'What time?' fearing she may not reply because quite possibly she's already ended the call.

'Eleven o'clock,' she says and then, just like that, there's silence on the other end until another thunderbolt thrashes the evening sky, making Harriet cower and Maisie scream.

I spend the first part of the night not sleeping, but rather staring through the window as the rain falls, scouring the backyard for a man in a hat and gloves. Certainly something triggered this sighting from Maisie. Or was it simply an illusion, a figment of a little girl's imagination? I can't say for sure, but as the night goes on and no man comes to call, I start to have doubts about the veracity of the words that emerge from Maisie's mouth. I want to shake her as she sleeps, to shake her awake and demand to know if she really saw a man in a hat and gloves, or if that was only make-believe.

And then at two in the morning, after four restless hours in and out of bed, I decide that I can't leave fate to chance. I have to know.

I make sure the kids are asleep. I slip down the stairs, ease my feet into a pair of Nick's old work shoes and my arms into his coat, find a flashlight and step outside into the storm.

I have to know.

Harriet follows reluctantly, and for this reason I don't feel quite so scared or alone. I close the front door and lock it, sliding the keys into the pocket of my coat. I stand by the door and listen for the faint sounds of a baby's cry, but there are none. I pull the coat's hood over my head, and immediately the wind rips it right back off again, the air whizzing past my head. As I step from the covered front porch, the rain pelts me from all directions. It doesn't take more than a minute or two until I am soaking wet and cold.

I use the flashlight as a guide. Harriet follows closely behind, and I don't know who's more nervous, her or me.

With every step, I plunge deeply into the mud, the mire getting stuck to the soles of my shoes, making it hard to move. I sink as if it's quicksand, my eyes sweeping the property for any signs of a man with a hat and gloves. Is he here? *Was* he here?

I don't know what I'm looking for. I tremble inside and out, cold and wet and scared, praying I find nothing, that at the end of this expedition I can chalk the man in a hat and gloves up to Maisie's imagination and not let it obsess me. *No one is here*, I try hard to convince myself, wishing I had stayed in bed, that I was tucked beside Maisie and Felix, that I was safely inside and dry. But instead I'm outside as the thunder grumbles through the sky and an explosion of lightning lights up the night, and I cry out in fright, certain an evergreen arborvitae is *him*, the bad man, taking a minute to realize that it is only a tree, tall and thin like a man, motionless, watching me.

It's not him, I tell myself.

No one is there.

The rain taps on rooftops, a marching band's drum line. The water comes pouring out the gutter's downspout, creating a flood in the flower beds, into which I sink, getting soaked halfway up my calf.

My heart throbs quickly as a noise from behind sends me spinning in a complete three-sixty, flashlight and eyes scanning my sight line, finding nothing.

'Is someone there?' I call anxiously over the sound of the wind and the rain, and then immediately after, 'Who's there?' finding myself scared stiff. Beside me, Harriet whines. She's drenched like me, wondering why she followed me outside. The fur of her legs and the pads of her feet get coated in mud. She wonders what we're doing. Even I don't know for sure what we're doing, but I have to know if someone has been here watching Maisie, Felix and me. For the children's sake, I have to know.

For my safety and for the sake of my sanity, I have to know.

'Who's there?' I call again, but no one replies. From across town, I hear the sound of the train's wheels bustling down the tracks, oblivious to the wind and the rain that all but brings me to a standstill.

I walk the periphery of the house, staying close. I use the flashlight's dull glow to examine the yard, Maisie's play set, the trembling trees. I round the second corner of the home and, opening the fence, let myself into the backyard where the rain turns to penny-sized hail and I can hardly see, thanks to the precipitation in my eyes, my unrestrained hair, which thrashes around my head like a leather whip.

I'm starting to feel certain that I'll find nothing, and this will all be for naught. It comes with great relief, knowing with certainty that there is no one here, that there *was* no one here, that Maisie was wrong. Maisie was being silly, I reason. She was confused. She saw something on TV, and her imagination is to blame for this, for bringing the man with the hat and gloves to life. My heartbeat decelerates. I stop shaking. I smile.

There is no man with a hat and gloves. No one has been here watching us.

And that's when I catch sight of the mud.

I freeze in place, my legs going numb.

There sit three glops of mud, trampled across the back patio, three large footprints of mud imprinted on the brick pavers beneath the pergola where the slats of wood have deflected the rain. Not in the yard as they should be, but pressed up closely to our home, coming to a dead stop beside the kitchen's bay window, where only hours ago I stood with Maisie, listening to the rain. The footprints are squashy around the edges, losing shape. By morning they will be gone, trace evidence of our visitor washed away by the storm. I could call Detective Kaufman and have him come in the morning, first thing to see, but what are the odds that by the time he arrives the footprints would still be here? He wouldn't believe me. Detective Kaufman would stare at me with those somber eyes of his and tell me again that I am wrong. *There is no case*, he would say. *You know what I think happened? I think your husband was driving too fast and took the turn too quickly.* And then he would apologize for my loss.

I shine the flashlight on the footprints and force myself to step closer to examine them closely. It's a lug sole, like you might find on a hiking boot or a heavy-duty work shoe. The three steps are spread wide, farther than my own legs can span. I set my foot beside the print, measuring the length, easily reasoning that they belong to a man, for the size bears a striking resemblance to Nick's shoes on my own feet.

In my hand, the flashlight battery dies, and my world turns to black. I peer around, utterly blind. 'Is someone there?' I call out, but no one replies. But someone was here. That I know for sure as I call for Harriet, and the two of us hurry back to the front door and inside.

Someone was here. But who?

NICK

BEFOЯE

I make the difficult decision, the one I've been trying to avoid. I've put it off as long as I possibly can. I can't keep paying Connor for work that I can do, and so around noon, when the office is empty, I ask him if I can buy him lunch, and there in a crowded Mexican restaurant over a plate of nachos supreme, I tell him I have to let him go. His eyes grow wide at first, and then he laughs, thinking that this is some kind of joke, that I'm screwing with him maybe.

'Funny, Boss,' he says, chuckling as the waitress brings glasses of ice water and then leaves. We've known each other for years, and that's the kind of thing we used to do. Pull pranks on one another. But this time it isn't a prank. The look on my face is serious, and I tell him no, it's not a joke.

'I'm sorry, Connor. I have to let you go,' I say again, telling him how it will be easier for him if I lay him off rather than having him resign, as if I'm doing him some sort of favor, which in all actuality, I am. He just doesn't realize it yet. I tell him this is for the best. Being laid off is indicative of the shortcomings of our practice, not him; resigning is a reflection of his work ethic and stamina, his staying power. But already I see his hands clench up into fists on the table slab, his face become red. He flexes and then clenches the hands, again and again, gearing up for a fight. He reaches for a napkin and wads it into a ball, tossing it back and forth between his hands.

'You can't be serious, Nick,' he says to me, eyes steely but also stung. 'After everything I've done for you,' he bleats, and it's conjecture only when my mind goes immediately to Clara, to my life with Clara. That if it weren't for Connor, Clara and I would never be.

Though he doesn't say it, that's exactly what he means.

Clara was working at a kiosk in the mall when I met her, trying hard to sell some sort of high-end perfume to passersby. It helped put her through college, the commission she made off of sales, which wasn't a lot, but as she told me later that day in the food court over limp slices of pizza, *It was better than nothing.* Connor claims he saw her first, but if so, it was seconds before I spied her long, lean legs that stretched out from beneath a miniskirt whose hemline landed high above her knees. *You can have her,* is what Connor said before we'd even exchanged a word with Clara, as we stood, backs pressed to a railing that overlooked an open space and four floors of stores. He saw exactly what I was looking at, and though his comment didn't bother me at the time, in the coming years it did, this constant reprise that Clara was mine because Connor had let me have her, as if she was his to give. As if, if he hadn't been so charitable that day at the mall, she might otherwise be his. He always said it with a smile, too, so that the line between sarcasm and truth blurred. Did he mean it, or was he only joking? I could never tell.

I look him in the eye now and say, 'Don't make this harder than it has to be, Connor. The business is a mare's nest right now. You know that. We're losing patients left and right. It isn't personal. I can't afford to keep you on board.' And then I make all sorts of promises I'd make if I had to let anybody go, how I'd write a letter of recommendation, I'd put in calls to a few colleagues around town.

Connor's eyes avert from mine, and he raises a hand to get the waitress's attention, ordering a Dos Equis when she stops by. A Dos Equis. It's only noon, and Connor has patients to see later today. He's trying to provoke me, to get me to tell him what he can and can't do. 'Connor,' I say to him. 'I don't mean today. I'm not laying you off *right now*. There's time to find a new job. I didn't mean so soon.'

He shrugs. 'Who said I had any plans of leaving today?'

The problem with Connor has to do with a problem with authority. A disregard for it. Connor doesn't work well when he's under someone else's leadership. He wants to be the guy in charge. His last position he was fired from—or rather, asked to resign—because he went head-to-head with the boss too many times. Connor works well with me because I never treat him like an employee; we're far more of a partnership.

Connor hasn't held the same position for any two years in a row now, and this laundry list of jobs on his résumé will soon raise red flags.

'You have patients to see this afternoon, Connor,' I remind him. 'You know I can't let you see patients if you've been drinking,' I say as the waitress delivers the green bottle to his hand, and he raises it to his lips, taking a long, slow swig. He maintains eye contact all the time, staring at me, a challenge.

'Then fire me,' he says, with a look in his eye I really don't like. One that's charged and combatant, looking for a fight, and I know what that guy in the bar must have felt like months ago as Connor sidled up behind him and jabbed him in the nose.

'Oh, wait,' Connor says now, laughing, 'you already have.'

But the laughter dies quickly, and he stares at me in a way that doesn't back down.

'I didn't fire you,' I say. 'This is different. You know that, Connor. You know I wouldn't do this if I had some other choice. This isn't personal,' I tell him, pushing the plate of nachos supreme away. I'm no longer hungry.

'After everything I put into the practice,' he says, and without meaning to, I ask, 'What? What did you put into the practice?' which makes him more mad.

'The patients I brought on board,' he spits, though the number of patients Connor brought into the practice was negligible. Most of the patients we have are mine, who I gladly share with him. Except that now I need them back.

'You wouldn't have Clara if it wasn't for me,' he reprises, Connor's favorite refrain. 'You wouldn't have Maisie or that baby.'

'Leave my family out of this,' I say, voice composed.

'Your family is already part of this,' he says. 'Your family, my family. We're all family,' he tacks on, and then he laughs in that arrogant way that he does sometimes, asking,

'Do you ever wonder how Clara's life would have been different if she picked me instead of you? I bet she does. I bet she asks herself that all the time,' and it takes every ounce of self-control I have not to hit him.

He's hurting, I tell myself. It's an act of self-preservation, that's all. I've fired him. I'm the asshole here, not Connor.

'My back is to a wall,' I say. 'I don't have any other options,' which I don't. The way things are going, there's a chance I'm going to be taking money out of Maisie's piggy bank to cover Connor's salary this year. I try to explain this to him, to remind him of my family, my mortgage, how I have a baby on the way, but it's something he doesn't want to hear.

'I have obligations, too,' he says, and that's when things get even more personal, my unintentional implication that since Connor isn't married and doesn't have kids, he is of less value than me.

'I didn't mean it that way,' I say, but no matter what I say, he's going to assume I did. The space between us drifts to silence as he pounds back the rest of his beer and asks for another.

'I'm sorry, Connor,' I say. 'I really can't tell you how sorry I am that it's come to this.'

At that he leans across the table, so close that I can smell the jalapeños on his breath, and says, 'You know what, Boss? It's fine. It's not a big deal at all. You know why?' and I ask, drawing away from his advance, 'Why?'

'Because sooner or later, you'll regret this. You'll see,' and he rises from the table to leave, shoving the wooden booth into my gut as he goes.

* * *

It comes to me in the middle of the night, what I need to do.

It comes to me in a circuitous sort of way because I'm thinking of horses. Actually, what I'm thinking about is our unborn baby's bedroom, and how I swore to Clara that I'd have it painted, and now here we were, mere weeks until launch, and the room had yet to be painted. I'm thinking about how much something like that costs—professional painters—because Clara wrongfully assumed I was too busy at work to do it myself, and suggested I hire someone to do it for me. I'd put off so many other tasks on the house—installing the crown molding that Clara wants, maintenance checks for the aging appliances, the sump pump, the hot water heater, the air conditioner, all for lack of money and not time. Clara had already picked out a color for the baby's room—*Let It Rain*, it's called, a delicate gray to pair with the pricey new quilt—so all I needed to do was pick up the paint.

It won't take more than two hours to paint, I'd told her. *Don't hire someone. I'll do it.*

So there I am lying in bed, thinking about the paint and the paint store, and I start thinking about the horses we drive past on those country roads that lead to the paint store, back where Clara's parents used to live. I think of Maisie, in the back seat of the car, always so excited to see the horses. 'Look, Daddy, brown one!' or, 'Horsey with polka dots,' she'll scream, pointing, so that I find myself enamored by the smile on her face. Horsey with polka dots? Of course there's no such thing. But I look anyway because that's what Maisie wants me to do.

But thinking about the horses makes me think of horse racing, and though I don't know a thing about horse racing, I decide it's something I can learn.

I don't actually bother going to a racetrack, but rather find an offtrack betting site online, one that links directly to my bank account so I can easily withdraw money to bet with, and have the winnings just as easily transferred back in. In the morning I stop by the bank and set up a separate account, only in my name so that Clara doesn't see the comings and goings of cash in our personal accounts, not that she ever looks anyway but just in case. For whatever reason, I set up a POD at the banker's suggestion, a payable-on-death account to keep my funds out of probate court in the unlikely chance that I should die. I name a beneficiary. Clara.

I'm not trying to be scheming, because that's not the kind of man I am, but I don't want Clara to worry about our financial woes; between her mother and the baby, she's got enough on her mind right now and doesn't need to be stressed about a problem I can solve. I just need to earn enough money to pay my debts, to get my practice back on track, and then I'll be happy.

I do research on horse racing; I learn the vocabulary, backstretch and pari-mutuel, bankroll and trifecta. I create an online account and link it to my new bank account. I set myself up in my office during a forty-minute gap when I don't have an appointment, and discreetly turn the lock on the door. I get to work.

In order to bet, I need money I can bet with. Clara's savings account has already been drained. My money market, too, has been liquidated and poured into this dental practice. What we have in our combined checking account is barely enough to pay the mortgage and electricity and the rising cost of groceries. I leave it alone, knowing we need to eat. The last thing in the world I want is for Clara to go to the grocery store and have the clerk tell her that the credit or debit card has been denied. She'll fill with shame and embarrassment long before she fills with anger or dread. I see her there, my beautiful wife with Maisie by her side—Maisie already fussing because of how much she hates to grocery shop—and Clara's fair cheeks flaming red because everyone is staring at her for the denied payment. I hear her words, the shaky rhythm of her voice as she says to the clerk, *There must be some mistake*, and asks the clerk to run it again, only to go through the same shame a second time around. I won't do that to Clara.

The way I see it I have two options: Maisie's 529-college savings fund, and my life insurance plan. My first thought is to go for the life insurance, to surrender the policy for its cash value. It's not like I intend to die anytime soon. It's a whole-life insurance policy, like life insurance and a savings account rolled into one, or at least that's the way I explained it to Clara years ago when I sought coverage. Instead of a policy for a fixed time—say until our children turn eighteen and become financially independent—I opted for the whole-life policy, a decision that is paramount now. The cash is far more valuable in my hands than sitting squandered away, tied up in a life insurance policy I may never need.

I fill out the necessary paperwork to surrender the policy, though it will take time for the insurance company to pay out. In the meantime, I start slowly with Maisie's college education fund; the loss is less than withdrawing from my own retirement fund, and so it seems like a smart choice, the lesser of two evils.

By the end of the day I've made about seventy-five dollars, which somehow feels like a million bucks. It's a good day, I tell myself, until an hour or so later when Clara calls, scared out of her mind, saying her mother got ahold of the car keys again and took the car out for a ride.

'I thought your father did away with the car keys,' I say, and she rejoins with, 'That's what I thought, too.'

Turns out Tom forgot to hide the keys.

'They found her,' she assures me, but still she's scared stiff. 'One of these times she's going to get hurt. Really hurt.'

'Or hurt someone else,' I nearly say, though I don't want to be the Negative Nelly and remind Clara of this. She and her father both know how much is at stake every time Louisa somehow or other manages to find herself in the driver's seat of a car.

'Where'd she go this time?' I ask, and Clara reluctantly tells me that her mother was navigating the country roads out to the rental property that Tom still owns, telling a passerby when he found her pulled off to the side of the road, completely lost and disoriented, trying to find directions on the back of an old CD case as if it was a street map, that she was attempting to get home.

Where's home, ma'am? the passerby had asked, spotting the Medic Alert bracelet that Louisa wears and calling the toll-free number for help, but Louisa had only shaken her head and said she didn't know. She didn't have the slightest clue where home was, though she described it, the big, old farmhouse just a mile or so from my favorite shortcut through town, a forgotten, winding road that managed to circumvent nearly all of the town's traffic.

But Tom and Louisa didn't live there anymore; they hadn't lived there in many years.

But as with everything else in life, that was something Louisa couldn't remember.

CLAЯA

I wake to a knocking sound rapping on a wooden pane and, moving sleepily down the wooden steps, greet the flower delivery driver at the front door. It's the third time this week that he's come, his arrival always just shy of 8:00 a.m. Too early. He must sit outside in his car, waiting for what he deems an appropriate time to knock. Nobody wants flowers when a loved one has died, but still they come, these flowers, awakening me this time from sleep. I thank the deliveryman, quite certain he's grown tired of seeing me in my pajamas again and again, hair a mess, sleep in my eyes, mouth repugnant with morning breath. I close the door, staring out the window at the evidence of last night's storm.

It's everywhere.

Tree limbs have been wrenched from the arms of trees and tossed capriciously across the earth; a half block down the street, a power line is down, lying recumbent on the road. I reach for the chandelier's light switch and turn it on; the electricity is out. It will take hours for the electric company to remedy the situation, hours while Felix and Maisie and I have no access to light, to coffee, to TV. Important things. Across our lawn, the remains of an overturned garbage bin are strewn: a box, a fast-food bag, an empty container of cat litter; shingles are missing from the roof of a neighbor's home. There are puddles on the street, which little perching birds bathe in, splishing and splashing their wings in the turbid rainwater and then, like Harriet the dog, shaking them out to dry. The sun is out, trying unavailingly to dry the earth. It will take time. A red-winged blackbird sits beside the puddle, watching me through glass.

I take a peek out the back door, beneath the pergola, to see if the man's muddy footprints are still there. They're not there. They've been rinsed away by the storm, as I convince myself that they *were* there, that it wasn't only a dream. Nick's muddy shoes beside the front door are proof of this, as is his rain jacket looped over a door handle. I didn't make it up.

There is evidence of the storm inside the house, as well. Harriet, terrified of thunder, has defecated on the rug. She's taken to chewing the arm of the sofa, too, and Nick's forgotten gym shoe so that pieces of fabric upholstery and synthetic fibers litter the room like the garbage on the lawn. Harriet's muddy paw prints are trekked across the foyer floor.

In Nick and my bed upstairs, Maisie, up half the night cringing at the wind and the rain, still sleeps, the door to the bedroom now pulled to. In the middle of the night I heard her crying and the muted rustles of *no, no, no, no, no* as she kicked angrily and unconsciously at the sheet. With the air conditioner out of commission, and the windows closed to stave off the rain, the house has become unbearably hot. Throughout the sleepless night I watched the thermostat move up to eighty-four degrees, listening as fifty mile per hour wind gusts rattled the home. As we slept, the sweat collected between my legs, making them viscous like hands coated with a thick emollient, the thin sheet clinging to my legs until Maisie in her restlessness yanked it from my skin.

And then I lay in bed, still sleepless, trying to remember what it felt like when Nick lay beside me, the sound of his ever-so-soft snore and the impression of his body, pressed against me, arms, torso and legs parallel to mine.

But I found that I could no longer remember.

Our town doesn't have the best track record for good weather. Twenty-some years ago, a tornado plundered our community, putting us on the map. Nobody had heard of our little town before the twister hit, an F5 that lifted houses right off their foundations and catapulted cars across town, killing dozens of people and injuring hundreds in its path. Now our town is synonymous with tornado just as New Orleans is with hurricane. I walk throughout the house picking up the mess left behind in Harriet's terrified trail, feeling grateful it was just a thunderstorm and nothing more. It comes as no surprise to me that when she awakens, Maisie doesn't want to leave the safe confines of our home. But with the electrical outage comes an advantage; without electricity there can be no microwave pancakes and no TV: no *SpongeBob*, no *Max & Ruby*. Instead, there is the promise of a glazed cruller from Krispy Kreme and a trip to the park. And so, reluctantly she comes, changing out of her pajamas and into a pair of soft cotton shorts and a sleeveless T, and the four of us settle into the car, Felix, Maisie, Harriet and me. To keep her content, I hand Maisie my phone.

It's not yet ten in the morning, and so after we gather our donuts and coffee, I make the decision to drive out to Harvey Road. It isn't a thought that comes to me in that moment, but rather something I'd been thinking about all night, tossing and turning as the summer storm raged outside. And now, it returns to me as I drive through town and toward the site of Nick's crash, the familiar scene creeping slowly into view. The horse properties manifest themselves on the sides of the street, along the straightaway before that dreadful bend. They are large homes, renovated, or modern farmhouses with horse stalls, barns, fenced pastures and an assortment of other outbuildings I can't identify, placed in an unincorporated part of town. It's different here than it is elsewhere around town. There is a distinct lack of commercial structures: no stores, no gas stations, no water towers. Everywhere I look, I see only houses and trees, houses and trees, and of course, horses. There is a church, a singular Presbyterian church abutting a small cemetery, which appears oddly welcoming with its wrought-iron gates and its bushes and shrubbery. The streets are narrow and empty, and as I open my window and let it in, the air smells fresh and clean but tinged with the distinct metallic remains of last night's rainfall.

Today I don't drive so far as the bend, though I see it up ahead and I wonder if Maisie, too, will see. Will she recognize this scene? My roadside memorial slopes in one direction, compliments of the wind and the rain. The flowers that I laid before the white wooden cross are scattered now across the roadside, but they've also multiplied in number, making it clear that someone else has also been here, leaving flowers at the place where my husband died. Many people, it seems, for the gifts and flowers are profuse. A soggy teddy bear, a cross manufactured from twigs. More flowers. A Chicago Bears cap sits positioned on the top of the white wooden cross, the blue-and-orange wishbone C staring back at me. Connor has been here, Connor who shares Chicago Bears season tickets with Nick, two seats on the thirty-yard line. They spend every other Sunday afternoon at Soldier Field together, August through December, eating hot dogs and drinking beer.

Instead of driving onward toward that bend, I pull into the neighborhood and, before one of the large homes, put the car in Park. Maisie looks up from over the top of my phone. 'Where are we, Mommy?' she says, her eyes appraising the homes, seeing a horse off in the distance that catches her eye. A Clydesdale, chestnut in color with white feathering on the legs. I know a thing or two about horses, thanks to a childhood obsession with them. I collected figurines and buried myself in books.

'We're just going for a walk,' I say now as I remove the double stroller from the trunk and get Felix first and then Maisie situated inside, and put Harriet on a leash.

If Detective Kaufman isn't going to canvass the neighborhood, I've decided I might as well try. Tucked here so closely to the crime scene, I find it impossible to believe that nobody heard the crash or saw the debris lying across the street. Certainly somebody heard something; somebody saw something. I head out like a political candidate barnstorming a community to gather votes, with my dog and children serving as my campaign tactics.

Maisie doesn't put up too much of a fuss this time—she likes going for walks far more than she does grocery shopping—and as long as she can hang on to my phone, gathering her bits of candy and swiping them from the screen, all is right and well in the world. Her eyes rise from the LCD screen to scan the street quickly, and I make believe I know what's going on in that mind of hers as she regards the smattering of parked cars, looking for a black car as I've already done.

But there is no car here, not so far as I can see.

The morning is quiet and still. In the fenced pastures, horses roam, gnawing on the sodden grass. Harriet cowers; she isn't brave. I pull on her leash and call for her to come.

The first door I come to belongs to a picturesque farmhouse with a detached garage, lemon chiffon in color with trim the color of rust. The trees in the yard are enormous, and the driveway is long and wide. My troop meanders to the front door, and I turn to Maisie in the stroller, lugging her small frame from beneath the lap belt, and telling her to take my phone under a tree to play. I point to it off in the distance, thirty feet away or more, a tree with scaly brown bark and tiny clusters of flowers, most of which have been knocked to the earth in the storm.

'There's more shade. You'll be able to see the screen,' I say, before my eyes trail Maisie to the dogwood tree, watching as she sits down, soaking the seat of her shorts. And then I knock on the door gently, feeling my stomach turn as before me the door opens, and a man appears, middle-aged with a rotund face and thinning hair. It's gray, as are his eyes. He appraises me, confused.

'Hello?' he asks, and I answer his next question before he has a chance to ask it. 'You don't know me,' I say, as a woman, too, appears at the door, her eyes also furrowed in question. 'My name is Clara,' I say to them both. 'My husband was killed down the street from here. Just a few days ago. A car crash,' I explain, though from the looks in their eyes, I need not say more. They know who I am.

As I peer off into the distance, I see that bend in the road glaring back and, beside it, the fated oak tree. From where I stand, I've got the perfect vantage point. A person could be sitting here on this porch, conceivably sipping from a glass of iced tea in the hanging swing and watching the wreck play out before them like a sporting event, a car or maybe two, hurling down the street at breakneck speed, the unforgiving impact, the air filled with debris; they might have heard the sound of the crash.

'We heard,' the woman says, stepping outside onto the porch beside me. I feel my heart hasten—*she heard!*—only to be let down again with these words, 'We heard what happened, dear. Such sad news. We weren't home when it happened, but saw it on the news. We couldn't believe it. Right down the street. Such a shame,' she says.

'What was it you were looking for?' the woman asks me, and I confess, 'I was hoping you saw something. That you might have seen what happened,' I say.

She sets her hand on my elbow. It's warm and kind but also strange, an unfamiliar touch. 'The newspaper said reckless driving was to blame,' she says sparingly, and I nod an inappreciable nod and whisper that it's quite possible the newspaper was wrong. In her eyes there is only pity and doubt. She doesn't believe me. She believes that I am wrong. 'Sometimes seeing is believing,' she says abstractly, and I pull away as she tells me she's so sorry for my loss, but somewhere deep inside I wonder if she really is.

I collect Maisie from beneath the tree and again we leave, Harriet this time taking the lead.

No one is home at the second home, and though there seems to be activity in the house after that, no one comes to the door. The garage door is open, a child's bike lying sideways on the lawn. From an upstairs window comes the sound of a guitar. I ring the doorbell, and then knock twice, listening for footsteps to come scurrying to answer my call. And yet they don't come.

I move on and on. Each yard in the neighborhood must be one or two acres wide. It takes time to walk from one house to the next, on the street because there are no sidewalks here. But that doesn't matter, because there are also so few cars that travel along this path. The owner of the next home, a thirtysomething woman already outside, stands feeding her Clydesdale a handful of hay, the same Clydesdale we eyed from a distance. She greets me with a smile, and I tell her who I am. 'Clara,' I say, 'Clara Solberg.' And then I whisper to her about my husband who is dead.

'Can I pet the horsey?' begs Maisie as she pushes herself out of the stroller and takes large strides toward the chestnut-colored horse, hand already extended.

'Maisie,' I say, stopping her advance, but the woman tells me it's fine. Maisie knows better than to pet a strange animal without asking first. But she did ask, I remind myself.

She just didn't wait for a reply. Typical Maisie, always antsy, always in a hurry, can't be bothered to slow down and wait. It's so hard for children to be asked to wait.

'Lady is gentle. She loves kids,' says the woman, finding a carrot for Maisie to feed the Clydesdale, while Harriet forces herself between my legs to hide. I find myself trying to make sense of Harriet's fears on occasion, her angst over loud voices, thunderstorms, creatures bigger than she, trying to put together the puzzle pieces of her life before Nick found her hiding in the back of a kennel, incapacitated, her legs unable to move. She was terrified, trapped inside one of those high-kill shelters with startlingly high euthanasia rates, where cats and dogs sat awaiting their time. Death row. It was only a matter of time before someone injected her with a heavy dose of sodium pentobarbital, or would have had Nick not found her in time. I rub my hand gingerly over her head; she was Nick's dog, not mine.

But now she's mine.

And now, with Maisie distracted, her hand moving gracelessly up and down this horse's hair, making it stand oddly on end, I ask this woman whether or not she saw anything, whether or not she heard anything, whether or not she was home. What I want to ask specifically was whether or not she saw a black car, lying in wait perhaps to pounce on Nick from behind the trees or tucked away on a narrow drive, concealed by leaves. But this I don't say.

'I was home,' the woman tells me, and, 'I heard the crash. It was just—' and she pauses, closing her eyes, shaking her head, and says to me, 'awful. That noise. But,' she says, 'I didn't see a thing,' and she leads us all to her backyard, where I can clearly see the red wood of a neighbor's barn smack-dab in the way, obliterating the line of sight. 'I looked, don't get me wrong,' she says. 'I wanted to know what had happened. I thought about getting in the car and driving around the block. I was curious,' she admits sheepishly, adding on, 'and of course concerned—but then the sirens came, ambulances, fire trucks, you name it, and I knew I would only be in the way. Help was on the way.'

'Thank you so much for your time,' I say as I gather Maisie and we prepare to leave. I say my goodbyes; she says she's sorry for my loss. Everyone is sorry. So very sorry. But they're also relieved it's happened to me and not them.

It goes on like this for three more homes—they were home, but nobody saw a thing—and at the fourth house, the house is quiet. The lights are off, the garage is down, a delivery sits there on the porch, sopping wet from last night's squall. *Janice Hale*, the address label reads, a cardboard box bearing a Zappos logo. Janice Hale has ordered new shoes.

I move on, knocking on the door of the next home, though no one comes, and by now I'm so far away from Harvey Road, it feels futile anyway. I turn to leave, but before I've taken three steps away I hear a voice, a woman yodeling at me, 'Yoo-hoo.'

I turn to see a window forced open, a face pressed to the fiberglass screen.

'Can I help you?' she asks as Maisie moves closer to my legs in fear. In the stroller, Felix sleeps, peaceful in the warm summer sun. Soon he will need to eat, though I've prepared for this, toting a diaper bag with bottles and formula and distilled water as the parenting websites told me to do.

'You're looking for Tammy,' she assumes. 'Tammy's

working,' this woman says, hacking into the palm of a hand. I don't bother to ask who Tammy is. In the other hand, she wields a cigarette, the end burning an amber red. The smoke drifts out the window to Maisie and me, who also coughs, an exaggerated cough, but still a cough.

'Go play,' I tell Maisie, ruffling the hairs on her head and gently shooing her away.

'When will she be home?' I ask.

'Tomorrow sometime, I assume,' this lady tells me. 'She's on reserve, you know?' Though, of course, I don't know. 'Had to fly out to Arkansas a few days ago, or something like that. Alabama. I can't say for sure. I never know where she is, if she's up or down anymore, on the ground or in the sky.' And when I give her a confused look, she tells me how much this Tammy hates it, the unpredictable nature of the job and the repulsiveness of those ugly monkey suits, the double-breasted dresses and the uniform scarves, she says. 'For as much as she hates it, you think she'd try to find something new.' And then, as if all one concurrent thought, Tammy's job and me, 'Something you need?' the woman asks of me, her voice gruff, manly.

'No,' I say, shaking my head, quite certain I won't find what I'm looking for here. I can come back, I decide; I'll come back in a day or two and ask to speak to Tammy. But then I change my mind, not wanting to let an opportunity pass by. As at the other homes, I step closer to the open window and tell this woman who I am and what I want, and leave it at that, waiting for her to fill in the gaps.

'I was at the store,' she tells me, 'picking up a carton of smokes.'

And I think that that's it, her answer is a clear no—she

saw and heard nothing, she wasn't even home—until she says, 'I was driving home just after it happened. I called the cops, you know? Saw that car smashed to smithereens.'

At this my heart stops. I envision smithereens spread across the concrete street. Nick as smithereens, small pieces of him everywhere. I gasp. I press a hand to my face so that I won't cry.

'Was there anything else? Anything else you saw?' I beg, my voice erratic, choking on words. I peer around for Maisie, to be sure that she can't hear about her father smashed to smithereens. 'Anyone else around?' I ask, and she thinks for a while before telling me that she passed a car on the way home, another car, a half or a quarter mile past the scene.

'Normally, it wouldn't have caught my eye,' she says, and yet it was the way the car swerved into her lane unmindfully, the way she had to veer into the gravel on the side of the road to keep from being hit. 'Son of a bitch was driving too fast,' she says. 'Probably on their phone, you know? Texting.'

She blew her horn and flipped the driver the bird, she says, and continued on. It wasn't three minutes later before she came to the bend where Nick was killed.

'Did you see the driver?' I ask, but to this she says no, that the sun was so dang bright that day, she hardly saw a thing.

'What about the car?' I ask. 'Can you tell me anything about the car?'

'It was dark,' she says, trying hard to remember. 'Something dark.'

I nod my head. 'Was it black?' I ask, yearning for an emphatic *yes*. I need her to tell me this car was black. I need proof, someone other than Maisie telling me what they saw, that this black car is real and not only a figment of a little girl's active imagination.

And that's just what she does.

She nods her heads and says yes, it was black. She thinks. Maybe.

'I think it might've been,' she says, taking a long drag on that cigarette and blowing it through the screen at me. 'I think it might've been black,' she says, and I decide *good enough*. That's good enough for me. For now it will do.

'Sorry I couldn't be of more help,' the woman says, but I assure her she's been more help than she knows.

'Thanks so much for your time,' I say.

'There's something else,' she says as I gather my troop and we start to leave. 'Something else I just remembered,' she says, tapping her temple with the point of an index finger. 'The sun was so damn bright I couldn't see much of the car. Had to look down, you know, at the street, so that the sun wouldn't blind me. But there's something I remember about that car. It was one of them cars with the gold cross on the front.'

'A gold cross?' I ask, and she says, 'Yeah. A gold cross. Like the logo or whatever you call it. The emblem. A gold cross,' and I beckon for my smartphone from Maisie's hand and type in those exact words, *car with a gold cross logo*, and instantly it appears on my screen, dozens of images bearing just that: Chevrolet's famous emblem, a golden bow tie. 'Like this?' I ask, thrusting my phone to the window so that she can see.

She smiles, revealing a row of bent teeth, yellowing quickly from the nicotine and tar. 'That's the one,' she says.

A black Chevrolet. That's what I'm looking for.

'Thank you again for your time, ma'am,' I tell the woman, tacking on, 'I didn't get your name,' and at this she says that it's Betty. Betty Maurer.

'Thank you for your time, Betty,' I say, and this time we leave.

NICK

BEFORE

June arrives, bringing with it all the heat and humidity of a typical summer in Chicagoland. Overnight, the mercury on the thermometer soars to eighty-some degrees in a climate known for having two seasons: hot and cold. I make the difficult decision to switch on the air conditioners in our home and the practice, though my mind calculates the sum of the rising cost of the electricity bills already, anxious long before they come. With the arrival of June, a lease payment was due, an imposing number that boggles my mind. I didn't have it to spare, though I was able to maneuver an extension of fifteen days. It buys me time. I'm hoping that by the fifteenth of June I have enough saved up.

But I'm not just thinking about this lease payment; I'm considering the bigger picture. I'm thinking of ways to save on rent and other expenses. Without Connor my patient load is again nearing full, though I'm waiting on pins and needles for some sort of discriminatory discharge lawsuit to arrive from a disgruntled Dr. C, as I'm sure it will. I've tried calling him to talk it out. Many times. He won't return my calls.

The good news is that I've been doing well on the off-track betting, though it's a slow accumulation, thanks to daily limits imposed on the online gambling site, a gradual buildup of money that I hope amounts to something before a complaint arrives from Melinda Grey. I've advanced from merely horse racing to placing bets on the NBA playoff games. I'm not much of a basketball whiz, but have inundated myself with rankings and statistical analysis, point spreads, to place my money on the teams with the best odds. The Warriors are a heavy favorite, and so I put my money on the Warriors and watch as they take the first game of the series in overtime. Clara sits beside me on the sofa as I press down hard on her sciatic nerve with the pad of a thumb, Maisie on the floor before us, scribbling in a coloring book. 'I never knew you were such a basketball fan,' she says, and I think to myself how suddenly there are many things she doesn't know.

* * *

'You have a new patient today,' says Stacy the next day as I step from the humid morning air into the serenity of the air-conditioned office. There is music on, some sort of ambient music that overrides the show on the wall-mount TV screen; the room smells of coffee, reminding me of the things I cannot have. Caffeine. A Weber grill.

Stacy smiles. A new patient is, of course, like gold dust around here. I shed my car keys and sunglasses, and she wishes me good luck. I return the smile. There was a time I didn't need luck, but now I do.

Coming into the open-concept office space, my hygienist does what she always does and introduces me to the patient, telling me something I don't already know about the patient's personal life, something other than what is happening with his or her teeth. It's rapport-building, a means of showing our patients we care. Not just about their teeth, but about *them*. Them as people. As human beings. And so my hygienist Jan says, 'Good morning, Dr. Solberg. We have Katherine here. Katherine Cobb, who's just relocated to the Midwest from the Pacific Northwest,' and as I drop down into my stool and extend my hand in greeting, I have the surprise of my life when, sitting there on the dental chair is not Katherine Cobb, but Kat Ables—the woman who, twelve years ago, I was absolutely certain I would spend the rest of my life with.

'Kat,' I say. My mouth gapes open; I don't have the wherewithal to make it stop. She looks unchanged to me, still eighteen years old and gorgeous. We didn't break up. I went to college. We said we'd keep in touch, and then, somehow or other, we didn't keep in touch. 'Kat Ables,' I say, though I know she's no longer Kat Ables. Worse so, I gather that she's married Steve Cobb who I also went to high school with, this larger-than-life presence that I hoped I'd never hear of again. He was a wrestler at the time, an imposing figure who walked the halls with a whole underclass entourage surrounding him. He always had a thing for Kat.

'Long time, no see,' she says, and she smiles this extraordinarily white smile, and I know the last thing I'm going to be able to focus on right now is her teeth. 'How are you doing, Nick?' she asks, and I send Jan on an errand so that for a few moments Kat and I can be alone. Jan takes her time; she doesn't hurry back, though the supply closet is right across the hallway, and all I asked for were more cotton pellets. Even Jan knows I don't need any cotton pellets.

'Well,' I stammer. 'I'm doing well,' though I step on the wrong foot pedal and force her head down when I meant to lift her upright. Kat laughs. She has the most melodic laugh, airy and carefree. Clara, thwarted by her mother's dementia and eight months of a wearisome pregnancy, rarely laughs anymore. But Kat still laughs, and the ease of it, the simplicity, makes me laugh, too.

'What a coincidence this is,' I say, knowing it's not at all a coincidence.

'My family and I just moved into the area,' she tells me, 'and I knew you were here. I guess you can say I've been cyber-stalking you,' and I blush because, instead of feeling any sort of ominous dread over the fact, I let it go to my head. I find that I like that suggestion, of Kat searching for me online.

'Cyber-stalking?' I ask, and she tells me abashedly how she Googled my name and, as luck would have it, stumbled upon my practice's website. She was due for an exam anyway, and needed to find a new dentist. She leans forward in her chair, and, like that, our professional gap transforms into something more familiar and intimate. Her fingers twiddle with the edges of the paper napkin that lies across her chest, though the Kat I knew was never fidgety, never nervous. She's changed, as have I. Twelve years ago she said she'd put her world on hold for me. She'd wait. But she didn't wait.

'I tried to talk myself out of coming here. I wasn't sure I was ready to see you,' she says, and then more softly, almost apologetically, 'I wasn't sure you wanted to see me.'

'Please, Kat,' I say, trying hard to be nonchalant. 'Of

course I wanted to see you. It's fantastic to see you. It's so good to see you,' though mostly what I remember of my relationship with Kat were stolen moments in the back seat of my parents' cars, romantic moments that were brief and hurried and filled with anything but romance, regular intervals of breaking up and making up, hurt feelings, teenage melodrama, walking around with her on my arm just for show. But still, there was something so exhilarating about being with Kat.

Even at the time I knew it wasn't love. But it felt like love for two teenagers who'd never before been in love. And then I met Clara, and suddenly love came with a certain clarity I'd never known before.

'I have a son now,' she tells me, and I tell her I have a daughter. A wife, a daughter and a dog. And another baby on the way.

'Tell me about your son,' I say and she does. He's the antithesis of everything his father is, she says. 'You remember Steve?' she asks, and I nod and say that I do. Gus—Kat and Steve's son—doesn't like sports. Unlike Steve, he's narrowly built, tall and thin and more musically inclined, the kind of kid obsessed with video games and his air guitar and Harry Potter books. That's the way Kat describes him, and from the impression my mind forms, I like this kid already. He's my kind of guy.

'He looks nothing like Steve. He acts nothing like Steve. He's shy, sensitive. All Steve wants to do is teach him some basic wrestling skills, but at twelve Gus shows no interest in wrestling at all.'

Kat and Steve started dating about three days after I left for college, she tells me—he apparently swooped in just at the right time, while Kat was grieving my loss—and before she knew it, there was a baby on the way. It's the reason she never answered my emails or returned my calls. 'Steve wanted to make an honest woman out of me, and I said okay. You remember my parents,' she says, with a roll of the eye. I do remember her parents. Strict and demanding of total obedience. They scared the heck out of me. I can see why she and Steve decided to get married, but hope for her sake that she was at least in a little bit of love.

'You're happy?' I ask, and she shrugs her shoulders and says sometimes. Sometimes she's happy, though I have this sense that there's so much more she wants to say.

'You?' she asks, and though there's a part of me that thinks she wants me to say that I'm not, I say that I am. I'm happy. I have a beautiful wife and a child and another on the way. Of course I'm happy.

'I'm so glad,' she says and then she presses a warm hand to either side of my cheeks as she used to do, and forces me to see her eye to eye. 'I've always hoped that wherever you were and whatever you were doing, you were happy.'

'I'm happy,' I say again with a smile.

And it's then that I catch the sound of applause, of movement in my purview. It's Jan, I'm sure, returning for the dental exam, and I half expect to see her standing there with cotton pellets in hand. Except that when my eyes cast a glance toward the doorway it's not Jan, but rather Connor, standing there in his dental smock, clapping his hands at me. An ovation. Suddenly Kat's hands feel like fire on my skin, and I draw back quickly and rise to my feet.

'What are you doing here?' I ask, my voice circumspect,

but also panicked. What did Connor hear, and what did Connor see?

'I have patients to see,' he says, his voice composed as he turns and parades down the hallway.

'Give me a minute,' I say to Kat, circling the end of the dental chair. 'I'll be right back,' and I leave before she can say anything. I follow Connor down the hall, calling to him, though he doesn't stop. I jog to catch up.

I set a hand on his shoulder and force him to look at me.

'Does Clara know?' he asks and I don't reply. He shrugs, jaw set, eyes wide. 'Far be it for me to give marital advice, but I think you know as well as I do that sooner or later, the wife always finds out in the end.'

I'm speechless. I can't reply. My mind is rattled by the fact that Kat Ables sits in the very next room. A vision floods my memories then—the last time I laid eyes on Kat—overcomplicating my thought process, Kat's skin as a pastel painting, the spindly bones of her vertebrae as she stood, back to me, undressed save for the flimsy sheet she held around her waist like a toga, gazing over a shoulder as I left. *Until next time*, she'd said, and I'd replied, *See ya*, because it didn't occur to me that I might never see her again, not for over twelve years when she showed up in my dental chair.

'If you don't mind,' says Connor, drawing away, a patient file in his hands. He flips through it breezily. 'I have an appointment,' he says.

'The hell you do,' I snap, feeling suddenly angry, trying to reach across him and snatch the file out of his hands. On his face is this goading look, a challenge. He's wondering what I'm going to do about it, and whether or not I have it in me to make him leave. 'You don't work here anymore,' I say, 'or have you forgotten that already?' And somehow in that moment I forget completely that there was a time that Connor and I used to be friends. I expunge from memory all those late-night confessionals over endless bottles of Labatt Blue. I cross my arms across my chest and take a step closer to him. Connor isn't bigger than me, but he is stronger, a rock climber and a motorcyclist, the kind who believes he's invincible and has nothing to lose.

But in this moment, I, too, have so little left to lose.

'I'd hate for Clara to find out about the blonde,' he says, but I call his bluff on this and say, 'You wouldn't.'

He assures me he would.

'I'll give you three seconds to gather your things and leave,' I say, as the office ladies step foot into the hallway to see what the fuss is all about, 'and then I'm calling the police.'

He stands there, holding his ground, hands placed on his hips. I forget about Kat in my dental chair, my wife at home, combing through endless parenting websites for the perfect baby name. I forget about horse races and basketball games, and think only of what it would feel like for my fist to connect with the side of Connor's face. There is so much anger in me in this one single moment, so much rage I didn't know I had.

And then I begin to count, grateful that by three he leaves, though there's a nagging thought in the back of my brain that Connor and I aren't through yet, and that he's only toying with me, planning his counterplay.

CLARA

The phone in Maisie's hand rings as we drive to the park. It's my father, *Boppy*, I tell Maisie, who squeals and claps her hands in delight, handing me the phone. *Boppy, Boppy, Boppy!* Maisie loves her boppy. Boppy is even better than Candy Crush to Maisie.

'How are you doing?' he asks me as I answer the phone, and I lie and tell him we're doing fine.

'Running errands,' I say, also a lie as I steer the car in the direction of the park, speaking on the phone while driving, which I know I shouldn't do. I hear the detective's words, reminding me that Illinois is a hands-free state. I shouldn't talk on the phone or text while behind the wheel of a moving car.

But I don't care. The clock on the car's dashboard nears eleven o'clock; we are due soon.

'I'm glad to hear you're getting out and about,' says my father. 'It's good for you, Clarabelle. Keeping busy. It doesn't help anyone to be home all day, reveling in misery.' He means well; I know this. My father always means well. He has my best interest in mind. And yet the words come out abrasively, like steel wool scrubbing at my heart. *I can revel in misery if I so choose*, I want to scream. My husband is dead. I can do whatever I want to do. But I don't say this. I don't say anything.

'Your mother,' he tells me, a filler for the silence that follows his opening line, 'has been asking for you relentlessly. Your name has come up more times than you know.'

'I'm sure,' I say. This always seems to be the case until I actually appear, and then she doesn't want a thing to do with me. Even with me standing right there, three feet before her eyes, she still begs for Clara, adamantly sure it's not me.

'It would be nice if you could come by sometime. She would appreciate a visit,' he says, and at this I groan, reminding my father that my mother doesn't know if I'm here, there or anywhere. When I'm in her presence she doesn't speak to me; she only eyeballs me like I'm a stranger in the room, some amorphous shape standing in the way.

It wasn't always this way. The first manifestations of her dementia were slight: driving straight past the gas station on the way to get gas; forgetting to show on the occasional days she and I planned to meet for lunch or coffee or tea. Sometimes she just plain forgot, but other times she couldn't find her car keys, or she'd found the keys and was driving in circles around town, not able to remember where she was going or how to get there. Twice my father received a phone call from her on some busy street corner in downtown Chicago—and once from a shady area of Garfield Park—the haste of the city pervading the phone lines. She'd come to meet me for coffee in a little hipster coffee shop in the western suburbs, but got confused along the way, hopping blindly onto the expressway and soaring thirty miles in the wrong direction, caught up in the flow of traffic. By the time she found a phone and called, she couldn't explain to him where she was or how she'd come to be there and a passerby had to get on the pay phone and explain to my father just exactly where she was so he could come lay claim to her and bring her back home.

'I'll try my best,' I say, the third lie of many, and then my father's voice softens, and he asks how we're eating, sleeping, whether or not everything is really okay.

'Have you told Maisie?' he wants to know, and though I consider lying, I tell him no. I haven't told Maisie about Nick. 'When, Clarabelle?' he asks, and I say, 'Soon.'

'She needs to know.'

'Soon,' I say, asking then how he and my mother are doing. My father shouldn't be worrying so much for the kids and me; he has enough on his mind. Though I mailed a check to cover the debt to Dr. Barros, I'm still worried about my father's financial state, as well as his cognitive one. Is he eating okay, is he sleeping okay, I ask, but don't want to add insult to injury and mention the bounced check.

'Of course,' he says. 'I'm fine, Clarabelle. Why do you ask?'

'I worry about you,' I say, 'as much as you worry about me.'

'You don't need to worry,' he tells me. 'Your mother and I are fine. Just take care of yourself and the kids,' he says, telling me how he and Izzy will be taking my mother for a haircut this afternoon at one o'clock. They thought it would help lift her spirit. 'She's been feeling down lately. Depressed. I was going to take her myself,' says my father, 'but I don't know the first thing about hair. Izzy is the expert there,' he says, and I'm just the slightest bit piqued that my father didn't ask me to come along, though I would have said no, thinking of some excuse as to why I couldn't go. I envision Izzy's hip bleach-blond pixie do, and know she was the better choice anyway. I see myself in the rearview mirror. I haven't combed my hair today.

We end the call, and I give Maisie the phone, but it's not in her possession for thirty seconds when it rings again, and this time, when I go to snatch it from her, she puts up a fight. 'Give it to me, Maisie,' I demand. She clutches tightly to the phone so that I have to reach backward and wrench it from her hands. As I do, a fingernail grazes her hand by accident, and she grips tightly to that hand, crying that it hurts. She accuses me of scratching her. She screams.

But the tantrum doesn't have a thing to do with her injured hand. She and I both know that.

'Quiet, Maisie,' I say, and then press the phone to my ear. 'Hello?' I ask, out of breath, Maisie in the background kicking her feet at the back of the passenger's chair and moaning.

'You hurt me!' she cries as from the other end of the phone line comes a voice, the staid voice of Detective Kaufman asking me if everything is all right, and if I didn't know any better I'd think he knew I was intentionally breaking the law, talking on the phone while driving.

'Yes,' I say, though clearly everything is not all right. 'Just fine,' I say, hoping he doesn't hear the car's engine as we drive on toward the park.

The detective has called to tell me two things. First, the

man with the black car, the one with the tribal tattoo and the Budweiser beers—he has an alibi, airtight, for the day that Nick died. He was with his audiologist in Hinsdale at the time of the crash, which Detective Kaufman has confirmed with the doctor's office.

'Are you sure?' I ask, and he says, 'I'm certain of it. You must be mistaken about this man's vehicle,' at which I peer into the rearview mirror to see Maisie glaring back at me with resentment. She's mad that I scratched her; she wants the phone back. She wants to play Candy Crush.

'There's one more thing, Mrs. Solberg,' says the detective. 'I was doing a little research, digging up some information. I took the liberty of speaking to a few of your neighbors. I hope you don't mind. I've noticed that your husband has a history of speeding,' he says, and already I know where this conversation is going. Nick has a lead foot; I know. I've nagged him about it since the day we met. 'Two speeding tickets in the last year, four over the last three years,' he tells me. 'He was one more traffic violation away from having his license suspended.'

This was something I didn't know.

Nick received a speeding ticket about six months ago. I was in the car with him at the time, begging him to slow down, but he didn't. He was trying to outrun a train, to get through the crossing before the train inevitably stopped on the tracks. A cop had a speed trap set up on Route 59 and caught Nick going nearly sixty when he was meant to be going forty-five. But these other tickets and the threat of having his license revoked, these were things I didn't know.

'You said you spoke to my neighbors,' I say. 'Why?'

'We had two complaints on file. One from a Sharon Cadwallader and one from Theodore Hart.'

Theo. Emily's husband.

Theo and Nick have never liked each other much, and yet it seems completely ludicrous that he called the police on Nick, and we didn't know. Or maybe Nick did know, and only I didn't know, I think, wondering why in the world Nick wouldn't tell me if a neighbor had phoned in a complaint to the police about him. Maybe Nick felt guilty, maybe he was embarrassed. Nick was never one for gossip; he always tried to see the best in everyone, no matter what they'd done.

'What?' I ask, utterly surprised. 'Complaints for what?'

'Complaints for speeding,' Detective Kaufman tells me, and I envision Nick driving the car too quickly down the curling streets of our neighborhood, eager to be home. Even I have nagged him about this, worried for the children playing baseball in the middle of the street.

Sharon Cadwallader I can certainly understand. Sharon Cadwallader, a high-ranking official on the neighborhood council, and the one who fought to have traffic calming measures installed around the community: speed humps or traffic circles, or those ridiculous speed display boards that flashed when one drove too fast. She purchased her own radar gun and sat on her front porch, vetting every car that drove by. I'm quite certain she called the police about everyone who breached the twenty-five mile per hour speed limit.

'Mrs. Cadwallader clocked your husband going forty-eight miles per hour on your street. That's nearly double the legal limit,' the detective says to me. 'And Mr. Hart says there was some run-in with his son. Just a few weeks ago. The boy's rubber ball had rolled into the street, it seems, and when he went to fetch it, Nick came tearing around the bend.' He concludes with this, 'It was a close call,' and an exaggerated sigh through the phone line. And I picture the speed of Nick's passing car creating a breeze, eddying the brown hairs on Teddy's head, his eyes wide with fear as he groped for the ball. Theo in the background, screaming, and Emily at a window, watching the commotion from afar. Did Theo and Nick exchange words in the middle of the street? Was there a blowup, name-calling, or were punches thrown? Did Emily know, and if so, why didn't she tell me? I have a hard time picturing it. Nick is a pacifist. He avoids conflict at all costs, and is quick to apologize even when he's done nothing wrong. Anything to avoid a fight. I have no doubt that he was speeding through the neighborhood, whizzing home at forty-eight miles per hour to see Maisie and Felix and me. This comes as no surprise to me.

But I also see him rushing out into the middle of the street to see if Teddy is all right; I envision him apologizing demonstratively about the near-miss with Teddy and the rubber ball. He would have apologized for it all; he would have atoned for the misdeed.

So why call the police?

'Seems your husband had quite a history with speeding,' Detective Kaufman says, and I hear the words he says but also those he doesn't say: Nick's frequent speeding is the cause of the crash out on Harvey Road. It's Nick's fault that he's dead. Nick took the turn too quickly and lost control of the car. His speed is the reason he ran into that tree.

All roads lead to Nick.

I think of the woman I've just met, in the window, smoking her cigarette, and about the car she'd seen leaving the scene of the crash, veering into oncoming traffic. A black Chevrolet.

'I've taken the liberty, Detective Kaufman,' I say, echoing his own words, 'of speaking to some of the residents who live off Harvey Road. Just to see if anyone saw or heard anything at the time of the crash.' His sigh is long and loud.

'And?' he asks, his words stultified. I'm boring him, it seems. I reach into the back seat to pat Maisie's knee. *Almost done*, I mouth. Almost done, and then she can have the phone back. Almost done, and then I can ask about her injured hand.

'There was a woman,' I tell him, 'driving home from the market at the time. She came upon the scene just seconds after the crash, passing a black car along the way. It was driving erratically down the road. A black Chevrolet,' I say, pushing from my mind the drug possession charges I spied online for Melinda Grey, wondering if it's at all possible Nick was under the influence of something at the time of the crash. I won't put this suggestion in the detective's mind.

'Did she get a license?' he asks, but I tell him no, blaming the sun. It was so bright that day she could hardly see a thing. 'Then how did she know it was a Chevy?' he asks sagely.

'Well, that she saw,' I say, knowing how foolish it sounds. 'The emblem on the front of the car was easy to see. She remembers seeing the golden bow tie.'

'What is this woman's name?' he asks, and I tell him. 'Betty Maurer,' I say, and he promises that he'll speak to her. 'Many cars travel on that road every day,' he tells me. 'It's a shortcut, a nice alternative to highway congestion. Just because it was there, passing by around the time of the accident, doesn't make it a crime,' he says, but I press again, asking if he'll speak to Betty, and he says that he will. I thank the detective for his time. He says, 'Just doing my job,' and we end the call.

As I pass the phone back into Maisie's expectant hand, asking whether or not her scratch is okay, I'm floundering and confused. Did Nick die because he was driving too fast? He had a history of speeding, that much I know. But there's so much more to consider, from the canceled life insurance funds to the agent's suggestion that suicide or homicide are to blame. And then there is the restraining order, and the fact that some man in a hat and gloves has been skulking around my home.

Was Nick driving too fast because he was chasing someone, rather than the other way around?

Was he the pursuer and not the pursued?

And then Maisie's words come to me again, about the bad man following her and Nick, the obvious fear imbuing her eyes. That can't just be for show. Maisie saw something that terrified her.

I watch in the rearview mirror as Maisie—happy as a lark now, having forgotten all about the pilfered phone—points out the window and says to me with decision, with arrant conviction and delight, her voice decked out in a sing-song cadence, canarying the words, 'An elephant, Mommy. Look, Mommy, an elephant's in those trees,' and God help me, I look, even though of course there isn't an elephant in those trees. An elephant wandering around in suburban America? How absurd.

'You silly girl,' I say soberly, watching the way the day's sunlight glints off the white of her eye. 'Why would an elephant be here?' I ask, and as she chirps, 'Just taking a walk, Mommy,' I'm filled suddenly with a sense of unease.

Did she tell Nick that there was a car following them? Did she make it all up, and for this he drove faster, manically, anything to get away from the phony car?

For the first time, I ask Maisie. I ask her about the car. My words come out guardedly, carefully chosen, cautious not to use the wrong ones. 'Maisie, honey,' I say, my voice purring the words, 'did you see the black car like you just saw that elephant in the trees? The car that was following you and Daddy?' but at the mention of a black car, she goes silent. She turns away from me and peers out the window, any sense of a smile washed clear from her face.

No, I tell myself. No. Of course not. Nick is much more commonsensical than this. He would never give in to the whims of a child.

But then I see them in the grocery store together, Maisie set in the basket of a shopping cart, begging, *Faster, Daddy, faster*, and I see Nick run like greased lightning up and down the aisles, not caring what other shoppers thought because all he cared about was his little girl in the shopping cart, happy, smiling, laughing.

This has happened. Many times this has happened.

And now, from the back seat comes Maisie's crooning voice again as she spots the playground off in the distance, the one we're en route to, the slides, the swings, the monkey bars mere specks on the horizon. 'Faster, Mommy, faster,' she squeals, eager now for a day at the hippo park as my foot presses down on the gas pedal without intent, and the car casually picks up speed.

NICK

BEFORE

Driving home that night, I have every intention of telling Clara about Kat. Every intention in the world. It's one of the cardinal rules of a happy marriage: no secrets, and this detail—a visit with a former flame—seems too large, too uncontainable, to omit. It's not the same as the imminent malpractice suit or the sorry state of our finances. This is different. If Clara found out some other way, she'd be hurt, and a completely meaningless reunion would alter into something more, something sordid and wrong, something unforgivable. And so I fully intend to tell her.

But as I come into the house, I find Clara sound asleep on the living room sofa, her back pressed into the cushions for lumbar support. It's later than I usually get home. I phoned Clara hours ago and told her that I'd be late—thanks to a few emergency evening appointments, I claimed, when what I really needed to do was cool off for a bit, to collect my-self. And I did, thanks to a single dose of Halcion I pulled from the locked storage cabinet once the office ladies left for the night. It made me calm, sleepy and forgetful all at the same time.

I probably shouldn't have driven myself home, but I did.

When I finally get home, it's after eight o'clock, and Maisie is in bed. Harriet the dog greets me at the door, but the house is quiet, the TV turned on but the volume low. A box fan sits on the floor, plugged into the wall and aimed in Clara's direction, and though it's warm in the house, it's far from hot. The breeze from the fan ruffles her hair as I drop down to the floor before her body to watch her sleep, the flutter of her eyelids, the way her nostrils flare when she inhales. I'd blame the shortcomings of our aging air-conditioning unit for the reasons Clara is hot, and yet, more likely I tell myself, it's Clara's hormones, the fact that she's carrying twenty or thirty pounds of extra weight. She wears a tank top and a pair of stretchy pants that cohere with dog hair, and it's all I can do not to run my hand along the length of my baby boy, press my lips to Clara's midsection and whisper to him hello.

But instead I let her sleep.

I put off any idea of waking her and telling her about Kat. There's always tomorrow.

For now I watch her sleep, enjoying the stasis of the moment, the tranquility, and as I lay myself down on the floor before the sofa with a bolster pillow and a throw blanket, not sure if I can spend the night alone without her by my side, I whisper to her, 'Sleep tight.'

CLARA

What I discover is that she's beautiful. Utterly stunning, in an exquisite, fine-china sort of way. The woman with the Seattle phone number who knows my name, sitting in a chiffon tank top and a pair of formfitting jeans beside a boy on a park bench, a boy whom she calls Gus. Gus looks to be eleven or twelve years old to me, stuck in that gap between childhood and adolescence, wearing a black polyester T and a pair of shorts. His legs are long and lanky, a set of earbuds plugged into his ears so he can mute the outside world. He holds two figures in his hands, two molded green army men who duke it out on his kneecap, punching each other in the face until one falls to the concrete below.

My breath catches; I try not to make more of this than there is.

There must be billions of little green army men in our town alone. This means nothing. These army men have nothing to do with the one I found in the plastic sack of

Nick's possessions, given to me from the morgue after he had died.

Or do they?

The woman looks to me like she stems from one of those countries that produce tall, light-haired, light-eyed people by the yard. Her hair is so blond it tends toward white; her eyes are blue like beach glass. She says to Gus, 'Go play,' and he mopes, yanking the earbuds from his ears and abandoning them along with the army men on the park bench, rising lethargically and meandering to a swing. Maisie, on the other hand, takes off full tilt, headed toward a sandbox where she wiggles out of her hot-pink Crocs and gets down to work.

The woman says that her name is Kat; I say that my name is Clara. She has the most perfect posture, and though it isn't intentional, her hair, her clothing, her eyes make me feel subordinate. I sit beside her and cross my feet at the ankles, feeling huge in the woman's presence, my midsection still round and flabby. I try to ignore the charm of her adorable espadrilles and to avoid looking at my own bloated feet, the polish chipping quickly off the nails. The baby weight weighs heavily on me, my breasts engorged with milk. Just because I've begun feeding Felix formula doesn't mean my body has adapted to the change. Not yet anyway, and so I fill to capacity with surplus milk, my breasts flattened beneath an old sports bra that only adds to my revulsion. I haul Felix from the stroller and feed him a baby bottle to satisfy his needs while my own stomach growls, a reminder that I've eaten nothing today, nearly nothing this week. I should eat, I tell myself, knowing I won't eat.

Harriet lays herself in the shade beneath a tree.

'Who are you?' I ask the woman as we watch her boy, Gus, descend upon Maisie in the sandbox, asking indifferently if he, too, can play. I half expect Maisie to say no and throw a fuss that some newbie has infringed upon *her* sandbox, in an attempt to maraud the best, wet, packable sand, and I ready myself with the need to intervene, to explain to Maisie about sharing and playing nice, and how this sandbox isn't all hers as she's convinced herself it is.

And yet she doesn't make a fuss but instead nods her head okay, and together she and Gus begin to build. *Good girl, Maisie*, I silently say.

'Nick and I were friends way back when,' Kat says to me as she picks at the flat-felled seam on a pair of vintage wash jeans. She doesn't look at me, her eyes instead placed on the jeans. Her fingernails are freshly painted, a dark grape, freshly manicured.

But this is too ambiguous to me, too abstruse. *Way back when.* 'When?' I ask, needing specifics, and Kat reluctantly tells me how she and Nick went to high school together.

'Where?' I ask.

'Seattle,' she tells me. 'Bainbridge Island. We were close,' she says. 'Good friends,' though I wager a guess from the tears that fill her eyes that they were more than good friends. I'm afflicted with a sudden pang of jealousy; were Kat and Nick better friends than Nick and me? But, no, I reassure myself, thinking of Nick and me lying together in bed, my head on his chest as he stroked my hair with those gentle, loving hands of his, the same hands that held our wrinkly baby boy all covered in vernix days later when he finally emerged from my womb after eighteen hours of painful labor.

He married me. We had a child together. Two children. He loved me, not her.

'You've kept in touch all these years?' I ask, wondering why Nick never mentioned Kat before. I think hard, trying to decide whether he did tell me about Kat and I wasn't listening. It's not like me not to listen, and yet I'd been so consumed in recent months with the pregnancy, with my own expanding body, with my mother's ever-failing mind. Maybe he mentioned a Kat, and somehow or other I didn't hear.

But she tells me no. 'My husband and I, Steve,' she says, 'Steve and Gus and I just moved here, to town. He's in accounting, my husband. Steve,' and her words come out unmethodically, a series of ramblings that I must put together, like puzzle pieces. Her voice shakes. She is nervous, sad and scared. Why is she scared? Does she have a reason to be scared? Or maybe it is only the nerves masked in fear.

'He was transferred?' I infer, and she says yes. 'When?' I ask.

'We've been here nearly eight weeks,' she says. 'Two months,' and in my bitterness I want to tell her that I know that, that eight weeks is two months, that I can add, that I'm not an idiot. The words nearly snap out of me as the anger in me begins to rise, all but reaching a boiling point. Kat has done nothing to harm me, nothing that I know of for certain, and yet my dislike for her builds and builds. I'm tired and hungry, I rationalize in my head, and my husband is dead. I have every right in the world to be grouchy, angry, to snap at people I hardly know.

'And you and Nick…' my voice trails off as I search for the word I need. 'You reconnected?' I ask, reading between the lines. The question comes out more pointedly than I'd

intended—an inquisition—sharp like a scalpel. I envision
some chance encounter at the tire and auto repair shop,
which I only imagine because I remember Nick running
over a mislaid nail on the interstate one day, eight weeks
or two months ago, and coming home with a flattened tire.
Or maybe it was at the post office, the Saturday afternoon
he mailed a package to his father, an autographed glossy
photograph of Dave Krieg he found at a sports memorabilia
store on the highway toward Joliet. Maybe she was there
browsing through boxes of NFL trading cards, finding one
to give to Gus, Nick staring through tempered glass at expensive items on display. A chance meeting. Kismet.

'Yes,' she says, nodding her head. 'In a way. We ran into
each other at his dental practice, of all places,' she says,
smiling cannily without realizing it, as she says to me, 'He
hadn't changed a bit. Nick was still Nick.'

'You've seen him many times since you've moved to
town?' I ask, trying hard to curtain my jealousy and distrust. Why didn't Nick tell me about Kat, Nick who told
me everything? *No secrets*, he always said. *None*. But now
I'm beginning to believe there were secrets indeed. Many
secrets. Had he been lying to me for the last eight weeks,
the last two months, or for many years? All these women in
Nick's life about whom I knew nothing, Melinda and Kat.

Were there more? What else don't I know?

'Yes,' she says, and then, 'no,' settling finally on, 'a few.'
She and Nick had seen each other a few times since she
moved to town. She, Steve and Gus, Kat goes on to tell
me, are living in a suburb that lies adjacent to ours, one
with home prices that soar upward of a million dollars and
property taxes that are heinous, ones that fund the superla-

tive public school system in town, the best one around. She doesn't say this to me, but I know. Nor does she describe her home to me, but still, I picture it, some palatial home in one of those newer, gated subdivisions, the ones making a grand show of their upscale homes and on-site amenities, the tennis courts and heated pools and the elitist clubhouses flanked in glass and stone.

When I ask Kat about her last phone call with Nick the day of the crash, she describes it for me, the sounds she heard that day over the phone: the shrill screaming and the wreckage of the car as it slammed against the tree, 'like refuse in a garbage truck,' she tells me, 'being compacted beneath the force of the metal pusher plate, times infinity. That but worse,' she says decisively, her eyes set on Gus and Maisie in the sandbox and not me.

Much worse.

She doesn't apologize for her candor, but says it like she means to leave this horrid visual in my mind, Nick's broken body whisked together with leftovers and rubbish and trash, being compressed inside a garbage truck's hopper with a bounty of hydraulic power, until there was nothing left of him at all. Flat Nick, is what I imagine, like the well-traveled children's book character, Flat Stanley, and I envision my Nick as a card-stock clone that I can carry around in my purse and pose for photos with beside the Golden Gate Bridge, Rockefeller Center and Soldier Field.

'After that there was only silence,' she says, her hands trembling and her eyes turning red as a merciful breeze blows through the stagnant air. 'The silence,' she says, voice quivering, 'was somehow or other even worse than the noise. I called to him over the phone,' she tells me, but there was nothing, no crying; no screaming; no strained breaths or gasping for air; no staticky noise from the car's radio.

No Nick.

And then she is quiet, watching the children play.

There are questions I want to ask but don't. They aren't questions about the crash but rather: Are she and Nick really just friends, and how does her husband feel about this friendship, or does he even know about Nick? I'm struck with sudden pangs of jealousy, wondering if she and Nick were only friends in high school as she's said, or if there was more to it than that, sweethearts, homecoming king and queen or teenage lovers who made out in the back seat of a parked car on some bluff overlooking Puget Sound? I have to know as my mind invents details, picturing it then and finding that I can't get that image out of my mind: Nick's hungry, naked body raised above Kat, the rhythmical movements, the earthy and untamed moans that scream suddenly and uninvited into my ear. Eighteen-year-old Nick, wide-eyed and gung ho, full of potential, twelve years ago or so, a gamely boy slipping his hands up under the cotton of a burnout T to graze the slender, curved bones of Kat's young rib cage, moving eagerly upslope toward her chest.

This is what I'm envisioning as my eyes rise up and greet Maisie's eyes there in the sandbox, as I grab Harriet by the leash and call for Maisie to come, needing more than anything to get away from this woman, knowing for certain that she is the one with whom Nick was having an affair. Not Melinda Grey as I initially assumed, but Kat.

A flush creeps up my neck and into the connective tissues of the lobes of my ears, making them redden and burn, prickle and sting. 'Come on, Maisie,' I call for a second time, my voice quivering, feeling this woman's eyes on me, needing desperately to get away, to get out of here. To seek solace in the only unfailing arms I know.

My father's arms. They will protect me.

'Please, don't go,' begs Kat, rising to her feet, saying, 'There's more.' But I hold up a hand. I can't bear to hear more. What would she possibly say to me? Tell me where and when they committed their acts of adultery, and how Nick was going to leave me for her. How Nick loved her more than he did me? Is that what she plans to say? I can't stand to hear it, her confession.

'I have an appointment,' I claim, finding it hard to speak and even harder to breathe, the oxygen keeping me at an arm's reach. 'I really must go,' I gasp, hurrying to the sand-box to draw Maisie away by the hand, letting her walk bare-foot through the park, carrying her shoes in her hand. 'I'll call you,' I lie. 'We'll meet for coffee,' I claim, praying I never have to lay eyes on this woman again. I get into my car, racing in the direction of my mother and father's home.

I won't tell my father about Kat and Nick. I can't. But he'll see the sadness in my eyes, and he'll hold me tight, and for one brief moment I won't feel so alone.

* * *

It's nearing one o'clock as we drive through town, and it isn't until I arrive at my parents' home and see the drive-way vacant that I remember my mother's haircut appoint-ment. They won't be home. Izzy and my father have taken my mother to the salon. I pause in the drive, breathing hard, trying to remove the lewd images of Nick and Kat from my mind as I take in the small, one-story home—no stairs down which to fall—adorned in vinyl siding and fake brick.

My parents moved here five or six years ago, when their previous home became too big for them, too much work. They no longer needed twenty-five hundred square feet for just the two of them and decided to downsize to a ranch in an active adult community, the kind that offered exercise classes, bingo night and craft workshops, none of which my parents attended.

'Boppy!' Maisie screams, recognizing the home, but I tell her that Boppy isn't here right now it seems, and I'm about to pull away when suddenly, amidst Kat's unspoken words, which muffle all rational thoughts in my mind—the unsaid admission of adultery, the blow-by-blow of her intimate moments spent with Nick—I remember the scrap of paper that bears the password to my father's bank account in a desk drawer, and it's a great reprieve when I do, a way to divert the unwanted thoughts that fill my mind. I didn't go to their home planning to seek out the password, but rather for the comfort of my father's arms.

But now that I'm here, I can't just leave without it.

I put the car in Park. I tell Maisie that Mommy just needs to run inside real quick and find something for Boppy.

'You stay here and keep an eye on Felix, okay, Maisie?' I ask as I step from the car, putting the windows down so the kids don't overheat. 'Can you do that?' I ask. 'Can you be a good big sister and watch Felix?' Maisie smiles and nods her head, reaching over as far as she can to set a hand on Felix's arm. He's fast asleep.

I knock once on the door to be certain no one is home, and then scurry to the garage keypad and type the familiar pass code in. The door springs open. Once inside, I take the shortest route to my father's office where there is a desk but also a twin-size bed, which is where my father sleeps these days, no longer able to sleep with my insomniac mother.

I don't delay. I find the slip of paper in the top desk drawer, where my father keeps a listing of his passwords. I snap a picture of it with my smartphone, and, sliding it back into the desk drawer, I leave.

* * *

That night I don't bother going through the motions of climbing into bed, of closing my eyes, of fooling myself into believing that sleep is within reach. Sleep is not within reach. I tuck the children into bed and sit instead at the breakfast nook with a cup of tea. Beside me is Nick's phone. I've never been one for snooping, and yet I press in his password and begin scouring all the information I can find on the device. I gaze through his calendar searching for dates with Kat; there are none. I check his call log, I read his emails for sappy notes to and from Kat. Again there are none. I check his internet browser, wondering what I might find among his most recent searches, and as I do, three windows load, one bearing basketball scores, and another for the Chinese restaurant where Nick would have eaten his final meal, the restaurant menu loaded onto the screen. But it's the last one that knocks the breath from my lungs.

A search for suicide statistics among dental professionals. At this I gasp out loud, dropping the phone from my hand. Suicide statistics. Dental professionals. Nick.

It's true then, I reason. Nick took his own life, and he did it with Maisie in the back seat. He risked our child's life, and suddenly I'm not only sad but also completely incensed. He nearly killed my child. All other possibilities go scurrying from my mind: Maisie's suggestion of foul play, the ridiculous idea that Nick gave in to the whims of a four-year-old child and sped recklessly at her suggestion. Of course that couldn't possibly be true. Nick panders to Maisie, yes, and yet he's far more commonsensical than that. Far more commonsensical, and yet also desperate. Desperate enough to kill himself. But why? It must have had something to do with Kat, I reason. He was stricken with guilt, or maybe she threatened to tell me about their love affair if he didn't leave me. He tried to pay her off, perhaps, with the life insurance payout, but even that wasn't enough for Kat. The only way out was suicide.

Kat admitted as much at the park. She said that there was more she had to tell me, but I said no, that I had an appointment, that I had to leave. She was going to tell me about their affair.

It's clear to see now that there was never a bad man.

Nick was the bad man. Nick did this.

The tears fall freely from my eyes as I reach for my laptop in an effort to quell the thought, to not think about Nick intentionally plowing into a tree at the side of Harvey Road, to not imagine Maisie dead like Nick. I open my laptop and pull up my mother and father's account on the bank website, to be sure they're not in any sort of financial distress. My father is far too proud to tell me if he's having money trouble, but after the missing check and the bounced check, I have to know if he needs help. With the sting of Nick's betrayals, he's all that I have left. I type in the log-in and the password and the account opens before my eyes. At seeing a balance of over a thousand dollars, my immediate reaction is relief. I exhale heavily, not aware until that moment how long I'd been holding my breath.

If I wasn't facing a sleepless night, that might have been the end of it. But as it is, I have nothing better to do with my time than to sip tea and stare at the clock until morning finally comes, and so I start scouring the statements in reverse, taking note of weekly cash withdrawals, all for three hundred dollars. Some months the account shrinks to near nothing before the pension check arrives and the rent payment from Kyle and Dawn. My father is old-school, as many men of his generation are; he likes to carry cash. That much I know, but a weekly allowance of three hundred dollars seems like a lot of money to have on hand. What is he spending three hundred dollars on each week, twelve hundred a month, over fourteen thousand dollars a year?

But that's not all.

Scrolling backward, I find a payment made to a local jewelry store in excess of four hundred dollars, nearly two months ago. Two months or eight weeks. I'm overcome with the strangest sensation of déjà vu, thinking only of the receipt to the very same jewelry store tucked away beneath Nick's undershirts in the dresser drawer. The receipt for a four-hundred-dollar pendant necklace. In the moment I can't be sure that the dates of purchase are the same, or that the value amount is identical down to the penny, and yet it seems far too analogous to be a coincidence. My mother doesn't wear much jewelry, nothing other than her engagement ring or items with sentimental value, such as her mother's wedding ring. My father tried giving her a string of pearls once when I was a teenage girl, Tahitian pearls that most certainly cost him a lot of money, but my mother was too penny-wise for such a thing and made him bring them back. I felt sorry for him, remembering for years to come the pained expression on his face when my mother scolded him for the gorgeous string of pearls, never once saying thanks or acknowledging the generous gift.

But now, knowing this, I find it impossible to believe that my father spent four hundred dollars at the jewelry store on my mother, fully aware of her antipathy toward it, and yet maybe he's taken advantage of her dementia to spoil her rotten with flowers and jewelry, and other things she'd pooh-pooh were she still of sound body and mind.

But, no, I realize then. That can't be. My father is far too practical of a man for this.

And that's when the suggestion starts to gnaw at me, that Nick has somehow used my father's credit card to purchase this necklace. Nick was in some sort of financial crisis, that much I now know. But was he in enough financial crisis that he had the nerve to steal my father's credit card and buy a necklace for Kat with it? Had Nick been panhandling money from my father, or just outright stealing it? It's the latter, to be sure. Nick was stealing from my aging parents. I fill to the brim with embarrassment and shame as well as anger. It reaches a boiling point and begins to overflow.

Not only has Nick wronged me, but he's wronged my family, as well.

My father was right all along. Nick could only bring me down.

* * *

It's nearing one in the morning when an inconspicuous knock comes on the kitchen window. At the sound of it, I leap from my skin, goose bumps forming on the flesh, the hairs of my arms standing on end.

The breakfast nook lines a bay window. It's surrounded

by glass on three sides. The noise is jarring like a shock of electricity jolting through my body. My first instinct is to blame my imagination for it, but then it comes again, far less inconspicuous and more pronounced this time, the heavy smite of knuckles on glass so that my heart picks up speed. Harriet's heavy head rises from the floor, and her ears stand at attention. Harriet heard it, too.

Someone is here.

I turn apprehensively from the laptop and peer outside. My eyesight is diminished by the lights of the LED screen so that I can hardly see, my vision hindered by spots and blotches. It takes a moment for my eyes to adjust, but as they do, I make out a light on in the Jorgensens' home behind us, though the Jorgensen home is likely a hundred feet away and with windows closed to repel the heat, there's no chance they'd hear me if I screamed.

And that's when I make out a nebulous shape standing just outside, eight inches away or less, and at seeing it, I press my hand to my mouth and gasp.

Instinctively my hand reaches for the phone, thumb hovering above the nine until my eyes make out the shape, the brown eyes and the brown hair, the indulgent smile as the contour of a hand rises up to wave hello.

Connor.

And though I should feel many things—relief among others—it's unease that I feel. Anxiety. What is Connor doing here at one in the morning? Butterflies pulsate in my stomach as I rise from the nook and move to the back door, pulling it to. There he stands on the back porch plucking the motorcycle gloves from his hands one finger at a time, and as I ask, 'What are you doing here?' I see that his eyes have a drowsy look to them, glossed over. As he welcomes himself inside my home, he stumbles a bit, grabbing the door frame for support. Not much, for Connor is no stranger to drinking and his tolerance is high, but enough that I know he's had a drink or two before he came here.

He steps from his shoes and into the kitchen. 'Do you know what time it is?' I ask, and, 'Why didn't you call?'

'I saw a light on,' he whispers to me, his breath laced with the bitter smell of beer, which leads me to believe that Connor drove past the house for the sole purpose of seeing if I was awake, leaving his motorcycle in the drive and tiptoeing around the side of the house to see my silhouette through the kitchen window.

How long was he watching me?

He pulls me into him, an awkward hug, and instinctively I draw away. 'You okay?' he asks, sensing the way I tense up at his touch, but I shake it off and tell him I'm fine, as good as to be expected anyway. Unable to maintain eye contact, my eyes drop to his shoes.

A pair of classic Dickies, the color of wheat. Heavy-duty work boots with a lug sole. Instantly my mind goes to the muddy footprints beneath the pergola the night of the storm. I think of Connor's motorcycle helmet, his black leather gloves. A man in a hat and gloves, as Maisie had said. It was Connor, standing in the rain, watching me through the window, and at once I want to know why, though there's a part of me too put off, too confused to ask. I feel my cheeks redden at the thought, Connor staring through the window, watching me.

'I wanted to see if you were okay,' he says as he leads the way unhesitatingly to the refrigerator, where he pulls on the door's handle to help himself to one of Nick's Labatt Blues. Thanks to Connor, they're dwindling in number. Only four remain, and those will soon be gone, too. And then what will I do? Purchase another case to mislead myself into believing that Nick is still here?

I find a bottle of Chardonnay on the wine rack and pour myself a glass. Felix is no longer nursing, and so there's no longer a need to abstain. I press the glass to my lips and sip, letting the anesthetic fill my veins, trying hard to forget the events of the day, from the discovery of the black Chevrolet, to meeting Kat, to Nick's many indiscretions. It's all too much to handle—my mind bounding back and forth at all the possibilities, confusing me, making me feel crazed—and at seeing tears fill my eyes, Connor asks, 'What is it, Clara?' while setting his beer on the countertop and again pulling me into his arms, his hands locked around the small of my back. There's an awkwardness in the way he latches his hands together behind me, so that for a brief moment I think I couldn't get away if I wanted to, and I feel instantly suffocated. Smothered. It's too much. He holds too tightly and for too long, and my first instinct is to blame the alcohol. He's had too much to drink. His hands stroke the small of my back in a way that's far too close, far too intimate for me.

Memories return to me then. We've done this before, Connor and me.

'He was having an affair,' I say, and this time Connor nods his head and affirms that it's true.

'I saw them together,' he says as I draw away to look him in the eye. 'At the office. I don't know for certain, but it looked suspect to me.'

'He was going to leave me?' I ask.

Connor shrugs his shoulders. 'Maybe,' he says, and my mind leaps instantly to the notion of divorce lawyers and divorce proceedings, alimony, child custody, irreconcilable differences. Nick and I didn't fight, hardly ever. Our differences were slim, irreconcilable or not. We were never truly at odds, and yet, in the final days and weeks of my pregnancy with Felix, as I pushed a nearly nine-pound baby from my body, were these the thoughts that occupied my husband's mind? Leaving me so he could be with another woman? The word *dissolution* flits around in my mind, a marriage dissolving like instant coffee.

He comes for me again, trying to wrap his arms around me, to comfort and console me, but I step away, out of his reach, and his hands come up with nothing but air. 'What is it?' he asks, this time meaning my avoidance, and as my eyes move again to his shoes, I say that it's been a long day. There's only so much one person can take.

'I just need to be alone,' I tell him, wanting more than anything for Connor to leave. The discomfort is overwhelming, a feeling in the pit of my stomach that something isn't right. And it's not just the alcohol this time. It's something more. The closeness of Connor to me, the presumption of his hands. Knowing it was Connor who watched me through the window, staring, saying nothing. What did he see?

Connor doesn't take to this well. He shakes his head; he tells me no. 'You can't be alone now, Clara,' he says. 'You and me, we're all we have left. We have to stick together,' he says, reaching out again to clamp my hand, squeezing tightly so that I can't let go. 'We shouldn't be alone at a time like this,' and as he runs a hand along my hair, he whispers, 'You were always too good for him anyway,' and though it's meant to appease me—comfort me in the wake of Nick's affair—it strikes me as an odd comment to make. Connor is Nick's best friend. We don't say bad things about our best friends, least of all when they're dead.

The thought that comes to me then is that summer when I was expectant with Maisie, in those early days when only Nick and I knew, too terrified still to share the news and jinx it. It was early in the pregnancy, though the merciless morning sickness had finally relented as I crossed that viaduct between trimesters one and two. I was feeling good for the first time in a long time, no longer bilious and green, and yet consumed with fears that I had yet to share with Nick. I'd become pregnant sooner than expected; Nick and I planned to wait until after our thirtieth birthdays to conceive. And yet here we were, in our early and midtwenties with a baby on the way. To call Maisie a mistake seems cruel, and yet that's what she was, a miscalculation of dates, a forgotten birth control pill, a romantic night with an expensive bottle of red wine. I wasn't sure if I was ready to be a mother, though I never told this to Nick, who was so excited to be a father he could practically burst with pride.

Instead I told Connor one summer evening at an outdoor gathering at the home of a mutual friend, a garden party where I was the only one who hadn't been drinking, and Connor stumbled upon me in the kitchen, drinking tap water and trying not to cry. I confessed to him about the pregnancy, that I was terrified to be a mother, that I was consumed with all the things that likely could and would go wrong. Being responsible for another human life was a formidable task. I wasn't sure I could do it.

But Connor's words were rational. *Nobody knows what*

they're doing the first time around, he said. *You're a smart woman, Clara. You'll figure it out.* And then he held me while I cried. He stroked my hair and comforted me. He told me I would be the best mother, that there wasn't anything in the world I couldn't do.

Until that moment, our relationship was purely platonic. We were merely friends.

But as Connor held me there in the kitchen with everyone else safely outside beneath a set of string lights, he nearly kissed me. Not quite but almost. His eyes drifted closed, his inhibitions lowered by the excessive alcohol consumption, leaning into me, though I pressed a gentle hand against his chest and whispered, 'Connor, please, don't.' His only reply was to clutch me by the waistline and pull me closer, to attempt to draw his lips to mine. Connor was the kind of man who was used to getting what he wanted. Women didn't tell him no. He was drunk, I reasoned at the time, and come morning, he wouldn't remember. But I would.

I can't tell you how long I've wanted to do this, he breathed deliriously that night as if he didn't hear my rejection at all, as if he couldn't feel the palm of my hand against his chest. His eyes stayed closed until a noise jolted them open again, Sarah, the owner of the home, stepping in through the sliding glass door with an armful of wobbly plates balanced on her inner arms, threatening to fall. There was a tower of them, eight plates or more, stacked precariously on top of each other. Connor stepped away from me, moving quickly to Sarah's side to rescue the plates, though she was so blitzed she didn't even notice, just as she didn't notice the near-kiss.

We never spoke of it. It never happened again.

I didn't think twice about brushing it under the rug. We all do stupid things when we've had too much to drink, don't we? In time, I forgot it happened. I never told Nick, and Connor became like a brother to me, the brother I never had.

'You shouldn't say that,' I tell him now, slipping my hand from his, though he steps forward as I slowly retreat. 'He was your best friend,' I condemn, and though Nick has hurt me, a thousand times over he has hurt me, there isn't a thing for Nick I wouldn't still do. I avert my eyes from his, looking anywhere so I don't see the way he stares at me, making me feel uncomfortable. I want to ask him to leave. I stare out the window, at the clock, at Connor's abandoned gloves. I stare at Harriet sound asleep.

'Nick was many things,' he says. 'But he wasn't my friend,' and at this I turn to ice, wondering just what exactly Connor means by this. Of course he was Nick's friend.

'Of course he was,' I say, but Connor responds with, 'I thought he was, too. Turns out we were both wrong,' and before I can press him on this, before I can demand to know just what he means by these words, his hands fall to my hips, and he pulls me into him with so much impetus I gasp, his lips moving toward mine. The yeasty smell of alcohol on his breath is nauseating; he's had far too much to drink. His lips press me in a way that is sloppy and shapeless, his lips wet with beer. I push him away, and as I do he breathes into my ear, 'I've envied Nick many things, but most of all was you,' and it's then that I know why Connor was standing at my window the other night, watching as I argued on the phone with the life insurance man. Watching as I called Kat. Watching as I comforted Maisie in the heat of the storm.

It's because of me.

Connor is in love with me.

And at once I feel many things, from guilt to sadness to despair. Have I done something to deserve this? Have I led Connor on in some way? Is this my fault? I see the pleading in his eyes, the unspoken words. *Let me be your Nick*, he silently begs.

And then suddenly the words are spoken, as Connor says to me, a forced whisper so that I feel the breath of his words against my skin, 'Let me take care of you, Clara. You and the kids. I'll take such good care of you,' and I know he would. That's the hardest part. I know that in the wake of Nick's transgressions that Connor would take the very best care of the children and me, but I can't bear to imagine myself in another man's arms, in another man's bed.

There's so much hope in his eyes, hope and desperation, a toxic combination, it seems—so much to gain, so much to lose.

And I know that when I deny him, I'll lose Connor, too. My words get lost in my throat. I can't speak because when I do, I'll break both of our hearts.

After tonight, Connor and I can no longer be friends.

And then I hear a noise. My saving grace.

It's a meager noise like the scritch-scratch of a house mouse trying to worm its way into a bag of birdseed. Connor hears it, too, a noise that makes his hands suddenly stop their digressions so that he can pause to hear. His ears perk up; he listens, and it comes again, the scraping sound of paws on the hardwood floors. Harriet, I think, but no, Harriet is here, on the kitchen floor fast asleep. Not paws, then, but feet. Human feet. Tiny human feet, and then a voice, a quiet, unobtrusive voice as if not wanting to interrupt, not wanting be a bother. 'Mommy,' says the voice, and I realize then, as I stand there in the kitchen, holding my breath, that it is Maisie. Maisie is here.

She appears in the doorway, hair in shambles, clutching her derelict bear, and says to me, 'Mommy, I can't sleep.' She catches sight of Connor and grins, and though I want to run to her, to gather her in my arms, to thank her for her timing, for saving me from this awkward fate, my voice remains staid.

'Did you try?' I ask, and Maisie nods her head, saying that she did. She tried. I run my hand the length of her hair, staring at her gratefully as her eyes become hopeful and she begs of me, 'Mommy, you go to sleep, too?'

I nod my head. There is nothing in the world I would rather do.

With shaking hands I turn to Connor, and I tell him how I really must go, how Maisie needs me, thankful he doesn't object, though his face falls flat and there's a great letdown at this. Connor doesn't want me to leave, to attend to Maisie. He wants me to stay. I appease him by saying, 'I'll call you tomorrow,' knowing I won't call.

'Of course,' he says, nodding his head and drawing away, and I grip Maisie by the hand—wanting to tuck myself between my children and slip into oblivion, a restless sleep no doubt, if sleep even comes—as we watch him slide his feet back into the muddy work boots and leave the same way out in which he came.

I close the blinds so that no one will watch as we sleep.

NICK

BEFORE

It all goes wrong at the same time.

An official medical malpractice complaint from Melinda Grey arrives, delivered to me by a man who presses it into my hand and tells me I've been served. There's no one around when he does it, and yet I imagine that everyone can see. I imagine that everyone knows, but in truth, only I know. My hands sweat, and my mouth turns to cotton as I take the complaint in my hands and, for whatever reason, thank the man for bringing it to me.

I squirrel myself away on a laptop in my office and get busy on the internet, researching the effects a malpractice suit has on doctors and dentists—financial and otherwise. They're debilitating, though they don't surprise me in the least bit because I'm already feeling every one of them. Practitioners who have been sued for malpractice have higher rates of suicide, as in my mind I think of ways to end my life. Dentists already have one of the highest rates of suicide of any profession, thanks to the self-sacrifice required and the extremely competitive nature of the job. I know; I've lived it firsthand. The easy access to drugs is also an advantage; sitting behind a locked storage cabinet in my office are all sorts of pharmaceuticals that could end my life if I so chose.

But a malpractice suit makes it even worse. Dental professionals lose happiness in a career they once loved, and depression ensues. Many leave the profession. For the rest, a rift forms between doctors and their patients, a wall of distrust. And then there is the financial impact, the loss of a reputation.

Soon, I think, this will be me. Depressed and suicidal, having lost enjoyment in a career I once loved.

I phone an attorney, and the discovery process begins, though we won't go to court, the attorney tells me, because juries have been known to award upward of a million dollars for legitimate malpractice suits, whereas out-of-court settlements are usually less. I have malpractice insurance, which covers me up to a million dollars, though it doesn't cover the cost of attorney fees, the loss of patients while I'm trying to save my reputation and practice. But whether or not to settle will be up to the insurance company to decide. If a jury awards Ms. Grey more than a million, or if the settlement demand exceeds that amount and I'm deemed to be at fault, the difference is mine to pay.

And then there's the fact that my malpractice insurance rates will soar steadily, sky-high until I can no longer stay afloat. The fifteenth of the month draws near, meaning I owe the landlord rent. I still don't have it, and I'm running out of time. I need to make quick decisions now, trying to turn an easy profit, and so I place the maximum I can on the Warriors in tonight's NBA finals, though they're in a do-or-die situation—down two games to one. I figure it's fitting because I am, too.

More patients disappear, having caught wind of the referral giveaway across town, I tell myself, trying hard not to take it personally. It's about the grill, not *me*. But maybe it is me.

Each day another poor rating appears online, and I try to convince myself that Melinda Grey and Connor are not in cahoots, putting their heads together to think of ways to ruin my life. I call Connor, once, twice, three times a week to try to talk this out, but he doesn't answer his phone. The office ladies seem upset that the congenial Dr. C is gone. They don't tell me directly, but I hear them talking about it when they think I'm not in the room. We never talk about the scene they observed in the hallway, me threatening to call the police on Connor if he didn't leave. But we're all still thinking about it, especially me. I hear them talking to clients on the phone. 'No, I'm sorry,' they say to a patient who's called to make an appointment. 'Dr. Daubney is no longer with us. But I can schedule an appointment with Dr. Solberg, if you'd like,' and then inevitably the conversation drifts to quiet as the patient decides whether I'm good enough for them to see. Connor was always the more charming of us, the more witty and gregarious. The children loved him; he made dental exams fun. But not me. Sometimes these patients schedule an appointment with me, but other times I hear Nancy or Stacy explaining how they don't know where Dr. C has gone or if, wherever he is, he's taking new patients. There's nothing in his contract that prevents him from usurping patients of mine, not that I could blame him if he tried.

At night, I find it harder and harder to sleep, my rest obstructed by the thoughts that fill my mind, that and Clara's body pillow that lies between us like a third spouse. I end up spending half of my nights on the living room sofa or the floor. Halcion is my only saving grace, two pills before bedtime, swallowed secretly with a swig of water from the bathroom sink, to help cross that bridge to dreamland. I take the pills from work before I leave, not bothering to make a note on the inventory log. Since I'm the only one dispensing drugs these days, no one will know that it's missing. It's a lifesaver for many of my phobic patients, making them oblivious to what happens in the dental chair, and yet fairly alert by the time they go home, though someone else always has to drive them there. They're never allowed to drive home alone.

The little pills sedate me deeply but only for a short time—creating an amnesiac effect, the hours between eleven and two lost to thin air—so that when I awaken in the middle of the night to Clara's agonizing cries about another leg cramp, I easily come around to massage the pain away. And then, when the pain passes, I watch as she settles back in for sleep, my fingers tiptoeing down her back, slinking around her swollen midriff and along her inner thigh, in the hopes that she'll turn to me, drawing my attention away from the thoughts of delinquent payments and professional misconduct that fill my mind. 'I'm so tired,' she drones, slipping away from my advance, legs woven around the pillow instead of me. 'Another time, Nick,' she purrs into the pillowcase, and like that, she's asleep, breaths flattening, a restful snore.

And I'm left alone to think, swallowing two more pills so that I stop thinking.

* * *

One morning a few days later I receive a text from Clara while I'm at the office, hands buried deep inside a patient's mouth. 2 cm dilated, 40% effaced, she says, and only then do I remember an appointment with the obstetrician. I told her I'd try to make it, but I didn't make it.

You're almost there, I type into the keypad after my appointment is through. Soon I will be a dad. Again. Though I'm debilitated by a sudden pang of guilt, seeing the world into which my baby will arrive, one that is clearly not up to snuff.

I don't have much time left to get this right.

And then later in the afternoon my cell phone rings, and I answer the call, expecting Clara, but am surprised instead by the melodious voice on the other end of the line.

'Nick,' she says, 'it's me. Kat.' My heart rises and falls all at the same time. I had hoped I'd heard the last of Kat, and have the sudden sense of swimming upstream, of digging myself into a deeper and darker hole. It isn't about Kat, but right now I don't need any more complications in my life.

'Hi, Kat,' I say, and it's then that her voice catches, and she says, 'I need to see you, Nick,' and I know I'm in a jam here, having seen Kat two times now without ever telling Clara. I try to put it off, to tell her I'm swamped at work, that I don't have the time. But Kat, oddly reminiscent of eighteen-year-old Kat, begins to cry.

'Please,' she begs over the phone. 'Just for a few minutes,

Nick. There was something I should have said the other day,'
she says, her words hard to hear through the tears.

And so I say okay. I say it so that she'll stop crying. I tell
her that I can meet for one quick drink, but then I have to
split. We make plans to meet at a little bar down the block
after my last patient is through, and after I apply sealants
to a seven-year-old's teeth, I make haste and leave. I don't
want Clara sitting at home, wondering where I am. From
the parking lot, I send a text to Clara that I'll be home soon.
Be there in an hour, I say, and scurry in to join Kat, wishing and hoping that I could wake up from this nightmare
of mine, and that it would all be a dream. A bad dream, but
still a dream. I wish that I could forget somehow—the sad
state of my finances, the feud with Connor, the medical
malpractice suit. I wish that I could get away from it for a
while, that I could take a breather. Drown my sorrows in a
bottle of booze or find something else to take my mind off
of this shit storm that is now my life, if only for a while.

And that's when I spot Kat sitting all alone in a corner
booth, waiting for me.

She looks stunning as always, and for one split second
she takes my breath away, there in the dim bar lights, wearing this gauzy pale pink dress that, in combination with the
blond hair and fair skin, makes her look angelic. A tress of
hair falls across a single eye, and she leaves it there, a lock
of hair that is undeniably sexy and appealing.

My knees buckle for one quick moment, and just like that
we're eighteen years old again, wild and reckless, living
only for the moment, not caring what tomorrow may bring.

CLARA

At eight in the morning the doorbell rings, and of course I'm expecting flowers, the poor deliveryman waiting with his idle van parked outside, about to greet me in my pajamas for the forth time this week.

But it's not a delivery of flowers.

Standing outside on my front porch is Emily, dressed in black running shorts and a fleece half-zip hoodie that is certainly too thick for a day like today. On her feet is a pair of pricey running shoes, and she jogs in place, warming up for a run, her hair pulled back into a loose ponytail, strands escaping here and there and falling into her face. It's only 8:00 a.m., and already the heat and humidity rush in to greet me, fusing together with the inside air, which is already hot. Maisie bounds down the stairs at the sound of knocking—a hungry Harriet hot on her heels—her sweaty hair stuck to her forehead. 'Why don't you go turn on the TV?' I tell her, and she nods her head a sleepy okay, as Emily and I step outside and I gently pull the door closed. The sun is brilliant this morning, dazzlingly bright, and I curse it for having the audacity to show its face after everything it has done. It's the sun's fault that Nick is dead.

Or maybe not.

The first thing I see are the red marks singed into Emily's skin, reaching from the edges of the fleece hoodie, which is doing a piss-poor job of concealing them. That is its purpose after all, not to keep Emily warm on this hot day, but rather to hide the red marks, as she tugs indiscreetly at the zipper to make certain it's up as high as it will go, which, as luck would have it, isn't high enough. There are bruises there, small but visible to the naked eye, discolored skin from bleeding beneath the surface where her husband's fingers pressed on the windpipe, paring down the oxygen supply, making her gasp for air. She tugs again at the hoodie, trying hard to shroud the bruises, but she cannot undo what has been done. It's too late; I've already seen. The fleece is two inches too short, and we've had this conversation before, Emily and me, her wine-induced disclosures of how during intercourse Theo would throttle her from time to time until she felt a tingling sensation throughout her body and an overwhelming sense of vertigo, coupled with the all-consuming fear that she was about to die. And then he'd release her. It was meant for pleasure, hers and his, but only one of them thought it was fun.

She confessed this to me long ago, a year or more, one afternoon while Theo was traveling—Cincinnati that time—as she and I sat together in her backyard watching the kids play a game of chase. Teddy was *It*, and he sprinted quickly and clumsily after Maisie, who clung to a nearby tree that they'd deemed to be base. Emily and I were drinking that day, a day not so different than this one—hot and sunny—some kind of cooler she'd concocted with peach juice and pineapple juice, but also a long pour of Moscato wine. I'd confessed something trite about Nick—how he left his gym shoes lying around, how he mislaid used articles of clothing here and there, somehow or other unable to locate the hamper in our master bath—and Emily countered with this: how Theo had a fetish for asphyxiaphilia, a word she had to explain to me because I couldn't imagine such a thing would ever exist. It sounded primeval to me, violent and heathen, something ancient Vikings might do when they weren't pillaging others' homelands. It was the stuff of high school house parties when parents weren't home—reprobate teenagers without a clue about the fragility or the sanctity of life, getting blitzed and taking part in madcap sex games as if they were immortal—and not what middle-class suburbanites did while their children slept soundly in the room next door.

That day, I took in the coral-colored bruises left behind by Theo's aroused hands, and I could see in Emily's eyes that she was scared. After I'd left, I spent days trying to imagine it, Theo near killing her and then bringing her back from the dead. Again and again. For pleasure and fun, as well as something else, I assumed. Dominion and control.

'I thought Theo was traveling?' I say now, standing outside on the front stoop beside Emily. 'Massachusetts for an auto show.'

She nods her head and says, 'He is. He was. He came home last night, early. He wasn't due until tomorrow afternoon. It isn't what you think,' she says quickly then, one concurrent thought, as her hands move to her neck and she feigns excuses: she lost her balance, took a nosedive down the basement stairs, Theo tried to break the fall. She knows how I feel about this custom of theirs, this strange tradition. *You should leave him if he scares you*, I'd told Emily once, twice, three times, and every time she looked at me despairingly and said how she'd never be able to support herself without Theo around, how Theo would take Teddy from her. Emily had worked for years as a pediatric nurse, a position she left upon marrying Theo, and in the subsequent years her nursing license expired. She was no longer able to practice as an RN.

I told her once that if she didn't leave him I would call the police.

Emily called my bluff.

'I'm lucky I didn't break anything,' Emily says now, and I give in to this myth of hers about the fall and the basement stairs.

'Quite fortunate indeed,' I say, and then there is silence.

But Emily didn't come to speak about Theo. She came to see if I was okay, for the last time she saw me I was standing in the doorway to her home, sobbing while Maisie and Teddy watched on in their magician costumes. 'I hated for you to leave like that,' she says, and it comes rushing back to me then and there, in that one single moment, the fact that Nick is dead, that I'm a widow, that Maisie and Felix are one parent away from being orphaned.

Maisie's nightmares fill my mind, the image of a mysterious *bad man*, the suggestion that Nick didn't die but that he was killed, purposefully, intentionally and with malice. But now I've begun to think that Maisie is wrong, that Nick himself was the bad man: abusing drugs, cheating on me, stealing from my father. Contemplating suicide. As the police have said, Nick is to blame for his own death, though even they don't know the reasons why. In my mind I hear Detective Kaufman's words over and over again, goading and tormenting me, *You know what I think happened?* he asks. *I think your husband was driving too fast and took the turn too quickly... I'm so sorry for your loss*, he says, sitting across the room from me, laughing a heinous laugh, so that I'm no longer certain what's real and what's not real, what has happened and what has not happened. I haven't slept in nearly two weeks, this much I know, and I'm hampered by sadness, insomnia, an overwhelming sense of fatigue. My body hurts, physically, mentally, emotionally, and the only thing in the world I want to do is crawl between the sheets of my bed and die.

And suddenly I begin to cry.

'What is it, Clara?' asks Emily. 'What's wrong?' She sets her hands on my hands, and though part of me wants to pull away and sequester myself back inside my house all alone, I don't. I lean into Emily and confess to her what I know about the accident, how maybe—just maybe—it wasn't an accident at all. I tell her about Maisie's dreams, and the black car, the Chevrolet. I tell her about my meeting with Detective Kaufman, confessing to Emily that I never went to the grocery store in search of bananas the other day, but rather the police department. It's a relief saying the words aloud to someone who will listen, like purging oneself of too much food. It feels good, absolving, cleansing and purifying, so that maybe after this grand confession I'll be able to get into those skinny jeans again, and accept the reality that has become my life. I tell her about Connor, I tell her about Kat. Except I don't confess to Emily about the drugs, the suicide or the stealing because of the way I stand here, staring disdainfully at the bruises Theo has left behind on her skin with his hands.

Emily would find me to be sanctimonious. A hypocrite. Nick has turned me into a hypocrite.

What I'm expecting is for Emily to cascade with empathy, and tell me how awful this is, how she's so sorry this is happening to me. It isn't pity I'm looking for, not at all, but rather someone who will listen, someone greater than four years old to share this secret with me. Someone who will look at me with sensitivity and compassion rather than the way the detective looks at me, with my pie-in-the-sky idea that Nick was murdered. I want Emily to help catalog the clues for me. I need for her to tell me that I'm wrong about Kat, that there was nothing unchaste about her relationship with Nick, that they were merely friends as Emily and I are friends. I want her, Emily who stands before me with big, disbelieving eyes, her husband's hands impressed across her neckline, to assure me that Nick loves me the most. Not Kat.

But Emily only releases my hands. 'You know that can't be true,' she says to me defensively, as if she herself is the one who killed Nick. Her voice shakes as her eyes dither between her home and me, so that I think if I blink she might just flee. In the distance, her house is quiet, a Queen Anne Victorian with all the curtains pulled to. At 8:00 a.m., I imagine Teddy may still be asleep, cocooned in bed beneath his sheets as Theo prepares for work.

'Well, why not?' I ask, wondering why it can't possibly

be true. Of course it can be true. My voice shakes, too, but this time with irritation.

'The police decided,' she says, as if the police are some all-knowing deity, as if the police never ever make mistakes. 'They said it was an accident.'

'They don't know,' I assure her.

'So you'd believe a four-year-old over the police department?' she counters, and at this I want to rage, for many reasons but mostly because it's so unlike Emily to take a stance on much of anything, wishy-washy Emily who never wants to muddy the water, who always wants to appease people and make them happy. But this makes me very unhappy, the way she stands before me and questions my credibility and Maisie's credibility all in one fell swoop while lying to my face about the bruises on her neck.

I have a feeling in my bones. A hunch. Something isn't right here.

Emily is covering for herself or for someone else, and at once my mind races back to Maisie's mention of a bad man. Maybe Nick didn't commit suicide, but maybe he was indeed killed. The words ricochet back and forth in my mind—murder, suicide, murder, suicide—like a tennis ball alternating over a net, and each time I think I've got it figured out, someone swats it with a backhand stroke, making my thoughts, and with it, my sanity, bounce back.

Emily sees my anger; it's transparent. Her face softens, and she takes a step closer to me. 'Clara,' she says, her voice calm as she reaches a hand back out to mine. 'I just don't want you to mislead yourself,' she placates softly, and then the stages of grief are mentioned as Emily speculates out loud that I'm stuck somewhere in between one and two:

denial and anger. 'It's a defense mechanism,' she says. 'It's okay, Clara, it's perfectly normal,' she assures me, though I pull my hand back with haste—I don't want to be analyzed. 'I'm worried about you, that's all,' she tells me, her words attempting to sound apologetic, and maybe they are, but still, I don't want to be placated. I want to be listened to. 'Have you told Maisie yet?' she asks me. 'About Nick,' and she means have I told Maisie yet that her father is dead. I don't reply, not right away, because I know that my answer would only substantiate her theory that I'm in denial, spinning yarns to abate my loss.

It doesn't matter.

Across the street and two doors down, Emily's garage door opens and Theo appears behind the back fender of a fancy sports car, something red, though what it is specifically, I can hardly see. He has a work bag strapped over a shoulder, a pair of leather driving gloves in his hands. *For better grip*, Nick told me once when I asked why in the world the man always wore gloves to drive. But me, I was pretty sure Theo just wore the driving gloves because he had an ill-conceived notion they made him look cool. As a writer for some automobile magazine—*Car & Driver*, *Road & Track* or something of the sort—Theo schleps home a new car on loan nearly every week, so that he can draft a review. When they met, Emily has told me, he was working as a car salesman, a writer trying to hone his skills. He had a degree in journalism, and an uncanny ability to talk a buyer into near anything they didn't want or need, a used Caddy when they wanted a minivan, or a minivan when they wanted a sedan, doing it all sans charisma and charm but rather with scare tactics and coercion, quite in the same way he convinced Emily to marry him, I'm sure. He's handsome, of course, and has a smile that could move mountains, but my guess is that it wasn't the smile that made Emily say *I do*. Theo's own car is tired, a wannabe sports car, which he keeps hidden in the three-car garage while he drives whatever car he's been entrusted with that week.

The sun glints off the cherry-red door of the car as he opens it, his line of sight aimed at Emily and me. He hollers for Emily, slipping a newsboy cap on his head, and she runs. I can't help but stare as he reprimands her there at the end of the driveway, she in her wasted workout getup, and he in a hat and gloves. *A hat and gloves.* Is it possible, I wonder, and can it be? Was Theo the man in the hat and gloves watching Maisie and me through the window of our home? Was it Theo and not Connor? Have I gotten this all wrong?

Emily winces as Theo quietly degrades her—it's far too early in the morning to yell. If Nick were here he would want to intervene. Nick who hated Theo just as much as Theo hated Nick. But Nick is not here, and so I can only watch on, feet frozen to concrete, unmoving.

I watch then as Theo kisses Emily coldly on the cheek before climbing into the fancy red car and driving away, leaving her alone on the driveway. As he passes me, eyes glaring at me like a hungry hawk, I speculate on what kind of cars Theo has driven in the last few weeks.

What are the odds that one was a black Chevrolet?

NICK

BEFORE

As Kat waves at me from the corner booth of the bar, I'm transported back in time, to twelve years ago when Kat and I were a thing. There was a park back on the island that Kat and I always liked to go to, set on the northeast side of Bainbridge Island that overlooked both the Cascades and Puget Sound. It closed at dusk. When we went, always well past dusk, the place was empty. We had it to ourselves, and there, on the beach with its piles of driftwood and sand, we did things that I'd never done with anyone but Kat. Things that even now, twelve years later, made me blush.

I slide into the booth and feel my knee graze hers, and it's instinct that makes me pull back. What happened between Kat and me all those years ago is over and done with.

On the wooden block between us sits a photograph, which she slides toward me as the waitress draws near to take our order.

'Who's this?' I ask Kat before the waitress arrives, staring at a boy with shaggy blond hair, a school photograph with the standard blue backdrop, a boy who didn't smile when he was told to smile. In the image, his face falls flat, his lips tugging downward at the edges, his eyes sad. He has that whole teenage ennui to him already, a clear dissatisfaction with the world around him, though he's younger than a teenager, displaying evidence of adolescence.

'That's Gus,' she says, and her eyes rise from the photograph to meet mine. 'He's your son.'

And with that the waitress arrives, and I ask for a Death in the Afternoon—Hemingway's hybrid of absinthe and champagne—because it feels entirely fitting for this moment in my life.

'What do you mean he's my son?' I ask in a forced whisper, hissing the words across the table so that only Kat can hear. I look around the bar to be sure that I don't know anyone here, that a neighbor or Jan my hygienist isn't sitting at the booth behind me, eavesdropping on my conversation with Kat. 'He can't possibly be my son,' I say, but I'm no idiot. I know in my heart that he can be my son. Kat and I were stupid teenagers, the kind who believed nothing bad could ever happen to us. Sometimes we got caught up in the moment; we didn't always take precautions. We didn't play things safe.

'That night,' she tells me, as under the table her knee presses into mine, and I pull back. 'That night before you left for college. My parents had gone to the ballet,' she says, and she stops then. She need not say more. I nod my head slowly. I know. I remember. They'd gone to see *Coppélia*, and after they left I stopped by to say my goodbyes. It was Kat's parents' anniversary, and so they planned to stay in the city for the night, at the Four Seasons. It wasn't the kind of thing they ever did, but that night they were celebrating twenty-five years, and so it was something out of the ordinary, something special, and Kat and I decided to celebrate something special, too. Kat had a bottle of Goldschläger that she'd taken from her parents' liquor cabinet, knowing it was something they didn't drink and wouldn't miss. Kat and I had never been alone together for so long. We took the bottle to her bedroom, doing things slowly for once, feeling like we had all the time in the world. In the morning I awoke and boarded a plane bound for Chicago; three days later Steve took over my spot in Kat's life.

'How can you be sure he's mine?' I ask, and I hate the words even as they come out, this shirking of responsibility. It isn't me. But twelve years ago is a long time. If Kat had called me up twelve years ago and told me she was pregnant, things would have been different.

I don't wait for her reply. 'Why now?' I ask, feeling irate. 'Why are you telling me this now?'

In the corner of the room is a TV. On the screen are sportscasters, wagering their bets on tonight's NBA finals game. My eyes putter to it to see that the odds are not in the Warriors' favor. The favorite for tonight is the Cleveland Cavaliers, the team with the home advantage, and at this my hands turn clammy and my heart sinks. The room starts closing in on me as I think of the hole I've dug myself into, financial and otherwise. All these secrets I've kept from Clara that I can't now confess, after the fact. The fiscal state of the business, firing Connor, my reunions with Kat. Two of them now. Two reunions with Kat. Two times

I've seen a former girlfriend, the mother of my child—my *other* child—and I've never mentioned them to Clara.

The waitress meanders by, and I ask for another drink, Jack and Coke this time, which I down like it's ice water and I've just been on a five mile run. I've begun to sweat. There is a countdown on the corner of the TV screen, reminding me that it's eighteen minutes until tip-off. Eighteen minutes until I win or lose all that matters to me in the world.

'I don't know if I can stay with Steve,' Kat tells me, adducing the number of arguments they've had lately as the reason she can't stay. He's under a lot of pressure, she says, with a new job, and he's taking it out on her and Gus. 'His temper,' she adds on. 'He's always short of patience, with me, with Gus. He has a short fuse. And he's never home. He's always gone. Always working.' She reaches a hand across the table to touch mine, and I quickly disengage, pulling back and placing my hands in my lap so that she can't reach them. 'Gus needs a father figure in his life. A father. He's twelve years old. I don't know the first thing about raising twelve-year-old boys.'

I shake my head quickly. I can't do this. This can't be happening to me. 'I already have a family, Kat. A wife, and a child. Two children. I love them,' I say. 'I love my wife—I love Clara. You kept this from me all these years, and now you just expect me to slip into the role of father? I can't do that,' I insist, smacking my hands on the table too loudly, so that a man at the table behind us turns to see. 'Don't you get that? Don't you see? I have a family.'

It's all coming at me so quickly now, my life spiraling out of control. I place my head in my hands to make it stop, but it doesn't stop. In fact, the world keeps spinning until I feel like I could be sick.

'We were happy once, Nick,' she says. 'Don't you remember?' she asks, but instead of replying right away, I yank my wallet out of my pocket, find a twenty in it and lay it on the table.

'We were kids, Kat. We were stupid kids,' I say as I stand quickly, telling her we'll talk about this later, that I have to go. 'I'm in love with Clara now,' I stammer. 'Clara is my wife.'

I hurry away, mumbling over and over again to myself as I leave, *I already have a family. I already have a family.*

'Nick,' she calls after me as I push past people out of the bar and into the oppressive June air. I clamber into my car, the inside nearing a hundred degrees in the evening sun.

How will I tell this to Clara? How will I explain? Not only is Kat informing me of my paternity of a twelve-year-old boy, but she's telling me she wants me to be a father figure—an actual father—in Gus's life. What do I do? Give her money and tell her no? I have no money to give to her.

Clara will leave me. Clara will leave me if she knows.

I can't live without Clara. Clara, Maisie and my baby boy. These are the only things that matter. I turn on the car and start to drive. I spin out of the parking lot, needing to get away, the tires skidding as I press down hard on the accelerator, the engine moving faster than the tires can go, leaving black marks on the concrete. I pull out onto the highway and floor it home, the world coming at me quickly, trees blending together into a mass of green, buildings and houses becoming one. All I want is to be home.

Evening traffic is a mess as always, scores of cars lined

up at red lights going nowhere. I watch as other drivers check incoming texts on their phones. They listen to the radio, bebop music turned all the way up, the heavy bass making their cars shake. We sit frozen in a line, and my patience starts to thin. The train has no doubt stopped on the tracks again, making it impossible to get to the west end of town, where I need to go. Where Clara is, and where Maisie is. Home. I picture them sitting side by side on the sofa, waiting for me. *I'm coming*, I think, and then, when the traffic finally starts to clear, I gun the engine and press down hard on the gas. I swerve in and out of cars to get to Clara and Maisie.

The radio is tuned in to some AM sports station, and they're giving the play-by-play of the basketball game. It isn't going so well. It's all I can do not to scream.

I drive past the grocery store, the library, the post office, the elementary school and a public park. The highway turns residential, but I don't slow down my pace. The streets become pockmarked but wide, lined with dozens of full-grown trees. In the distance I spy my house. I keep my eyes on the house the entire time. I hold my breath and dig down deep onto the accelerator. The speedometer surpasses forty-five miles per hour, reaches for fifty. I close in on my house. The finish line.

What I fail to see is little Teddy from across the street, scampering out from behind a tree. Two steps ahead of him bounces a red rubber playground ball, which Teddy trails blindly into the middle of the street. It happens so fast. I don't have time to react.

First there's nothing, and then there's a boy, a four-foot, forty-pound figure standing in the middle of the street with eyes terrified, his mouth formed into a silent scream. Staring at me.

If I hadn't had two drinks at the bar my response time might have been quicker; if I weren't under so much stress I wouldn't have been driving so fast. But as it is, I'm slow, my movements asthenic, and it takes time to react. Time to raise my foot off the accelerator and move it to the brake. To press down hard on the brake pedal. To divert the steering wheel from its course. The car slips past Teddy by mere inches, and as it does, I hear the boy finally scream.

I come to a stop on the lawn of a neighboring home, missing their mailbox by a hair. My hands are shaking, my legs like sludge as I thrust the gearshift into Park and open the car door, tumbling out onto the street below, my feet barely making contact with the road. 'Teddy,' I say, lurching around the side of the car to find the boy lying on the concrete in the fetal position, embracing the ball. For a moment I think he's hurt, maybe even dead. I've hit him, and I start running to his side, saying his name over and over and over again, 'Teddy, Teddy, Teddy,' and I fall to my knees to shake him awake, to bring him back to life. I'm about to employ my resuscitation skills, but then I notice that Teddy is breathing, and there is no blood. He's okay, he's okay, I tell myself, and I feel a smile cross my lips, a relieved, thankful smile. Thank God he's okay.

'Get your fucking hands off my son,' says a voice, and my head rises sharply to see Theo marching into the middle of the street toward me, arms already swinging. His fist connects with the side of my head, and before I can react the world spins. I stagger, and Theo comes at me again, connecting this time with my gut so that I bowl over in excruciating pain, clutching my stomach. I'm apologizing profusely, spouting a surfeit of confessions and excuses. 'I'm sorry,' I say and, 'I didn't see him,' and then I place the blame on Teddy and claim, 'He came out of nowhere.'

'I saw you,' barks Theo as he lifts Teddy from the concrete. 'You were driving too fucking fast, and you know it,' he says, and then he steps closer to me, and I prepare for another beating, in the mouth this time or maybe the nose, as his fist forms and he leans in close to me. By now Theo's wife, Emily, has stepped from their house, and Teddy leaves his father's arms to run to his mother, who collects him in a maternal embrace. My car, ten feet away, still idles, keys in the ignition, engine running. My own house is quiet; Clara hasn't seen a thing.

'If I ever see you speeding again,' he says, face pressed so closely to mine that I can see the pores of his skin, the way he salivates in anger. His eyes are more than just angry, but irrational and deranged, the very same way I'd be if someone ever messed with my kid. Emily calls to him, 'Theo, enough,' but like a belligerent dog disobeying its owner, Theo doesn't come.

'If I ever see you speeding again on this street or anywhere ever again,' he says, stepping somehow even closer now so that his spittle flies into my eye, 'so long as you shall live,' as Emily encroaches on the conversation now, tugging desperately on Theo's arm to try to bring him inside, 'I will kill you. I will fucking kill you, Solberg,' he says, and Emily's and my eyes grow wide, fully dilated, at exactly the same time.

I have no doubt in the world that he means it.

CLARA

My father calls. It's midafternoon.

'Daddy?' begs Maisie at the sound of the phone ringing, but I say no, it isn't Daddy.

'Boppy,' I say, and Maisie smiles gaily.

'Your mother has been asking for you,' my father says, 'again,' though we both know this isn't true. She isn't asking for me so much as she's asking for Maisie, for the four-year-old version she believes is still me. We feed into her delusion sometimes, letting her believe that Maisie is me because it's far easier than telling her the truth.

My mother is not that old, and yet it's hard to remember sometimes when her mind has stopped working and her body is quickly following suit. No one knows for certain how much time she has left on the ever-dwindling hourglass of her life. Some doctors say five years, others say seven, though one way or another she's simply biding time as we all are, biding time until we die.

'You'll come see your mother?' my father asks, and I say that I will.

* * *

I open the front door to step outside with Felix in my arms and Maisie on my heels, and, as luck would have it, a black sedan sweeps down the street, a chauffeured car that stops three houses away at the home of Jake and Amy Lawrence, a childless couple in their thirties. They're business moguls, and one or the other of them always seems to be on the road. Amy leaves their house towing a rolling suitcase in a pair of sling-back heels. Today it's her turn to go.

But none of that matters. What matters is that Maisie sees the blackness of the car as it drives slowly past, tortoise-like and deliberate, the driver's eyes converging with hers, and now her eyes are locked on that car as it hovers down the street waiting for Amy, Maisie's knees trembling, her eyes filling with tears. She says nothing, and yet her body language says it all, the distress and the agitation as she turns on her heels and begins to run. She's fast, much faster than me, as I lug Felix in my arms and attempt to pursue her throughout the home. I call to her over and over again, Felix frightened by my screaming, and so he, too, begins to scream.

I find Maisie under the bed, a spare queen-size bed in a guest room where no one goes. 'Maisie,' I say to her, dropping down to my hands and knees to try to meet her eyes, 'please, come out,' but she buries her face into the carpet and cries. 'Boppy is expecting us,' I say. 'Please, Maisie. Please. Do it for Boppy.'

What I don't do is ask her why she's scared; I know. I don't tell her that everything is going to be okay, because I'm not sure that it is. I raise my voice once and demand that she come out, and when she doesn't, I beg. I offer treats;

I issue threats. And when all that fails I lie on the floor at the edge of the bed, and reach a hand out to hers and pull, and my Maisie cries out this time, not in fear but in pain. That hurt. She bawls, saying how it hurt, how Mommy hurt her, and I tell her that I'm sorry, that Mommy is so sorry.

But it doesn't matter; Maisie is still rooted firmly under the bed.

I want to tell her that she's wrong about the car, that there was no bad man in a black car trailing her and Nick. Nick was the bad man, I believe, but as always I'm confused. Did Nick end his life, or did someone do it for him? I have to know, feeling that the uncertainty is slowly driving me mad.

Closure is what I need. I need closure.

More than thirty minutes later my father calls again, wondering where I am. I slip from the room to retrieve my cell and answer the call. 'I thought you'd be here by now,' he tells me, and this time I confess that Maisie has cloistered herself beneath the bed and won't come out. My voice is panicked as I say it, tired, frustrated, panting, with Felix serving as background noise, quietly lamenting. She is a smart girl, my Maisie, hiding under the bed because she knows I've mastered removing the hinge pins from the doors.

Nick would know what to do. Nick would slide his body under the metal bed frame and join Maisie beneath the bed, or he would lift up the mattress and box spring with a single hand, and the situation would resolve with laughter before they'd make a fort out of the blankets and sheets and pillows that were now cluttered around the guest bedroom.

But not me. I can only beg.

'Oh, Clarabelle,' my father says empathetically, and it's decided that my father and I will swap places. He will come to cajole Maisie out from under the bed while I stare into the addled eyes of a woman I once knew.

* * *

I come into my parents' home to find my mother shored up on an armchair, Izzy beside her, painting my mother's fingernails a cherry red. Izzy gazes at me with her heavy-lidded eyes and a compassionate smile. She has a big bust and fullness around the middle, but the legs that emerge from beneath a denim skirt are disproportionately slim, like the legs of a giraffe.

My mother was born Louisa Berne, the only child of Irish parents who imparted to Maisie and me our green eyes and red hair, and a face full of freckles. She married my father over thirty years ago, he a former business exec and she a happy homemaker, the type of woman who could do most anything on an hour or two of sleep and a good cup of tea. Her dementia developed slowly at first, a few forgetful moments that spiraled into something more over the coming years.

Izzy smiles at me and says, 'Look how lovely our Louisa is,' while my mother watches on, staring at me with a confused and yet hopeful look in her eye because she doesn't know me from Eve, and yet she's waiting for a response, for me to also say that she's lovely.

'Beautiful,' I say, though she's not. This woman is not my mother.

My mother is self-sufficient and adept; she doesn't need some woman to paint her fingernails or to introduce me when I step inside.

'It's Clara, Louisa,' Izzy prompts. 'Clara's come to see you. You remember Clara,' she adds while my mother de-

cides point-blank, exhaling heavily like Izzy and I are both
a bunch of idiots, that I am not Clara.

'This is not Clara,' my mother insists, and Izzy tells her,
'Well, sure it is. This is Clara.' I stand pressed to a wall and
awkwardly smile, an outcast in the home. My mother has no
memories of me, not the twenty-eight-year-old me at least.

There are bruises on my mother's arms, bluish bruises
on the pale skin that lines her tender forearm, and as my
eyes move to them in question, Izzy explains, 'She's been
clumsy lately. Not so good on her feet anymore,' which of
course is an effect of the dementia. My heart sinks. This is
something the neurologist has been forewarning us about
for a long time now, how my mother would need more and
more help performing those everyday tasks she used to
do on her own with ease, how her mobility would become
stunted, how in time she might be bed-bound.

'She fell?' I ask, and Izzy nods her head.

'The doctor said it's a problem with her depth perception,'
Izzy tells me, though I wonder why I have to hear this from
Izzy and not my father. Why didn't my father tell me? Like
Nick, has he been keeping things from me, too? 'She runs
into doorways, mistakes shadows on the floor for things,
tripping over her own two feet.'

The expression on Izzy's face is grim, and I wonder how
in the world she's able to deal with this, day in and day out.
I couldn't do it. And yet there's a stoicism about her, the
way Izzy feeds and clothes and cleans my mother without
complaint, all the while being called names like *idiot* and
imbecile, which are my mother's preferred epithets these
days. I think of a young Izzy, caring first for her ailing father and then her mother, and losing both in the end. I can't

imagine how hard that must have been. I can't bear to think what will happen when my mother and father are one day gone. I smile at Izzy and say, 'We're lucky to have you,' knowing I don't say it as often as I should.

'It's me, Mom,' I say to my mother, forcing a smile on my face. 'Clara.' But to my mother I'm an outsider, a pariah, a leper, and the expression on her face is one of cynicism and doubt. I am not Clara. I am persona non grata. I don't exist.

I talk to my mother anyway. I tell her about Felix, the way he sleeps with his mouth open wide—a robin fledgling begging for food; the gentle whistle of air that flutes through his nose as he dreams. He hasn't smiled yet, nothing intentional at least, but rather thanks to an unconscious reflex or the passage of gas, but when he does I'm certain it will be Maisie's big, bright grin he smiles at first. 'You remember Maisie?' I ask my mother, but she doesn't reply, eyes lost on the curtain rod above my own head, and in time I give up.

'She's usually like this,' Izzy says as a means of reassurance, and yet it bothers me that Izzy knows my mother more than me. 'She doesn't say much.'

'I know,' I say. These days my mother doesn't even remember that she has dementia. This is a blessing, I suppose, the perquisite of being in the advanced stages of a dreadful disease. The memory lapse is only part of it. There's also her irascible nature, that quick-tempered tendency of hers to become mad and curse and cry, my mother who was once nonconfrontational to a fault. Now she sits propped up in a chair unquestioningly—her fifty-five years taking on the semblance of someone who is seventy-five—letting a woman comb through her hair while I sit on the edge of a sofa and behold the scene: the way that Izzy knows my mother's mannerisms and oddities by heart, how she can predict my mother's anomalous habits, like asking for tea and then refusing to drink it, reading the newspaper upside down. Izzy seems to know before my mother when she will stand up and how she will aimlessly pace, the irrational path she will take around the room, Izzy two steps ahead of her all the time, picking up fallen throw pillows so that my mother will not trip.

It's then that, to my horror, my mother finally returns to her seat and peers toward Izzy reverently, saying to her, 'Can you be a good little girl and get Mommy her slippers, Clara, dear? My feet are cold.'

And Izzy looks at my mother and at her feet, already clad in a pair of nonslip, suede slipper clogs, with the most luxurious-looking fur lining on the inside, and says, 'You already have your slippers, dear,' as she reaches for her necklace with its *Izzy* charm, her hand coming up empty. The necklace is there, but there is no charm. Like so many other things missing around the home, the charm is gone.

But Izzy doesn't miss a beat. Instead, she says, 'It's Izzy,' to my mother, while stooping down to stare her in the eye. 'Remember, Louisa? Izzy. Clara's over there,' she says, motioning to me.

But whether or not my mother remembers is impossible to know.

'Don't take it personally,' Izzy says to me then, smiling this uplifting sort of smile that's meant to improve my mood, though of course I already have. I've taken it very personally, knowing how it must feel for my father when my mother looks at him, calling for help, saying there's a stranger in her home, a burglar, meaning my father. How alone he must feel. Heartbroken and alone. 'Most of the time she doesn't know me, either,' Izzy says, and then she excuses herself to brew hot water for tea, my mother's favorite elixir. She pauses once in the doorway and says to me, 'She doesn't even know me now. She thinks I'm you.' I know she means well, that this is supposed to make me feel better, and yet it's a sorry consolation prize. I watch as she goes, seeing a weightlessness about her, though she's not small by any means. And yet she's airy, unhampered by the mishaps in her life—the untimely death of her own parents, the responsibility of caring for a younger sibling—while I'm weighted down by mine, feeling buried alive.

My mother is watching me. I know I shouldn't cry, but I can't help myself. Big, fat tears fall from my eyes while her eyebrows furrow and she rises from her chair. My first instinct is to call for Izzy, worried that my mother will do something unexpected or that she will trip over her own feet and fall. But that's not what happens at all.

She takes a series of small steps toward me, and sits down on the sofa by my side. She takes my hand into hers, her movements steady and sure. She knows what she's doing. Her pale green eyes fall on mine, and for this moment in time she knows who I am. I can see it in her eyes. A second hand skims the surface of my hair as she asks of me, her words lucid and clear, 'What is it, Clara? What's bothering you?' pulling me into her gentle embrace. Her arms feel light on mine, weak and anemic, and yet in them I feel undeniably safe. Like my father, she's getting too thin, her body lost in the fabric of a soft sweat suit.

'Mom?' I ask, choking on the word, crying. I wipe my eyes on the sleeve of a shirt, and beg, 'You know me? You know who I am?' Behind us, the window is open, a gentle breeze blowing in, a zephyr passing through the curtains so that they billow into the room. Motes of dust hover in a narrow beam of sunlight like glitter, suspended in the air above our heads.

She chuckles, her eyes filled with unassailable recognition. She *knows* me, and whether it's the four-year-old me or a twenty-eight-year-old me, I don't know and I don't care. She knows me. That's all that matters.

'Of course I do, you silly goose. I wouldn't ever forget you. You're my Clara,' she says, and then she asks, 'What's making you so sad, Clara, dear?' But I can't bring myself to tell her, knowing how this moment is as reliable as tabloid magazines, and that chances are good her memories of me will disappear just as quickly as they appeared. And so I revel in it instead. I take pleasure in it, my mother's hand on mine, her arm draped around my back, her eyes staring with cognizance rather than confusion.

'Nothing, Mom,' I tell her. 'These are happy tears,' I say. 'I'm happy,' though I'm not really happy, but rather a dangerous cocktail of happy, sad and scared.

Izzy appears in the doorway with tea in hand, but upon seeing my mother and me, she retreats, not wanting to steal this moment from my life.

NICK

BEFORE

I'm falling apart.

I can't sleep.

In the morning I stumble down the stairs, disoriented and unsteady on my feet. My head aches. I'm delirious from lack of sleep, thinking already how I need to take something stronger than Halcion to get me through the night, how if I don't sleep soon I'll lose it completely.

Clara is at the breakfast nook when I come down, talking into the phone. It's her father, I can tell from the worry lines on her face, as she drops her head into her hand and frowns.

'What is it?' I ask when she ends the call and sets the phone on the table, but my headache is so immense I can hardly see straight, much less think straight. The early-morning sun blazes through the window like little scalpels stabbing me in the eyes. I trip over my own two feet.

'My father,' she says, as if this is something I didn't already know. 'He's misplaced a check from the tenants,' she tells me. 'Their rent payment. He endorsed it and left it out to deposit, but now it's gone.'

For years Tom has hung on to Clara's childhood home, an old farmhouse that was fully renovated and rented out for an additional income for Tom and Louisa. It isn't too far away from our own home, in an unincorporated part of town, one of the few areas left in the community that hasn't yet been overrun by new construction and big-box stores. From the front porch of the farmhouse, you can see cornfields still, horses, the occasional John Deere driving down the middle of the road. But it became too much work for a man of Tom's age and Louisa's health. At Clara's suggestion, Tom made the tough decision to lease it out and move to the retirement community where they now live, though Tom hates it, the kind of community with Bingo night and bunco games. Newlyweds rent the farmhouse now, a couple by the name of Kyle and Dawn, who I met once when I helped Tom with some electrical issues in the home. Tom used to handle the upkeep all on his own, but these days and at his age, there's not much he can still do.

'Your mother?' I ask because this isn't the first time we've heard of Louisa losing things. Louisa loses many, many things, and half of them they find later, hidden in strange places, and the other half they don't find at all. My stomach churns, and I try to remember what I had last night to eat, or whether it's all anxiety and nerves. I feel for Tom, knowing what it feels like to lose money. I've been losing my fair share of things, too.

'Seems so,' Clara says, and then she tells me how she plans to go there today, to comb through the house and see if she can find the check. It's the least that she can do, she says, shaking her head, saying, 'I just feel bad for them. What if they're having money trouble, Nick?' she asks. 'My father would never tell me. He's too proud to ask for help,' she says.

'You want me to talk to him?' I ask, but she shakes her head and says no. We all know how Tom feels about me. The last thing any of us needs is me checking up on Tom's finances. But I ask anyway in the hopes that Clara won't think she's in this alone.

And then, rising from the breakfast nook, Clara changes the subject and tells me how she's gone ahead and hired someone to paint the baby's room. They're coming today. By the time I arrive home, the baby's room will be gray. This is supposed to make me happy, but instead all the air gets sucked from the room and I snap.

'I told you I'd take care of it,' I say to her, more angrily than I wish I had, and she comes back with, 'The baby is coming soon, Nick. We can't wait anymore.'

The baby is coming soon. I can see it in Clara, in the way Baby Doe has moved inside her, dropping down into her pelvic area so that she's in noticeably more pain. She waddles when she walks, the baby's head shoved somewhere into her crotch. The heaviness of the baby is tangible, even to me. I can feel him vicariously through Clara's trudging movements.

'Do you have any idea how much professional painters cost?' I say, my voice elevating as I move toward the coffee maker and reach instinctively for the fully caffeinated coffee grounds.

'We have money,' she asserts. 'It's not like we don't have money.' And then, 'I thought we weren't drinking caffeine,' she says, standing before me in her nightgown, her belly as fully extended as it can possibly get. She looks tired, hand pressed to the small of her back as if she can carry this baby weight no longer. Across the taut nightgown I spy ripples of movement, our baby reaching his hands and toes to get out, alien-like. He's ready. I look down at the bag of coffee grounds in my hand. Dark roast, it says; not the decaf. 'Have you been drinking caffeine all this time?' she asks, and I almost laugh at the inanity of it, how I have an illegitimate son, my practice is in shambles, I'm being sued and I almost plowed down a neighborhood kid, but what Clara is concerned about is my caffeine intake. But I haven't even been drinking caffeine. Of all the things I've done wrong, this is the one thing I've done right. I stayed true to our vow. I didn't drink caffeine.

And then I do laugh, this odd, manic laugh that doesn't sound like me, tossing the coffee to the floor so that the bag cracks open and grounds spill out everywhere. 'What has gotten into you?' Clara asks, her face shrouded in worry and disgust.

'Into me?' I demand. 'Into me? What has gotten into *you*?' I ask, using some sort of defensive tactic of spinning the conversation in my favor. 'I told you I was going to paint the bedroom. Why in the hell would you hire someone else to do what I can clearly do?' I grab a dustpan and broom from the pantry wall. I drop down onto all fours to clean the mess.

'Stop being an asshole, Nick,' Clara growls, holding Harriet back as she tries to get at the coffee grounds, to lick them up off the floor as she licks everything up off the floor.

'Oh, I'm being an asshole?' I ask. 'I'm the one being an asshole?'

'Yes, Nick. You're being an asshole,' Clara asserts before she gathers Harriet and leaves the room.

I try to follow her, to reach for her, but instead feel the cotton of her nightgown slip through my hands as she disappears.

CLAЯA

'What's going on?' begs my father hours later as I step into the kitchen to see him standing before the stove, pouring a box of uncooked pasta into boiling water. I notice how loosely his pants fit, hanging on to near nothingness, merely skin and bones. He's becoming too thin. His eyes look tired, his skin aging quickly, getting covered in liver spots and wrinkles. His hair thins with each visit, the fatigue weighing heavily on him. My mother no longer sleeps, which means my father no longer sleeps, and they're both aging far more quickly than I'd like them to. I've told him before, *Your health is important, too*, but my father rejoined with, *This is what people do when they love each other. Self-sacrifice*, he said, telling me how there was nothing for my mother he wouldn't do.

In the next room, Maisie watches TV. I'm not sure how, but somehow or other she's no longer stashed under the guest bed. Now she's out, her face radiated by synthetic light, and on her lips is a smile—not for me, but for the characters on TV. She clings to her scruffy teddy bear, one of its decrepit ears stuffed inside her mouth, wet with saliva. She doesn't see me as I pass by. I pat her head; I say hello. On the floor, spread across a hand-knit blanket, Felix is asleep.

'What do you mean?' I ask my father now, standing in the kitchen, though I know exactly what he means. When my father arrived to take my place, taking on the task of wheedling Maisie out from under the guest bed, I didn't tell him why she was there or what had triggered her meltdown. I simply said that she was under the bed and that she wouldn't come out, and he arrived under the pretense that Maisie was being insubordinate rather than what she really was: scared.

'Are you in some kind of trouble that I don't know about?' he asks as he sets the empty pasta box down on the countertop and looks me in the eye before I quickly avert my gaze. I can't meet my father's eye. Not now. 'You can tell me, Clarabelle,' he says. 'You can tell me anything,' and I wonder instantly what Maisie has said to my father to make him believe that I'm in trouble, that we're in trouble. I reach into the cupboards and begin pulling bowls and plates from the inside, vessels for the pasta my father is cooking us for dinner. The cupboard is a refurbished thing, one that came to us from Nick's grandparents. It was old when it arrived, but we stripped and sanded it and painted it brand-new. A second chance, a new lease on life.

'I'm not in trouble,' I mutter, but in truth I wonder if I am.

My father is staring at me, waiting for an answer, and I discover that my first response didn't suffice. He needs more than a halfhearted *no*. In his hand is a wooden spoon, and he stirs the pasta sluggishly. 'What did Maisie tell you?' I ask, and he confesses that Maisie didn't tell him much, but her quiet twaddle did, as she sniveled beneath that bed, crying about a *bad man*, calling again and again for Nick. The only way she came out from under the bed was with the promise of popcorn and *SpongeBob*, and so Maisie crawled out, and my father and Maisie and Felix curled together on the living room chair and watched TV. She didn't say a word more, and my father didn't ask, certain that broaching the topic would only send her straight under the bed again.

'What bad man?' he asks me point-blank, and I force a smile and tell him there is no bad man. It's only make-believe.

'You still haven't told her about Nick?' he asks, and I shake my head and say no. 'Oh, Clarabelle,' he says. 'Why?'

I want to tell my father. I want to tell him all of it, about Maisie's nightmares, and Detective Kaufman, and the implication that maybe Nick was being trailed, that he was killed, that his death was actually a murder. I want to tell him about Melinda Grey and Kat; I want to tell him about Connor. I want to tell my father all of this. To curl into a ball on his lap like I did when I was a child and confess to him that I'm sad and scared and confused. But I think of Emily backing away from my admission and the disbelieving gleam in her eye and know I can't do it. I don't know what it would do to me if my father repudiated me, too.

'You can tell me anything,' he says again, trying hard to convince me, but I shrug my shoulders and say that there's nothing to tell.

'You know Maisie,' I say. 'Such a flair for the dramatic,'

and I force a smile so that maybe, just maybe, my father will believe.

I change the subject. 'She remembered me,' I tell my father, and he asks, 'Your mother?'

I nod wistfully, knowing it may never happen again. 'She knew that I was Clara. She was sensible, clearheaded. She knew who I was,' and he says that he's happy I got the chance to experience this moment with my mother. These days, he says, they're few and far between.

'I'm sure it meant the world to her that you came,' he says, but as the lines of his forehead start to crease, I ask him what's wrong. Something is bothering him. 'These moments of lucidity,' he tells me, 'they come and they go. One minute she knows me, the next she doesn't. One minute Izzy is Izzy, and the next she's not. Three times now your mother has tried to call the police on me because she thought I was a robber.

'She got out again last night, Clara,' he says sadly. 'I'd hid the car keys in a kitchen drawer, but she managed to find it there and start the car. In the middle of the night. She put it in Reverse, the sound of the engine revving the only thing that caught my attention. I got to her just before she pulled out of the drive. She could have really hurt herself, or someone else. And then there's the credit card,' he says, voice trailing off.

'What credit card?' I ask, and he tells me how my mother opened a credit card all on her own, in her name. A Citi MasterCard. He never would have known about it until a notice of data breach arrived in the mail, made out to Louisa Friel. The credit card company was warning my mother that her account might have been compromised, and that she should closely monitor the statements for suspicious charges. Except that my mother wasn't meant to have an account of her own. Just like stealing the car keys and trimming Maisie's hair, it was something she did because she didn't know any better.

'How did she possibly…?' I ask, voice trailing off because I know that with my mother the possibilities are endless. There's no telling what she might do.

'A commercial on TV,' my father says. 'A telemarketer, an ad in a magazine.' He shrugs. 'I don't know.' And I think then of all the personal information she'd need to relinquish to apply for a credit card, and begin to worry. I wonder what, if anything, she's purchased with her new card, and what this has done to my parents' credit.

'Oh, Daddy,' I say, setting my hand on his. 'I'm so sorry, Daddy,' knowing how hard it is for him to confess these things to me when I have so many other things on my mind.

'I don't want to burden you with this,' he says, but I tell him he's not a burden, he's never a burden.

'Let me help you,' I beg, but he assures me as he always does that he and my mother are fine, telling me he was looking into additional resources for my mother and came across some extra security devices, like alarms and tethers so he can better monitor her movement at night. 'Is that necessary?' I ask, cringing at the suggestion of my mother in tethers, but he rubs at his forehead and says, 'These days it seems to be.'

* * *

Before he leaves, my father mentions that he'd like to sell my mother's car. It's old, he says, and without it lying around, there's less chance of my mother taking it for a ride.

'We should have gotten rid of it years ago,' he says, tacking on, 'We can use the money,' meaning me more than him; he wants to sell my mother's car and give me the money.

'Oh, Daddy,' I say, 'I can't possibly...' but he holds up a hand in refusal and assures me I can. But he'll need my help posting the car online; he asks if he can send me photos. I'm far from a technological savant, but I know my way around the internet far better than he, and he promises to email them to me just as soon as he gets home. 'How much?' I ask.

'Five thousand,' he says. 'It's not much,' he adds, 'but it's something, at least until Nick's life insurance pays out,' and at that I inhale sharply, wanting to confess to my father about the life insurance and how it's been canceled, how it won't ever pay out. But I don't. I bite my tongue and say nothing, knowing what my father would say if he knew about Nick purchasing drugs from Melinda Grey, about him sleeping with Kat, about the canceled life insurance policy, about Nick's duplicitous life. *That man will only bring you down*, he'd told me when I displayed my hand proudly before him nearly half a dozen years ago, one that flaunted a simple engagement ring, a timeless solitaire marquise diamond on fourteen karats of white gold. *Don't do this, Clarabelle. Don't marry him. There are more fish in the sea*, he had said, but I told him I didn't want any more fish. I only wanted Nick.

My father hugs me and thanks me for doing him this favor, though we both know it's him who is doing me a favor. In my arms, he feels rangy, as thin as a rake. My father used to be a marathoner, thin but robust. He could run for nearly forever without breaking a sweat. Now he's just thin, and I want to ask if he's eating okay, if he's sleeping okay, if he's paying enough attention to his own health or only to my mother and me. There are bags beneath his eyes, big, burlap potato sacks, and I wonder when is the last time he's been to the doctor. I touch those few strands of hair upon his head, a maternal gesture. 'It's the least that I can do,' I say, 'for all you've done for me,' and again we hug.

'I could do more,' he says, but I say no, he's done enough, and with that he turns and leaves. Before he's halfway to his own car parked at the end of the drive, he tells me that his HVAC guy will be here tomorrow at three, his treat, and it's then that I notice the sleeves of his button-down shirt thrust clear to his elbows, the dewdrops of sweat that bind to his skin thanks to our un-air-conditioned home. The heat is suddenly stifling, and I find that it's difficult to breathe. I never told my father that we were in financial crisis, and still he knows. He knows everything.

'I'd come,' he says, 'to keep you company while they're here. But I can't this time, Clarabelle. Your mother also has an appointment at three. The neurologist,' he says, and I shake my head and tell him it's no bother. I'm a big girl. I can handle this all by myself.

NICK

BEFORE

I get the idea at work as I'm sorting through the patient files for an afternoon appointment, one that my hygienist forgot to pull. I go into the stacks searching for the file for one William Grayson, and end up leaving a few seconds later with the file for Melinda Grey clutched in my hands, finding the two files perched side by side on the metal shelves in alphabetical order. In criminal law, it's all about intent—*mens rea*, or in English: guilty mind. It's something I don't have. I have no intent to harm Melinda Grey. I didn't even intend to pull her file from the stacks.

And yet here it is in my hand.

I tell Nancy to reschedule my appointment with William Grayson. I tell her I'm feeling sick.

* * *

The home is small and dated, a single-story house on the south side of town. It has big, squarish windows in the front, flanked with shutters, and a low roofline that hangs too low for my taste. The landscaping is mature but sad, the periphery of the home beleaguered by boxwood hedging. In the driveway rests a dark sedan, black or maybe blue, a forgotten sunroof left open, the interior leather absorbing the oppressive heat of the day.

I stop the car just shy of the house and put it in Park, sitting there in the front seat, trying hard to catch my breath.

As I step slowly from the car and make my way up the asphalt driveway, I have every intention of just trying to talk some sense into her, to try to get her to understand my position. To apologize, as all websites said was paramount to avoiding a malpractice suit. Maybe I should have just apologized in the first place. I never had the chance to explain.

And so that's my intention for coming to see Melinda Grey: to explain.

Malice aforethought, in the legal world, is a conscious intent to cause somebody harm, and that's not what I have. The thought never even crosses my mind, not until the door opens, and there she stands, Melinda Grey, glaring through the two-inch gap back at me, the weight of her body pressed behind the door in case I try to force my way in.

And then suddenly the only thing on my mind is causing this woman bodily harm, this woman who's trying to spoil my life.

'Go away,' she snaps through the doorway. 'Go away or I'll scream,' and she's saying it as if I've already hurt her, as if I'm trying to push that door open against the weight of her, though I'm not. I stand a good twelve inches away from the door frame, my hands in the pockets of my khaki pants.

'I just want to talk to you,' I say. 'See if there's any way I can make this up to you, without the need for lawyers and insurance companies and all that. Maybe we can work this out our own way,' I tell her, holding my hands up in deference and saying, 'I swear.'

But Ms. Grey will not talk to me. The two-inch gap becomes one, and though I use every ounce of self-control I can possibly manage, the toe of my loafer still collides with the front door so that it can't close. She tries to push, but still it won't close, and before I know what's happening, my hands are on the door, too, forcing it open, so that I see her fully, my six-foot frame overlooking her by a good foot.

'You seem like a reasonable person,' I say to her, 'a good person,' but she's backing away from me, and I find myself moving closer. There's a cat in the backdrop, a Siamese who sits perched on the top of a TV stand, watching me. A witness. 'I have more to lose than you can imagine,' I explain, telling her about my wife, my children, my practice. If I explain, then maybe she'll understand. Maybe she'll drop the whole suit.

But what I'm not thinking about is how much Melinda has to gain from the settlement: hundreds of thousands of dollars.

'You tried to kill me,' she says, and like that her benign eyes turn cancerous before my eyes. I see her for what she is: a liar and a con.

'You didn't return for your follow-up appointment,' I say. 'You were supposed to watch for signs of infection and call if you had any concerns. Any concerns, at all, I told you. I gave you my cell phone number,' I insist. 'I told you to call anytime. You didn't call. You didn't call.'

A smile dances on the edges of her lips as she replies,

'They told me at the hospital that I could have died. If that infection had spread to my brain, I would have died.'

And at that I feel something in me snap. It was avoidable, it was all so avoidable had she followed my explicit directions. But she didn't follow my directions, and it was intentional, a stroke of luck when she spied that infection starting to form inside her mouth and decided to do nothing about it.

'You bitch,' I whisper. 'You stupid bitch.' And I'm moving forward, closing in on her quickly as she backs away and into the open front door. There's nowhere for her to go. Her back is quite literally to a wall, and it's all I can do not to press my hand to her trachea and stop the airflow. I imagine her turning blue before my eyes, arms and legs flailing for air, her eyes gaping wide with fear. I all but feel the tautness of her skin beneath my hand, all those vital arteries of her neckline, the carotid artery and the jugular vein, fully distended as she sucks in to breathe ineffectively against the weight of my hand.

And that's when the cell phone in my pocket begins to ring.

* * *

Clara is laid out in the hospital bed when I arrive, wearing a light blue gown and socks. It's a large room, a private room, and the doctor, Clara's obstetrician, is attending to her as I trot in, out of breath.

'I'm not too late,' I beg, huffing the words out. 'Please, tell me I'm not too late.'

'Eight centimeters,' the doctor says, pulling a hand from between Clara's legs and draping a paper-thin blanket over them. 'You're not too late,' she assures me. 'Shouldn't be much longer now,' as she pats Clara's knees and smiles at me. 'You ready for this?' she asks, and I tell her that I am, rushing to Clara's bedside to envelop her in a hug.

Clara looks exhausted, but ready. She is a tough woman, a resilient woman. She can handle anything, and lying there in the hospital bed waiting for the next contraction to arrive, she has her game face on. She's ready for this. I stroke her moistened hair; she's been sweating. There's a washcloth set to the side of the bed, which I dampen with cool water from the bathroom sink and press to her head. I feed her ice cubes with a plastic spoon from a Styrofoam cup that sits on her table tray; the ice cubes have begun to melt and form a puddle at the bottom of the cup. The contractions are coming every few minutes, lasting thirty seconds or more, and within minutes I become a slave to the clock, knowing before Clara does when the next contraction will arrive. She grits her teeth and pushes through them while the nurse and I remind her to breathe.

'We don't have a name,' Clara gasps between contractions. 'We never gave him a name.' And there is panic in her eyes, as if without a name he might just *poof!* disappear before our eyes.

I have no good reason why we don't have a name. We had nine months to decide. Maybe we just need to see him and then we'll know, I rationalize, and suddenly I'm overwhelmed with a sense of eagerness and anticipation that soon my baby boy will arrive. I'm filled with pride. Soon I will welcome a child into the world, and I envision Clara, Maisie, my baby boy and me all curled together on Clara's hospital bed, and in that moment everything else fades away: the practice and Connor, Kat and Melinda Grey, the malpractice suit. There are voices in the hallway, two men, a new father and a new grandfather, moseying down the hall, discussing the game. I try to turn a deaf ear to what they say, to focus on Clara and only Clara, but I catch wind of it anyway.

They're talking about basketball. The NBA series. The Golden State Warriors have taken the lead in the series, and I feel this great relief at hearing those words, knowing that out there somewhere, in a POD account, is money. Money waiting for me.

As another contraction grips Clara, I feel the weight of the world lifted from me and, for the first time in a long time, a sense that this will be okay. That everything will be okay.

She cries out from the pain, and I hold her tightly and tell her that she can do this. 'You're the strongest woman I know,' I whisper into her ear, words that are altogether true. Clara is a fighter. If there's anybody in the world who can do this, Clara can do this. Her body is glossy with sweat, the paper-thin blanket now kicked from her legs and to the tile floor. She breathes heavily as the contraction passes, her rib cage expanding and contracting with each gulp of air. She lays her head on my shoulder, and I stroke her hair.

'Charles,' she whispers to me, gasping for air. 'Let's name him Charles,' she says. A concession. My father's name and my middle name. But I don't let Clara capitulate in fear.

'No,' I tell her, kneeling down so that I can see her eye to eye, the floor digging into my knees so that they burn. Clara's cheeks are flushed, the red spreading from her face to her chin and neck. Her eyes, always so sure, are consumed with fear and doubt and exhaustion. I hold her hand in mine, pressing it to my heart, and say to her, 'We'll know when we see him. When we see him, we'll know,' and in my voice, there's conviction, a guarantee, and she nods her head, believing.

'I'm sorry,' she says, meaning our fight this morning over coffee and paint. A dumb fight. An argument that means nothing. I tell her that I'm sorry, too. 'It was stupid,' I say, and she agrees, 'So stupid,' as our lips press together, erasing the moment from our minds for the time being.

The doctor returns again to check on Clara. This time, she's nine centimeters and nearly one hundred percent effaced. 'You're in the home stretch,' she tells Clara. 'We'll begin pushing soon,' and again she leaves.

Clara is thirsty, but only ice cubes are allowed, a sorry consolation prize for someone who's completely parched. I feed her the last from the Styrofoam cup and then tell her I'll be right back; I'm going to get more. But Clara clings to me, begging me not to go. The kitchen is just across the hall, just a quick hop, skip and a jump away I tell her, but Clara holds tightly to my hand and begs, 'Don't leave me. Please, don't leave me,' and I melt like snowdrifts on a warm spring day. I'm moonstruck. In all my life, I've never loved anyone as much as Clara. I fall again to my knees, swearing over and over again that I won't leave. 'I'm right here,' I say. 'I'm here. I won't go anywhere. I'll never leave you,' I say as the nurse takes the cup from my hands. I stroke Clara's hair as another contraction arrives, her fingernails bearing down hard on my skin, leaving their mark. But I don't mind. What I wouldn't give to do this for her, to birth our baby myself, to take the pain away. 'If there's anybody in the world that can do this, Clara, you can do this,' I say again into her ear as she screams through yet another contraction.

'Breathe, Clara,' I remind her. 'Just breathe.'

* * *

Maisie arrives in the room with her grandfather behind her, bearing a piece of construction paper in her hand. She comes in slowly, deliberately, her eyes locked on the new addition, a puckered creature who lies on her mother's chest in a blue blanket.

'What have you got there?' I ask Maisie as I reach out to gather her into my arms and place a kiss on her forehead.

'I drew a picture,' she says as she shows me her drawing. 'Our family,' she says, and I look down to see that in her drawing, our family includes four, and Harriet of course. 'Who's that?' I ask, pointing at each figure in a row, *Daddy*, and then *Mommy*, and then *me*, says Maisie, but when I get to the pocket-size figure in Clara's arms, no bigger than a mouse according to Maisie's drawing scale, she tells me that's Felix. A buck-naked Felix who, like a bug, has three body parts and maybe an extra few legs. The hair on his head far surpasses mine.

'Felix?' I say, as both Clara's and my eyes rise up to meet Maisie's at exactly the same time.

'Who's Felix?' asks Clara.

'That's Felix,' she says assuredly, pointing a green crayon at the baby in Clara's arms as if all along, while Clara and I sat on the fence undecided, she knew that the baby was a Felix. 'Like Felix from ballet,' she says and Clara and I release a simultaneous, *Ohhhh*. Felix from ballet. The sole boy in her class, with his footless tights and his white T-shirts. The love of my four-year-old's life.

I hear Clara's voice parrot the word. 'Felix,' she says, and there's a lilt to it, a rising action instead of what has always followed my name suggestions: a firm, deflating no. I turn to Clara to see that she's reached a hand out to Maisie's drawing to see if the mousy figure in the palm of her illustrated hand is indeed the same one as the baby sleeping soundlessly on her chest. Her lips display a measured smile, as I set Maisie down and she climbs clumsily onto the hospital bed to join her mother and her baby brother beneath the sheets. Clara looks to me for approval, and I shrug my shoulders and say, 'Why not?' Felix. It's the perfect blend of traditional and trendy all at the same time, and as I lean in closely to stare at the thin, gossamer eyelids of my sleeping baby boy, I see that he really is a Felix. All along he was a Felix.

'Felix Charles,' says Clara, and in that moment, it's decided. 'Welcome to the world, Felix Charles Solberg.'

I sit on the other side of Clara, and Maisie sneaks awkwardly across and climbs up on my lap. Clara lays her head on my shoulder. I set my hand on Felix's arm, and even in sleep he kicks a firm hello. 'Hello, Felix,' I say and Maisie giggles, a sound that is melodious and majestic and pure.

Our family, I think, telling myself how this is the only thing in the world that matters. The rest of it is just packing materials, the upholstery, a filler. It means nothing.

And for one single moment there is bliss.

CLARA

The night comes and the night goes. I sleep, though my dreams are full of zombies, of the undead walking the earth. I dream of Nick as a zombie, alive but dead, in a state of decay. In the dream, his eyes and skin are missing because those things no longer belong to him; they've been gifted to someone else. Nick's blue eyes now disassembled and sent in opposite directions—the cornea one way, the sclera another—so that in my dream an eyeless Nick tracks and trails me, groaning, groping the hollows of his eyes with decomposing hands. Behind him stands a whole horde of zombies, a herd, grotesque figures with rotting, discolored skin, moving in an unwieldy shuffle, as they reach for me, hungry for my flesh.

I wake up screaming.

In the morning, Felix, Maisie and I go through the motions. We eat and turn on the TV, staring vacantly at the animated cartoons that fill the screen. I let Harriet out. I let Harriet in.

It's then that I remember my father said he'd send photos of my mother's car to post online. I rise from the sofa to retrieve my laptop and, returning, sit beside Maisie on the sofa where she presses up close to me and snuggles tight.

The truth is that I'm desperate for money, for five thousand dollars to hold me over until I can find another way of earning an income. I hate to take money from my father, and yet desperation prevails. I need the money. I pull up my email to find the same correspondence there that also infiltrates my mailbox: bills and sympathy greetings. I delete them all, delete, delete, delete, looking only for an email from my father. Sure enough, there it is, an email with the photographs attached, and as Maisie clambers awkwardly onto my lap, settling herself somewhere between the keyboard and my legs, she asks, 'What's that, Mommy? What's that?'

The images slowly load, one pixel at a time, and as she points a gooey, butter-coated finger at the snapshots that start to take shape, I say, 'It's your grandma's car,' and then we wait for the car to appear as if by magic, the internet connection sluggish, so that by the time the car finally does arrive, Maisie has almost lost interest, eyes reverting from the laptop back to the TV screen.

Almost. But not quite.

I feel the urine well before I, myself, lay eyes on the car. It comes streaming out, a torrent of warm urine with an immediately pungent smell, settling on my lap and dripping into the crevices of the sofa cushions, turning the space between Maisie and me into a tepid lake. The urine is followed by the scream, this desperate, high-frequency scream that makes even the glassware in the dining room's sideboard sway, a bellow that comes again and again with the only saving grace the breath Maisie summons between each scream, this millisecond of silence as she gathers the oxygen to scream again. And again. And again, and I can say nothing for I, too, would like to scream as my eyes cross over my father's note—set there above the four photographs taken of the car from all angles, inside and out—the wording he'd like for me to use in the ad. A 2006 Chevrolet Malibu sedan. Four door. Five speed automatic with 94,271 miles.

Black.

And I'd tell myself it was a coincidence, a simple fluke. I would reprimand Maisie for both the accident and the scream, for the urine that becomes subsumed by the sofa cushions so that I'll never get them clean and that smell will forever persist, were it not for the golden bow tie insignia that greets me in the eye, emblazoned across the front of the car's radiator grille.

The woman, the one woman, the only person in the world who was a near witness to Nick's crash was sure she saw a black Chevy pass by mere seconds before she came upon the accident, a car in a hurry, scuttling quickly away from the scene, swerving wildly into oncoming traffic, forcing the other vehicle off the road. A black Chevrolet.

And I find that I can't get this sinking feeling out of my mind, a vision of my mother snatching the car keys from a forgotten coat pocket while no one was watching—napping perhaps, or consumed with a show on the TV—and deciding to dust off the old car and take it for a spin.

Nick didn't kill himself after all.

He was killed by my mother.

NICK

BEFORE

The day that Clara and Felix are released from the hospital, I drive them home and tell Clara I have a few errands to run, and she says to me, 'Okay.' Unlike Maisie, who came home from the hospital vociferous and emphatic, making her needs immediately and desperately known with a cry that could go on for hours, Felix is quiet.

'Can you get milk, too?' Clara asks before I leave, rooting around inside the refrigerator to see that we're in short supply.

'Sure thing.' I kiss her on the lips and then go.

From my cell phone, sitting in the driveway before I pull out onto the street, I place a call to Kat. It isn't that I'm trying to shirk responsibility. That's not what I'm doing; that's not it at all. If it turns out I am Gus's father as she says I am, then I will welcome Gus into my life. I've been thinking about it, sprawled there sleepless beside Clara's hospital bed, imagining this newcomer Gus sharing our lives. Split custody arrangements and visitation. Every other weekend and school vacations. It's a strange prospect, envisioning myself playing catch with a boy I don't even know. I've only seen a photo of the boy. I have no idea how tall he is, what he sounds like, smells like, whether or not he can even catch a ball. But if he's mine, then I'll do it because this is what decent men do. They take care of their own. They clean up their own messes. I'm not trying to neglect my responsibilities. It's just the opposite. I'm trying to claim them, to make what's mine, mine.

But first I have to be sure.

We meet at a DNA diagnostics center, and for the first time in my life, I meet this boy Kat calls Gus. He's a spindly boy, tall and thin as am I, but his features—the eyes, the hair—are Kat to a T. It's easy to see they belong together, but the question is: Do I? We greet each other in the waiting room, and Kat introduces me to Gus as *her friend*. I wonder if he's heard of me before, if she's ever mentioned the name Nick. Not around Steve, that's for sure. But maybe around Gus. Maybe she relayed to Gus memories of her own childhood, how she and her friend Nick did this or did that. There's wariness to his eyes, a laziness and indifference in the way he reaches a hand out to greet mine.

Kat rises from a chair in the waiting room and says to me, 'I hear congratulations are in order.' I never told her I had a new son, but still she knows.

I avert my eyes, staring at Gus instead, on his chair thumbing through a magazine. 'Thanks,' I mumble.

I wonder if Gus knows anything about this appointment. Why else would someone meet a stranger at a facility to have the inside of their cheek swabbed? But then again,

Gus is twelve, and I'm guessing the notion of sex is just beginning to dawn on him, though thoughts of paternity are still far away. I try to talk to him. 'What grade are you in?' I ask, and, 'What's your favorite food?' but his answers are all one-word answers, and any two-way conversation is missing, though whether it's due to immaturity or timidity or disinterest, I don't know.

'Sixth,' he tells me, and 'Bacon,' and I feel my heart beat hard, knowing that bacon is my favorite food, too. Are these things hereditary? I don't know. I try another one to be sure, as if my own evaluation might negate the paternity test we're about to undergo, as if I can tell after a five-minute conversation whether or not this kid is mine.

'Favorite color?'

'Black.'

'Favorite sport?'

He shrugs, though it's clear to me that he's thumbing through a sports magazine, staring at a glossy image of LeBron James. 'I don't play any sports,' he says and, as if to prove the point, he tosses the magazine aside and reaches deep into the pocket of his shorts to produce a couple of green army guys, the very same kind I played with when I was a boy.

I nod knowingly, feeling somewhere deep inside like we could forgo this paternity test right here and right now. Steve is big, brawny, an athlete to boot. I'm not. I tried out for the middle school basketball team eons ago and didn't make it. All but one kid did: me. It was a degrading feeling, being singled out as a loser. I never played sports again, not competitive sports anyway, though I did sometimes just for fun, always with Connor. Racquetball at the gym, running the occasional 5K. I find myself thinking about Connor then, as I sit and wait for Gus and me to be called, wishing I could call him up and tell him about Felix, about all of this, and together we'd both commiserate and celebrate, and he'd laugh about the irony of it in usual Connor candor, how suddenly I had two sons with two women and he had none, sons or women. And we'd chuckle while throwing back a beer.

But that won't happen.

'I used to have those when I was your age,' I tell Gus, 'except that mine were brown. I'd line them up across my bedroom floor and play war games. You have the tanks, too?' I ask, like the whole collection of miniature World War II tanks that used to occupy my bedroom floor. My mother, coming in to make my bed or fold the laundry, would step on them and get mad.

Gus shakes his head no; he doesn't have the tanks. He motions to his army men. 'I've never seen ones that were brown,' he says, and then the nurse calls our names.

Gus goes first, and then me.

When I come out of the exam room, Kat and Gus are gone. In his chair, where he sat only moments ago, remains a single green army man. I pick it up and slide it into the pocket of my jeans. Whether he left it on purpose, or if it was unintentional, I don't know. Maybe it was an accident, or maybe it was a gift.

The results, I'm told, will be posted online in just a couple of days.

In a couple of days I'll know if Gus is my son.

I have two more stops before I go home. The first is the jewelry store, from which I purchased a necklace months ago for Clara. She eyed it herself just weeks after she became pregnant with Felix—a month max—a silver necklace with a duo of heart-shaped tags. 'Would you look at that,' Clara had said, pointing to it through the store's glass display. We didn't go to the jewelry store looking for necklaces, but rather to have her wedding band resized. She stood there, ogling the necklace, then smiled at me and said, 'Two hearts. One for Maisie, and one for baby,' while rubbing a hand wishfully over the tiny peppercorn in her womb.

The next day, without Clara around, I returned to the store and bought the pendant necklace on the sly. There wasn't anything I wouldn't give Clara if I could. I hid it away in a dresser drawer for the next eight months, knowing that as soon as the baby had a name, I'd get the heart tags engraved. The time has come. I swing by the jewelry store and leave the necklace for engraving: one heart for Maisie, and one for Felix. And then I show him a picture of my kids because I just can't stop myself from gloating. It'll be a week or two before they're ready, and then I can surprise Clara with the gift. The store owner winks at me and says, 'You know we sell the charms individually. You can always add more hearts if need be,' and already I'm thinking that might be something we'll one day do. One day there may be more kids for Clara and me. Maisie, Felix and baby.

And then I stop at a convenience store to pick up the milk and go home.

* * *

I spend the couple of days following Felix's birth at home, a paternity leave of sorts. It's not easy to do. Without anyone to fill in my shoes while I'm gone, Stacy and Nancy are left to reschedule dozens of patients. 'If anyone calls with an emergency,' I tell them over the phone early in the morning, while sipping my very first mug of caffeinated coffee and staring at the day as it stretches out before me, long and wide, full of opportunity, 'call me. I'll come in. Only for an emergency,' because sometimes there are things that can't be put off for a week. Melinda Grey is proof enough of this.

I've been served with an Emergency Order of Protection from Melinda Grey, a sheet of paper that's stashed between the pages of an old dictionary we never use, and I'm waiting on a hearing date, just as I'm waiting on a date for mediation in the malpractice suit. I can't let this bother me. I feel grateful that the emergency order—a *restraining* order—arrived the day after Felix was born, as I left Clara and Felix at the hospital for a quick breather, just enough time to drive home, shower and change my clothes. He was waiting for me in the driveway when I arrived, a different messenger this time who also pressed the order into my hand and told me I'd been served. I was just so grateful Clara wasn't around to see, and that Maisie wasn't here to ask questions. *What's that, Daddy?* and, *Why was that man here?* I found a safe spot for the order, a place where it will never be seen.

We spend the days together, morning, noon and night devoted to holding my baby boy in my arms and watching my daughter spin across the room in delight. 'Look at me, Daddy,' she begs. 'I can fly, I can fly.' And then she asks if I want to fly, too, and I tell her yes, that there's nothing in the world I'd rather do. And so, handing Felix to Clara, I stretch my arms out beside Maisie, and together we fly, spinning wildly around the room. The days are warm, stretching out before us like an open country road, full of nothing to do.

There's no better feeling in the world. I spend time catering to my wife's needs, changing my son's diaper, holding him while he sleeps, coloring innumerable pictures with my daughter, watching TV. In the afternoons, Maisie and I slip outside and play games of tag and chase until we are both sweating and exhausted. We bike to the playground; we turn on the sprinkler and take turns leaping through the water's icy spray. I prepare hamburgers on the grill for dinner, and we all four eat on the patio table with the umbrella pressed all the way up to keep the sunlight out of Felix's dozing eyes. And as I become rapt in this—in my family—the extraneous worries start to slip away, and I'm only even vaguely aware that the Golden State Warriors have won the NBA finals, and that all that money I bet on their team was not for naught, that sitting in a bank account is enough money to cover my debt, to replace Maisie's college education savings and start contributing to a new life insurance fund.

My gambling days are through.

I go through the ways I will tell Clara about Gus. I practice in the bathroom mirror, confessing to her first about my run-ins with Kat, and then the declaration that Gus is my son. I don't know whether or not this is true—I still have yet to hear the results of the paternity test—and yet somewhere deep inside, I know it's true. Clara will be angry. It will take a while to process the fact. But then she'll come to realize that what happened between Kat and me was many years ago, long before I first laid eyes on Clara and knew at once that she was the one for me. She'll grasp that I haven't kept this knowledge from her for twelve years, but that Kat has kept it from me.

That evening, Clara falls asleep with baby Felix in her

arms. They're on the sofa, Clara's head lying peacefully on a throw pillow with Felix pressed against her chest, her arms locked tightly around him even in sleep. The peace and tranquility are palpable, and it takes everything I have in me not to force myself onto the sofa beside them and join them in dreamland. The exhaustion of having a newborn around weighs heavily on me, those long, interrupted nights, sleep always just out of reach.

And yet I wouldn't trade it for anything.

Outside it is evening, just after eight o'clock on a muggy summer night. Even from inside through the cracks of an open window, I can hear the sound of crickets and cicadas. Harriet lies on the floor, pressed against the sofa; she will not leave Clara or the baby's side. Our guard dog. I pat her head, and whisper to her, 'Good girl.'

Maisie comes stampeding down the stairs like a herd of elephants being chased by a lion. She's loud, laughing hysterically. As always Maisie is dressed in her ballet leotard and tutu, and she asks *pretty, pretty please* if we can go to ballet. She pliés before me; she attempts a clumsy pirouette and falls.

I laugh, pressing a finger to my lips to quiet her down. 'Today is Monday, silly,' I say, taking her by the hand and drawing her away from Clara and Felix, who are sleeping. I heft her into my arms and carry her from the room. 'Tomorrow is ballet,' I say, but I have another idea, a way to freeze frame this moment in time. Seven thirty is usually Maisie's bedtime; somehow or other, in the excitement and delirium that follows childbirth, we forgot to put her to bed. I haul her into the kitchen and set her on a kitchen counter where she sits, little piggies kicking the cabinet while I rummage around for the things I need. A glass jar and a pair of sharp scissors. As I use the pointed end of the scissors to poke holes in the stamped steel lid, Maisie asks, 'What are you doing, Daddy?' and, 'Why are you doing that?' but I tell her simply that she'll see. I want it to be a surprise.

We find her pink sandals and step outside. Oftentimes Harriet would follow, but today she has a far greater task to do: protect Clara and the baby, and so her ears don't budge; nor do her eyes look to Maisie and me as we go. Outside, Maisie and I become enfolded in the heat of the day. Though the humidity has relented somewhat, the evening remains hot. A couple of American goldfinches perch on the bird-bath, taking the last few sips of green algae-tinged water. I make a mental note to clean the birdbath soon, to refill the birdseed, and then I hoist Maisie onto my shoulders with the jar in hand, and she asks of me, 'Where are we going?' and I say again that she'll see.

I lead Maisie into the thicket of trees that surround our yard, where the fireflies like to frolic at this time of night, playing with their friends. 'What are they doing?' asks Maisie as she points her fingers intermittently at the light as it appears and then disappears, appears and then disappears, and I say to her, 'They're talking. This is how they talk with their friends,' and I see Maisie contemplating that, thinking what fun it would be if some part of her lit up to say hello. Her head or her hands or her toes. I lift her up into the trees and tell her to grab a handful of leaves, and she does—asking, of course, 'Why, Daddy, why?'—and to-gether we drop down onto the earth to fill the glass jar with sticks and leaves. The grass doesn't grow here, where we sit, and is always austere, just a few blades poking out of the parched dirt. The tall trees prevent the sunlight from reaching the grass, preempting it from growing tall and strong. 'There are things,' I tell Maisie as she helps me stuff handfuls of leaves into the jar, 'that every creature needs to live. Food, shelter and oxygen are a few. We put holes in the jar so that the firefly can breathe, and these leaves are for food.'

'Can we catch one?' she asks, and I ruffle her hair and tell her, 'Of course we can,' and then we rise from the earth, and I show her how. Darkness closes in quickly, though the moon is bright, a crescent in the nighttime sky. The black-blue sky abounds with stars, helping us see, as somewhere off on the horizon, the sun fades away, leaving only faint traces of light, which will soon disappear, too.

'Cup your hands together,' I tell her, 'like this. But not too tightly,' I caution. 'We don't want to hurt the firefly. We only want to catch him for a little while, and then we'll set him free.' I spy a light radiating through the air, and I catch it, this beautiful beetle that climbs easily across my hand. I show Maisie, and she giggles as the firefly spreads its forewings and flies, and she chases it through the yard, the skirt of her tutu fluttering in the nighttime air.

'My turn! My turn,' she says, skipping back to me, and again I show her how to cup her hands. She tries, but her movements are too slow, too timid, the firefly always one step ahead of her unwieldy hands. And so I catch it for her, and let it climb onto Maisie's tiny hand. She laughs. 'That tickles,' she says, as six jointed legs creep across her skin. I'm not sure whether or not she likes it, not until she says, 'Hi there, Otis,' pressing her face close to the bug's tiny face to greet him in the eye.

'Who's Otis?' I ask, and she raises her hand so that I can see.

'This is Otis,' she says. 'This is Otis, Daddy. Can we keep him?' she asks, and I nod my head as I help Maisie set Otis in the jar and screw on the lid.

'Just for a little while,' I explain, as Otis clambers on a stick and drops down into our glass house, making himself comfortable in this temporary home. 'But then we'll have to set him free. It's fun for a little while, but Otis doesn't want to live in a jar forever.'

'Why not?' Maisie asks, staring curiously at me. This one is an easy one.

'Would you want to live in a jar forever?' I ask, and she shakes her head a firm, decisive no. 'Why not?' I ask, and she happily explains, 'Because I want to fly!' as she twirls around and around through the yard, arms extended, until she becomes dizzy and falls.

'Daddy, fly with me?' Maisie begs, and I can't help myself. There's nothing I'd rather do than fly around the backyard with my girl. I help her rise to her feet and set her on my shoulders, spinning around and around through the lawn. Around us fireflies dot the sky as Maisie calls out, 'We're flying! We're flying, Daddy,' and I laugh and tell her that we are. We're flying. For just one minute I imagine our feet leaving the earth, Maisie and me soaring together through space.

'Look at the stars,' I tell Maisie as if she and I are one with them, the stars and us, and Maisie exclaims, 'There's the moon!' and we make believe we're in a space shuttle of some sort, circumnavigating the moon. We laugh, giddy, silly, happy.

I can't remember the last time I've ever felt so happy.

How long we fly, I don't know. Until I'm wobbly on my feet and Maisie has had her fill. 'That's the best thing,' Maisie says, and I ask, 'What is?'

'Flying!' she screams.

'Can I bring Otis to my bedroom?' Maisie asks as I return her to the ground and she sits cross-legged on the lawn, leaves in her hair, and I mull this over, thinking Clara wouldn't like it in the least bit if I let Maisie bring a bug into her bedroom. But Otis is in a jar, completely harmless. And it's only for one night. If she were awake, I'd ask her. I'd plead Maisie's case, about how we should let her keep Otis in her bedroom for one single night, and then tomorrow we'd set him free, return him to the trees to play with his friends. But Clara isn't awake, and I don't want to wake her. I picture her in my mind's eye sleeping serenely with Felix in her arms. It's been a while since I've seen Clara so peaceful, so relaxed. The last thing in the world I want to do is wake her, and so I make a judgment call and tell Maisie yes.

'Yes,' I say. 'We can keep him for one night,' I tell Maisie, and I hold out a pinkie finger for her to grasp with her own, 'but we can't tell Mommy. Okay? Pinkie promise we won't tell Mommy about Otis,' and she does.

'Why not, Daddy?'

'Mommy doesn't like bugs,' I say. 'This time tomorrow night, we'll set Otis free. Deal?' I ask, and she says, 'Deal,' as we tiptoe back into the house, up the wooden stairs and into Maisie's bedroom where we set Otis in his jar on the edge of her dresser, and I tuck her into bed. It's a compromise; Maisie would like for Otis to sleep under the covers with her, but I smile and say no. 'This way,' I say, 'he can watch you sleep.' I pull the blanket clear up to Maisie's chin and say to her, 'Snug as a bug in a rug,' and she laughs and reminds me of Otis the bug in a jar, in case I've somehow already forgotten about Otis.

'Sweet dreams, my love,' I whisper to her as her eyes drift sleepily closed. 'Good night,' I say as I stand in the doorway, watching as a chemical reaction from inside Otis's abdomen illuminates Maisie's night.

CLAЯA

This afternoon my mother has a neurologist appointment at three o'clock, the very same time that the HVAC men are to come to my home and bless me with an operable air-conditioning unit at my father's expense. But the memories of the HVAC men evade me as I maneuver a sleeping Felix and a completely crazed Maisie into the back seat of my car, not thinking of anything but that car, the black car, my mother's car. Maisie is beside herself, absolutely unable to calm down for anything, not a sticker or her teddy bear or the promise of ice cream. She hasn't stopped crying, a paltry cry but still a cry, as if she's truly scared out of her mind. She kicks in my arms as I set her in the back seat of the car, and, as I attempt to strap the harness around her lobbing body, she gets me in the nose with those hot-pink Crocs of hers. I recoil, and she begins to whimper, petitioning desperately and to no avail for Daddy. 'Daddy, Daddy, Daddy,' she begs.

As I stand there on my driveway, both sweating and out of breath, trying to close the back door against the weight of Maisie's foot, Emily comes scurrying down the street, tugging little Teddy by the hand. 'Would Maisie like to come over and play?' she asks, as if she's plain forgotten about our rift the other morning, as if it didn't happen. Teddy stands beside her with pleading eyes, telling me how he and Maisie are going to do another magic show as if it's already been discussed, which of course it hasn't, but I'm shaking my head before I can stop myself, and already I'm telling them no. 'No, Maisie can't play today,' I say. 'No.'

As if it matters, Emily tells me that Theo isn't home.

I step past her and say that I'm in a rush. 'There's somewhere we need to be.'

'Clara,' she says, latching on to my arm. The bruising is still there, decorating her neck like festive garland. My eyes fall to it and then glance away quickly, as Teddy presses his face to Maisie's side window and makes a silly face. From the interior of the car, I hear Maisie squeal in delight, clapping her hands. How she adores sweet Teddy, so much so that already she's forgotten about kicking me in the nose. Oh, how easy it is for Maisie to forget. 'I just couldn't bear to think of it,' Emily says to me. 'A murder,' she whispers, so that Teddy won't hear, 'so close to our homes. We're not that type of community.' I think to myself, easy for her to say. Hers isn't the husband who's dead. 'It isn't that I didn't believe you,' she says. 'It's that I didn't want to believe. Theo and I picked this area to live because of the low rates of crime. Some vandalism, arson, auto theft. Sure. But murder, Clara? I can't imagine. There just has to be some other way,' she goes on, though I excuse myself; I don't want to hear it. I say I have to go, stepping into the car and driving away quickly, leaving Emily and Teddy standing awkwardly on my drive, wondering whether her words were a failed attempt at an apology, a rationalization or something different. Something else. Something more.

I think of Theo with his rotation of loaner cars. His petulance and temper. The fear in Emily's eyes.

Theo is no stranger to brute force; the bruises on Emily's neck are proof of this. He and Nick were never friends; he called the police on Nick. He had a beef with him. Maybe he wanted to get even, to seek revenge.

And suddenly my mind is swimming, all logical thought and sensibility sinking beneath the water, drowning a slow death. I can't think. My mother killed Nick, of this I was certain just moments ago.

But now a new thought crosses my mind, one that doesn't replace the first but only distorts it somehow, turning it ogre-like before my eyes.

Theo killed Nick.

And I find that it's like radio static somehow, all sorts of white noise and other disturbances interrupting the ordinary processes of my mind. Crackling noises. Interference. Background noise. Drugs and adultery, lying, stealing, cheating. Who is this man I'm married to? Who killed Nick, or did Nick kill Nick?

My mother killed Nick.

Theo killed Nick.

Or maybe someone else killed Nick, I think as I see Emily and Teddy shrinking away in the car's rearview mirror as I drive slowly down the street. Emily's eyes are aimed in my direction, watching as I go. The hem of her long skirt blows in the wind, getting wrapped around her legs.

Maybe she isn't trying to cover for Theo.

Maybe she's trying to cover for herself.

She would do anything for Theo, out of fear and out of necessity. Maybe Nick threatened to go to the police if Theo ever laid a hand on her again. Emily has confessed to me that she couldn't live without Theo, not because she loves him but because he pays the bills, he puts food on the table and a roof over their heads. He's the sole breadwinner in the family, and without him, Emily believes she has nothing. Believes she is nothing.

Maybe Nick told her he would turn Theo in for spousal abuse, for child abuse.

Maybe Emily killed Nick.

A dozen radio stations play simultaneously in my mind, each playing a different genre, a different song, not in harmony but, rather, fighting each other for airtime, the volume turned all the way up so that it's impossible to think or to hear, and it all becomes one thing: noise.

A migraine forms in my head. It's all too much to handle. It's all I can do not to scream.

'Mommy, play a song?' begs Maisie from the back seat of the car, and I think to myself, *How can she not hear it? The radio is already on.*

NICK

BEFORE

I stand in the doorway to the bathroom, watching as Clara forces Maisie's hair into twin pigtails with adroit hands. Maisie, excited for an afternoon at ballet, is completely incapable of standing still, though Clara reminds her countless times, 'The sooner we're done here, the sooner we can go.' She forces a pair of white tights onto Maisie's legs, then slides on her leotard and the pink tutu. Maisie begs Clara for lipstick, and at first Clara hesitates, but then she relents, painting a pale pink lip gloss across Maisie's lips.

My heart stops. My little girl is all grown up.

'Look at me, Daddy,' she says, and I smile at her and tell her she's beautiful. I smile at Clara and tell her she's beautiful, too, though she scowls at this, wearing her maternity clothes still because it's the only thing she has that will fit. On her bottom half is a pair of sweatpants, and up top a spit-up stained shirt. Her hair is unwashed, oily, and she looks whipped. She hasn't showered; she covers the smell with deodorant and perfume. In the past four days, she's slept much less than me, awake at all hours of the night to feed Felix. I've offered to help, but there's only so much I can do, and so I make every attempt to stay up and keep her company, but inevitably my eyes drift closed while Felix is still imbibing his nutrients from Clara's sore chest. Her eyes are weary, and her mood is starting to sink.

I pull her into an embrace and tell her it's true, she does look beautiful, but she draws away and says that she has to change before she can take Maisie to ballet.

'I can't be seen in public like this,' barks Clara as she rummages through the closet for something to wear. I see my own reflection in the bedroom mirror. I, too, am looking worse for wear. My hair is slovenly, my face covered with so much stubble it now resembles dirt. I can't even remember the last time I've shaved. My jeans are slouchy where they're not supposed to slouch; it's quite likely I've worn the same pair of denim every day this week, tossed over the end of the bed at night only to be slipped back on, come morning. There are pit stains on my shirt, and even though I have plans to go nowhere, I can't stand the smell of my own body odor. I yank the shirt over my head, toss it to the floor and slide into something clean, a blue polo shirt that smells of lavender laundry detergent.

Ballet class is only an hour long, and with the commute either way, Clara and Maisie will be gone less than three. Clara has got it all timed out down to the minute, a chart left on the breakfast nook for reference. Felix has just been fed and burped, and is fast asleep on a blanket on the living room floor, which should be enough to tide him over until she gets back home. Then he'll need to eat again. 'If he wakes sooner,' she says, having yet to start using the breast pump we rented from the hospital, 'call me and I'll come home.' She quickly ushers Maisie down the stairs, and they grab the ballet slippers. She tells Maisie to use the bathroom.

'But I don't have to go,' says Maisie, arms across her chest, pouting, as if using the bathroom is the worst thing in the world.

I tell her to try.

Clara's purse and the car keys have been gathered; Maisie's feet are stuffed in her pink sandals. They're all set to go. They're halfway to the door when, from the living room, we hear the sound of a baby's cry, soft and subdued at first, but quickly growing more needy, more insistent, as we stand by the garage door and listen. It's instantaneous, the way the worry lines besiege Clara's face. 'Don't worry,' I tell her, setting my hand on her arm. I've been a father before. This isn't new to me; I've done this all before. He can't possibly be hungry, but is instead fussy, lonely, plagued by gas.

'He'll be fine,' I say, but still she's worried. 'He can't be hungry,' I assure Clara. 'He can't. I'll rock him. I'll settle him down. It will all be fine.'

But by now Felix is wailing, and I can see in Clara's eyes that this will not be fine.

'He needs me,' she says, nervous, as beside her Maisie's face reddens, and she begins a mounting tantrum, sure that if Felix is crying she won't be able to go to ballet. Her eyes plead with mine, and it's easy, a no-brainer, when I lean into Clara and whisper, 'You stay. I'll go,' and Clara and Maisie both turn to me at the same time and ask, 'You will?'

I've never been to Maisie's ballet class before. I've never met the four-year-old Felix who Maisie is crazy about; I've never met the other moms with whom Clara finds conversations therapeutic, a way to combat all the monotony of motherhood. I've never laid eyes on Miss Becca, and so I tell them that I will.

We say our goodbyes to Clara, who hurries off to tackle Felix, and as she goes I hear her say, 'It's okay, Felix, Mommy is coming, Mommy is here.'

Grabbing Maisie by the hand, we step outside. I decide to take Clara's car to ballet because her car is parked at the edge of the drive, roasting in the hot summer sun. It'll be like an oven when we step inside, the interior a smothering eighty or ninety degrees. 'Come on, Maisie,' I say, tugging on her hand as she stops to snap a dandelion from the yard. 'We have to hurry so we won't be late to ballet.'

At that she picks up the pace, letting go of my grasp as she rushes ahead of me and toward the car, yanking on the locked door handle as I fumble with the car keys to let her in. But I have Clara's car keys, and so finding the right one isn't as easy as it seems.

'Come on, Daddy,' says Maisie, bouncing back and forth between her feet, and I tell her I'm coming.

I'm not halfway to the car when I see a black Beemer inching its way down the street, the tinted windows rolled down, Theo staring out at me from behind a pair of aviator sunglasses, moving in slow motion. At seeing me, he stretches out an arm, a finger pointed at me like the barrel of a pistol as he cocks the imaginary hammer and shoots. I flinch instinctively, and Theo laughs, this patronizing laugh that's hard to hear from the distance. But still I see it. Even Maisie sees it, as her eyes wander from Theo to me and back again, and I think to myself, *God, how I hate him.*

I remember Clara's comment from months ago as we stared out the window at Theo and the Maserati he had at the time. *It's not like it's his*, was what Clara had said. Clara, if possible, hates him even more than I do. Theo could never afford his own BMW, much less a Maserati, but he always has some fancy loaner that he likes to cruise around town, purporting it is his, letting it go to his head like a boy with a toy. What I want to do is tell him to fuck off or to give him the finger, but with Maisie standing there, tugging on the car handle, waiting for me to unlock the door so she can climb inside, I can't. I'm better than that.

I try hard to ignore the threat—*I will fucking kill you, Solberg.* I turn away from his bullying eyes, telling Maisie as I grope for the car keys, 'Just a second,' when, before I take two steps, I see the Beemer swerve onto the end of my blacktop, the hood aimed momentarily at Maisie. It's a jerk, a simple tug of the steering wheel. It happens so fast, as Maisie sees the car coming at her full throttle, her skinny legs crumbling at the knee as she drops to the ground face-down, covering her head with her hands. The engine revs, a loud, hostile sound. By now I'm running, and just as quickly as it began, it's through. Like that, Theo tugs on the steering wheel once more, rerouting the car less than three feet from where Maisie lies, and this time I hear his laugh out the window as he calls out to me, 'See? See that, Solberg? How does it feel to be on the receiving end for a change?'

'Why don't you pick on someone your own size?' I carp, muttering under my breath *asshole*, so that Maisie can't hear it, though somehow or other Theo does. Or maybe he doesn't hear the word so much as he sees it form on my lips.

'What the fuck did you say?' he demands. 'What did you

fucking call me?' he asks, but I hardly pay any attention to him because already I'm hurrying to lift Maisie from the hot blacktop. I gather her shaking body in my arms as Theo slams on the brake and the car comes to a complete stop. He thrusts the gearshift in Park and steps from the car, towering over Maisie and me on the drive. Maisie clings to me like a baby chimpanzee, fingertips sinking into my skin, confessing, 'I'm scared, Daddy,' and though I don't admit it to her, there's a part of me that's scared, too. There's a threatening look in Theo's eyes.

'I'm not the asshole,' Theo says, as I lower Maisie into the car and turn back to look him in the eye. Except that I don't look him in the eye because Theo is a good three inches taller than me and likely another fifty pounds.

From behind I hear Maisie wince, and before I can tell her everything is okay, everything is all right, Theo shoves me against the car and tells me, 'You're the asshole, Solberg. You got that? You're the asshole. Not me.'

'Not in front of my kid,' I plead, but Theo doesn't care who's around to see. His hand forms into a fist and before I can react, he gets me in the lip. Maisie screams out loud, pressing her hands to her eyes so that she can't see what happens next, which just so happens is a good thing for me because it's a gut reaction this time when my own hand follows suit, and I jab Theo in the jaw. Three times. With all of my might. He staggers, but comes back at me with a hook and uppercut, putting the weight of his entire body behind the blow so that the car behind me is the only thing that keeps me upright.

He laughs as I wobble, calling me a sissy, a pansy, and I'm about to hit him again when Maisie cries out, professing loudly this time that she's scared, and Theo retreats a step, saying to me, 'We're not through here. This isn't done,' before waltzing away, back toward the car, smug as can be, thinking he's doing me some favor by not beating the life out of me in front of my kid. I'm transported back to ninth grade when some asshole told me to meet him at the flagpole after school so he could beat the crap out of me, and I let him, unable to put up much of a fight. I've never been a fighter. I always had guys around like Connor to do it for me, except that this time Connor isn't here.

Theo laughs arrogantly, sure that he's won this round, but when his back is turned, I consider tackling him, taking him down with a chop drop or an elbow drop, catching him when he isn't looking and turning the tide in my favor. It's the only way I could really win, with a cheap shot or a low blow. I have a vision of him lying facedown on the burning concrete like Maisie just a minute ago, bleeding out, crying uncle.

I start to advance, but as I do, Maisie whispers, 'Is he gone, Daddy?' and her words freeze me in my tracks. I can't move.

This isn't something Maisie needs to see.

Theo gets in the car and slams the door. He steps on the gas and disappears down the street. 'It's okay,' I tell Maisie, stroking her hair, seeing that her pigtails are all out of whack, the knees of her tights smudged with dirt. 'You're okay. He's gone.' I peer up and down the street to be sure he's gone, and like magic, Theo and his black car have disappeared from view, the only sign of him the unmistakable smell of burning rubber that lingers in the air.

'Why did he do that, Daddy?' Maisie asks, her voice

shaking, as I secure the straps, wiping the tears from her eyes. I hold tight to Maisie. It was such a close call. Just one more second and Theo would have hit my girl. 'Why, Daddy?' she begs with this childlike innocence that reminds me that in Maisie's world, bad things don't happen. Bad people don't exist. Maisie hardly knows Theo. He's Teddy's daddy, and yet we don't let Maisie play with Teddy when Theo is home. Maisie has hardly laid eyes on him, and I plan to keep it that way.

As soon as I get home, I'll tell Clara what happened, even though it means I'll have to come clean about my run-in with Teddy. She should know. Maybe it's time to activate the home security system, too, just in case there's a psychopath living across the street. Maybe it's time to put the house on the market and move somewhere new.

Three feet. He was less than three feet from hitting Maisie. I could tell her it was an accident. I could make a story up, how a squirrel had darted into the road and he was trying to avoid it, how he didn't see Maisie. But I don't.

He wasn't going to hit her, I tell myself. It was just a threat. But still…

'He's a bad man, Maisie,' I say, because for once I can't think of anything better to say, some way to sugarcoat this situation for Maisie's delicate ears. I want her to know. I need her to know. Theo is a bad man, and under no circumstances should she ever be around him. I look her straight in the eye. I need to be sure she hears. 'He's a bad man, Maisie,' I say again, point-blank. 'That's why.'

And then I close the door and take one more look up and down the street to be sure Theo isn't around as we take off for ballet. I don't need him following me there.

CLARA

As I pull down the quiet residential road on which my mother and father live, I find only one car in the drive: Izzy's old wreck of a car, a clunker that must be older than she. It has character, as does she, for it's a gaudy green with fuzzy purple dice hanging from the rearview mirror. The fender is lined with bumper stickers, one for every single day of the week. One reads *Free Spirit* and another *Dead Head*. It's a used car, a hand-me-down, pre-owned or maybe passed on from another generation, with paint that is chipping and a wheel well corroded with a reddish brown, flaky rust.

But what matters most to me has nothing to do with Izzy's car. My father's car, which he always keeps parked on the south side of the driveway, isn't here, and, to me, that's all that matters.

I park on the street. I leave the children in the car with the windows opened a crack, and take myself to the front door, cutting across the lawn.

I knock, and Izzy answers. She stands before me in something that's clearly handmade, a skirt and a shirt and an antiquated fashion vest, all in a hodgepodge of patterns: argyle and damask and polka dots. She radiates panache. Izzy smiles and says to me, 'Hello, Clara,' and I reply with a curt, 'Hi.'

There's a warm, wonderful aroma wafting from inside the home, and she tells me that she's cooking dinner for when my parents arrive home from the appointment. 'It's a long drive from the city,' she says, 'and they'll be famished by the time they get here. I wanted to be sure I left them something to eat.' She asks if I'd like to come inside and wait. But I say no, for some reason put off by her efficiency and good manners. If I was half the woman as she, I would have thought to bring my own parents dinner, and yet I didn't.

I carry my camera. It's a heavy thing, a Nikon DSLR with a black strap that crisscrosses my frame. 'My father wanted me to place a classified ad for my mother's car online,' I tell her. 'I needed to snap a few quick photos of it, if you don't mind,' I say, though what I fail to say is that my father already sent photos, that I have more than I need to post the classified ad and that that's not the reason I came.

Izzy smiles and says *sure* and *of course*, and gives me the green light to let myself into the attached garage and take the photographs. She asks if I could use a hand, but I say no. She asks if I need her to open the garage door for me, but I say no to this, too—I know the code—and we part ways, me heading to the garage by way of my own car parked in the street, where I pass my cell phone to Maisie through the open window to keep her company and take a quick peek at Felix to ensure he's fast asleep.

I continue on to the garage door keypad and type the familiar numbers in, four digits that are also my birth date, the very same PIN as for their debit cards, my father's cell phone, the computer's log-in. *It's not very safe, having passwords that are all the same*, I'd told my father long ago, saying how if someone got access to one, they'd have access to them all. My father pooh-poohed the idea, saying it was easier to remember this way. He's far too trusting, not disillusioned like me. The only one that varies is the Chase password, on account of the bank's guidelines and not my father's intuition.

The door lifts open, and there it is, my mother's car, a black Chevy sedan, the bow tie insignia glaring back at me, baiting me. A tease. I was in college when my mother bought this car. I didn't help her pick it out, nor did I sit idly by, bored out of my mind, while she and my father finagled with the salesman over a deal. I missed out on a test drive. The times I've been in it are few and far between, and so long ago that I can no longer remember where or when or why. I'm certainly no car connoisseur; I couldn't care less what kind of car I drive so long as it's dependable and safe.

Is this the car that took my husband's life?

I check my watch and wonder how long I have until the HVAC guys phone my father to tell him I skipped out on our appointment and that I wasn't home when they came to call. How long do I have until my mother and father finish up with the neurologist and hurry home? Already it's three thirty in the afternoon.

I hurry. I waste no time.

I examine the exterior like a dermatologist giving a full-body exam, running my fingers over the burnished steel, searching for signs of damage: a dent or a ding, chipped paint, a missing hubcap. But there are none. I get down on my hands and knees to examine the underside of the vehicle and the tires, all-season tires that look like they've seen better days. The depth of the tread is negligible, though still I find fragments of gravel embedded there, and I think of the gravel fringing the sides of Harvey Road, the sand and crushed stone and clay that span four feet or more on either side of the street. I pluck a piece of gravel from the tire with a fingernail and slide it in a back pocket of my jeans like a crime scene investigator collecting soil samples. Where did these rocks come from? I wonder.

I rise to my feet to continue my search, and I discover a single leaf—the leaf of an oak tree—tucked beneath the blade of a windshield wiper like circulars in a grocery store parking lot. I pluck the leaf from the glass and examine it in my apprehensive hands, a mossy-green leaf mottled with blisters, scaly yellow abscesses that rise from the surface. It's a fungus, I believe. The white oak tree on the side of Harvey Road was ripe with leaves when I last saw it, some green, some yellow, drooping with thirst. I'll bring this leaf with me; I'll compare it to the leaves of Nick's tree. If it's a match, then I'll know. This leaf, I tell myself, along with the gravel, will be all the proof I need to confirm that my mother has done this to me, somehow, in some insoluble way; she has taken Nick from me.

I find nothing else outside the car.

In the distance, I'm quite certain I hear a phone ring, and I peer toward the outside world, away from the garage, waiting for Maisie to joyfully answer my phone with a merry, 'Hello, Boppy!' But from the car, there is only silence, and

I worry now about the children overheating in the car, wondering how long I've been in the garage, how long I've left them alone. I can see Maisie's little head through the back window, and there is movement. She's moving her head. Not much, but a slight sway. Enough that I know she's okay.

I set my hand on the car door's lever and pull swiftly, opening the door. The car beeps as an interior light illuminates the dark cavern of the car. I gaze inside.

The inside of the car is nearly empty, save for an array of road maps and the casing of a Simon & Garfunkle CD left open on the dash, my mother's favorite. If I were to put a key in the ignition and start the car, I'd hear 'The Sound of Silence' playing through the speaker system, timeless voices filling the space. There isn't much to see inside the car, but I go through it with a fine-tooth comb, just in case. I open the glove box and rummage around inside, finding nothing. What I'm looking for, I don't know, though my brain is moving a mile a minute, confused with thoughts of Theo and my mother, images of Kat and Melinda Grey. How in the world could my mother have intentionally pushed Nick from the road? It couldn't have been her; it just couldn't have been. My mother doesn't do anything these days with intent. It's all random and involuntary.

But then it strikes me: maybe it wasn't intentional at all. It was a mistake. The rental property—the home my parents used to own—is a mile or two from Harvey Road. It was just a rotten break that Nick and my mother happened to be driving down the street at the very same time, Nick heading to our house, my mother trying to find the old farmhouse she mistakenly believed was still home. There was nothing calculated about it. It was just bad luck, and I'm afflicted with a sudden pang of sadness, wondering who I feel the most sorry for, Nick or my mother or me.

But there must be proof. I need something tangible so that I will know. Something conclusive. Because without it, my mind keeps spinning, a montage whereby I see half a dozen different faces behind the wheel of the very same car. My mother. Nick. Even Maisie. Even four-year-old Maisie clutching her hands around a leather steering wheel of a car whose accelerator she can't reach.

I have to know for certain. I have to know once and for all.

I keep searching the car, finding thirty-eight cents forgotten in a cup holder, a wad of chewed gum swaddled in the wrapper beneath a seat, piquing my interest. What else might be hiding beneath the seat?

I reach my hand as far as it will go under the passenger's and then the driver's seats, scratching a forearm on the jagged parts beneath that seat, feeling blindly and coming up empty, or almost empty until a single finger grazes something cold and flat beneath the chair, a thin slice of metal no bigger than a key chain or a pocket mirror. I pinch it awkwardly between my fingertips and pull, coming up with far more than I'd ever expected to discover.

I gather the item in a hand before stepping out into the dim light of the garage to see, like an archaeologist peeking through a sieve, looking for treasure.

But this isn't treasure.

At the sight of it, my fingers and legs go lame, unable to move. My heart beats its wings inside my chest, in a panic, quickly taking fright, a trapped bird unable to fly as a predator watches on from a distance. The afternoon sunlight smuggles its way into the garage and hits the object square on, refracting its light toward me, and just like that, I am blind. I lose the ability to see. The world around me becomes a shiny, golden yellow before it fades to black.

My head can no longer think straight, my eyes can no longer see as I realize that the answer to my question lies there, clear as day in the palm of my hand.

NICK

BEFORE

The dance studio is located in an old furniture factory in the town next to ours. It's a three-story redbrick building that lines the railroad tracks. It's been refurbished and flaunts all those exposed beams and ductwork that people want these days. The floors are a dark wood, the office spaces bound by glass. The upper floor of the building is loft apartments, but down below are a photographer's studio, a home decorator, attorneys, dentists and more. And a dance studio, of course. I can't help but wonder what the lease payment is on a place like this, though I also wonder how much traffic comes and goes through. The building is off the beaten path; without a devoted client base, there's no chance in the world of ever being found.

The whole way to ballet, for fifteen miles and nearly thirty minutes, I stared in my rearview mirror, searching for signs of Theo and his Beemer. Nearly every black car I saw scared the daylights out of me, as I was half sure it was Theo coming to get even with Maisie and me in case we weren't already even. I'm not the only one who's scared. In the back seat, Maisie sits with her eyes pinned to glass, quiet like Maisie is never quiet. She holds tightly to my hand as we walk inside, peering over her shoulder. I can feel my eye start to swell, a shiner taking form.

Inside the building, in the common space, there are signs posted—*No tap shoes in the hall*—and yet a group of girls scurry down the corridor, tapping their toes and giggling. As we walk down the hallway, Maisie becomes giddy with anticipation, forgetting about Theo as she skips along.

The other mothers eye me as I step inside the lobby of the dance studio, looking me up and down before they smile. They say a soft hello to Maisie as I help her into her ballet slippers, and she disappears with her friends behind a closed door, where I stand and watch through a pane of glass as the teacher, a pretty woman no more than twenty-one or twenty-two years old, leads the ten girls and one boy through their ballet positions. The women make small talk while we wait, asking me how Clara is feeling and whether or not the baby has arrived. I pull up photos on my phone, and they pass it around, oohing and aahing as they gaze at my boy. 'He looks just like you,' says one of the women, and another says that he's a cutie-pie.

As I stand and watch the ballet class, I feel the week start to weigh heavily on me. I'm tired, and yet I have no good reason to complain. Clara is the one who has tackled all those late night feedings while I've tried to keep her company—tried and failed. But still, I'm tired. I find a couple of quarters in the pocket of my jeans and step toward a vending machine, pressing in the code for a Mountain Dew. I'm not one to drink soda—I know exactly what all those sugar byproducts do to the teeth—but right now, a jolt of caffeine is just what I need. I watch as the plastic bottle falls down into the chute, twist the cap off and quaff half the bottle in a single gulp, sliding the cap into my pocket beside Gus's abandoned green army man that I picked up the other day. There's also a couple Halcion pills stuffed in there, which I plan to flush just as soon as I get home. That's something I no longer want or need.

I wonder when I will find out if Gus is my son.

It's a sinking feeling, knowing that if he is I'll have to confess to Clara about it. I'll have to come clean. I didn't do anything wrong—I didn't even know Clara twelve years ago—and yet this little boy will change the future of our marriage together. There will always be a reminder that before Clara, I'd been with another woman. Clara wasn't the only one.

For the last five minutes of ballet, we're allowed inside the classroom so we can watch the kids perform. The mothers and I line up against a mirrored wall as our children begin to twirl gracelessly to the sound of a Disney soundtrack. I can't take my eyes off Maisie, the awkward and yet adorable way her spindly arms rise up above her head, the way her knees buckle as she bends down to plié, the torn knee of her tights reminding me of Theo, though I try to push his face from my mind and to focus on Maisie and only Maisie. She smiles at me, feeling like a princess, like all eyes are on her and none of the other children. It's spellbinding; I'm hypnotized by my little girl as she peers behind me to see her own reflection in the studio mirror. She waves, and the little figure in the mirror waves back. The other mothers take notice and smile. I pull my phone from my pocket and take a video, thinking how I will show this to Clara when I get home, and then I silently thank Felix for his fussiness this afternoon, knowing that if it hadn't been for Felix and his ravenous appetite, I would have missed out on this moment of my life. Watching Maisie dance.

Back in the lobby, I tell Maisie to sit so I can help her with her shoes. 'Miss Becca says we're going to have a recital,' she's telling me as I remove the slippers and force her foot into the pink sandal. 'She says we get to dance on a big, big stage and wear a pretty dress.'

'Oh, yeah?' I ask, and Maisie says, 'Yeah.' I ask when, but all she does is shrug. She says she's hoping for a pink dress. Pink or purple or bright blue. With sequins and a fluffy tutu.

My stomach grumbles, and Maisie's stomach grumbles, and I realize then that it's nearly five o'clock. Traffic will be a mess on the way home. 'I'm hungry, Daddy,' says Maisie, and I say to her, 'Me, too.'

I call Clara for a quick check-in before Maisie and I leave. She answers on the second ring.

'Hey,' I say to her, and she replies, 'Hey yourself,' though the words are hushed and hard to hear, a forced whisper, and I know right away that Felix is sleeping.

'How's everything going?' I ask, picturing her and Felix at home, on the sofa, watching TV, Felix in her arms or on the floor, maybe, swaddled in a baby blanket.

'Just fine,' she says, and I hear that overwhelming fatigue in her voice, so tangible, like she could close her eyes right now and drift off to sleep.

'Is Felix asleep?'

'Yup,' Clara says, and I do the math in my head, easily

suspecting that if Felix is asleep now, he'll be up half the night, and therefore Clara will be, too.

'Maybe you should wake him,' I suggest, as twin ballerinas wave goodbye to Maisie and drift through the glass door. The room is loud and crowded, so many mothers trying hard to force shoes onto their ballerinas' feet, nobody wanting to go.

'And how should I do that?' Clara asks.

Her words are snappy, and yet I know she doesn't mean for them to be. I don't take it personally. Clara is tired. In the last four days, she's barely slept, and she's still recovering from the pain and ordeal of childbirth. I don't have the first clue what that must feel like.

'I don't know,' I concede, as I force the second of Maisie's sandals onto her feet, and whisper to her, 'Let's go potty before we leave.'

'But, Daddy,' whines Maisie, as expected. Maisie never ever wants to use the bathroom, not until it's an absolute emergency or she's already had an accident. 'I don't have to go potty.'

'You need to try,' I say as I help her to her feet and watch as she disappears behind the ladies' room door. 'Should I pick up something for dinner?' I ask Clara as again my stomach rumbles. I could make something at home, hamburgers on the grill again, but with traffic, I'm guessing it will be six o'clock before I make it there, nearly seven o'clock before we eat. From the other end of the phone, there's no response, and I envision Clara on the couch with Felix in her arms, eyes drifting off to sleep. 'Clara,' I say, deciding for her, 'I'll pick up something for dinner. Maisie and I will be home soon. And then you can rest,' I say as

Maisie arrives through the heavy bathroom door, and I grasp
her by the hand to leave. Tonight, just as soon as I get home,
I'll take Felix from Clara's arms and tell her to lie down
for a while, to get some sleep. She won't be able to keep up
this pace much longer if she doesn't get some sleep soon.
'Chinese or Mexican?' I ask as Maisie and I head off, hand
in hand, through the concourse of the old furniture factory.

Clara says Chinese.

CLAяA

'I've been wondering where I left that,' a voice says. Izzy, whose necklace lies splayed across my hand, her tone icy as I spin around and see her standing behind me, in the doorway that separates the garage from the inside of my parents' home. The temperature inside the garage begins an upsurge as beneath my clothing I begin to sweat.

The realization settles in slowly, an awakening, as I stare at the word *Izzy* now spread across the palm of my hand in curling silver. Izzy's charm somehow disengaged from the chain. She wears the chain, thumbing at it now, though it's only a chain, a silver chain without its charm, the jump ring that holds them together now missing.

'I've been looking everywhere for it,' she says. 'Thank you so much for finding it, Clara,' and she reaches out a hand, waiting to reclaim the charm, thinking I'm just going to waltz right over and hand it to her. 'My mother gave that to me, you know?' she asks, though of course this is something I don't know. 'When I was just a girl. I couldn't stand the thought of losing it,' she adds, and the realization settles on me then with striking clarity. It was Izzy all along. Izzy who killed Nick. Not my mother. Not Theo Hart. Izzy.

'You did it,' I say to her, clutching that charm in my grasp, squeezing tightly, feeling the silver dig deep into my skin, drawing blood. I wait for silly and contrived excuses, but they never come. She doesn't blame my mother, my father for her necklace being inside the car. She doesn't hold up her hands and say, *I didn't do it*, or, *It wasn't me*. I found the proof, evidence that nearly puts Izzy at the scene of the crime, and now the onus is on her to refute it. I wait in vain, but the rebuttal doesn't come.

'What are you talking about?' she asks as she steps fully into the garage, letting the door slam shut behind her so that I flinch from the force of the noise, the impact making the tools that line the wall on a wooden pegboard shake— a screwdriver, a hammer, hand rivets and hex wrenches.

'I knew all along that it wasn't an accident,' I say brusquely, sure to keep one eye on Izzy all the time. I don't know what she's capable of. 'I just didn't know who, but now I do.

'Why?' I implore, speaking louder now, my words angry and aggressive. 'What did Nick ever do to you?' I can't make sense of it, why Izzy, of all people, would want Nick dead. Nick was always so pleasant to her, always so kind. He paid more attention to her than the rest of us ever did. Sweat begins to pool beneath my arms, my shirt sticking to me in odd places, making it hard to move. I pluck the shirt from my skin, fighting for oxygen in the stifling air. I can't imagine why Izzy would have any sort of acrimony toward Nick,

any discord. It couldn't have been about money because
there was no money. Nick and I have no money; we verge
on broke. But maybe it was the impression of money—
Nick's private practice and our ample home. Maybe this
is the reason why Izzy decided to take his life. My mind
then springs in a dozen different directions—an unrequited
romantic gesture, hush money, ransom, unfulfilled promises of giving her our firstborn child and more—but none
of them make sense. It's all so farcical; there could be no
sound reason why Izzy would want Nick dead.

'Why did you kill Nick?' I demand. 'Why, Izzy, why?
What did he ever do to you?' The expression on her face
shifts, and suddenly she looks confused. She's a good actress, I'll give her that, but also a murderer. 'How did you
do it?' I ask. 'Did you trail him to ballet? Follow him home?
That's premeditated murder,' I tell her, and I'm crying now,
though I don't want to be crying, but there are tears snaking
down my cheeks as I speak, imagining a run-in between
Nick and Izzy, some blowup outside the ballet studio for
reasons I don't know. Did Maisie see? Did she catch sight
of Nick and Izzy in a tiff? Or maybe it was something that
happened during class, and Maisie, tucked safely away with
Miss Becca, didn't see? I think back to our last conversation, Nick and me on the phone, talking about dinner. Just
an ordinary, mundane conversation, like any of the other
thousands of conversations we've had. He didn't know he
was going to die. Whatever transpired between him and
Izzy that day hadn't yet begun. It happened later, I tell myself, after he left ballet. There was never a bad *man*. It was
a bad *woman*. Izzy was the bad woman, but thanks to the
sun in her eyes, Maisie couldn't see.

'What are you talking about, Clara?' Izzy asks. 'I didn't kill Nick,' she says. 'Nick killed Nick. We all know that.'

'No, Izzy,' I snap. 'You killed Nick. You. In this car,' I say as I thrust a hand toward my mother's Chevrolet. 'I have proof,' I spit, telling her Betty Maurer spotted a black Chevrolet leaving the scene of the crime, and how the silver *Izzy* charm puts her inside the car. The murder weapon.

'Oh, Clara,' she says, this odd combination of indignation and pity. 'You're just as crazy as your mother,' she says, and I take great insult at this, not for my sake but for my mother's. This is the woman who is supposed to love my mother, to care for her better than my father and I can. 'Everyone knows Nick was a lousy driver. He killed himself,' she says, but of course she's wrong. I can't let her sidetrack me, as she reminds me how Nick and Maisie were all alone at the time of the accident, how, as Detective Kaufman has already told me more times than I can count, it was Nick's reckless driving that caused the car to hurl off the side of the road and into the tree. Nick is the only one to blame. 'You're imagining things, Clara,' she tells me. 'You're in denial. You have to accept the facts, Clara, and not let these fantasies mess with your head. Nick killed Nick,' she says. 'He's the only one to blame.'

But, no, I tell myself. It was Izzy. She killed Nick. It's so utterly obvious. Of course she did. I've connected her to the murder weapon. It has to be.

'No, Izzy,' I snap. 'You did it. You,' and then I interrogate her, demanding to know why she was in my mother's car if what she says is true, and why her charm was under the seat. 'Why?' I shout, starting to lose all sense of self-control. I reach for a baseball bat leaning against the garage wall, and think of coming at Izzy with it until she confesses, of swooping the bat at her again and again, trying hard to take her down like a group of black-capped chickadees mobbing a hawk.

But then I think of the kids, of Maisie and Felix, trapped inside the stifling car. How long have they been there? Ten minutes? Thirty? An hour? It wasn't meant to be this long. How long does it take for children to die in cars? I made sure to leave the windows down, but the eighty-or ninety-degree air outside is no better than that which is in the car. I've lost track of time, and now I envision them, sweating, dehydrated, convulsing, their breathing slow and shallow as their body temperatures soar to 105 or 106 degrees, and I begin to panic, knowing the wretched death that comes from heatstroke.

Izzy doesn't answer my questions but instead she screams at me, 'You're such a fool, Clara. Such a fucking fool,' as that sweet, obliging composure starts to wane. 'You don't know anything,' she insists.

'Then tell me,' I insist, stepping toward her with that bat in hand. I don't mean to do it, but the bat rises suddenly and sharply in my hands, the arch of the bat's swing now aimed at Izzy. She flinches, though I stop there, never swinging. Merely holding the bat in my hands. A threat. 'Tell me,' I say again, and when she doesn't, I say, 'See? You're a liar. You were in the car because you killed Nick.'

'You couldn't be any more wrong,' she snaps, and there's this holier-than-thou expression on her face that I despise. A smug, arrogant mien that I want to displace. 'You wouldn't hit me,' she haughtily assumes, and so I do. I clip her with the bat, that's all. A mere graze, though from the look on her face you'd think I hit her with all my might. It swells there at the point of impact, on her arm, that's all, and she grabs for it, mouth agog, saying, 'You hit me. You hit me, Clara,' and I nod knowingly, because of course I know that I did.

And like that the smugness of her expression is gone.

'I did,' I tell her, 'and I'll do it again,' as I wind up for another swing. She flinches this time before I even have a chance to think about striking, telling me to stop. Telling me she'll scream. Telling me she'll call the police.

'You're going to call the police and turn yourself in?' I ask, laughing, though it's not funny at all. There's nothing funny about it, and yet, I'm laughing. 'Please, do,' I say as again the bat descends through the air, meeting Izzy this time in the hip. There's a noise when Izzy and the bat connect. The hollow clapping of wood on wood, of Izzy screaming in pain.

I've hit bone.

'What are you doing?' she squawks, her voice desperate and shrill as her legs nearly give from the force of the hit. She reaches out blindly for something, anything to hang on to, to hold her upright, but finds nothing, her hand writhing through the air. 'Go away, Clara. Go away,' she says, voice catching on the last words of her plea so that if I didn't know better I'd think she might cry.

She's a good actress, indeed.

I stop laughing. 'Why were you in the car, Izzy?' I ask a final time, and this time she calls out, voice quivering, any sign of condescension gone, 'Mine wouldn't start,' she claims, 'I couldn't get the damn thing to start, and Louisa had an appointment. Your father wasn't home because, Clara, he was with you. *You*. I had to get Louisa to the doctor. We took her car,' she states, though I know a liar when I see one, and Izzy is a liar. Her nostrils flare, she bites her lip, clutching her hip, no longer standing upright but now hunched to the side, suddenly unable to meet my eye.

'You're lying,' I scream. 'You're a goddamn liar. Tell me the truth,' I demand. 'Tell me why you were in the car. Tell me why you killed Nick,' as I toss the baseball bat on my shoulder, a batter ready and waiting for the perfect pitch. And then it comes, apparently, a curveball from the pitcher's mound, and I strike, getting Izzy in the thigh. She emits a savage sound, something tameless and brute. Unhuman. An animal dying.

'You want to know why I was in the car?' she blubbers this time, eyes locked and steady, bracing her leg. 'To get the VIN number. To find the insurance cards. Before I got rid of the car. That's why, Clara,' she screams, and this time I know she's not lying.

'To hide the evidence?' I demand, seeing now how Izzy planned to get rid of my mother's car—to torch it maybe, or sink it to the bottom of a retention pond somewhere—so she could never be connected to Nick's murder.

But Izzy only laughs at me, a nervous snicker. 'What evidence?' she asks, eyes locked on the barrel of the baseball bat. 'This car? This old car? I was doing your parents a favor by getting rid of it, something your father should have done long ago. This car is hardly *evidence*.'

'It's the car that killed Nick,' I state, wanting to pluck the gravel and the leaf from my pocket and show her as proof that this is the car that killed Nick. 'The evidence that puts you at the crime scene.'

'Oh, Clara. Poor Clara. There was no crime scene, don't

you understand? Don't you get it?' The look in her eye is an odd combination of pity and loathing, hate and disbelief.

'No, Izzy, no,' I snap. 'I don't get it. So tell me,' I snarl. 'Tell me, Izzy. Make me understand,' as my knuckles turn white on the handle of the bat, my grip ironclad.

At first she doesn't tell me. She stands before me, thinking, staring. She isn't going to tell me, I think. She isn't going to confess.

I jerk the bat ever so slightly, wondering this time what I should hit: her head or her chest. Which one will hurt more, which one will elicit a confession?

'For the insurance payout, Clara,' she spits out, wincing at the small movement of the bat. 'So I could get money. It's the actual cash value at the time of the car's disappearance, you know. Nearly three thousand dollars, I assume, which isn't much, but it's something. It's more than I get from the agency for a month's worth of work. Cooking for your folks, cleaning up after Louisa, wiping her ass, all the while being called an idiot. Don't you think I deserve this?' she asks, though I can't make sense of it, what that payout has to do with Nick's death. Did Nick know she planned to claim the car stolen to take money from my parents? Did he confront her about it, and for this reason she drove him off the side of the road and into a tree?

'But you were in the car,' I insist. 'You were driving the car that killed Nick.'

'No,' she tells me, 'no. I was in the car gathering the information I needed to call the police and report the car stolen. That's all, Clara. That's all. I never even set the keys in the ignition.'

'But the car isn't stolen,' I say, confused, as the heat starts to get to me, weighing heavily on me, wearing me down. 'The car is here,' I insist, pointing to it as if Izzy can't see it there beside her, the black Chevrolet that ended Nick's life.

She laughs. It's the laugh of a narcissist, a high-pitched laugh that rattles my every last nerve. I step toward Izzy again, consumed with a sudden desire to strike her hard. Not merely as a warning or a threat this time, but to shut her up. To make her stop laughing. 'It isn't stolen yet, Clara,' she corrects. 'Not yet. Nick had to get in the way of my plan.'

'Nick knew? Nick knew you planned to steal the car?' I insist, putting the pieces together. Yes, that's it, I think. I was right all along. Nick knew about Izzy's plans to steal the car, and he confronted her on it and for this reason he's now dead.

'Oh, Clara. Sweet Clara,' she says in this trivializing way, downgrading me to a raving lunatic. And that's how I feel in the moment, like a lunatic, like all the answers are just out of reach, floating away like dust particles in the atmosphere. Like Izzy is speaking Japanese, and I have to take time to look her words up one by one, to translate them, to makes sense of what she means, but by the time I find the meaning of her words, they've changed course. 'Nick got in the way because he died. Because he killed himself. The last thing I needed to do was draw any more attention to your folks with a missing car. I was waiting for all the hoopla to die down.'

'The hoopla? Meaning us mourning Nick's death?' I ask, and she says yes. Nick's death is hoopla, a singular term that reduces it to nothing. To an inconvenience. A hassle.

'And once the hoopla died down you were going to get rid of the car?' I ask, making a slow connection. 'Then you were going to claim it stolen? For the insurance payout?' and she nods her head, clapping her hands at me, an applause. I've figured this out. Except I haven't. Not yet anyway. It still makes no sense to me why Izzy has taken Nick's life.

Or am I wrong about this still?

Was it not Izzy at all?

My thoughts revert to my mother, to Theo Hart, to Emily. Maybe it wasn't Izzy after all.

'It seemed the quickest and easiest way to get my hands on some cash,' she says.

'But the money would have belonged to my father,' I say. 'The check would have been made out to him,' I argue, knowing with certainty that when the insurance company did pay out for a pseudo-stolen vehicle, it was my father who would have received the three thousand dollars. Not Izzy. What did Izzy have to gain from getting rid of the black Chevy?

'You're so naive, Clara. So naive. You and your father both,' she says, and I feel the blood in my veins begin to boil because Izzy can say anything she'd like about me, but she cannot disparage my father. The last thing my father is is naive. 'As always, he'd endorse the check and leave it lying around to deposit. And when it went missing, as it no doubt would, we'd blame your mother. Poor Louisa who is forever losing things. Meanwhile I'd be at the bank cashing the damn thing.'

It's a realization that settles over me slowly like the dawning sun, one faint glimmer of light after the other.

This has nothing to do with Nick.

And then I understand.

Izzy did all of this. Izzy stole the endorsed check, she

made the regular cash withdrawals from my father's account, she opened a credit card in my mother's name. She bought herself jewelry, a bangle bracelet made of genuine jade, which glares at me now from the fleshy wrist, just inches away from my grandmother's wedding ring, which she also stole. She's been stealing from my parents all this time. My mother hasn't been misplacing things. Izzy has taken them.

'That bracelet?' I ask, to be sure. 'Where did you get that bracelet?' though again my thoughts are a jumble, not knowing what the jade bracelet has to do with the receipt for a pendant necklace I found in Nick's drawer. They're one in the same, aren't they? Nick used my parents' credit card to purchase the necklace, helping himself to hundreds of dollars of my father's hard-earned money. To buy a necklace for Kat, I'd assumed. Because he was sleeping with her. Because he loved Kat more than me.

Izzy thumbs at the bracelet. 'Your father bought this for me,' she says with a wink as my grip on the baseball bat again constricts, a boa constrictor squeezing its prey. I'm feeling dizzy, nauseous from the heat of the garage. I'm losing control, wondering again what Izzy's thievery has to do with Nick's death? Are they one and the same? Are they connected somehow? Did Nick know?

Or are they disjointed facts, and my imagination is to blame for fusing them together?

But if not Izzy, then who?

Who? I want to scream, or maybe I do scream it aloud for Izzy just stares at me with eyes gaping wide, listening to my breathless scream. *Who? Who? Who?*

'You,' I say, pointing a finger at her, thinking how worried I'd been about my parents' finances and my father's state of mind. 'You.' And at that I raise the bat to strike her in the chest, or maybe the head, and Izzy pushes me in return, her face turning florid, a frightening contrast to the white of her bleached hair. I stumble awkwardly into the hand tools that line the garage wall and at once a wheal begins to form on my shoulder, fiercely red and rising from the surface of the skin. I stare at Izzy in dismay; this can't possibly be the same woman who trails on the heels of my mother, predicting her every move. Gently, lovingly catering to her. Caring for her.

'Why would you tell me this? Why in the world did you confess?' I ask, though of course I know why she confessed. She confessed because I left her no choice. Because I threatened to beat the life out of her if she didn't confess, and now I'll do it regardless, confession or not.

'Because stealing, Clara, is a far cry from murder. I might be a thief, but I'm no murderer. I never killed Nick,' she says defensively this time, and for once I can't tell if she's lying or not. 'You have to believe me,' she begs, her voice suddenly desperate and pleading, and I find that in that moment I don't know what to believe, for it's happening so fast and I'm so confused, certain that Melinda was to blame, then my mother, then Theo and Emily and Izzy.

If Izzy didn't kill Nick, then who?

'Why would I believe you?' I ask.

'You said it yourself, Clara,' she says, confusing me. 'I had no reason to kill Nick. Nick, who was always so kind to me. I'm just as sad about Nick's passing as you are,' she claims as a puddle of phony tears fills the basins of her eyes and she begins to cry. It exasperates me, the bogus tears at my dead husband's expense. It makes me lose control. How vain to think that she is as saddened by Nick's death as me. He was my husband. He loved me the most.

And that's when I lose it.

I brace myself to strike. I'm feeling off-kilter, finding it hard to stand, much less think, as I raise the bat up above my head. I haven't slept in weeks, and the delirium and confusion and sadness chip quickly away at me, a wood carver with chisel, rendering me a skeleton of myself. I come at Izzy with all of my might, flinching as if it hurts me more than it does her.

I'm stricken by a sudden and visceral irascibility, and it hits me then: this is just as she did to Nick, though in my heart of hearts I know it isn't necessarily true, but I need someone, anyone, to take the blame for Nick's death. It's a means to an end, that's all. Killing Izzy because I so desperately need someone to blame so this can be over and done with. I need closure. Acceptance.

Self-defense, I'll later allege, though I'm not thinking about that right now.

Right now I'm only thinking that I need for this to be through.

NICK

BEFOᴙE

We pick up the Chinese food first and then head home. As expected, traffic is a nightmare, stir-crazed drivers at the helm, ready to be home. They accelerate quickly and then slam on the brake, going nowhere. The sun is bright this evening, the day still hot. The thermometer on my car's dashboard reads eighty-three degrees. As the sun sinks lower and lower into the evening sky, its glaring light lands in that cavity just beneath the visor's edge so that there's nothing there to dull the light. It disorients me as I drive on, having forgotten my sunglasses at home. I find that it's hard to see. I use the rear tires of the car before me as a guide. I can't see anything up above—not the houses or the trees—because the sun is there, turning the world into a sea of flames.

I take the back roads to avoid the gridlock of the highway, gliding down Douglas to Wolf Road. The car fills with the scent of ginger and soy sauce, and my stomach growls at the anticipation of food. Maisie sits in her car seat, kicking her little feet against the back of the passenger's seat, asking, 'When will we be home, Daddy?' and I tell her soon. 'I want to be home now,' she pouts, and again I tell her, peering over my shoulder to look her in the eye, that we'll be home soon. Her eyes are sad, pleading, desperate. 'I'm hungry,' she complains, and I pat my stomach and say that I am hungry, too.

'I'm starving,' I tell Maisie. 'I'm so hungry I could eat a horse.'

At this Maisie laughs, a high-pitched squeal, and comes back with, 'I'm so hungry I could eat a sheep,' and we both laugh.

'I could eat a pig,' I say, and Maisie says, 'I could eat a cow,' as the tires of the car in front of me come to a sudden halt, and I slam on the brakes, the car kicking up rocks as I swerve to the side of the road, missing the bumper by a mere three inches. I inwardly curse the logjam of evening traffic, this stop-and-go for no apparent reason at all. Car horns honk, and slowly, we begin to move.

And then my cell phone begins to ring. My first thought is that it's Clara asking me to pick up milk on the way home, milk as well as Chinese, but when the Bluetooth display bears the name *Kat*, my heart skips a beat.

It's Kat, calling finally to tell me if Gus is my son.

Just like that my hands begin to sweat, and I'm no longer thinking about evening traffic.

'Where are your books?' I ask Maisie before answering the call.

'Right here, Daddy,' she says, motioning to the basket of books by her side. Clara always keeps books inside her car for Maisie to read, something to keep her occupied so that Clara can drive. Maisie's never-ending questions are often a distraction.

'Can you read your books?' I ask, and she says, 'Okay, Daddy,' hoping that if she's concentrating on the pages of her picture books, she won't overhear the conversation that's about to transpire between Kat and me, words like *Gus* and *father* and *paternity* breathed into the air. Maisie's little hands reach clumsily into the basket, and she comes up with a red-and-green board book she's had since she was Felix's age. *Goodnight Moon.* She begins to read.

'Kat,' I say into the phone, answering it on the fourth ring. I disable the Bluetooth so I can speak to her through the phone, half the conversation muted so that Maisie can't hear. 'You've gotten the results,' I say. My voice is gasping, my heart beating fast.

This is the moment where everything changes.

'I got the results,' Kat begins, but Maisie is whining again from the back seat, claiming she's so hungry, she's starving, that she can eat a dog, a cat, a barn owl. She's trying to sidetrack me, to start up a game that I've already put the kibosh on. Usually I'd give in, but not right now. Right now I need to speak to Kat, to find out if Gus is my son, and so I press a finger to my lips to quiet her down. I whisper in an aside, 'Daddy's on a work call,' hoping that it means something to her, whether or not it really is a work call. But no; Maisie continues to plead her case, clutching her stomach as if besieged by hunger pains. I relent only to quiet her down, digging deep into the bag of Chinese food for fortune cookies, and coming up with three in my hand. A bribe. I reach into the back seat and drop them all to her lap, and she smiles mischievously; she got her way.

'What is it, Kat?' I beg. 'What did they say?'

She's quiet.

'The results,' she says, her voice hard to hear as I roll through a stop sign. I think she's crying.

'What is it, Kat?' I ask again, but before she can answer me, Maisie's voice comes again, so that I have to tell Kat to hold on. Maisie is upset again, but this time it has nothing to do with hunger pains.

'Who's that?' Maisie asks, her voice agitated as another car drifts past the median from behind, a little too close to my tail end for comfort, honking their horn and making a harebrained attempt to pass. What an idiot. He or she is going to get us all killed. It's a no-passing zone, the solid yellow line I can clearly see even with the blinding sunlight. It's not as if I'm driving slowly, but regardless I take the hint and pick up the pace, accelerating now down Harvey Road so that this jerk will get off my tail. But the car comes at me again, making a second attempt to pass, and this time Maisie is scared, truly freaked out, and she screams to me, 'It's the bad man, Daddy! The bad man is after us,' and I reach into the back seat and pat her kneecap, telling her everything will be fine. But I see it, too. I see exactly what Maisie sees as she says to me, 'He's going to get us, Daddy!' as a black vehicle soars around up from behind so that I have to tug on the steering wheel to get out of the car's way, again hitting gravel. It's Theo, Maisie thinks, but it's not Theo. It's just a black car. Just some driver in a hurry, trying like the rest of us to get home. I let up on the gas to let the driver pass, watching as he or she breezes by.

But before I can tell Maisie not to worry, Kat speaks.

'They were negative, Nick. Gus is not your son,' Kat

says, and as she begins to sob on the other end of the line, I'm speechless. *Gus is not my son.*

I'm wondering what I should say to Kat. This wasn't what I was expecting, a negative result. I thought for sure that Gus was my son. I'd convinced myself he was mine.

What I feel is an overwhelming sense of relief, the weight of the world lifted from my shoulders—again. A sense that for once in my life, I'm the luckiest man alive. The tide has turned. Good things are happening to me.

He is not my son.

'Are you sure?' I ask, and Kat gathers herself for a moment and says that she's sure, but then she sobs through the phone, telling me how much she'd hoped it was true. How much she needed it to be true, and I placate her by saying, 'Me, too,' though that's the last thing in the world I was hoping for. If he was mine, I would have manned up and done the right thing. I would have told Clara, and she and I would have welcomed Gus into our lives. But without Gus around, life is much less complicated, less complex.

I press down on the gas pedal, suddenly excited to be home. To hold Clara in my arms and know for the first time in a long time that everything will be all right.

This is good news, I tell myself, smiling broadly as the car skids off the side of the road, hitting gravel, and I right it quickly, forcing both hands on the steering wheel. I tell myself to focus, to drive in a straight line. To slow down a bit.

Clara will still be there whether I get there in five minutes or ten.

I picture Clara holding Felix in her arms, both of them half asleep, waiting for Maisie and me.

I try hard to put Kat and Gus out of my mind, though it's near impossible with Kat on the other end of the line crying.

'It's going to be okay,' I say drily. 'You and Steve,' I say, 'you'll be okay,' though what I'm thinking is how I will come clean to Clara about my meetings with Kat. Tonight. How I will wipe the slate clean with a confession, and then remove Kat forever from my life. There will no longer be secrets between Clara and me. It's one of the cardinal rules of a happy marriage. No secrets. A promise I made to Clara long ago, and one I plan to keep.

All I can think about in that moment is getting home. Of being home. Of being with Clara and Maisie and Felix. The loves of my life. Of sitting on the sofa with the three of them and Harriet by our feet. Of telling Clara everything, every last secret I've been keeping from her, every last lie. And even though Clara won't be happy about it, she'll understand. Because that is Clara. Indulgent and understanding.

And in that moment I'm hardly able to contain my excitement, wanting nothing more in that split second than to be in Clara's arms.

CLARA

In the end it's Maisie who stops me. My Maisie standing in the stifling garage, watching as I hoist the baseball hat over my head for the sixth or seventh time, while Izzy cowers in the corner of the wood-framed walls, hands to her head to protect it from my blows. There is blood. A steady stream of it that snakes from her nose. Bright red blood, red like red currants, that drips to the concrete floor.

'Mommy,' says Maisie, that simple word knocking me in the gut. *Mommy*.

In her hand, my cell phone. 'Mommy,' she whispers to me again, extending the phone, though her eyes travel from Izzy to me and back again, scared, so that I can see the way the phone shakes in her hand, and I know it isn't Izzy she's scared of.

It's me.

Her eyes are wide and terrified. They fill with tears. She stands in a princess dress because it was what she insisted on wearing today and I didn't care enough to object. It's a beautiful dress made of organza, a Halloween costume that Maisie considers appropriate for daily wear, with glittery rosettes stitched to the bodice and light-up, high-heeled shoes. On her head is a tiara. Lilac in color with feather trim and colored jewels. Perched askew on the top of her head, threatening to fall.

She's just a child. A wholesome child watching her mother beat the life out of another woman while the woman begs for her to stop.

'It's Boppy on the phone,' she says, trying hard not to cry, and in that moment I lose control of my body. My legs go weak and lame. The bat falls from my grasp. 'Tell Boppy I'll call him back,' I say as I shrivel to the ground like flowers withering in the heat of the afternoon sun, and Izzy takes advantage of this—bruised but not broken Izzy, who limps and bleeds but is very much still alive—to make a run for it. I don't have it in me to stop her as she hobbles through the house for her purse and keys, and heads for her car. I watch on as she climbs inside and fights the aging engine to start, driving off down the street, her *Izzy* charm still clenched in my fist.

Izzy can wait.

'It's okay,' I say to Maisie, extending my pinkie finger as only Nick would do. 'Pinkie promise, it's okay,' I tell her and, as she slips her tiny pinkie through mine, she smiles weakly, though her hand still shakes and on my fingertips there is blood.

* * *

I stagger into the police station with Felix in my arms and Maisie on my heels. The very same quasi-receptionist in uniform greets me, and this time I don't need to wait fifteen minutes to speak to the detective. Detective Kaufman is phoned without delay, and he quickly appears, standing before me, eyeing my children and me.

'Mrs. Solberg,' he says, and I'm not sure if it's concern that crosses his face or something more like disbelief or incredulity, but I don't care. My mouth opens, and these words come tumbling out, 'She did it. She killed Nick,' I say, and the detective asks, 'Who, Mrs. Solberg, who?'

'Izzy,' I say.

'Who is Izzy?' he asks cynically, and I don't respond right away for I can't find the words to explain. Again he asks, 'Mrs. Solberg, who is Izzy?' and this time I manage to tell him.

'My mother's caregiver. Izzy Chapman,' I say, and as I start to rattle off the woman's credentials, I wonder how much of it is true, or whether Izzy lied about them to deceive us, my father and me easily putting our trust in her because we were so desperate for good help we would have believed anything.

'And what reason would Ms. Chapman have for killing Nick? Did she have a motive?' he asks, stepping forward, and when I splutter, not willing or not able to hush my voice for the children's sake, 'I don't know, I don't know, but she killed him. I know she did,' Detective Kaufman leads me to an interrogation room and suggests we start at the beginning. But before we do, he phones for another detective, a female detective by the name of Howell—Detective Howell—to come and lay claim to Maisie. Maisie is too young to overhear the conversation that's about to transpire, and though she doesn't want to, it's in Maisie's best interest that she goes.

'I don't want to,' moans Maisie, eyes pleading with mine as Detective Howell reaches out a hand and says, 'I'm pretty sure I saw cookies in the vending machine. You like chocolate chip?' and Maisie gives in, only for the sake of cookies. Detective Howell has also promised to find coloring pages, and I wonder if, somewhere in another interrogation room much like mine, she will sit Maisie down and ask her about what she saw today, the bat and the blood, Izzy begging for me to stop.

With Maisie gone and Felix asleep in my arms, Detective Kaufman again asks me to explain, and I begin falteringly to recount my story of the black Chevrolet, the *Izzy* charm I found beneath the seat of the car. My words verge on incoherent. The detective only stares. He's unimpressed with my fieldwork and displays far more interest in Izzy stealing from my parents than her committing murder. The facts that he bullet points on the legal pad before him have to do with the stolen check, credit card fraud, insurance fraud and more, but when I raise my voice and insist, 'She killed my husband,' he gazes at me disinterestedly—or maybe it's with shame and pity—and asks to know about the blood on my hands.

I open my mouth and commit perjury. 'Self-defense,' I allege, saying how Izzy came after me with the baseball bat. How I was only trying to protect myself from her.

'She killed Nick,' I assert. 'I didn't know what she was capable of. I had to protect myself. I had to protect my children.'

'Did you hit her with the bat?' he asks, and I say, 'Of course not.'

'When is the last time you've eaten, Mrs. Solberg?' he asks, evaluating my dry skin, my hollow cheekbones, my tired eyes. Like magic the baby weight has disappeared from my stomach and hips, and instead of a potbellied pig, I've become gaunt. 'Have you been eating, sleeping? There are grief counselors, you know,' he says, but I snap at this, telling him I don't want a goddamn grief counselor. I want him to find the person who killed Nick.

'And where is Ms. Chapman?' he asks then, and I tell him she ran. 'Is she okay, Mrs. Solberg? Did you hurt her?' and I shrug drily and say, 'Nothing she won't get over,' but even this is something I don't know. How hard did I hit her? I wonder now, thinking of the fury with which I swung that baseball bat. Did I hit her head, or was it only her hands? Did her hands protect her head from my repeated blows? Or might there be damage, internal damage, far more damning than a bloody nose?

I check my watch. It's nearing four thirty. 'She could be anywhere by now,' I say, though I beg the detective to send an officer to keep watch over my mother and father's home in case she returns, and he relents, saying he will. He'll send someone at once. 'You'll look for her,' I insist. 'You'll arrest Izzy.' But all Detective Kaufman assures me is that if and when his officers find her, they'll bring her in for questioning in regards to fraud and theft. If my father chooses to press charges, that is.

'And murder,' I remind him, though the expression on his face says otherwise, and I think that maybe it's not murder after all, but rather manslaughter, vehicular homicide or some other designation of which I don't know. I've gotten the terminology wrong, that's all. The wrong verbiage.

'Not murder,' he says. 'Ms. Chapman didn't kill your husband, Mrs. Solberg,' the detective categorically states. He's inexpressive, staring straight-faced at me. He doesn't smile. He doesn't so much as blink.

'You know who did, then?' I plead, desperate for him to tell me without a shadow of a doubt who was behind the wheel of my mother's car when it ran Nick off the side of the road. If not Izzy, then it must have been my mother. Perhaps my first inclination was right as I sat on my sofa this morning with Maisie on my lap, watching the images of the black Chevrolet load on the computer screen. Perhaps it was my mother after all who slipped behind the wheel of the car, driving off down the road alone because driving, like riding a bike or climbing the stairs or playing the piano, is one of those procedural memories that require no conscious thought and therefore are far less easy to forget. She was trying to get home. To the home she still believes is her home. Is wasn't intentional, but a case of being at the wrong place at the wrong time. She could have easily taken out another driver, another vehicle on the road, and only by chance was it Nick. A tough break. Bad luck.

That's it, then. My mother has killed Nick. It wasn't Izzy. It was my mother all along, though all these presumptions, all this conjecture, is enough to make me go slowly insane. I'm trapped inside a fun house whereby everything is skewed, and my center of gravity is thrown off by centrifugal force. The floor beneath my feet moves, tilting me from left to right, up and down, threatening to plummet my body entirely through a trapdoor so that I'll soon disappear completely. Everything is distorted; I can't make sense of what I see.

I need closure. Acceptance.

I need to know with absolute certainty who killed Nick.

'There's something I need to show you,' the detective says, leaving the room and returning moments later with a laptop in his hands. He sets it on the table before me, typing in a password to bring it to life.

'This won't be easy to watch,' he says.

'What is it?' I ask as a video loads and a grainy thumbnail appears, and all I can make out are a fenced field and trees.

'The quality isn't the best,' he apologizes, explaining to me about a man and a woman, a Mr. and Mrs. Konig who live just off Harvey Road in a home that overlooks the road. He shows me a snapshot on his phone. A yellow farmhouse with trim the color of rust. I recognize it immediately, the lemon chiffon farmhouse with its dogwood tree in full bloom. I remember Maisie sitting beneath that tree, her shorts getting soaked by the marshy lawn in the aftermath of a storm.

'I spoke to the couple that lives there,' I say.

'Yes,' says Detective Kaufman. 'Mr. and Mrs. Konig. They remember you.'

I nod my head, thinking of the kind couple. I didn't know their names at the time, but now I do. 'They weren't home when the accident happened. They didn't see a thing.'

'That's right,' the detective agrees, and I recall what a great view they would have had from the farmhouse's front porch, how conceivably they could have watched the whole scene play out before their eyes if only they'd have been home. 'A strange thing happened,' he says, setting his phone aside as he strokes his mustache and beard, looking intently at me. 'Mr. Konig stopped by the station this morning. There was some vandalism on his property, you see. Spray paint on the barn doors, damage to the horse pasture.'

'What a shame,' I say, though the compassion is lacking from my voice because Mr. and Mrs. Konig suffered vandalism while I've lost my spouse. There's a difference, you see.

'It is,' says Detective Kaufman. 'Teenage pranksters, but as you can imagine, the Konigs were upset.'

'I can imagine,' I say, and though I feel sorry for the couple, this doesn't have a thing to do with me. The detective is stalling, finding a way to tell me he can't look into Nick's murder because he's too busy investigating the defacement of the Konig property. I'm about to make a scene, to demand to speak to someone other than Detective Kaufman, to another detective, one with a higher pay grade, or a captain or deputy chief. 'What does this possibly have to do with Nick's murder?' I ask, sounding incredulous because I am.

'Thankfully for the Konigs, they have a surveillance camera on the exterior of their home. Backing up to the main road, and in such an uninhabited part of town, this isn't the first time this has occurred on their property. Vandalism. Mr. Konig had the camera installed a few months ago so that he could catch the perpetrators, and he did. We have them on video,' he says, motioning to the thumbnail on the screen before me, a bird's-eye view of the Konig yard. 'Now we just need to identify them,' Detective Kaufman adds, and I look to him in question, my cheeks flaming red. He can't possibly think I have something to do with the vandalism to the Konig property. Can he?

I suck in my breath. I try not to cry. 'You think I know who they are?' I ask, but he shakes his head and tells me no.

'No, Mrs. Solberg. No, I don't. You see,' he says, handing me a tissue so that I can blot at my rheumy eyes, 'the surveillance camera records up to thirty days of continuous feed. After this latest incident, Mr. Konig sat down to watch the recordings, hoping to catch the person or people who trashed his yard. But as it turns out,' he says, pushing Play on the video and sitting back to watch with me, 'he found much more than he was looking for.'

The video begins. It's gritty, the images pixelated, but I can make it out nonetheless. Some techie has no doubt zoomed in on the scene the detective wants me to see, so that the Konig property becomes an afterthought, and instead I'm focused on a lonely, deserted road. The angle of the video is odd, so that the street slopes downward at forty-five degrees. It's a color video, the trees and the grass a fading green, the street a gray concrete. The wind swooshes through the leaves of the trees, and though the video lacks volume, I imagine I hear it, the rustle of the parched and papery leaves in the blistering air as a squirrel gathers a fallen nut in its greedy little mouth and darts quickly across the street without a sideward glance in either direction. Though the houses themselves have been cropped from view, I spy a mailbox, the edge of a driveway, refuse in the grass. A sagging wooden fence. There isn't a single car traveling on the road. For nearly two and a half minutes there's nothing to see.

The date stamp in the corner reads June 23. The day that Nick died.

The time is 5:47 p.m.

At seeing this, my breath leaves me. Though I try, I can't avert my eyes. I'm lost in a state of hypnosis, no longer feeling the chair beneath my frame. I've gone numb, paralyzed, frozen in time. The room pulls away from me so that it's only me and the video, the video and me, as I'm teleported to the side of Harvey Road on the afternoon that my husband died.

'Shall we continue?' the detective asks, his words muddied as if I'm swimming in water, overpowered by violent ocean waves, drowning. His hand reaches out to pause the video, and it's a gut reaction when I swat it away, my hand chafing his.

'Yes,' I say with conviction, my voice staid. 'Let it play.'

This is the moment I find everything out. This is the moment I will know who killed Nick.

Beside me Detective Kaufman leans back in his chair and folds his hands in his lap. He watches me, though I'm unable to meet his eyes, finding myself transfixed by the green grass and the concrete, a scrap of refuse that quivers in the humid breeze.

And then a vehicle enters the scene.

It's black, and my mind thinks of Maisie and her fear of black cars. It comes hobbling down the road quite slowly, and Detective Kaufman explains to me that they took the liberty of slowing down the clip so that it was easier to see. 'That car,' he says as he points to the black vehicle now taking center stage, 'was likely speeding,' though as the car approaches the bend, red lights illuminate on the tail end as the driver steps on the brakes to slow, rounding the corner and disappearing from the lower corner of the screen.

My eyes bound back toward the opposite corner, waiting for Nick and Maisie to appear, followed closely by the person who killed Nick. I envision my mother at the helm of her black Chevrolet Malibu, hunched white-knuckled over the steering wheel, feet likely barefoot or forced into the pair of suede slipper clogs, right leg depressed on the gas, trying desperately to get *home*.

I exhale long and slow, unaware of how long I've been holding my breath until I start to feel light-headed, carbon dioxide collecting in my blood thanks to a shortage of oxygen. My breathing is labored, but Detective Kaufman doesn't notice. I am the only one who knows.

A sliver of red appears at the edge of the video, and I gasp. My car, which Nick took that day to ballet. 'We can take a break if you need,' the detective offers, but I say no.

'Let it play,' I say.

The car moves at a snail's pace along Harvey Road. At least that's the way it seems to me, though again, the video has been slowed, and Detective Kaufman tells me that already Nick was likely driving fifty miles per hour or more. 'He was trying to get away,' I say, but the detective doesn't say yes or no. The dimensions of the video are wide, encapsulating nearly forty feet before the bend. Breathlessly, I wait for my mother to appear as Nick and Maisie roll into full view. Nick is there, just a silhouette of him blurred by the low quality surveillance video. I lean forward in my seat. I reach out a hand to graze my husband's profile one last time before he dies.

In this moment, did he know he was about to die?

Nick is there. Maisie, too. And there is the oak tree, tall

and portentous at the corner of the bend. There are signs of warning, noting the hairpin turn up ahead. Bright signs, a blatant yellow, impossible to miss, set beside an advisory turn speed sign that the detective points out for me, explaining that this sign dictates a twenty mile per hour speed limit around the curve. The angle of the turn is tight, easily exceeding ninety degrees.

But where is my mother? Where is the black Malibu? She should be here, hot on their heels well before Nick ever reaches the tree. My eyes scan the video, but there is no Malibu. My mother isn't here. 'Where is she?' I ask the detective.

'Where is who?' he asks.

'My mother,' I say, but he only stares questioningly, saying nothing.

The black car has come and gone. All that's left are Maisie and Nick as the car dips into a pothole and then comes rocketing back out, the performance tires straddling that solid yellow line that's not meant to be crossed.

As the car descends upon the turn, it slides sideways, leaving behind black markings on the concrete, the tires' tread imprinted at once across the street. There is no one behind Nick, no one beside him forcing him from the road.

It's only Nick.

Nick with his history of driving too fast.

There's a last-ditch effort made to slow the car, a burst of red brake lights, like an iridium flare in the nighttime sky, that comes and goes as the car lifts off from the earth and strikes the tree with so much force the tree itself staggers, losing leaves, bark getting shorn from its trunk.

And then all is quiet. All is still.

'I don't understand,' I utter. I click at keys at random on the laptop screen, certain I've missed something. I need to see it again. 'This is the wrong video,' I say. There's been a grievous mistake, and this car on the computer screen is the wrong car, another red car that also ran into the same oak tree, another driver who suffered a most gruesome death at the hands of that tree. 'There should be another car,' I insist, demanding to know. 'Where is the other car? Where is the car that pushed Nick from the road?' I urge, telling him how this is wrong, all wrong. How he's made a truly awful mistake.

But there are close-up snapshots, it seems. Snapshots pulled from the video feed and enlarged so that I can see. The license plate on the rear of the car. My license plate.

An image of Nick, face obscured by glass.

Detective Kaufman plays the video again, but this time it isn't in slow motion. This time it's at full speed. The red car comes tearing down the road all alone, losing traction as it skids around that sinuous turn, going airborne, flying into the tree. There is no other car around, no one following him, no one pushing him from the road. No bad man.

The detective's words come to me.

'It's as I've said all along, Mrs. Solberg. Your husband was driving too fast. He took the turn too quickly. I'm so sorry for your loss,' he says, gathering his things to leave. But before he goes, he says to me, 'There are grief counselors. Bereavement counselors. Someone who can help you find the closure you need,' as if he can read my thoughts, as if he knows exactly what I need. And then, with a pat to my shoulder, he's gone, and it occurs to me that Detective Kaufman was right all along. He told me long ago what happened to Nick, and I chose not to believe him, but rather to spin a different narrative myself based on lies and other fallacies.

This was never about Nick. It was about me.

EPILOGUE

CLARA

Morning rises. A new day.

The knock comes at the door early, and all I can think of are flowers. More flowers. But today it is not flowers, and as I dodder through the foyer and to the front door, I see her standing there through the beveled glass. Kat. I set my hand on the door's knob, but before I can bring myself to open it, I gather my bearings. What in the world does she want?

I open the door, welcoming in the morning's sun and, with it, Kat. She comes alone this time, with no Gus in tow. Outside, down the street and across, Emily stands in her drive, clothed in a thin robe, waving goodbye to Theo as he takes his latest plaything for a spin, a nimble red two-seater sports car, the aerodynamics of the car making it zoom down the road. My eyes revert from the car to Emily, and still she stands, on the drive, this time with eyes on me.

Her hand rises in a timid wave. I wonder if ever again we can be friends.

'When we met,' says Kat, 'I wasn't completely honest with you. I wasn't being frank.'

I don't remember inviting her inside, and yet there she is, feet in my foyer, closing the front door to partition us from the hot summer air and the vociferous calls of birds and bugs. It's August now; fall will be here soon. But first we must survive the hottest month of the year, the dog days of summer, the time when cicadas come out to play, their drumlike tymbals already clamoring at eight in the morning like a rooster, waking those who sleep. Maisie. Felix. I hear them both, upstairs, in their own bedrooms, having conversations with themselves, being resourceful, keeping themselves entertained.

Kat looks nervous. Her hands fidget as she stands before me, unsure what to do. I come to her aid, not having it in me to put her through this agony. It's hard enough to have her stand before me, much less utter the words out loud. *I slept with your husband. He loved me, not you.* 'I already know about you and Nick,' I say before she can say it. There was more she wanted to say to me that day at the park, but I couldn't bear to hear it. This is what she wanted to say. She wanted to confess to adultery, to tell me she was sleeping with Nick.

'What do you know?' she begs, the lines of her face becoming creased, her eyes wide. She sets her hands inside her pockets; she pulls them out. She crosses her feet at the ankles, her arms across her chest.

'He was going to leave me,' I say, though no one has told me as much, but still, I know it to be true, 'for you.'

And I try to be casual about it. I try not to let my emotions get the best of me. There is much I need to come to terms with, from Nick's death to his betrayal and more. I've spoken to Jan at Nick's office, who told me the truth about Connor, how he had long since been let go, and it was then that I knew there was only one thing left to do: sell the practice. It was Nick's practice, not mine. Without him here, it's time to be through.

Jan also told me about Melinda Grey. 'She's just a patient,' she said when I asked.

Nick was in love with Kat, and it was only later, when sorting through his files, trying to put his past behind me, that I discovered a complaint from Melinda Grey, a complaint for medical malpractice. Then I knew.

'Oh, Clara,' Kat says now, her blue eyes filling with tears. It's a confession, her entry of a guilty plea. *I did it; I'm guilty*, say the eyes. She steps toward me; she sets her hands on mine. 'I loved him,' she says, and it strikes me that I'm supposed to embrace her, that I'm meant to hold her, to tell her I'm oh so very sorry for her loss. That I'm supposed to gather the dead flowers from my front foyer and give them to her. Kat is the bereaved, not me.

'I loved him,' she says again, just in case I didn't hear it the first time. She wants to be sure I know. The silence that follows is endless. I'm certain it will go on forever, that Kat and I will remain in the foyer for all of eternity, this awkward confession frozen in time. 'I loved him,' she says then for a third time, choking on the words. The tears fall freely from her eyes, a Victoria Falls of tears. 'I loved him, but he didn't love me. He loved you. He loved you, Clara. Not me.'

And then she explains.

* * *

We're about to leave the house when the home phone rings. 'Hello?' I ask, as I watch Maisie hunched over Felix's baby carrier, playing peekaboo. She covers her eyes with her pudgy little hands, asking singsongingly, 'Where'd Maisie go? Where's Maisie?' before pulling her hands away and hollering, *Boo!* He starts every time, eyes growing wide, tiny baby feet kicking in their navy socks. He can't laugh yet—though he would if he could—and so his lips part into a toothless grin, his own hand latching on to Maisie's pinkie finger by chance.

'Look, Mommy,' Maisie says, smiling wide. 'Felix is holding my hand.'

I mouth the words as the man on the other end of the line begins to speak: *He is.*

'Is Mr. Solberg there?' he asks, and I feel the sting, wondering if ever a time will come that my heart won't break when someone calls, asking for Nick.

'No,' I say, stepping into the adjacent room so I can explain just exactly where Nick is without Maisie overhearing. Later I will tell her. Soon.

'Ah,' says the man, explaining that he's been leaving messages on Nick's cell phone, messages I have yet to hear. After retrieving the information from it I needed, I let the battery die. I didn't hear any incoming calls. 'I'm calling from Mark Thames Jewelers,' he says, 'about a pendant necklace your husband purchased,' and I feel this instant recoil, remembering the necklace, the one he supposedly bought for Kat. Except that by Kat's own admission, Nick didn't love her. He loved me. 'It's ready to be picked up,' the man tells me, and at this my next query—*Why would*

Nick buy Kat a necklace if he didn't love her?—disappears completely.

The necklace is there. In the store. He didn't give it to Kat.

'I'll be right there,' I say, loading the kids in the car post-haste and taking off for the jeweler. The cemetery is where we were meant to go, but for now the cemetery can wait. I phone my father and tell him we're running late.

The jewelry store is located in an out-parcel just inside the grocery store's parking lot. I park the car and carry Felix inside, Maisie rambling behind. 'I'm Clara Solberg,' I say to a gray-haired man behind a glass counter, and he plucks a jewelry box from beneath the register, setting it in my hand. 'How much do I owe?' I ask, but he tells me it's already been paid for—which, of course it has; I've seen the receipt—and I hold it skeptically, not sure I'm ready to see what awaits me inside. I would like to tuck it in my purse to open at home alone with a glass of wine—just in case—except that the gray-haired man's eyes are watching mine, smiling deliberately, more eager than I am to see.

'Aren't you going to open it?' he asks as Maisie parrots, 'Open it, Mommy. Open it,' and so I do, slowly gathering the courage to lift the lid from the box. Inside lies a silver chain and, attached to it, two heart-shaped charms, one for Maisie and one for Felix, their names engraved in a play-ful, cursive font.

All the oxygen leaves my lungs. My legs buckle at the knees, threatening to give.

I've seen this necklace before.

Tears rush to my eyes, and only then do I know with absolute certainty that it's true.

Nick loved me the most.

* * *

The cemetery is near empty when we arrive. It's quiet, the only sound the rustling of the breeze through the trees. My mother and father are out of the car, perched on a concrete bench beneath the shade of a maple tree. In my mother's grasp rests Felix, my father's arms around the both of them as an extra safeguard. Felix's eyes are wide with wonder, staring quizzically up at a new face, one he's yet to see. He smiles a toothless grin, and at seeing this, Maisie points and says, 'Look, Mommy. Felix likes her,' and I say yes, yes he does, wondering if Felix can like Grandma, then maybe Maisie can, too.

'Maybe you want to sit by Grandma when we come back?' I ask, and Maisie shrugs her shoulders and says, 'Maybe.'

'We'll be right back,' I call to my father as I take Maisie by the hand, and he tells me to take my time.

'There's no hurry, Clarabelle,' he says, though when we return, we've promised Maisie ice cream. *But first*, I'd told her, *there's something we have to do.*

I haven't been here in weeks. The land that was once bare is now a patchy green, Nick's resting spot no longer looking so new. The headstone can't be placed until after the ground has settled, and so for now it's simply a depression in the earth littered with sprouts of grass. I lead Maisie over the sloping lawn to find her father. *Where's Daddy?* Maisie has asked, a hundred times or more. Today I will sit her down beside his grave and tell her about Nick.

'What are we doing here, Mommy?' she asks as we come to the spot, and I tell Maisie to sit down beside me, and she happily obliges, dropping quickly to the ground. A red-winged blackbird perches in a nearby tree, black, button-like eyes watching Maisie and me. I turn to the bird, raising a hand to shield my eyes from the sunlight, and it calls to me, a lilting trill, its beautiful bold colors conspicuous in the green tree. Above us the sky is a brilliant blue that enhances the green of the trees, marred only by the contrails of a passing jetliner. There's not a cloud in the sky as we watch the bird spring from the treetop and disappear into the afternoon, wings extended, soaring freely through the sky.

'You've been missing Daddy,' I say to her, and already my voice is quivering, and my eyes fill with tears. 'You've been asking about Daddy,' I say, to which she nods her head and smiles, her eyes brightening with the belief that Daddy is here, as she peers over her shoulder, eyes scanning the horizon for signs of her father, sitting beside a tree or cresting a faraway hill.

He's not there. Her smile fades, and her eyes grow sad.

'Where is he, Mommy?' she asks. 'Where's Daddy?' and this time I tell her.

She doesn't cry. She stares quietly up at the bright blue sky, eyes set on that blackbird as it soars through the atmosphere, wings extended, merely drifting through the sky, disappearing until nothing remains of it but a speck of black amidst the blue.

'You know what I think, Mommy?' Maisie asks, and even before she speaks, I know she's going to say something timely and brilliant, as only Maisie can do.

'What's that, honey?' I ask, stroking her hair, and as the bird passes completely from sight, she smiles and says to me, finger pointing at the long-lost speck.

'I think Daddy's flying.'

* * * * *

ACKNOWLEDGMENTS

It goes without saying that publishing a novel is a collaborative experience. I'm forever indebted to my amazing team for all of their hard work and tenacity on this project. *Every Last Lie* wouldn't have been possible without the patience, diligence and extraordinary intuition of Erika Imranyi, who tirelessly reads and edits my manuscripts time and again to make sure they're top-notch, providing brilliant insight into the lives of my characters, or my incredible literary agent, Rachael Dillon Fried, whose constant reassurance and enthusiasm (late-night phone calls, flying hundreds of miles for lunch and a pep talk) keep me doing what I love to do. Thank you to the HarperCollins and Harlequin teams, and to the wonderful folks of Sanford J. Greenburger Associates for their continued support. I couldn't be more proud to be part of your families. Special thanks to Natalie Hallak for the fabulous editorial assistance, to Emer Flounders and Shara Alexander for the amazing publicity, and to the sales and marketing teams, both locally and abroad, for sharing my books with the world. And to all of those who have had a hand in the publication process—copy editors, proofreaders, the ingenious crew who designs my lovely covers—thank you, thank you, thank you!

In the last few years I've had the chance to meet truly exceptional booksellers, librarians, bloggers and readers across the world, all of whom have graciously hosted me for book signing events, read and written reviews of my novels, done giveaways, welcomed me into their book clubs and suggested to a friend that he or she read my books. It truly takes a village to make a novel successful, and to everyone who has played a part in spreading the word—none of this would be possible without you!

Finally, a huge shout-out to my family and friends, especially Dad and Mom, my sisters, Michelle, Sara and their families, the Kyrychenko family, and Pete, Addison and Aidan for the unvarying support, for being the most vocal advocates of my books and a constant sounding board for the ideas that fill my mind and for driving to every single bookstore and library in Chicagoland—and elsewhere—to hear me speak. Though I might not always say it, it means the world to me. Love you all!

'FANS OF *GONE GIRL* WILL EMBRACE THIS' —LISA GARDNER

Mia Dennett can't resist a one-night stand with the enigmatic stranger she meets in a bar.

But going home with him will turn out to be the worst mistake of her life.

An addictively suspenseful and tautly written thriller, *The Good Girl* reveals how, even in the perfect family, nothing is as it seems.

ONE PLACE. MANY STORIES

Bold, innovative and
empowering publishing.

FOLLOW US ON:

@HQStories